The Journey: Erudite

David Cocklin

 FriesenPress

Suite 300 - 990 Fort St
Victoria, BC, V8V 3K2
Canada

www.friesenpress.com

Copyright © 2020 by David Cocklin
First Edition — 2020

All rights reserved.

No part of this publication may be reproduced in any form, or by any means, electronic or mechanical, including photocopying, recording, or any information browsing, storage, or retrieval system, without permission in writing from FriesenPress.

ISBN
978-1-5255-6943-2 (Hardcover)
978-1-5255-6944-9 (Paperback)
978-1-5255-6945-6 (eBook)

1. FICTION, LITERARY

Distributed to the trade by The Ingram Book Company

Other Books by David Cocklin

The Cottage: Recondite
2016 Friesen Press

Vargas Hamilton: Life Is A Gas
2018 Friesen Press

Available at:
www.DavidCocklin.com

To my children, Meagan and Brendan
Shape your journey, for life is not only worth living, but worth forging.

To my sister Debra, and to Andrew,
for guidance, detection, and amelioration

To Sarahjo Stott, an angel of inspiration,
motivation, and revelation

Table of Contents

Prologue	1
A Providential Journey	5
Chasing the Sky, Finding a Star	13
Chasing Redemption	23
A Tangled Mess	29
Selim and the Silver Spear	37
Talia Twists and Travel	49
Emotional Servitude	57
Talia Travel and Twists	67
Ladies Lost, Love and Luck	73
You Are What You Are	81
Thank You, Mr. Mayor	95
Chasing Illusions	105
Talia Words and Wishes	119
Chasing the Mist Behind	127
Safa, Good and Evil	141
Julian and the Improbable Encounter	151
Heading Home	161
The Journey Full Circle	173
The Human Condition	185

Sarah	**193**
Sharif in the Clutches of Kindness	**201**
Sarah, Sarah	**211**
Sharif in the Clutches of Indifference	**221**
Sarah, Sarah, Sarah	**233**
Sharif in the Clutches of Cruelty	**243**
The Language of Opportunity	**253**
Sharif and the Improbable Encounter	**267**
Talia and the Traumatic Truth	**279**
Footsteps and Shadows	**285**
Talia Full Circle	**293**
Julian and the Rays of Fate	**303**
Jubilation, Revelation, Destination	**311**
The Journey Parallel	**319**

Prologue

The Journey: Erudite is a companion book to an earlier novel; *The Cottage: Recondite*. It is intended that the reader does not have to read *The Cottage: Recondite* in order to follow and enjoy this book. It would, however, provide much greater insight into the main character's backgrounds and formation, as they travel through their current adventures.

In *The Cottage: Recondite*, despite a family environment void of love and nurturing, Julian grows to adulthood through a strong internal compass; a longing for an alternative existence, strengthened by independent ambition and a general kindness, and always lured by curiosity. His obsession with traveling and *"seeing the world"* is a driving force in his life. The initial adventures he undertakes in *The Cottage: Recondite*, represent a departure from a loveless childhood, the introduction of joy and purpose into his life, and the initial steps in self-actualization. His first foray into the outside world forges a foundation for the building of his character and competencies. It is just the beginning. The maturing process and independence achieved during *The Cottage: Recondite*, enables

Julian to set out for the world across the sea. The final piece to his puzzle is a veteran stranger named Tection, who, following his own journey, becomes part of Julian's life, encouraging both travel and enlightenment. Herein lies Julian's journey of self-discovery, of revelation; his erudite journey.

Nearly two decades before *The Journey: Erudite* begins with Julian travelling across the sea, his friend and mentor, Tection, does the same. He wanders aimlessly among strange lands and unusual people. He develops friendships and attachments, but always leaves them behind before they become too strong; preferring to be a stranger and thus, becoming a *veteran* stranger. In *The Cottage: Recondite*, Tection climbs from the ashes of his childhood, shattered and orphaned by the fire that has destroyed his family. His formative years are an opportunity to make something of himself, though he has to do so by fighting for everything he gets. As he becomes proficient in physical confrontation with other boys, he also learns how to manipulate his fellow orphans and the Brothers who supervise the orphanage. He turns the cruel discipline of an orphan's upbringing into admiration and respect from them. He studies diligently and through a scholarship to seminary, creates a potentially rewarding future for himself in the priesthood. Like a stained-glass window, however, that future is fragile. It is shattered when he uses his fists to end the life of a vile and demented clergyman, appropriately named Winter, who has abused him emotionally and physically during his formative years. Although Tection's action is recognized as justifiable, and he suffers no official consequences, the blow to his own psyche is devastating. A self-imposed exile follows, and his sojourn across the sea begins. Herein lies his journey of resolution, of absolution, and his road to becoming a veteran stranger, before eventually returning to his homeland. It is a journey that will ultimately deliver some exculpation and eventually unite him with a family he does not know he has; his erudite journey.

Prologue

Tection's history before *The Journey: Erudite* and his life afterwards, are both well documented in *The Cottage: Recondite*, where his formative years and his post-journey encounters are bookends to the travels recounted here.

The journeys that Tection and Julian experience in *The Journey: Erudite* are many years apart, yet touch people and places in a paradoxically random dance of serendipity, sewn together with symmetry and fate. It is intended that the reader also take a journey with them, weaving in and out of their lives in a gallery of episodes and adventures that appear indiscriminate, but are eventually revealed to be inextricably linked to Tection and Julian, and their destiny.

A Providential Journey

"G'day Julian. You seem a little less jovial this morning than what I witnessed at last night's revelry. Is everything okay with you?"

"Thanks Cap, ya, I'm fine. I guess I'm just feeling the finality of leaving behind my previous life."

Julian leaned forward onto the bridge railing as the impact of those words danced on his consciousness. His hand reached inside his shirt to feel the medallion hanging around his neck; representative of both the community left behind and the pilgrimage taking form.

The morning sun did its best to lend blindness to his forward vision of this distant land; the destination of his journey. Still, progress steered the boat through the waters as the waves were pushed aside, and the shore to which they travelled bent slowly over the horizon, gradually taking shape and form, stoic and eternal, without expectation of their arrival or guarantee of anything more than an end to this particular voyage.

It was a return home for some, who were anticipating a reunion with loved ones, sharing some lunch, some laughs, or perhaps some hot chocolate with anxious children. For others remaining on board to navigate the vessel, this was but a midpoint in their short journey. They would spend the night onboard the creaking and slapping boat, seeking tomorrow and its promise of a return to the shore they had left behind a short time ago.

For Julian, turning in limbo as he surged toward the third decade of life, this was the fulfilment of a promise, an important promise; one he had made to himself several years before, in the bowels of an old church with his friend John P, spinning a wobbly globe with his rugged hands, hands too calloused to be those of a fifteen-year-old, and realizing that any spot, any place noticed on the turning sphere, other than where he stood, was a worthy and desired destination.

Julian travelled solitary now. He had set out from the small town he and John P had eventually relocated to. They had left home together, on the very day Julian was of age, and managed to ramble for a few days from where they began, before settling into new lives of independence, coming of age at an accelerated pace, while still handling the unavoidable sense of responsibility and emotional impact of separation from childhood comforts, with less volatility than they had expected. Julian had been anticipating the severance of contact with his previous life and the parents who seemingly regretted his existence. He had chased the dream of escape from their clutches for several years. A few years older, John P had shared his initial adventure for different reasons, lured by the call of adulthood without anchors to hold him back. His mother had died unexpectedly some time earlier, and his father had been unknown to him. Except for the local priest, Joseph, with whom John P lived after his mother's death, there was no reason to delay the call towards the future. The tragic death of Joseph and the eventual revelation that he was actually John P's father, shaped John P's destiny in a different form and direction than Julian's. Their parting had been sorrowful and emotional but seemingly inevitable.

Julian had built up a small business, a café in a local town, through hard work, recognition of opportunity, and the kind and generous support of the now-deceased previous owner. Good fortune had surely smiled on him, though his own work ethic, commitment to responsibility, and attention to detail were unusual for someone so young and were the drivers behind the café owner's decision to leave the café in his will to a surprised, but fully appreciative, Julian. Without relatives or heirs, the café owner had developed a close relationship with Julian and saw no reason to do otherwise with the café following his death.

The owner had encouraged Julian to pursue his dreams of travel and adventure, lamenting his own inaction on such ambitions. So, when the opportunity arose later, for Julian to sell the café, with enough remuneration to support his foray into the extended world, Julian seized it. A recent friend and mentor, Tection, who was in the process of establishing a family with his son, Nicholas, and the boy's estranged mother, Sarah, proved to be the perfect buyer. He would take over ownership and maintain the spirit and integrity of the café, while providing enough funds for Julian to venture out onto the waiting horizons.

Tection had just appeared one day, fresh off a journey of his own. His had been one of redemption, not of adventure, though the two could easily be confused with one another. Over the next year, Tection had regaled Julian with numerous stories about other lands and peoples. He had fueled Julian's long-held desire to travel and experience something other than his own small community. Even though Julian had left home early, breaking away from a wretched childhood full of hardship and loveless relationships, he had grown into a kind and considerate man. Tection joined him in his wonderment of one's nature; how it was seemingly entrenched at conception, influenced only slightly by the world surrounding them. Tection already knew some of what Julian would discover; that the experiences of life and the actions and consequences surrounding them may be cast out of one's memories, but they are not so easily exorcised from the soul, always hovering silently, just beneath consciousness.

Contrary to John P, who had found some purpose and direction in a new life and new town, Julian was unwilling, or perhaps unable, to relinquish his dreams of travel. Tection nourished that with his stories and then funded them, through the purchase of Julian's café. Julian was now heading in the same general direction that Tection had ventured in, nearly twenty years earlier.

As he continued to rub the medallion around his neck, the one Tection had given him on departure, promising him it was a symbol well received in lands across the sea, Julian wondered if he would encounter any of the people Tection had on *his* journey. Would they remember Tection? He laughed to himself. *Of course they would*! *He was larger than life.*

Among the limited belongings Julian travelled with, necessarily limited so he could manage the weight without assistance, was a newly acquired journal. It was full of blank pages, which he was bent on filling with the anecdotes and adventures this journey would surely deliver.

And so, here he was. Enclosed by this boat he travelled on, building a growing desire to reach shore and begin his discovery of the world he had only known through books and maps. He was both nervous and excited, exhilarated and filled with anticipation, unaware of and unconcerned with any dangers lurking in foreign lands, or days of solitude to be endured.

As the advancing shoreline lumbered slowly but relentlessly forward, Julian's thoughts fell into a vivid recollection of random moments of his past; an indiscriminate dance of reminiscence, flashbacks of jagged shards of his existence, oscillating between childhood and travel, parents and perceptions, friends and fate. Each momentary thought, regardless of its distance from his present, was as clear as if it was happening just off the stern of the boat beneath him. He was unsure why these particular moments sprang forth from the archives of his experience. That could be analyzed later perhaps, for now he was consumed by the internal mosaic and intrigued by the seemingly random and unrelated pattern.

Of course, these were all memories of his, in whatever manner they were now recalled. Memories were not a reflection of reality, not a chronicle of events, but rather a perception of experience, moments in time, a personal version of external events, forged and shaped by a combination of physical encounter and the corresponding mental and spiritual interpretation of it, or interaction with it.

When Julian roused from his ruminations, the distant shore was still slightly elusive and incomplete. He had wandered through those random memories with the physically incomprehensible speed that a mind can produce; a mind not bound to the mechanical clock or the beating heart. That his entire existence, every moment of it, from deliverance from the womb to the ticking of time that fell in front of him now, was somehow organized and filed somewhere within himself and sometimes retrievable, was astounding. No, it was outstanding! These mental documents of what made him who he was, which shaped the descriptions he offered of himself and the analysis he applied to his history, were limited only by the amount of time that he had existed. Curiously, he noted, some of these memories even had variations, so that he was not always sure exactly which one was more a reflection of some reality, rather than a perception of some experience. Some of his more frequently accessed memories even carried a dual identity, buoyant and appreciated at times, but perhaps sullen and depressing under some alternative context and light.

His disappointments were nourished by a lack of instant recollection when sought, a youthful reminder of the battering old lives took when time eroded the avenues of memory recall, and by the imposition of reminiscence, especially when undesired, some memories surfacing to consciousness despite protective efforts to obscure them behind an emotional filter. Opposite, and occasionally contradictory encounters with the same memory, shared the same narrow, connecting corridors of self-realization.

Some memories and reflections were welcome to the explorer, either as joyful experiences to be re-lived, or perhaps relevant and necessary to support sagacity. Even unfavourable recollections could be drawn upon to serve as reminders of past hardship, as warnings against repetition, or as self-admonitions. Sometimes memories were so vivid, or so disquieting, that they forced themselves into the consciousness on a regular basis, never wished for but often ubiquitous; strengthened by the very desire to be unrecognized. Even more distressing was the arousal of those oppressed memories that hibernated within, coiling unceremoniously in a tensioning process, boxed and buried as it were, hidden from the files of experience. At times these segregated experiences burst from their spiritual isolation and drove into the psyche, wreaking havoc on the unsuspecting self. They were not merely unwelcome visitors to the conscious mind, they could be life-altering encounters, sometimes even triggering unnatural physical reactions and uncharacteristic behaviours.

Many wandered through a lifetime without ever creating such experiences, without ever experiencing such creations. It was some kind of combination of events, impressions, perceptions, and reality that created such latent, but potentially explosive memories, parked below the unconscious surface by an inherent drive towards self-preservation and moral humanity. Some fortunate souls could indeed build such pathological potential but keep it repressed throughout their lifetime, letting the beast come to an inauspicious end along with their physical selves.

Julian was not completely unaware of his own beast within. He had experienced the sense of lost control once before, venting some unrealized anger upon an innocent, unsuspecting cat. Julian had hurt the animal, and although he made every effort to successfully bring the feline back to a happy, sleepy existence, his act of violence left him greatly perturbed. The act of hurting such a defenseless creature carried enough impact, but it was the realization that he was even capable of such an action that impacted his psyche most. He had not recognized the hidden drama that swirled within his character, as he came to terms with parents who didn't want him and the accompanying childhood of abuse and exploitation. On the surface, he had dealt with the emotion of his loveless childhood and he had bid farewell to his parents both when leaving home and during an unexpected encounter with them sometime after that. He had lauded himself somewhat for the strength he had shown in dealing with the last encounter, maintaining a sense of decorum despite an escalating emotional condition, and a strong hunger to inflict some physical retribution for the perceived wrongs of childhood.

When his parents had departed for the last time, he convinced himself he was done with them, and finally closing that chapter in his life, a life that was now happy, anticipating adventure, and gaining some sense of purpose, or even fulfilment. Unfortunately, the impact that his experience with a loveless childhood had on his soul was not so easily discarded, and the remnants remained deep within, festering just below the recognizable self. His repressed unconscious resentments, driven by the realizations that he was an unwanted addition to the throng of humanity, verbally and physically abused by distant, unloving parents, could not be appeased by the strong and genuine friendships he had developed, or the good fortune he had experienced since severing his relationship with his family.

I've moved on from that part of my life, he promised himself, but he could no more exclude his past from who he was, than deny the waters that floated the vessel he travelled upon. Leaving the sea behind would not make it disappear, nor settle its movements. Storms would come and go, despite the fact that they might only impact Julian when he was dancing upon their waters. Julian opened his journal and made his first entry.

Chasing the Sky, Finding a Star

The sky was flawless as Julian stepped from the boat, planting his feet for the first time on soil from a new land. The boat ride had signalled the beginning of his adventure, but this earthly contact with a place previously known only as *"across-the-sea,"* was almost electrifying. Others around him pushed by, only slightly upset with his slow pace and seeming bewilderment. But they were not guests on a new, long-anticipated expedition to the unknown. It was not only the unknown bustle of life happening beyond Julian's understood and accepted world, it was the lure of cultural, religious, linguistic, and perceptive challenges that awaited, both an opportunity to embrace a new focus on lived reality and perhaps an unrecognized desire to dismantle a previous one.

Julian's reflections on this transition would surface and bear contemplation soon enough, but right now the impact of his decision to venture out to find the rest of the world was just settling in. His step from the boat was the ceremony of separation, the rite of passage, from the safe, albeit somewhat disjointed history of his life, up to this moment, to this juncture, with an uncharted and unfamiliar landscape.

Eventually, he stepped slightly to the side to let the throng of foot traffic avoid him and his curious gawk, while he soaked up the scene of a busy, perpetually moving mural; each new person apparently late for their destination or task, as they hustled along the avenues of industry and commitment that littered the entire landscape visible from his current vantage point. He needed higher ground, or at least a loftier perch, from which to view the surroundings.

Farther up the main thoroughfare, Julian could see a building of some height, certainly higher than the grounded flow of commerce. He marched purposefully towards it, careful to guard his bag closely, somehow comforted by the closeness of his belongings and the past life they represented. Finding an entry to the multi-story dwelling and an accompanying stairway, he began the climb upward. He passed a few levels and several curious sets of eyes, leaving him uncertain as to whether he was treading on something more private than he deserved to share. The end of the stairway was still encased by the building itself, and the lack of view it offered was disappointing. A mildly desperate search of the top floor found a smaller, less conspicuous staircase, leading up towards the roof. Perfect! Julian climbed it slowly, glancing back towards the hallway to ensure he was not disturbing the apparently mundane corridor, then leaping the final two steps as he pushed open the squeaky door that guarded the exit.

Immediately the landscape took on an entirely new appearance. Gone was the crush and scurry of activity that defined the port and accompanying marketplace, replaced by the panoramic vista of a city beyond anything he had previously witnessed. Certain thoughts struck him immediately. He was but a few meters higher than before, yet now he had an entirely new understanding and consequently, a new expectation of the same place he'd left behind. His first revelation was that the port area, the modest district he had landed in, was actually but a small corner of a much larger environment. He never would have realized this without his new vantage point. He wondered if a similar, minor elevation in intellectual or spiritual development might likewise provide an immense clarity on issues and a divergent impression on their conceptualization.

This drew Julian into further reflections and he sat for some time, half aware of the bustle of life sprawled out before him and half lost in a wide-eyed contemplation of the allegory he was developing. Like the city fanning out wide and far from his view, so surely must the spiritual realm blossom well beyond his current understandings. Even if he had grown up in that port neighbourhood and became fully fluent on its surroundings, knowledgeable of every street and every doorway, he would still remain familiar with only a small part of what was a much larger, greater, and complete metropolis. Any venture to the other parts of the city would find him with some bewilderment and perhaps even a bout of disorientation, until he became familiar and comfortable with his expanded surroundings.

Would this same analogy apply to the metaphysical? Would he necessarily expand his understandings of the spiritual domain by including a broader, more distant, and perhaps contrary belief system? And was such a *contrary-belief-system* actually contrary, or was it just a divergent observation of the same truths, wrapped in cloaks of another colour, upside down or inside out from what he was formally familiar with?

And if encompassing, or even embracing, a wider spectrum of acceptance provided some enlightenment into the mosaic that was humanity, some insight on the formation and value of personal beliefs, would an elevated observation of the same spectrum equally enhance the clarity and eventual understanding of these continually diverse convictions? Would a journey towards faith and fellowship be lengthened, yet also strengthened, by such an expanded frame of reference? Such challenging of entrenched beliefs and perceived truths would confront Julian's travels throughout his exploration of this new land, and beyond it. His pen frantically scribbled notes into his journal.

Julian's introspection was shattered by a sudden bark of words, then a repeated challenge in a language he didn't understand, but with an inflection that was unmistakably hostile. He slid his journal into his backpack, then spun around from his observational perch and was confronted by three youths, obviously locals, who were fanned out in a predatory pattern. One of them, the assumed leader, brandished a small piece of pipe, holding it directly by his side but with a tightened grip, as though there was an impending use for it. Julian assumed that use was as a weapon to batter him. He wasn't sure why these lads were behaving so aggressively, but he determined it was some sort of territorial claim. They repeated their demands, once again in a language he could not understand. Their eyes were clear enough, though, and Julian backed up the short distance between him and the rooftop wall behind him. His eyes darted from one assailant to the other in some kind of assessment of the anticipated battle, seeking a potential weakness in their defense to be utilized as the gateway to an escape. None was evident. They moved cautiously towards him with a constant chatter, which remained incomprehensible to Julian. Julian held his hands up in a surrender statement, hoping to provide some diffusion to the situation.

As the circle slowly shrank and Julian resigned himself to the inevitable attack, he heard another voice, calm and almost musical. He wasn't sure what the words meant, but the approaching boys immediately stopped their advance and relaxed their physical tensions.

Julian released his stare from the boys and looked out and up towards the source of the voice. He was shocked to see a young girl, woman actually, sitting on a slightly elevated stairway that led from their rooftop to another one, slightly higher. The midday sun reflected off the whitewashed wall below her and cast a hue of deflected light across the battlefield. She spoke again and rose confidently, stepping down the short distance off the stairway and moving directly towards Julian. She spoke once more, waving her hand as if dismissing a group of beggars who had overstayed their welcome, pushing past the pipe-wielding youth without concern and moving up beside Julian. She did not look back at the now uncertain group, but took Julian's arm and directed him back towards the city view. He glanced back at the boys, unsure of what had just transpired.

"Look out at the city," she said, with a calm but forceful expression, stretching her arm across the horizon in a single wave, as if inviting Julian to take in the entire vista. "I explained that you are my guest, so they will not bother you." She delivered the words perfectly in Julian's language, and so matter-of-factly that Julian could do nothing but believe her. "You should have been careful not to wander up here into a private residence." She held his arm, her admonitions delivered as if a comment on the spectacular view as opposed to the social faux-pas. "Slip a smile onto your face and let's leave together."

She tugged gently at his arm and they turned to face the three boys. The boys remained curious, but it was clear that they were more relaxed and would not hinder this young lady from passing through them with her *friend* in tow.

She led Julian, without conversation, back down onto the busy street, tugging his arm slightly, imperceptibly to passersby, but clearly directional for him. Eventually they came to a side street, littered with cafés along the road, which was actually just a broad sidewalk of sorts, void of any vehicles. She turned north, tugging him forward until she reached the cafe of her choosing, plopping him down into a slightly rusted steel chair, before slipping into its cross-table twin.

"I guess you just arrived?" She stated the obvious as a question.

The Journey: Erudite

"I guess you've been here for some time," Julian replied, self-congratulatory in his witty retort.

She looked at him curiously and tilted her head like he was a new type of animal, just discovered in her previously serene jungle. The waiter asked something in the same unfamiliar language and she replied without looking at him. Her eyes were on Julian, looking directly into his, while her brain engaged the waiter and ordered what sounded like two coffees. Julian held her stare, although he realized the onus would be on him, as the visitor, the rescued visitor actually, to be the first to drop his eyes. He did so after what he determined was an appropriate time, long enough for her to know that he was sincere and un-shifty, yet soon enough to save her any need to become more aggressive in her own stare.

He returned his eyes to her with the relevance of the staring discarded, and realized that she was quite a striking individual. Her slightly rounded face was framed by a head-covering that was unfamiliar to him, with eyes deep and dark, and lips large and naturally reddened. She wore a slight smile, revealing the tips of perfect white teeth, stretched from one side of her mouth to the other. She blinked infrequently. *Funny*, Julian thought, *most people blink so often we don't even recognize it, but this woman almost never blinks, making the lack of action so noticeable.* She smiled wider at his renewed stare, a stare with completely different context, and Julian felt a small wave of embarrassment as he realized he was being a little impolite.

Her hand slid out, over Julian's tapping fingers, bringing calmness to the moment and effortlessly reminding him that he had no need to remain nervous. He had not realized the involuntary rat-tat-tat he was drumming on the woven metal table top, remnants of the adrenalin rush brought on by the rooftop confrontation.

"Thank you," he finally uttered, ambiguous as to whether he meant for calming his finger tapping, or saving his body from the rooftop assault.

She looked at him a little more, keeping her smile constant, before responding. "Ha," she laughed, "You were in the wrong place back there."

"Why?" Julian asked, before realizing that being in the wrong place was not the important question. "why did you help me?"

He is so serious, she thought. "I'm the one who would have been left to clean up the bloody mess," she replied, smiling even more broadly with her own humour.

Julian smiled a little sheepishly as well, again realizing that it didn't really matter why she had come to his aid. Then they looked at each other, hesitated, and both laughed a little more heartily at the absurdity of the situation and her reply.

The ice was broken, the air was clear and the coffee was strong, much stronger that Julian was used to. They chatted for some time; where she had learned his language, who they both were, where they came from, where they were going, how they would get there, all in a symphony of speculation, half-truths, and reminiscences. Afternoon turned to dusk and afternoon coffee to dinner; dinner to a last bottle of wine and a quiet visit to her place, all hushed and secretive. Yasmine was stunning, her body like an oasis Julian had read about, a splash of cool water on the dry and dusty road he had travelled internally, despite riding high on the watery waves of an undulating sea, since leaving his life and friendships behind.

He imagined spending a lifetime with her as they wrestled across their bodies, caught in the passion of the night, tangled in the attraction that so unexpectedly captured them both. They explored each other repeatedly, each bringing previously unexperienced insights into their love-making; each sharing a limited history, a cultural intimacy with the other. When they finally lay back, exhausted but still excited, they looked at one another again, heads symmetric on the soft pillows that supported them.

The dawn crept silently through the window above, carving shadows and chiseled features onto their faces, reminding them visually of the attraction their bodies had already forged. Julian leaned over to kiss her; a gentle touching of lips. But that was not to be. Their kiss moved from gentle to passion once again, and they welcomed the rising sun for breakfast, along with their rising desires.

Julian ran down the wooden path, something chasing him; something unseen and unheard. He turned to look but saw nothing. He couldn't focus his vision behind as he pumped his legs forward, his head bobbing with the impact of the elevated cycle his legs were engaged with. From the corner of his eye he caught a momentary sparkle of light, out and across the large room he was running through. He realized he was at the far end of the room. It expanded away from him in a seemingly endless series of rows; perhaps a storage facility for bags of grain or crates of manufactured goods. He was slightly elevated, the pathway built on raised wooden tracks.

He looked out towards the light and saw a solitary female figure, brandishing what appeared to be a long silver spear, cocked and ready to throw. He slowed to a stop. She delivered the projectile with an amazing show of force and it hurtled through the dimly lit room with the vibration of flight it generated. Yet, somehow, by some unexplained bending of the vision, the spear travelled in slow motion. Julian could see it rumbling through the air with purpose and destination, but he could not move. He was also in slow motion. It was only his brain that was working in real time, perhaps even accelerated time. He could see the spear was heading straight for him but he could not move quickly enough to avoid it.

Just as he recognized his own resignation to the inevitable impact, a huge dragon-like creature burst from the bowels below the wooden pathway, rising high above him, staring into his cowering eyes, and snarling with jagged teeth. The creature lunged towards him just as the spear found the back of its head, bringing a sudden cloudiness to its eyes and complete relaxation to its frenzy. The creature fell sideways onto the path behind where Julian stood, the spear projecting straight out from the rear of its skull.

Julian looked up. The woman who had thrown the projectile was gone. Could she actually have anticipated the creature's arrival and released her throw before it appeared, knowing she would bring it down; or had she intended to kill Julian and the creature just happened to rise up in front of the spear? Equally possible, but permanently opposite.

Julian resumed his flight. He spotted a sliver of light emanating from what appeared to be a small doorway some distance down the pathway. He dashed for it, once again finding his actions in normal flow, no longer under the spell of slow motion. He reached the door and pushed it open as he slid onto his side to slow his forward momentum, nearly bursting past the doorway altogether. He peered out through the edge towards the light.

―

Waking, Julian became aware of Yasmine, busy at the sink across the room, her naked body dancing in an effort to prepare breakfast in the kitchen portion of her flat. Julian's head hung over the edge of the bed, sunlight from the mid-morning sky illuminating the room. It was a most revealing dream, he knew that, but he didn't know exactly what it revealed. The silver spear was significant, but he could not find any relevance to his life so far. And what about the dragon-beast; what, or perhaps who, did it represent? That was all food for future thought. Right now, all he could see was this erotic creature in front of him, and he smiled as his attention moved quickly from esoteric dream to ribald fantasy.

Chasing Redemption

Leaving his past life behind was less painful than Tection had expected, anticipated. His commitment to being a priest was one that had been thrust upon him. He had originally, perhaps unconsciously, viewed the possibility as one of escaping from the alternative careers available to an over-aged orphan; those being military service or manual labour. His scholarship opportunity was a great gift to him, and he cherished it, making the most of it.

He was not aware that the scholarship was, more realistically, a banner used by the orphanage to demonstrate their capabilities and success at turning poor, raggedy youth, into statues of fortitude and faith, fully capable of contributing to the social fabric of their community; thus, garnering additional funds from the church to continue their *'important'* work. The reality was somewhere in between supporting a disadvantaged youth and waving a banner of institutional success. Tection was, after all, a gifted individual, who through various moments of fortune and fate, climbed upwards from the well of despair his youth languished in, to find purpose and empowerment from adherence to a faith-based structure.

The Journey: Erudite

He flourished at the top of his class, studied faithfully, and embraced the full dogma of his particular Christian faith. His own lack of a structured family upbringing had left him uncertain about many social and spiritual matters. He grew up in an orphanage, where the mantra was self-preservation, every boy for himself, much of the time. The friendships and social skills he did gather from that period in his life were all rooted in some sort of *'self-first'* mentality. It had to be that way, because there was no parent or older sibling looking out for him, warning him of pitfalls or consoling him after calamity. Although Tection himself became a mentor for several younger boys in his senior years at the orphanage, he could not be mistaken as a suitable substitute for a loving and giving parent.

Growing, even surviving, without such mentorship was difficult enough, but doing so without any true spiritual development as well, was a struggle at best. When all this was combined with the kind of abuse and mistreatment that permeated the orphanage infrastructure, especially at the hands of Brother Winter, it was a miracle, of sorts, that any young man was able to lead a fulfilling life afterwards.

Tection's void of spiritual development, or more accurately, his regression in spiritual matters, left him hungry for something to grasp, something to hold on to that would allow him to be included in the world at large and give him common ground with those around him, who had lived in a more fortunate upbringing. And so, it was his time spent in the seminary that rewarded his longing with a suitable and acceptable belief system. His close adherence to the rules and dogma of his newly acquired understanding of faith resulted in much praise for him, and this in turn fueled his effort and intent to accelerate his studies. It was not really so surprising that he should complete seminary as an outstanding student and move on to become an equally outstanding priest. He received many accolades, always with the observation that he had accomplished his success despite his shattered youth.

Chasing Redemption

When Tection struck down Brother Winter years later, while the evil man was in the process of abusing a different young boy, it was an act of violent revenge for the years of sexual abuse he himself had suffered. The blow was struck in a moment of anger, and the fall that killed Winter was not planned or intended, but Tection knew in his heart that it was the result he had wished for. The fact that Winter struck his head while falling from Tection's blow did not make the death *accidental*.

'*Thou shalt not kill.*' It was an ominous commandment, without ambiguity or room for interpretation. But Tection *had* killed. The circumstances surrounding the why and how of it became less important to him than the fact that it had been done. He had great difficulty in facing that reality. He had killed someone. Despite numerous words of support from numerous people of importance, Tection could not find the same justification within himself, could not find forgiveness or embrace absolution.

He had built his adult life around the principles of his faith, and '*Thou shalt not kill*' was a fundamental one. This left him in deep internal conflict. It was not a perfidious act, but it was contrary to his belief structure. The fact that it was fundamentally contrary to his acquired beliefs was part of it, but there was another aspect that haunted Tection. He now realized that he was capable of such an act. It scared him, chilled him, to think that his kind heart and spirit were capable of finding enough rage to kill someone. Such a conflict. Of course, he tried to convince himself that he had not meant to deal a blow bringing death, but that was an inadequate reprieve.

He would chase redemption for that act, for that wish, for a long time. He was unaware that the conflict was not between the belief structure he had been taught and the action he had taken, but rather between the morals he had been indoctrinated with and those that had developed in him naturally. '*Thou shall not kill*' was an absolute. Tection needed his own addendum; '*Unless justified.*' It would be a long journey to discover that.

The Journey: Erudite

Despite the quiet acceptance and murmurs of justification, the hierarchy of the church deemed that his actions made it necessary to remove Tection from the public service he was so adept at, and bury him in the bowels of the institution, handling mundane administrative tasks. It was a bitter blow to his spirit. His inability to find redemption, combined with his ostracization from the life he enjoyed, left Tection restless and unsettled.

———

A fierce wind blew across the surface of the earth. Small whirlwinds sprang up and danced randomly, shifting direction on a whim, forming and dissolving without pattern. Dust streaked through the sky from the ground to the clouds; dark clouds that would not rain, but would not sail away either. Tection stood in this wind, turning his back to it, but the wind was blowing in the other direction as well, always head on. It was blowing in all directions at once. There was no escape. Dust flew into his nose. He covered it, opening his mouth to breathe, but it filled as well. He spat out the rough dirt, but it was no longer dust. When mixed with his breath it became a paste, like a tar-based substance, dripping and drooling from his lower lip. Tection tried to bite it off and spit it out, but he was no more able to separate from it, than it from him. He staggered along the edge of a valley. Below the ridge was a raging flow. It was not water, nor fire. It was an energy, moving at a tremendous speed, banging the sides of the ravine as it flowed onward. Tection tried to jump into it. Anything to provide respite from the ceaseless dust storm. His feet would not move. The tar substance continued to flow from his mouth. It slid down into the ravine, tickling the edge of the energy stream. Eventually, the tar flowed into the stream and began to get caught up in the flow. At first, Tection's mouth just produced more and more tar, allowing it to ride the flow without dragging him with it, but eventually he could not keep up. He was sucked towards the flow but his feet were anchored. His body was parallel to the ground and being pulled apart. His hands flew up to try and rip the tar away from his mouth, but they only became stuck in it. The pressure was mounting. He could feel his waist stretching, his soft belly about to be separated from his hips.

From the corner of his eye Tection spotted a branch slowly rolling by, riding the wind. He managed to liberate one hand from the tar and reach out for it. The first grasp missed, but the second attempt was successful. As his hand closed over the object, he realized it was not a branch, but the leg of an animal. What animal was unclear, but it was still warm, with small patches of blood coagulating at one end. Tection was disgusted, but unable to release the severed leg. He raised his hand and tried to shake it off, without success. As the leg rose again, it came in contact with the tar, easily severing it and freeing him from the pull of the energy stream. Tection felt his stomach return to normal, like an elastic returning to its original form. His feet were released as well. He began to shuffle backwards away from the stream. The tar was still dangling and growing from his mouth. He brought the severed leg up towards his face and moved it over his lips. The tar fell away and fresh air rushed into his lungs; air so fresh it was like water. The wind died down, the sun began to creep through the clouds, the ravine now held a cool stream of sparkling water. Tection was confused, dumbfounded. He looked at the severed leg, it was now a silver spear. He pulled back and threw it, watching it float off into the sunshine. It travelled in slow motion, making a wide arc, and returning directly to his hand. He did not grasp it. It just hovered above his hand, waiting.

When Tection woke, he was holding a rolled-up paper scroll. The dream was clear and vivid at first, but began dissolving with every moment of consciousness. He tried desperately to hold it, to imprint it on his memory, but to no avail. After a few moments, there was only a faint memory of tar, energy, and a silver spear. The paper in his hand was rolled up tightly, and Tection laid it out on the table,

The Journey: Erudite

anchoring one end with a book and rolling it out over the surface. It was a map. Basically, a local map, but one including several other lands across the small sea that bordered his home. Was the map also the silver spear? What could it possibly mean? At that moment he decided to travel. He decided to visit these other lands, to find some truth there, some purpose, perhaps even some redemption. His mind was made up. He left behind all he had worked for, all he knew, all he possessed; they all seemed so meaningless at that moment.

He said his farewells to an uproar of opposition and set out on a short journey of erudition; a journey that would last many years!

A Tangled Mess

Julian and Yasmine spent the next couple of weeks together, intermittently. She had her work, which was as a tour guide for foreign visitors, and he had his curiosity, which was endlessly evident. She spoke four languages with equal ease and had both the appearance of an angel and intelligence of a scholar. She was ideal for the work she undertook. As one of the few locals who could communicate with visitors from other places, she was respected and somewhat revered, although her beauty may have had some significant influence on the reverence as well.

Julian squandered his days with exploration of the city, an exerted effort to learn a few key words and phrases in the local language, and the occasional *accidental* bump onto the path that Yasmine used to guide the tourists through the winding streets and hectic marketplaces. He was comfortable staying with her, and although he had rented his own small room, he spent most nights in her warm arms, under the hymn of her purring breath.

Yasmine was busy many evenings and Julian did his best to avoid prying into her activities. She didn't offer any explanation so he assumed it was private. Perhaps she was visiting a sick relative, a prisoner of illness among hospital life, or maybe a younger sibling, still at home, lost in her studies and in need of tutorship. In any case, he was content with the free time he had to explore and investigate this new land, while still reaping the benefits of her companionship and zealous libido.

One evening, without purpose or destination, Julian wandered down one of the main thoroughfares of the city. He strolled past shop windows and restaurant doorways, seeking nothing more than the passing of time, anticipating Yasmine's return from her evening's diligence. As he peered into the various establishments, enjoying the window into other lives, people who were chatting and conniving towards their futures in unheard conversations, he imagined what each group or couple was discussing, creating irregular adaptations of their presumed conversation.

Somewhere between the curious cured meats which hung in a butcher's window, reminiscent of his own childhood as the offspring of sausage-producing parents, and the laughter bursting from two couples exiting their favourite restaurant after a happy night of dining out, Julian spotted Yasmine. She was sitting inside a small bistro, wine and water sprouting from the table, a small meze of local dishes easily recognizable, and most importantly, a young man languishing over her, their hands interlocked, their eyes engaged. Julian was dumbfounded!

After a frozen moment, he realized he was staring at them openly, and he moved off to the side of the window, turning his back slightly but keeping his eyes glued to the two of them. They were unaware of his scrutiny. *How could she do this*? He choked on the thought. *How could she be seeing someone else*? His surprise turned to shock, turned to anger, to resentment, to sorrow. He watched a while longer. She leaned in to kiss her companion, not a soulful kiss perhaps, but neither was it just a friendly peck for a brother or cousin. Julian was disheartened. He returned to his small room and moved directly from the door to the bed. He brought the pillow over his face and tried desperately, but fruitlessly, to push the vision of Yasmine and her perceived lover from his head.

Julian wandered in and out of sleep. Three weeks ago, he was about to get physically manhandled by a rooftop gang, and now he was getting emotionally pummeled. He wasn't sure which was worse. But why was he so attached to this young lady? What had Yasmine ever done to make him so jealous? He had never felt this way before, and he didn't like it. He found himself feeling anger towards her, even chasing random thoughts of bringing her harm. He was not happy with such thoughts and even less happy with the fact that he could have them. He pondered more as time went by, as sleep was lost. *Wait, am I in love with her? Is this what love is; an emotional attachment so strong that one could wish harm on the other if the bond was broken or beguiled?* A curious thought for Julian. He digressed from his anger and disappointment long enough to formulate an opinion on such powerful emotions as love, hate, anger, betrayal, deception; a litany of powerful and reactionary elements of life. Yet he could find only one positive, at least an assumed positive, reflection among the bunch; and that was love. There were no other emotions that drove such a physiological reaction. Happiness, joy, laughter, wonderment, pride, bliss, exhilaration; these were all pleasant but much less powerful than the dark emotions. Only love, as a positive and wonderous emotion, also reigned within the inner circle of aggressive and negative emotions. An interesting observation indeed!

Julian remained in hibernation for two days. Normally, he would be waiting for Yasmine as she slipped home from work, sometimes holding a small gift of chocolate or a flower, sometimes humming a little tune to her, and sometimes physically excited enough to begin demonstrating his intentions before she managed to get all the way through the door. She scolded him, but she adored the attention. On occasion she would say that she would be home too late to visit and he would find alternative diversions, but always with her in mind.

Yasmine worried about Julian, she had not seen him for nearly three days and in the entire time they had known each other they had never been apart more than one, and only then when she had evening clients to entertain. She liked Julian. He was attentive and energetic, always happy to see her and bearing small gifts of sorts, not to mention the fabulous time they spent in her bed. She wasn't sure if he realized that she was an escort in the evenings, providing private services for more wealthy visitors, but never including sexual contact.

She would show them the sights, enjoy dinner with them, and perhaps some entertainment later if they desired. She was their friend away from home, so to speak; a comfortable and knowledgeable person to spend their free time with, fluent in their language and educated in the ways of conversation. Many tried to take the evening into the night, but Yasmine had strict boundaries about that and never veered from them. She felt such deviation would become known and begin the disintegration of her comfortable business venture.

Her concern for Julian was sufficient to steer her towards his rented room to knock on his door. Julian was startled. He did not receive visitors and the landlord was interested only in the prompt payment of rent. He opened the door and looked into Yasmine's beautiful face, but it had somehow changed. He did not see the same beauty as before; her eyes were less vivid, her hair less shiny.

"Hey there," she said quietly, "I've missed you. Are you alright?"

"Ya, just feeling a little under the weather," he lied. The look on his face revealed that right away.

"Has something happened?" she queried.

Julian turned and moved back into the room. Yasmine debated whether to enter or not. He seemed rather strange. She stepped inside and closed the door, moving over to him and placing her hand on his shoulder.

Julian spun around when he felt her touch and blurted out, "How could you be seeing someone else!"

Yasmine retreated. "What do you mean?"

"Don't lie to me, Yasmine, I saw you in the restaurant the other night. The night you were *unavailable* for me."

"Are you tracking me Julian?" she asked quietly, tilting her head slightly to the side to emphasize her sarcasm.

"I was walking. I saw you through the window."

"It was just a client, Julian; it is just private tourists who hire me to escort them through our town. I see many clients in the evening."

"No doubt," he replied with his own sarcasm mounting. "Do you accompany these men for money?" He dropped the sentence with an awkward connotation.

"I do," she replied without defense.

Julian was surprised. He had expected her to resist a response, to redirect the lingering tension. "Do you sleep with them too?"

Yasmine stood straight. She held her head high in a clear demonstration of disdain and recalcitrance. "I sleep with whomever I wish, and that is not your concern." She still did not defend against the connotation of Julian's remark. "And by the way, young man, it seems that affording you the privilege to spend time with me was a mistake." She turned to leave.

"Wait." Julian pounced out ahead of her. "What are you doing with these men?"

Yasmine pushed him gently aside. She reached for the handle and turned it but did not open the door immediately. She turned to Julian, still calm and matter-of-fact in her demeanour. "I do for them exactly what I do for the bus-loads of tourists who venture a visit to our city. I take them on a tour, explain the sights, and instead of just recommending good restaurants to eat at, I bring them there and enjoy a meal with them. Instead of just recommending some evening entertainment, I join them. In return, they pay me and thank me. I also get a small commission from the restaurants and bars that I bring them to. That is my job." Yasmine opened the door and pushed out into the hallway.

"I saw you kiss him," Julian said, almost as if one final comment would somehow prove her explanation less than completely true. He realized it was the wrong thing to say, as the words left his lips.

Yasmine looked at him and smiled.

Julian's eyes dropped to the floor.

"Bye Julian."

Julian sank into his bed feeling more than foolish. If he didn't believe her, why was he so unhappy, and why was he thinking of chasing after her? He realized her goodbye was meant as a permanent one, but he also knew it would be too painful for him to let her go without some further contact. He eventually slept, but only with the firm commitment to see her in the morning.

Julian was at her door as the sun began its ritual rise. Her light was on, indicating she was up, so he knocked. She answered without surprise and walked back into her flat without saying anything, but clearly implying that he should enter. She continued her morning ritual of getting ready for work and Julian sat uncomfortably on one of the kitchen chairs. She walked by him a couple of times, looked at him, but said nothing. He would have to initiate a conversation. Just showing up wasn't enough to smooth the air.

"Maybe I misunderstood," he finally said, again recognizing his comment as poorly chosen. It was neither an apology nor an absolution. "I mean, what would you think?" Again, the wrong words were flowing from his mouth.

Yasmine sat down across from him at the table. She took his hand and played with the back of his knuckles. "Look," she finally said, "I have my work and I handle it the way I want. If the man is a gentleman, generous and kind, I don't mind to give him a kiss to say thank you."

A Tangled Mess

Julian looked up at her, feeling relieved that she was taking the time to explain herself. But before he could speak, she squeezed his hand and continued, "Look, we've had some good fun over these last few weeks. Really, it's been a real treat, but I think we should take a break." She said it without a speck of sorrow in her voice, almost as if she were a mother speaking with her son who had left his room messy.

"What? Why?" was Julian's first response. "I'm sorry," he finally continued, "I'll never question you again." He was not ready for this and it showed.

"That's cute," she said, "but I'd just prefer to let things end here. I mean, you were sort of lost and in need of someone, and I was in need of someone, but it's passed now Julian. I just want to be back *single* again. Don't make it difficult...please."

"No, no...of course not," he said, in a bit of a daze over what was happening. He had thought he might be in love with this lady, and she was casually reminding him that it was a three-week-long, *weekend*-fling. He rose from the table, unsure what to say, and backed towards the door.

Yasmine got up and headed towards the bathroom. She wasn't even going to watch him leave.

Julian walked for some time that morning. He walked for several miles, chasing dust and pebbles up and down the roadway. He stopped into a small café, not unlike the one he used to own, and ordered a beer in his new-found language. He sat quietly for a while and then glanced out at the horizon. He could see the edge of the harbour and various boats shuttling in and out. He looked farther out across the water, remembering where he had come from. His journal was building text with each passing day. *It hasn't even been a month since I left*, he thought, *and I've already managed to find a tangled mess for myself*. He laughed. *This is going to be more of an adventure than I expected.*

Selim and the Silver Spear

The sun was hot. Selim and his brothers continued to load their wares, but their speed diminished with each passing minute. The heat of the day was directly related to the pace of their labour, and they were losing the battle. They finally gave in to the burning rays and decided to take a few hours to let the sun wane in the late afternoon sky, electing instead to have a cool drink and well-deserved chair. They entered the café, three of them, under the scrutinizing eyes of the patrons inside.

Selim and his brothers were not local, they were part of a nomadic tribe, living from place to place, touching civilization from time to time, as if the wind was their guide. Their tents and livestock were seldom seen by residents of the towns and cities. They were not versed in the ways of city people and they were not really welcomed by them either. Still, on occasion, they had to trade livestock for funds, in order to acquire items not readily available to them on the open landscape. They were young men, with Selim being the senior, having just completed his thirtieth year.

The Journey: Erudite

They ordered their drinks, paid with cash drawn from a healthy bundle, freshly built from the sale of the livestock they had herded into town and sold off earlier in the day, and went to a small table to relax. They ignored the stares, especially from a small group of rather ugly men sitting across from them, with their dusty pants and dirty bandanas. The brothers had used part of their money to purchase some needed goods, much of which remained outside, yet to be loaded, and they were now waiting for the cool drink and hot sun to both diminish a bit. The bundle of cash they held would be used sparingly throughout the season, supporting their tribe when needed and bringing some comforts to the hard and difficult lives they led. The first drink went by quickly, quenching their heavily parched throats, and they managed a second drink. Once again Selim paid from the large roll of money he held in his pouch. The group of ugly men looked on with hungry eyes indeed.

Another man, one seemingly unusual for these parts and clearly a stranger, lingered by himself at the end of the bar. He watched the process as it happened, the payment peeled from a large stack of money, and the eager stares from the dusty spectators. He knew there would be trouble; he could taste it in the air, sense it on the surface of his skin. He had felt the presence of evil many times before, and had been penetrated by it, even though he remained on a futile journey to rid himself of it. He had fought many battles in his life and had grown strong and skilled with his fists, but running from the evil within as it sat comfortably, like a sheathed knife deep in his heart, was a futile voyage. He had not yet learned that there was no escape from it, no liberation, only entombment and hopefully, guardianship.

Selim and his brothers enjoyed their second drink with a little less anxiousness, savouring the sips and conversation before returning to their labour. With the last of their supplies finally loaded, they set off for their tents and their tribe; the dusty locals not far behind. The brothers were not so familiar with the treachery of city life; the loss of humanity and the insensitivity that urban life often delivered. They were nomads, children of the earth, completely loyal to one another and fully reliant on their extended family to share their life and love together. Highwaymen were not part of their culture, although they had heard stories from other unfortunate victims.

Somewhere between the city and the camp, the robbers struck. They did so with lightning speed and a coordination that unmistakably demonstrated experience. There was no threatening of the brothers, just an attack without notice, bashing into them with force and fury. The brothers were struck down without warning and the thieves ransacked their pouches, collecting all the valuables, especially the funding for the tribe for the ensuing season. The loss of this money would be devastating.

Selim was half-conscious. He made out the figures of the men as they lifted their booty, and he tried valiantly to rise in defence of his family currency. One of the robbers turned and moved towards him, his weapon raised, but before he could strike Selim again, another man appeared, almost from nowhere, delivering a resounding blow to the thief, sending him to the ground, motionless. The man's arm appeared as a silver spear, darting from his body but recoiling with equal speed and strength. Selim fought to clear his mind, to focus his vision. The other robbers returned to confront the stranger who had interceded in the events, but they too were struck down, the silver spear darting out and recoiling with rapid succession. All three thieves were victims of this stranger with the powerful fists.

Selim felt the man come to his aid, lifting him to his feet and then helping his brothers also to rise. Only when he was so close did Selim recognize him as the stranger who had sat quietly at the end of the bar in town. The brothers reclaimed their money and left with much haste, anxious to put distance between these city men and the recovered cash. They knew there would be safety in numbers at their camp. Their departure was delayed by the stranger, this avenger, who left with them only after he took significant time to ensure the thieves were not dead or heading towards it. Selim urged him away, calling out that these men deserved their fate, but the stranger completed his maintenance of their condition until he was certain they would suffer no permanent effects.

The stranger travelled with the brothers, dispensing water to focus their consciousness and with a careful eye to the past, ever scanning the horizon for any sign of the dusty bandits. There was none; they were gone.

The stranger wore several silver bracelets on his right arm. Selim was uncertain of their meaning, but he recognized them as the silver blur that preceded the impact of the man's fists, forming the impression, under the veil of his blurred vision, of a silver spear. It was obvious this stranger was skilled in fighting. He was large and well built, with a seeming disregard for his own safety and welfare.

Selim and his brothers rejoiced at their escape and tried to reward the stranger for his assistance, but he would not accept any payment. He insisted it was what any man would do. He did, however, accept to share food with them and perhaps a warm bed for the evening.

As they eventually slowed to a normal pace, the brothers pulled alongside the stranger. Selim touched his chest and pronounced his name so the stranger would understand. He likewise pointed to his brothers, Attayak and Ahmed.

The stranger returned the introduction. "Tection," he said out loud.

Selim repeated the name, and Tection nodded, confirming his pronunciation was correct.

Tection was received as a king. The three brothers recounted the entire affair to the huddled tribe, as they all gathered late into the evening enjoying a lavish feast. They were celebrating the end of the season, the reward for their labours, and the recovered, provident funds they had kept secure through the efforts of Tection. He was honoured repeatedly, to the point where his embarrassment was becoming evident. Selim's father, the shaykh, or leader of the tribe, finally stood and made a declaration to all, indicating Tection had been properly thanked and while his name would remain in their hearts, no one should further single him out this evening. Tection wasn't sure exactly what was said, but he recognized the change in demeanour immediately. He was most pleased with that.

Tection was uncommitted in life. He was leaving behind tragic circumstances, which had altered his life course so dramatically that he was only beginning to reconnect with his own spirit. He valued the sanctity of life more than the life itself. The potential sacrifice of a single life, in order to maintain the principles of living, was not a foreign concept. It was important to him that he live his life according to the values and character he felt devoted to, regardless of the risk that doing so entailed. It was the force that had driven him to assist the brothers, but also the impetus for his departure from a previous life into the arms of this newly embraced, capricious wandering.

With little else to form a foundation and no destination to lure him, Tection found himself remaining longer with the tribe than expected. He and Selim became good friends, sharing basic, hand-enhanced conversation, until Tection was able to gain a rudimentary knowledge of Selim's language. Once some basics were learned, more sophisticated understandings blossomed. His daily interactions with the tribe left no alternative; it was a combination of study, explanation, and osmosis that led him to the point of conversation. He received additional high praise for his rapid comprehension, and his status as a cult hero was only enhanced by his deemed prowess in matters of the mind.

Selim had a wife named Fatima and two daughters; Malika, who was eight years old and Aliya, still just an infant. It came to pass that Tection wished to return some of the good fortune he had been gifted with from the tribe. Although he had performed a single, perhaps heroic act, it was not enough to sustain the caring and giving nature he possessed. He tried to work alongside the other men, but they would not have it. Each one would be frowned upon if they let him assist them, for he was an honoured visitor and not expected to do so. He tried to help the women in their daily undertakings, but again he was hushed with whispers and doted on, as though his desire to help was actually a call for attention.

Finally, like a harsh whisper from a lonely cloud passing overhead, Tection realized how he could contribute. He would teach Malika his language. A second language was not widely needed in her life right now, but it was certainly an asset that could assist her in a future endeavour. Besides, Tection thought, it would assist with the maintenance of his own lexicon and ameliorate his understanding of Malika's language. Selim was delighted. Anything that elevated his daughter also elevated him. Fatima was slightly more apprehensive, wondering if these lessons would detract from Malika's other schooling, or her daily chores, but Tection coordinated a time slot that did not interfere with her responsibilities, and the lessons began.

Malika was excited to learn the new words. She was also excited to miss a few moments of her rather mundane existence. As was true for any of the children, a new experience always brought sparkle to the otherwise bland flow of days.

Teaching was difficult because Tection did not have a very complete vocabulary of her language. He knew nouns, places, things, but verbs and their tenses were not yet his strength. Still, with the passing of time and the efforts of their collective wills, Malika soon gained a basic working knowledge of Tection's mother tongue. She was ecstatic when she could talk to Tection with it at the table, somehow feeling superior to her friends and even parents, smug in the knowledge that she had something none of them possessed. It was a natural attitude for one so young, and Tection smiled and laughed along with her illusion of ascendance.

Selim and the Silver Spear

Selim and Fatima were again overly grateful to Tection. There is no greater gift to parents than that which supports their child. For Tection, still single and fatherless, the chance to interact with a child, to enjoy the simplicity of life, unburdened by experience or chafed by reality, was as refreshing as any cool pool was to dusty flesh. He found simple joys and basic laughter, all delivered by a tiny speck of a person; a random soul in a world full of indifferent and remote humanity. It was a cleansing of sorts, something that brought him forth from the doldrums that hounded him, loosened the ties of memory that bound him to his past. It was a symbiotic relationship, and both Malika and Tection grew quite fond of each other.

On one otherwise undistinguished day, Malika *graduated*, complete with an appropriate ceremony and her recital of a rehearsed speech, which was translated into her language by Tection, in his own confirmation of linguistic growth. Selim was ecstatic. He made Tection an honorary member of the tribe. It was a distinction bestowed on very few in the long history of their tribe, and Tection valued it as such. It was a gift of affection, friendship, acceptance, and love, which held more value for him than any sum of money, any form of physical riches. Tears were shed, laughs were howled, and way too much drink was consumed.

During the celebration, Selim noticed a medallion Tection was turning casually among his fingers. He had seen him fondle it before, but had not paid attention. Selim moved in and asked to see it, holding it up to carefully view the face. It was a crescent moon, with a five-pointed star keeping watch over it; an iconic symbol of Selim's religion. He was surprised to see it living around the neck of Tection, knowing he was not of the same religion, yet also realizing Tection was surely a man of significant faith just the same.

Days later, when the drink and revelry had receded to temperance and purification, he asked Tection about it. Tection recounted the story of its acquisition; a gift from another young boy in the orphanage he'd grown up in; a boy who had joined them from his own unfortunate circumstances. Tection felt his relationship with Selim was far enough developed to allow him the relief of telling Selim his harsh tale. It was a discussion he seldom had, preferring to maintain a certain solitude about himself, but he always felt a renewed relief whenever he had the inclination and opportunity to share his story.

Tection explained that he had suffered greatly as a young child. His family had been erased by a fire; his parents and sister consumed by the flames that had ravaged their home. Tection's *good fortune* at being outside when the blaze occurred, was something he questioned frequently during his life, often wondering if it would not have been better to perish with them as a family unit; close until the end. Instead, he had been raised in an orphanage; a place where children of unfortunate circumstance were kept collectively under the auspices of men of God, keepers of faith.

Selim had difficulty understanding such a concept. In his world, any child of such unfortunate circumstance was gathered in by the tribe and nurtured collectively.

Tection was not so fortunate. And within this orphanage, where the world was ruled by men of varying characters, there were some who abused the situation, who took advantage of the young boys and worked them beyond expectations, punished them with impunity, and emotionally carved them from the innocence of their youth. Tection did not reveal that he had also been sexually assaulted by one of these deliverers of faith; these purveyors of the truth. He still harboured too much guilt and shame from that episode in his life to allow it to be regurgitated from his bowels. He consciously reminded himself, probably on a daily basis, that none of that misfortune was his own fault. It was something perpetrated on him by someone abusive and disturbed. Despite that clear understanding and his eventual capacity to move beyond the burning memories of the abuse, he had not yet forgiven himself for eventually killing the perpetrator. He realized killing him had been an accident; a blow from his fist steeped in rage and reaction, but he could not escape the feeling that taking the life was ultimately more hideous than his own sufferings. He had run through the whole spectre of justification; he had probably saved others from the fate of abuse, the culprit deserved what he got, even that God had intervened and made his blow more powerful than otherwise possible, thus ending the life of the man, the priest. Still, when speaking to Selim, he painted the story black enough, possibly exaggerating certain other physical abuses to overcome the lack of revelation about molestation and his darkest of moments.

He did not give specifics, but he did reveal to Selim that he had killed one of the brothers, one of the faith fathers, who had significantly abused the privilege of scholar and caretaker, bringing great harm to many young men in his care, providing lasting scars, physical and emotional, to tarnish their young lives moving forward. He had done so after his release from the orphanage, after he had built a valuable and happy life.

Selim was shocked. He knew Tection well enough to know he was a good man, one of character, of principles, one with a good and honest heart. He remembered how Tection had carefully examined the bandits to ensure they were not in serious condition. Only a good heart would demonstrate such care for an enemy. He asked Tection why; why, after surviving the hardships of the orphanage and finding the fortitude to build a life of value and reward, had he resorted to such an act?

Tection went on to explain that he had witnessed the brother applying the same evil affliction to another young boy, a mere wisp of a lad, helpless and innocent, just as Tection had been, just as Malika was.

Invoking her name gave immediate impact to the story and helped Selim understand the anger that Tection had faced. Tection knew the pain and confusion this Brother was delivering into the lives of many others as well, and he had snapped. He had reacted without conscience, without regard for his own soul, delivering a blow for all who had suffered at this monster's hands. He had not intended to kill him, at least he did not think so, although that question remained an unresolved internal controversy as well.

Unfortunately, the blow to the monster had really been a blow to Tection. He had not been charged with the murder, as others were equally aware of this monster's crimes against innocence, and protected the truth with a veil of accidental death. But Tection had loosed upon himself that which he could not escape; the fact that he was capable of an anger, a pent-up emotional outburst that was uncontrolled. Tection had run from the situation. He had left behind his comfortable world. He had wanted to outrun his dark side, the part of him that enabled him to kill, to overlook the sanctity of life as though he were judge and executioner.

Selim was dumbfounded. Tection was such a kind and gentle man. Yes, he was strong and agile as a fighter, but only when circumstances offered no alternative. But a killer? It didn't seem possible. He recognized that Tection was a stranger now, not from Selim and the tribe, but from himself. He was lost internally, holding dear the characteristics which he believed defined him, which gave him purpose in life, yet recognizing that other characteristics lurked within, their release uncontrollable by him.

Selim shared some sorrow with Tection. He tried to comfort him, to offer some sage advice on what the future could bring and the happiness and purpose he could find with the tribe, but Tection knew his stay with them was temporary. They had been his salvation of sorts, his sanctuary as he dealt with the internal battle he was constantly waging.

On the day Tection decided to leave, he surprised everyone. Why had he not given them notice? They would surely have convinced him to stay. Was he not well enough treated? Did he need a wife? Yet, all of these things were the very reason he did not provide any advance notification. He wished not for such fanfare or parting sorrow.

His last conversation with Malika was more revealing to Tection than he realized at first. She was very sad at his planned departure and cried inconsolably. Tection tried comforting her, confirming their paths would cross again, telling her she was special and now, armed with another language, could communicate with an entirely new segment of the wide world, one she knew nothing about yet.

Malika regained her composure. She told Tection, in the words only innocent children could muster, that he was the best person she knew and that she hoped one day to be like him; so kind, generous, and loving, attentive to others and selfless in his needs. Tection was surprised at her comments and received them with a question mark as always, uncertain if all she said was really true for a murderer. He told her he was not always the best person, not always flawless in his nature.

"You are what you are," she said. "You give what you give, that is all I can know of you. I have not seen anything bad from you, not ever. So, if you have something bad," she reached over and touched his chest, "you have it somewhere where I cannot see it, where I cannot know it. Please keep it there always." She smiled.

Tection could not resist, he lifted her in a powerful hug, perhaps too powerful, and began to cry. He did not want to, but he could not prevent it. Others nearby thought he must be crying at the sadness of their final goodbye, but his tears were for the powerful understanding that came from the young girl, the window she had opened into his soul, with her innocent and uncorrupted observation of his character. He felt certain he would one day have a child of his own. Children were amazing!

Upon his final goodbye to Selim, the man took Tection's hand, and placed a small cube into it. "This was given to me many years ago, when I was a young boy."

Tection looked down. It was a dice-like cube, with various symbols depicted on each face. One side had a crescent moon with a single star; there was an eight-spoked wheel of Dharma; a cross; an Aum symbol; a taijitu, or ying-yang circle; and a six-pointed star.

Tection wasn't certain what all the symbols meant, but he immediately recognized that they were symbols of faith. "I cannot accept this from you Selim, it must be very important to you."

"It is important to me, and that is exactly why I want you to have it. I could give you many expensive gifts, but they would not be worthy of what you have given me and my family. Only a gift of personal importance is worthy." Selim looked at Tection. The large man was about to offer more words of protest, but Selim continued. "It is not intended as any repayment or any such notion. I know you have given of yourself to us. It is not a thank you for saving us from bandits nor even in appreciation of all that you have taught Malika. It is something from my heart to yours, something to help you cover the lost ground you have bypassed, something to remind you, no, to reinforce within you, that the world is a better place because you are in it. Please take it, and you will give it to someone later, someone you want to share the path with."

Tection was astounded. Selim appeared to be such a simple family man, a member of the collective, devoted to his tribe. His perception and understanding of Tection's dilemma was evident, even profound.

Tection hugged the man, one last time. "Thank you."

Nothing more was needed. He departed to loud cheers, endless waving hands, and somewhere on the side of the crowd, quiet tears on the face of one young girl.

Talia Twists and Travel

Andela danced and whooped a little, racing around the yard like a random tomcat, leaping here and pouncing there. Talia laughed as she watched, trying to imitate her moves but realizing it was not possible. Andela had no earthly responsibilities. She was void of attachment to gravity and completely without need for oxygen or caution.

Talia heard her mother call out from the rear of the house, forewarning her of the impending end to her morning folly. Andela heard her as well. She tumbled again, leapt up towards the small cluster of strawberry vines, and slipped out of sight, back to her realm of the unknown and unseen. She would be safe there, tucked away in the soft light, just out of mind's thought, but merely a moment from a young girl's wishful thinking, waiting patiently for Talia to coax her once again into the private world they shared. Talia's mother called to Talia again, beckoning her inside for her mid-day meal. Andela would have to return to temporary hibernation until she and Talia could once again join forces in their imaginary world of enchanted lands and mythical adventure.

Talia and Andela danced and romped through a timeless succession of childhood adventures. Andela's lack of attachments to the earthly world of Talia also meant that she was not affected by time and the slow but steady passing of it. Talia, however, grew in age and empathy, absorbing the world at her pace, embracing her physical growth with much wonder and curiosity, while Andela languished in a gradually diminishing role. Imaginary friends, although immortal, were nevertheless subject to lengthy abandonment. Perhaps Andela's most reasonable fate was to be a fragment of memory at some distant time, during some reflective moment. But Talia had other plans for Andela!

As Talia grew into a young lady, everyone told her how beautiful she was, how she was going to make some man very happy, deliver sparkling babies into the world, and make her parents proud. That seemed like quite a lot of responsibility for someone so young and unsure of what her true desires were. The thought of having her own family and sharing a lifetime with one person was a distant, if not absent, consideration. Her own parents' marriage was an imperfect union and Talia knew that, although she was not able to fully understand or articulate such matters internally. She wondered if anyone would ever ask her to get married.

Right now, she was young and wished only to be old enough to do as she pleased; to make decisions of her own choice and face consequences of her own making. She did not want to be the favoured child, gathered into closed situations under the watchful eyes of parents, relatives, servants, and, as she was constantly reminded, God himself. Although God was always referred to as He, Talia considered her god to be a she; it was the only way she was comfortable to speak with *her*.

Her wish to be old enough to make her own decisions and to chase her own future, was countered regularly by her father's constant contrary reflection, of wishing only to be younger, more energized, and free from the burdens of morning stiffness and aching

Talia Twists and Travel

muscles. Talia wondered what the *right* age really was. What was the balance between experience, vibrancy, responsibility, education, career, and family? Too many components to find consensus. Her father always told her to be patient, that life would happen as it was supposed to, *first-things-first*, and *all-in-due-time*. She was so tired of that rhetoric. She wanted it to happen now!

When Talia kept her eyes closed, she was free from the surrounding world. Inside, she could do and be whatever she wished. No parents to direct her, teachers to admonish her, or God to intimidate her. Even though she was told every Sunday that God was inside her if she let him in, which was quite contrary to the equally professed fact that God was only accessible through her priest, she felt confident that she was in complete control of her inner world, and the big God was only able to see her when she opened her eyes to *let* Him in. Despite that shadow of pre-eminence, she knew there was something very powerful and personal within her, though she was as yet unable to really determine what it was. She was fearless in her inner world. She could create great conquests and harrowing tragedies, endless romance and flagrant behaviour, charity of wealth and kindness of spirit. If only the real world, the *eyes-open* world, could be as easily navigated.

Talia, her mother Phoebe, and her father Nasos, lived in a very large house, built on many acres of cultivated land, complete with olive groves and several fields of tobacco. The land had belonged to Phoebe's late father, and he left it to Phoebe and Nasos when he passed away. It was leased out to a neighbour, who constantly approached Phoebe and Nasos about buying them out.

"No need," Nasos would always say. "You can farm it for us. Who knows when we might want to become farmers ourselves?"

The neighbour always smiled sarcastically, and returned to his affairs. But Nasos was not a farmer. He was a senior diplomat and constantly travelling on one mission or another, often gone for long periods. When they were first married and Phoebe's father was still alive, Phoebe would accompany Nasos on his missions. When Talia was born, she was soon added to the caravan. The rather nomadic life Talia lived with her parents made it difficult to build many friendships. She had only some neighbourhood friends back home, girls she had shared life's beginnings with, who had joined her in birthday celebrations or early school scribblings. During those first formative years the family was travelling much of the time.

Talia wasn't sure when Andela had appeared, when she'd first popped out of the roadside shrubbery of her current destination, but she had been a blessing for Talia and her hunger for companionship. Andela came out whenever Talia called to her and was exactly the person and persona that Talia needed, or more precisely, wanted. The only other person who knew Andela existed was Talia's mother. She didn't know Andela by name, but she often watched from afar as Talia and her imaginary friend shared time and space in the yard or perhaps in the corridor of imagination between Talia's bed and her window.

As Talia grew older, Andela did her best to keep pace, but she was destined to fall victim to time and circumstance. Talia was nearing young adulthood and polishing social skills that seemed only to deliver renewed acquaintances and interchangeable conversation at even the most formal and temporary of social gatherings. Talia called less and less to Andela, letting her languish for long periods in her dormant state, freed only for the occasional, short-lived adventure. By the time Talia's attention and considerations turned to young men, Andela was almost forgotten.

As Talia's education developed and her adolescence retreated, her need for imaginary friends, even one so long-standing and emotionally close, dwindled. Her childhood musings were replaced by the wonderment of adventure, fantasy, and curiosity. Her mind was opened by life and by living, and her questions about purpose, potential and destiny were gaining momentum. Talia was not satisfied with complacency and adherence; bound by the teachings chosen for her, the religion governing her, and the behaviour demanded of her. She wanted information and clarification. She wanted control and command over decisions and development. Unfortunately, these were beyond her youthful grasp, somewhat frowned upon by her mother, and especially frowned upon by her father. He often treated her as though she were still twelve years old, or at least that's how she felt. She was sixteen and easily carried herself socially with the maturity of a twenty-year-old. It was something she had learned from numerous diplomatic functions, and through osmosis from the constant instruction on protocol, presentation, and posture.

She was bursting from her childhood and embracing the beginnings of womanhood; something her mother sensed and tried to guide her into, unfortunately with poor skills and limited experience, as her own life had been one of even more strict diplomatic suffocation. Talia's father ignored his daughter's blossoming transformation and continued to think of her as his little girl, cute and quiet, a show piece for others, an affirmation of his character as a husband, father, and trustworthy individual. The ideal diplomat.

During this time in life, this period of self-discovery and esoteric questioning, Talia did not need an imaginary friend, rather she needed a guidance counsellor, a personal confidant, without judgment or discrimination, armed with knowledge and understanding. What she didn't realize was that Andela was also morphing; from bubbling buddy in the back yard, to staunch confident and universal consultant. She burst on the scene at some point during Talia's sixteenth year, full of opinion and suggestion, helping Talia decipher the enormity of change occurring to her, both physically, socially, and spiritually. Talia was forming the stamp of independence, gradually piecing together the fortitude, autonomy, and self-empowerment that would shift her from curious child to independent woman. Talia didn't necessarily recognize that Andela was also being transformed, even though she herself was affecting Andela's evolution, from imaginary friend to counselling conscience.

At some point along this ragged road towards adulthood, because of these two worlds, the eyes-open and eyes-closed worlds, Talia concluded that there must be two gods; the omnipresent God of omnipotence and omniscience, and the little god, the personal one, of empowerment, development, and fantasy. Furthermore, this inner god was not always right, and often delivered thoughts and revelations that were unintended and far from perfect. The real God would not be so flippant. He carried a great responsibility to all the world and especially those who served Him directly. He was engaged with battling the Devil, and surely was consumed with such an arduous task. Her little internal god was only responsible to her, growing with her and helping her with decisions, direction, and deviation. Her god was not there to battle demons and save her from any fires.

It was some time before Talia realized that her inner god, her counsellor and confidant, was amazingly similar to Andela, her childhood friend, all grown up and learned in the wrangling of life, inspiration, and imagination. As she reflected on that, she easily grew a smile; a great and broad smile. She was caught in the sudden realization of this ironic turn of personality. Andela, a forgotten whisper of childhood, morphed into personal goddess and guardian. What a curious but persuasive revelation. Talia was ecstatic! The big imperious God of myth, fable, and legend; giver of truth and wielder of reckoning, retribution, and forgiveness, shone in a blinding light over the eyes-open world, while her own little god, the transformed Andela, shaking out cobwebs and curiosities from her eyes-closed world, guided her to individual growth, advancement, and speculation.

This type of transformation was a journey that varied greatly in linear time, from one person to another, but it was a swift and permanent passage for Talia. Her mother could not keep up with

Talia's personal growth and was soon reliant on *her* for advice and consultation, in a role reversal that occurred spontaneously and comfortably for both of them. By the time Talia's father recognized there had been such a change, it was already complete and entrenched. He faced his own struggles in coming to terms with what he called, Talia's *sudden-independence* and opinionated expressions. Even though her metamorphosis had developed over a period of time, his emotional distance from her and lack of commitment to the family core, had left him unaware until the adult Talia, one day, just seemed to appear. He handled it poorly at first, but soon realized that she was past the childhood stage, and he began to include her with a more mature and balanced demeanour.

With her father unavailable as a confident and her mother unable to provide the kind of emotional guidance Talia needed, she began to develop her own methodology for confronting and navigating the feelings and perceptions she was experiencing. The evolution of Andela was essential. She was the cornerstone of Talia's jump to maturity and the go-to point for every situation. Her imaginary friend was reconstructed, the childish Andela buried in the past, transformed into a constant companion, cautiously supporting the confidence and courage of a young woman.

Once Talia completed her primary education and moved on to secondary school, she and her mother ceased to accompany her father on his long diplomatic missions. It was important for Talia to concentrate her attention on schooling and build the foundation of her future. With her father gone for significant periods, Talia and her mother developed a stronger and more resilient relationship, with Talia actually maturing into the alpha personality between them. Her mother was confused during this period. She was uncertain about Talia's transition and a little anxious about how her daughter would turn out. She sensed an edge of recalcitrance, of non-conformance. She didn't reveal this to Talia, but it was quite disturbing for her. She was also uncertain in her own marriage, how the future would unfold for her, and perhaps even a little uneasy with the idea of Talia moving on and leaving her to live in some lonely, self-imposed isolation.

Talia's father now recognized both subtle and significant changes with each return from his journeys. Talia no longer played the role of a daughter, full of anticipation and joy at the prospect of her father's return. She was a young woman with confidence and purpose as she managed the process of life; benevolent architect of her home environment and guardian of her mother and herself.

Talia's inner god was a strong and committed empowerment tool. She gave Talia a sense of self-worth beyond her years. Talia was able to call upon her in any circumstance, through any situation. She often wondered if others had a personal god as well. She once attempted to discuss this with her mother, but the complete lack of comprehension, and even some suggestion concerning Talia's well-being for having such thoughts, left the possibility for any further discussion adrift. Talia settled in with her god, and decided not to share her situation with others. Maybe no one else actually had their own god. Maybe she was unique in that sense. Of course, she still had the big, universal God, that everyone shared, but He was only there to keep away soul-munching demons, not to provide advice and empowerment to the young daughter of some random diplomat. Talia was happy to have her own god, and she spent much time sharing thoughts with her and listening to advice from her. Andela helped Talia make decisions on a daily basis, drove her forward with self-confidence, and generally enabled her to transition from teenager to young woman.

Emotional Servitude

Julian stayed in the city for another month. He even saw Yasmine a couple of times walking around town, but he didn't speak to her again, letting the emotion of separation settle into a quiet pond, from the raging surf it had been. Yet, he thought about her often. As he went about organizing his life post-Yasmine and the accompanying whirlwind beginning to his journey, he even arranged a tutor to assist in his understanding of the local language. He discovered that he caught on rather quickly. Once he learned the tenses and key verbs, he was comfortable conversing with some of the locals.

He frequented a small café near his room, a place he could venture to and have some idle chat with the owner, waiters, or perhaps a customer or two. Because he went there every day, sometimes twice a day, he became familiar with some of the other patrons. One in particular shared his conversation more frequently, and it wasn't until they were decently familiar with each other that the middle aged man let it be known his fluency in Julian's mother tongue was actually quite impeccable. Julian admonished him for not revealing that fact earlier in their relationship, in a friendly barrage of comments alluding to the deceit and cunning perpetrated on him. His friend explained that he recognized Julian was learning their language and he wanted him to practice. He heaped compliments on Julian's progress to dissipate any lasting concerns, and the two men continued to chat in the local language, reverting to Julian's only when Julian was stuck and exasperated on some point he wanted to make.

Nasim was older than Julian, perhaps in his mid-forties, but treated him very much as an equal. He had spent the bulk of his years in this one spot, dispensing his legal expertise when needed and sharing his wit and humour when desired. His status as diplomatic liaison for several foreign governments provided him with a steady cash flow, intriguing foreign contacts, and community status he would not otherwise have achieved, even as a highly successful business lawyer. His late afternoons in the café were his daily escape and the bridge from his busy corporate, professional life, to the simple, reflective, and often introspective lifestyle his middle age was manifesting.

Julian nurtured that part of Nasim that longed for understanding and insight into other parts of the world, beyond what could be garnered from reading, deduced by observation, or gleaned from the guarded conversations prevalent at his frequent diplomatic affairs. It was not just the physical and cultural differences associated with foreign societies; Nasim also relished the opportunity to gain insight, and consequently wisdom, from the younger man and his generation. He was interested in the abstruse nature of the human condition in other lands, and he could not realize that understanding from written word or cautiously scripted discussion. Julian was clearly not highly educated, his lexicon revealed that, but he was somehow quite worldly and conversant with matters of life unprotected by barriers of social caution. His remarks were always genuine and heartfelt, almost as if he were wise beyond his years

Emotional Servitude

on diverse topics, yet immature on matters of emotional reflection. Nasim enjoyed his company and appreciated his insights, even if they were slightly parochial.

Julian was not sure why, but he found comfort in recounting to Nasim his short but powerful relationship with Yasmine and the misery their separation was causing him. Nasim was attentive and careful not to make light of the situation, which was projected by Julian's expression as one of utmost seriousness. *Ah, first love; how I long for such sweet anguish again*, Nasim thought. He was careful not to trivialize the situation and sympathized with Julian while urging him to overcome the emotional negativity and replace it instead with the understanding that he had garnered both experience and education from the relationship, not to mention a plethora of physical recollections that could sustain him until another Yasmine entered his life.

Julian looked over at Nasim, unsure as to whether he was making fun of him or being wise and profound in his comments. Nasim looked back, stoic and stern in his facial expression. Julian cracked a smile. Nasim cracked a smile. The two men laughed out loud and ordered more coffee. Julian was not only getting over Yasmine; he was far more aware of the impact unbridled emotional attachments could have on the psyche. *I'll need to be more cautious on what I become entangled with*, he realized.

Later in the evening, after he had returned to his room, snacked on some flat bread and lamb slices moistened with humus, and washed it down with a healthy portion of wine, Julian reclined on his bed and gazed through the open window towards the twinkling heavens above. Stars danced in their sparkling flicker of light, inspired by the music of everlasting timelessness, and sister moon, only partially revealed this evening, sat comfortably on the edge of the night sky, rocking the world to slumber. His thoughts dwelled on the drama of emotions, the strength of unseen forces that shape our actions and reactions, and the endless effort to manage it all.

The Journey: Erudite

Julian knew he had an evil edge to his being, a hidden, or more accurately, buried component of his persona. It had surfaced very few times in his life, but he knew it was there. He had once kicked a startled and defenseless cat that had innocently tripped him, driving it towards some permanent injury. Even though Julian had made considerable effort to help heal the creature and provided care and comfort as he could, the animal was forever a reminder that he was capable of such evil action. His fleeting wish to bring harm to Yasmine for her folly was yet another reminder of his darker side. He longed for an opportunity to rid himself of it. He often felt the fear and adrenalin that accompanied its occasional rise to the surface, hungry for existence and careless in the journey upward, bumping and jostling both Julian and whoever else might be impeding its resurrection.

Of course, he could no more rid himself of this dark hunger than he could change his very nature. He was a kind, understanding, perceptive, and curious individual. He relished newly kindled relationships, whether casually friendly, scholarly, or emotionally binding. He cherished the importance these relationships brought him, recognizing his value and responsibility toward the other person, realizing that they too were committing part of their being, their existence, towards the interplay between them. All these people sharing lives together, and Julian with a seemingly unquenchable thirst for new encounters, new relationships; almost as if they were feeding his life-energy, chasing adventure of the body, the mind, and the soul.

He swirled this concoction of thoughts around internally until they began to morph into something else. He took the simplest expression or recognition, and bent it into a sub-condition, revealing a more esoteric revelation. At first, Julian paid little heed to such rambling diversions, shaking them from his evening's mental wandering. But he realized that he was the one driving these shifting manifestations, he was the only passenger on this voyage and

Emotional Servitude

was in control of the direction his thoughts were heading; perhaps not consciously in control, but spiritually unaffected or influenced by input from others.

Am I chasing new adventure, or am I running away from an uncomfortable past? Am I interested and inspired by others, or using their contributions to build my own ego? Can I allow others to gain access to my inner-most self, or must I maintain a barrier to guard who I am? Would their presence change me? Is it to be another who helps me rid the evil that lurks within? Am I capable of love, of unbridled commitment?

Many questions and few answers. Julian was not intimidated by this crush of uncertainty, he was secure in his conscious contemplations, though he recognized he was curiously inept at reflection on his unconscious deliberations and dilemmas.

He initiated some understanding of the moment, but the shift in direction his internal journey was taking remained unrecognized. Julian began building a reflection on emotional engagement.

We consciously control our actions and projections, yet we cannot access certain areas of our souls without the catalyst of emotional stimulation, and even though this is recognized, we cannot steer emotions towards any particular part of our internal landscapes; they dive and dart wherever they wish and pull up internal reactions wherever they touch. And exactly where does religion dance in this lifelong musical performance? Is it bound to finding ways to stimulate emotions within followers, so they can access certain internal areas that might otherwise be left in limbo?

Julian realized that a large part of growing, of maturing, was gaining a greater ability to control one's emotions. He thought it unfortunate at first, but came to a more sensible conclusion, that unbridled emotion let loose on the world might bring havoc and melancholy to humanity, rather than propitiousness and hedonism. He drifted back to his earlier reflections that the negative emotions were much more powerful than the positive ones. And they were much more prevalent; anger, sadness, disgust, fear, and surprise, all wrestling for emotional control, with happiness standing resolute to ward them off in a constant attack of shifting reality. Guilt riding a separate energy stream deep into the unconscious being; often an internal battle, openly un-manifested but internally corrosive. And where did that leave love and of course her siblings, joy, desire, adoration, and passion? Those were the good siblings! Lost love also delivered the most forceful opposites; anger, jealousy, vengeance, agony, and sorrow. *Love is a most powerful emotion*, Julian thought, *perhaps that is why it is so elusive and so misunderstood. No doubt Nasim will have some light to shed on this dilemma.*

Nasim was sitting in his usual chair, holding his tiny espresso cup with both hands, making it all but impossible to see. He spotted Julian from afar, hiking up the soft slope between the lower road and the higher one, head bowed, watching his own feet make their ritual march. As he reached the top of the small hill, Julian lifted his head and saw Nasim, unaware that Nasim had been watching his journey for a while. He waved in recognition of the older gentleman and headed to the same table, any thoughts of requesting whether Nasim wanted his company lost in the certainty of their friendship.

"And what is driving that most serious look on your young face this afternoon?" Nasim queried, half-serious and half-inspired as a conversation starter.

"Love," Julian replied.

Nasim looked at him, raising his eyebrows and squeezing his lips together slightly in an obvious recognition of the impact such topics might deposit on a casual café conversation.

"I think I'm beginning to understand why it is so elusive," Julian continued. He waited for Nasim to make some comment that would elicit additional disclosure on his revelations, but he offered none. Julian continued just the same. "It is such a powerful emotion that we are vulnerable and bewildered when it bubbles upward, while we remain helpless to prevent its rise within us and completely unprepared to handle the power it possesses, and the attention it demands." Again, Julian looked at Nasim, waiting for a partner in this conversation.

Nasim looked back with some anticipation etched on his face, curious to hear the rest of Julian's dissertation on this most powerful emotion; a long-lost distant memory for him.

"I cannot properly explain it with a few words," Julian claimed with some resignation, "But I have seen it manifest itself in a variety of ways, always dragging other emotions behind it."

Julian thought back to his own loveless parents, a void of love; the joy of reunification his friend Tection had enjoyed when meeting his son for the first time, love finally released; and his best friend John P, suffering at the moment of his father's death, a father he had not been aware of, losing a love that never arrived. So many variations; all powerful and compelling, yet diverse and distinct in the emotion being delivered. And then there was Yasmine, a new and fresh love, born from his flesh he realized, not his spirit. But it was still love, perhaps a kind of *young-love* as the terminology went, perhaps defined as just such, young and physical, animalistic and intense, but unbinding to the spirit, unchained from the heart.

Julian was a little lost in his thoughts when Nasim's voice brought him back into the as yet, one-sided conversation.

"The problem with love is not only our inability to recognize and control it, but equally our lack of desire to understand it. We do not question the emotion of it as it captures us, nor do we recognize it soon enough to prevent it. Even when we avoid that which we know we love, in some intellectual effort to reduce its power, we only strengthen its impact on our being. Running away from love while carrying it safely tucked in our hearts is a voyage doomed to failure."

Julian smiled at the simple irony of Nasim's last statement. He then switched languages to better convey the balance of his initial exposé. "It is the most powerful word in our language, our human language, regardless of what dialect is being spoken. It represents the binding of parent and child, siblings, and even favourite animals, yet is diverse enough to also encompass the passionate entanglements of lovers and beloved, conditions of time, and places of travel. It is a word used to occupy any place in our existence that generates joy and happiness, yet it also fuels the conflicts of life. The fierce engagements of armies over the love of *their* god, or *their* land, the battle between lovers who chase the same prize, the excuse for irrational behaviour of all sorts, and the very anchor of life-long commitment and even servitude. So completely encompassing, often debilitating, yet most desired whenever it is not present."

Julian's thoughts again returned to his parents, his childhood, and his endless desire for a family of loving relations of his own; things he thought were tucked safely away in his youthful archives. The relationship between hate and love was again at the forefront. His parents, as despicable as he perceived them, were forever his, even as an emotional burden to his psyche, even as a bad memory to his longings of life.

"She will become a reckless and incomplete memory, my young friend," Nasim offered, obviously referring to Yasmine.

"She is already that, Nasim. It is older and more permanent memories that are chasing my mind this day."

"Let them find you then. Confronting them, even embracing them, it gives you strength over them."

Curious concept, Julian thought, *that too will require some additional reflection. Perhaps burying my sorrows beneath my joy is only a camouflage destined to fall to the wayside from time to time, requiring continuous maintenance of my joyful overlay. If I can dig my joy as a foundation and let my sorrow lie upon it instead, perhaps I can tug joy up through the sorrow and set it asunder, crashed into a million pieces, shards of reality too miniscule to recognize and too blunt to penetrate my being.* Julian flashed back on a dream he once had. A dream of a friend, a saviour perhaps, who rescued him and then collapsed into just such an avalanche of a million broken pieces. He shivered.

After a complete lack of resolution to the dilemma of love, but with consensus on a decision to move to a lighter conversation, they

Emotional Servitude

enjoyed a long hour of banter and repartee. Nasim and Julian eventually parted company, both of them feeling enriched by their shared dialogue; Nasim enjoying the revelations of youth and the triggers to his own memories, and Julian thankful for this wise companion, who did not preach *to* him, but rather sparked the thought process *within* him. As they prepared to head in their separate directions, Nasim casually dropped an invitation to Julian. There was a diplomatic affair the next day, which was a social and entertaining event. Nasim had an extra ticket for the event, and Julian was in dire need of some escapism. At first Julian refused, feigning weariness and other unspecified responsibilities. Nasim reached into his pocket and pulled out a fair-sized stack of currency, one Julian had often noticed before. He peeled off a few bills and handed them to Julian.

"What's this for then?" Julian questioned; his hand hesitant to take the funds.

"Take it," Nasim said with some mock annoyance, jabbing his hand forward towards Julian's. "You will need a suit. There is a shop on the *Front de Mer* called Kaporal. Go there and see Taysir."

"I have my own funds," Julian said, even though he had no intentions of spending them on fancy clothing.

"Keep those funds for travelling and support, not for fancy clothing." Nasim laughed at his own remarks. His laugh was always larger than life.

Julian still hesitated to take the money. Nasim finally grabbed his hand and pushed the paper down into it.

"Tell Taysir you are going to my event tomorrow evening and need a suit. He will take care." Nasim looked Julian in the eye, widening his own eyes in mock anger this time. "Do it, and hurry. See him today and it will be ready tomorrow." He turned and marched off, still laughing in his friendly manner, "See you tomorrow at seven," he declared, without turning around. "I'll collect you in front of the café." And he was gone.

Talia Travel and Twists

Talia's newly found confidence was visible to everyone. She walked with purpose, spoke with assurance, and took charge of her personal environment without outside encouragement. Her mother was completely astounded with the changes occurring in her daughter. She became more reliant on Talia to direct the course of each day and allowed her to assume a role of schedule maker and daily planner. Talia's grades were superior and she did her home studies faithfully and diligently, without prodding. Her mother's anxiety over Talia's eventual development into a woman, and her uncertainty that she had handled everything *properly*, as expected, was washed away. She ultimately realized that Talia's development was one of independence and self-identity, and not rebellion. She relaxed noticeably, letting life once again sweep over her.

Nasos was also impressed with Talia, and this period brought a distinct change in his demeanour towards her. She was a little surprised when, following the completion of her school year, he invited her to join him on a mission of some distance; one that would take at least a month to complete. He did not invite her mother to join them, a point that was not lost on anyone. Her mother encouraged her to go, suppressing her own concerns of a personally lonely and solitary summer, while expounding on the possibilities for adventure, development, and experience Talia might encounter.

It was agreed, and Talia danced between the excitement of anticipation and the stress of apprehension, which thickened as the departure time neared. She bid farewell to her mother, the obligatory tears and lamentations delivered, and set out with her father and his entourage of support staff and diplomatic deputies; and of course, the ghost of Andela, now with god status, fully packed and ready to travel, brazenly reminding Talia of the adventures they might enjoy on such a distant journey.

Talia filled her role admirably during the trip; daughter of a senior diplomat, with protocol and behaviour perfectly honed. She had been to numerous functions in the past, always as a girl, but these were different. She was treated as an adult and developed separate conversations outside the social butterflying of her father. Initially, he always kept one eye out for her, but as their trip evolved and her social capabilities became evident, he relaxed his concerns. By the end of their journey he was quite comfortable with her wandering the social events under her own compass. Talia soon realized that these diplomatic functions were indistinguishable from one another. Some faces changed and the venues shifted slightly, but the core of each event was identical, and the behaviour of each individual predictable. Two events would have been sufficient to recognize this, but Talia was now on her sixth and final evening social. She had enjoyed the travel, spiriting quickly through new cities and landscapes, always lacking the time to explore thoroughly, and forever chasing the details of the day's itinerary. It was like travelling far to get somewhere and then reading a book about it, as you stood steadfast, watching it float by.

As this last evening gala drew towards an end, Talia stepped out onto a small solitary balcony and moved into a corner, allowing her vision of the sparkling sky, climbing out and above the distant sea, to blur into a mosaic of starlight and shimmer. She was lost in her tranquility when the balcony door was pushed open and a young man strode out towards the railing. He was seemingly lost in thought, sipping at a glass of alcohol.

"The lights are like jewels. If you just un-focus your vision for a moment and let the blur of their illumination merge, they appear as jewels," she said, breaking the silence of the evening and no doubt startling the young man.

He twirled and froze for a moment. Talia wasn't sure if he was upset that she was there, or more likely she figured, a little stunned by her presence, if not her appearance.

"I'm sorry," he said, half as a delay tactic while his brain assimilated what she had said, and half as a reality-check confirmation that Talia was real. She said nothing, He turned and looked out towards the sky as her comment received his reflection.

"Diamonds, no doubt," he finally said.

Talia liked his response and she liked his voice and she liked his appearance and she liked...she liked *him*. She wanted to say something equally as thought provoking as her original remark, but only managed a proper diplomatic comment.

"Are you visiting here, or do you reside nearby?" She felt foolish as the words escaped her mouth, *much too juvenile*, she thought.

"I don't know," he answered. "I mean, I do live here right now, but I am only passing through or staying for a short while. I mean, I don't know how long I'll be here."

He doesn't articulate things very well, she thought.

"I'm passing through as well," she replied. "My father travels constantly and this summer has me sharing his itinerary, ostensibly to enlighten my understanding of the world and enhance my otherwise academic education. But really, it usually just bores me to death." She laughed at her reply, not at the point she was making, but rather the nearly professional form her words were taking. How many times had she repeated that particular sentence? Definitely her father's daughter. "Are you travelling with your parents as well?"

"No, I departed from my parents immediately when old enough to do so," he said, without revealing exactly when that was. "Today I am a guest of our host, Mister Nasim. Do you know him?"

"I met him this evening. He is quite a jovial fellow, quick to laugh and obviously a happy person," Talia replied, sincere in her remark as she truly had enjoyed Nasim's nature.

He smiled at her comment. "Yes, that's him."

Talia reached out with her right arm, lifting it gently towards him. "I'm Talia, daughter of Nasos," she offered.

He took her hand and gently brought it to his lips in a ceremonial kiss.

"Julian," he simply replied.

They stood together on the balcony for some time, their glances awkwardly returning to the jewelled sky each time they caught one another looking at the other. Talia had a permanent smile across her lips, and she was feeling the distinct tingle of harmony flowing through her body whenever their arms or shoulders occasionally touched. He was handsome and young, and apparently pensive in his reflections, although that could have just been his internal panic at the possibility of saying something inadequate, or worse, inappropriate. Most of their conversation was question and answer, alternating between lives, although Talia was certainly providing more information than Julian was. He remained a bit of a mystery, which was much more appealing to her than the alternative. She reached out with both hands at some point and held his arm, pulling it gently towards her, extremely cognizant of the moment it brushed past her breast. She held it momentarily beside her. As she made some comment about the beauty of the evening, the balcony door opened.

She released Julian's arm immediately, and they both turned to see who had interrupted their privacy. It was Talia's father. He was a little angry, she could tell, although not sure if it was because she was with a young man in a secluded environment, or whether it was because she had abandoned the room full of diplomats, momentarily relinquishing her responsibilities. She introduced Julian and the two men exchanged standard pleasantries. Her father wanted her to return to the event and meet some people of significance. Julian held the door for them and followed them into the room.

Talia leaned in to give him a small kiss on the cheek as she began to move away, much to the surprise of her father...and Julian. Her body once again tingled with the contact, and she was certain her face must have flushed.

"See you soon, I hope," she commented, before following her father back to the important tasks at hand.

Talia thought about Julian throughout the balance of the evening and indeed, long into the night, as she lay awake in her bed. She eventually slid towards sleep with romantic visions of him shifting indiscriminately in her head, dancing from warm embrace, to frolicking with him in fields of grass and wind. She drifted from consciousness, a small smile still on her lips.

Ladies Lost, Love and Luck

Julian had not worn a suit since the funeral of his friend's father several months back, and even then, it was only one he had borrowed from a customer, a regular at his previous café, in his previous life. He had certainly never owned anything as spectacular as the suit he found himself dressed in, standing nervously outside the café, waiting for Nasim to arrive. He had managed to visit a barber, shaving off weeks of scruff and roughage, revealing his youthful and serious face.

Nasim was shocked. "My word, there is an actual person behind that rough garden you called a beard," he laughed.

Julian smiled, feeling somewhat inhibited, almost as if he was suddenly standing naked in front of the world. Nasim was dressed impeccably, head to foot, visibly shined, buffed, pressed, and no doubt, beneath it all, scrubbed to pink perfection.

The affair was beyond anything Julian had witnessed. People dressed in fine clothing, the likes of which he had never seen. Music of superior quality pulling dancers along as puppets, hopelessly caught in the pulse of notes springing from the musical instruments that fired them. Beautiful women, carefully manicured and landscaped into statuesque condition, seemingly afraid to bend or turn too quickly, less a lash or limb should fall off. The men, their suitors, wrapped in uniforms of diplomacy, ties and perhaps tails, responding appropriately to the curtsies with courteous bows. It looked completely scripted, each movement choreographed and every word rehearsed. Julian was not used to it, or familiar with it, or appreciative of it.

Nasim accompanied Julian for the first few minutes, introducing him randomly to the initial people they encountered, but he was soon off fulfilling his role as diplomat, and, as Julian soon discovered, host. Meanwhile, Julian hugged the sidelines of the event, casually strolling towards the buffet tables, lush with every imaginable food. He indulged for a while, carefully glancing up from time to time to ensure no one perceived him as gluttonous. After consuming his fill, and a few of the circulating glasses, he secured a stronger snifter of cognac and found a small door leading to a vacant balcony of sorts. A perfect spot to help in the passing of time. He certainly did not want to offend or criticize Nasim, especially after the generosity his friend had showed in securing his attire, and the insight he had shared in speculating on the inseparableness of life and love.

He leaned on the railing and gazed out at the city from his elevated vantage point, loosing himself in some recollections of the sea and her quiet power.

"The lights are like jewels. If you just un-focus your vision for a moment, and let the blur of their illumination merge, they appear as jewels."

He heard the voice but wasn't sure of its origin. He stood up sharply, suddenly refocusing on reality, and turned towards the young lady who had made the perceptive observance. She was exquisite; alluring without effort, graceful without movement. Julian stared momentarily. She smiled.

He shook his head as if to wake himself up. "I'm sorry," he finally blurted out. A rather useless bit of conversation, especially as his first words to this beautiful stranger. Even *he* wasn't sure if he meant he was sorry for delaying a response, as an apology for not hearing her comment and requesting her to repeat her observation, or just for being on this balcony with her and behaving immaturely. She smiled. He was immediately sure he had fallen in love... again. He looked back out towards the lights, ostensibly to reflect on her suggestion of a jewelry landscape.

He turned back to her. "Diamonds, no doubt." *A much better retort*, he thought, with some relief.

"Are you visiting here, or do you reside nearby?"

"I don't know," Julian said, again feeling he sounded somewhat the fool. "I mean, I do live here right now, but I am only passing through, or staying for a short while, I mean, I don't know how long I'll be here." He was obviously flustered by her presence, not her question, as that was as simple as she could muster.

"I'm passing through as well," she replied, seemingly unaware of how silly his response was. "My father travels constantly and this summer has me sharing his itinerary, ostensibly to enlighten my understanding of the world, and enhance my otherwise academic education. But really, it usually just bores me to death." She laughed a little giggle. "Ae you travelling with your parents as well?" she asked, making him feel he was younger looking than he expected.

"No," he said matter-of-factly. "I departed from my parents immediately when old enough to do so. Today I am a guest of our host, Mister Nasim. Do you know him?"

"I met him this evening. He is quit a jovial fellow, quick to laugh and obviously a happy person."

"Yes," Julian smiled broadly, "That's him."

Her name was Talia. They chatted for a while, which was actually an hour or more, and would have remained in conversation longer, had her father not found them on the balcony. He looked slightly angry at first, finding them secluded from the evening's festivities, creating an awkward moment before Talia slid over to hold her father's arm and introduced Julian to him.

"Father, this is Julian, a friend of Mister Nasim. Julian, my father, Nasos."

Julian being a friend of Nasim's certainly lightened the mood. Nasos extended his hand and the men exchanged grips, Julian careful to make his firm, but less so than her father's, looking him in the eye with all the respect he could muster. It was a skill he had fashioned and honed when living a life of service to his previous customers in his small café. A café that seemed like an eternity away now, but was actually just across the sea. Her father relaxed and finished the hello, but then urged her back to the room. There were some people he wanted her to meet before they wrapped up the event. Julian held the door for them and followed Talia back into the room.

As her father led her away, she leaned over and gave Julian a small kiss on the cheek. "See you soon, I hope."

And she was gone. Julian watched her glide across the floor toward the rendezvous with her father's acquaintances, feeling a spike of adrenalin when she looked back once and winked at him; a wink of innocent mischievousness, holding a promise of a future reunion. He raised his hand in a soft goodbye, *until then*.

Julian turned away from their direction with a plan to find Nasim, give his thanks for the evening, and make the accompanying farewell. Several guests were already leaving and enough time had passed to avoid any perception of his being an early departure. As he turned, he found himself directly in front of Yasmine! She too looked stunning. A rush of memories shot up though his spine and crashed into his brain. He tried to look nonchalant, but soon realized his mouth was slightly agape. He shut it. She smiled.

"Was that a new girlfriend?" she asked, obviously having witnessed his goodbye with Talia.

Julian looked back towards Talia, now far away across the room. "I suppose she is," he lied, feeling the joy of delivering some jealousy to Yasmine, somehow punishing her for the pain she had levied him. As soon as he said it, he regretted it. Not only was it not true, and possibly damaging to Talia's reputation, but he had delivered the comment with the intent to hurt Yasmine, something he did not want to do. His dark side in play!

He was about to rescind his affirmation when she leaned in and whispered to him. "I've missed you; I've missed our passion." She waited for him to move away but he didn't. "Come to my place tonight after two o'clock."

Julian felt the stirrings of passion, memories of their torrid past.

"Come on my dear, let's catch up with Arthur and Maude." Julian looked back. An older gentleman held Yasmine's arm and gently tugged her back towards the main room. One of her clients, no doubt. She kept her eyes on Julian for a moment, even as her body moved off with the stranger. She winked at him, a wink of overt sexuality, with a promise of memories revived. He raised his hand in a soft goodbye, *forever*.

Julian did not leave. He remained to the end, chatting with Nasim and some other guests he was introduced to. Nasim wondered where Julian had been for much of the evening, and Julian just smiled when Nasim suggested that perhaps a young lady had cornered him. Nasim could not know how close he was to the reality of the situation. Talia may have not cornered Julian physically, but she had certainly captivated him otherwise.

The evening finished without further adventure. Julian saw Yasmine leave with her customer and other friends, laughing and hugging as they descended the stairs, surely bound for another venue, perhaps music and dance yet to come. He also saw Talia leave, her soft, auburn-blonde hair bouncing across her bare shoulders, swaying to the music that continued to play despite the evening's conclusion. Her hair seemed to change colour, depending on the way the light shone upon it; a curious but most alluring quality. In the end, Nasim was the last to leave, and Julian remained with him until then.

When they departed, Nasim returned Julian to the café, where they mutually decided to procure one last coffee. The evening continued to pump in their veins and they knew sleep was a little way off yet. A coffee, though delivering caffeine, would still relax their heightened state and let them calm some stress. Julian was abundant in his appreciation to Nasim, and in spite of Nasim's calls for "no need," he lavished the older man with thanks. He hadn't realized Nasim's stature as a diplomat and citizen. The mayor and several civic politicians had been present, and the regional governors and indeed representatives of the executive, judicial, and legislative branches of power had all gathered to honour a sort of assembly of foreign diplomats. Julian wasn't entirely certain of the ongoing mission, but he did realize that this was at the highest level of the political world. He was a little in awe.

As they chatted idly before their good-night salutations, Julian managed to mention Talia.

Nasim smiled. "I knew it," he said, smug in his earlier reference to Julian's prolonged absence from the party. He let Julian's embarrassment fester for just a little bit, smiling at the casual discomfort. When Julian looked up at him, he delivered the exact comment he knew the young man was waiting for. "I am having lunch with a few people tomorrow," Nasim said, "including Talia and he father, Nasos."

He let that hang for a moment, watching Julian and seeing him build up the courage to ask for an invitation. He didn't make him do so. "Why don't you join us? You can wear the same suit, just change the shirt and tie, or better still, no tie at all."

"You really have been too kind," Julian said, his joy obvious and his mind already racing towards his expected path of conversation.

"Restaurant Les Gazelles at twelve sharp. Do you know it?"

"I do; it sits close to my lodging." Julian stood to leave. The end of the conversation had not been agreed, but he had all he needed for the rest of the night. Nasim looked delighted, shooing him off with a flick of the back of his hand and a smile on his face, driven once again by the reminiscences of youthful exuberance and vitality. He watched Julian walk away, certain that he spotted a small skip in his step.

Julian hurried home, anxious to fill more pages in his journal; something about being over Yasmine completely, but mostly about this new, amazing, and captivating young woman; Talia!

The next morning brought happiness and expectations of a fortuitous day, with hopes that such a disposition would continue throughout, being an exemplification of harmony, serenely pulling Julian towards the future in a dance of continuous fulfilment. He laughed at the bold expectation. He sat quietly in bed for a while, the prospect of such a day lingering with him, surprised at his own contentment and joy at the prospect of just seeing Talia again.

Am I in love? he thought, then quickly added the addendum, *again!* His thoughts turned momentarily to Yasmine as he realized he had not only passed on the opportunity to join her and wrestle with physical frenzy once more, but he had not even thought about her again, until this moment. *Indifference,* he confirmed to himself, *that is love's counterpart. Love and hate resting at point one and point three-fifty-nine on the circle, but indifference at point one-eighty, opposite of them both. That might explain the easy transition to, and difficult separation from, the love-hate relationship, with indifference being opposite and consequently fatal to either of them; both of them.*

The clarity of the moment was evident, but urgency jumped in, and reminded him he had to be at Les Gazelles at twelve; twelve sharp. He rose and showered casually, still confident that there was more than enough time. He lingered with his razor, ensuring every stray hair was scraped from his face, and then he dressed with purpose, retying his tie four times before remembering that Nasim had said not to wear one. He laughed at his state of fluster, feeling very much like the youth Talia had mistaken him for when they first met. He wondered how old she was, but reminded himself it was impolite to ask a lady's age. She was travelling with her father, but she seemed to be fulfilling the role of her father's confident supporter, rather than a daughter under his care.

He was dressed and ready to go when a knock hit his door. Julian was expecting no one, so he assumed it was either the landlord with a real-estate request, or a salesperson with a family to feed. He opened the door. Yasmine stood in front of him, already removing her outer garments.

"I missed you last night," she said, casually breezing by him into his room, dropping clothes as she went, and reclining suggestively onto his unmade bed. She looked at him, holding out her hand as an invitation to join her, her right leg swaying open and then closed in a rather wonton display. Julian continued to stare at her in some disbelief, realizing that he felt quite disinterested, realizing he was not at all aroused by her state of undress and open invitation.

He smiled at her. "Go home Yasmine," he said calmly, exiting the room and heading down the two flights of stairs to the street.

All thoughts of Yasmine, lying in his bed half naked, were replaced, somewhere between the first landing and the front entrance to his residence, by thoughts of Talia, sitting prim and proper in a restaurant chair, peeking across the table at him.

You Are What You Are

The road away from the tribe was a lonely one. Tection had thoroughly enjoyed their hospitality and was as close to being one of the family as one could be, being from another place, another language, another religion, and another culture; but still, he surmised, being a common member of the tribe of humanity. Malika was the most difficult parting moment. It was remarkable he thought, for him to be an important part of someone's young life, before that life had actually been shaped and hardened by its living. Just knowing he had afforded a positive effect on her nature, perhaps helped her be more prepared to engage the world, and revealed to her that good life existed outside the mobile corral the tribe surrounded themselves with, was most rewarding. He knew the lifestyle she was living was safe, but limited. It was without risk or outside engagement, but consequently, he feared, also doomed. She had shed too many tears.

Tection was also amazed at the astute and even profound understanding that she had of human nature. He weighed for some time the question of whether growth in experience did truly develop our understanding of our fellow creatures, or whether the education and experience life delivered actually built walls and shelters to keep out such understandings and protect us from the perceived hostility of the world. The fundamental indoctrination of religion and social responsibility was as evident in this nomadic tribe as surely as in the cathedrals of the Christian faith Tection had been trained in. The child, however, was full of wonderment and immune, or at least as yet unspoiled, by the tenets of her society or the guile of her religion. She was unfettered by cautious hesitation, free to reveal the truth in its raw and pure form. *You are what you are,* she had said, with the complete innocence and profound revelation that such a statement from a young heart deserved. Tection felt blessed for having known her.

His time with the tribe had been under a seemingly constant migration, from one grazing area to another, from one oasis to the next. Tection had spent little time calculating the geography of life, concentrating fully on its complicated human mosaic. Where he was did not matter as much as who he was; and who he was continued to elude him. The fall from personal grace the act of killing had incited, brought him close to thoughts of permanently ending the bizarre voyage his life was taking; fleeting thoughts of self-destruction occasionally crept into his brain, that part of his brain he could not control. His conflict, however, was that he embraced life, loved living, cherished relationships, and longed for new experience. It was the weight of a single act of violence, with the accompanying guilt and realization that such a capability lay within him, that hindered his happiness. But the young girl had driven some focus into his heart and he did, for the first time in many months, find a serenity with his internal contemplations.

Tection was educated, street-wise, independent, and confident in his social interactions, finding it easy to identify the nature of those he met, and then to morph his personality to foster a certain harmony. He was not pretending to be other than who he was, but he was identifying that part of him that might appeal to a new acquaintance, or at least not alienate them from him. Initially, he avoided matters of religion altogether, entertaining such discussion only after ensuring other aspects of the relationship were established, and there was some safe ground to resolve potential conflict. He had been schooled in the Christian faith, a priest at one time, before cursing himself with his anger and voluntarily renouncing his profession. The priesthood had been delivered to him from, and by, the orphanage. He was directed to seminary and coddled through three years of study, providing the Church with a vibrant and active priest, in exchange for the gift of education and reinstatement of personal self-worth that such an undertaking provided.

The slaying of his monster had ransacked Tection's soul. He was now running from the episode, yet, also carrying it with him. He perceived that, but was uncertain on how to overcome it and regain his joy for life. Initially, he felt a return to the orphanage and some perceived liberation of those poor souls housed therein would bring him relief and salvation, but he soon realized that was not the case. The boys living in the orphanage were indeed victims of life's circumstances, and although times were harsh there, at least life was allowed to be lived. Elimination of all human *monsters* was a dream, and not a very realistic one. Unfortunately, the alternative to an orphan's life was one of a street urchin, confronted with crime, servitude under men of prey, and probably even other monsters, somehow always lingering in the shadows, always on the prowl for the disadvantaged and the unprotected.

So, here he was. Ostensibly travelling to *find himself*, but actually running away from a past that haunted him. He knew, unconsciously at this point perhaps, but unmistakably, that he would return to his homeland at some point. The *when* and *how* were yet to be determined, but the certainty of it was never in doubt. In the meantime, he was seeking adventure, living with a carelessness that comes from lost concern about death. His tolerance for evil was almost nonexistent. He was fearless in its face and delivered restitution for its actions whenever he encountered it. At the same time, he was vulnerable to kindness, finding no reward too great to honour it, no road too far to embrace it; a very jagged path he travelled.

—

Tection moved slightly sideways into town. His eyes were seeking information about this place without any movement of his head. He gave the appearance of disinterest as he consumed the landscape. A dusty square, littered with people busy with their obligations, but without further information on what that might be. They seemed to be scurrying randomly among the arched doorways and cobblestone paths. Merchants in competition, mothers at market, officials on duty, and Tection, an experienced stranger, leery but weary, seeking refuge from the long trail he had travelled.

A young boy stood near the entrance of a restaurant, barking at him in a language different from Selim's, but close enough to support some understanding. He was chasing customers for the place, probably his father's, and Tection looked worn enough to be convinced. Tection was. He approached the boy, who immediately ascertained that Tection was both a foreigner and a hungry traveller. *Both of which allow for an inflated price*, Tection assumed. Tection, however, was wise to such strategy and spoke to the boy in the local language he had learned from Selim and Malika. The boy was shocked, expecting no such words to rise from this foreign traveller.

"Permit me a small menu please," Tection asked.

The boy immediately pointed to the far wall where a series of items were scribbled in words Tection could not read. Tection held his hands together and unfolded them, in the manner one would if opening a book.

The boy smiled. "No written menu, but I can tell you all that we have."

You Are What You Are

"Do you know the prices as well?" Tection asked.

"Do not worry," the boy continued, "the best prices in the city." He slid a chair out and Tection sat down, releasing a small sigh as his bones shifted position and relieved his weary feet. "You are tired," the boy stated, half asking and half telling.

"I am tired," Tection repeated with a smile, confirming the obvious.

The boy smiled too, then disappeared. In a flash he returned with a tall glass of what looked like water. Tection took a sip. It was not water, it was a mint tea, and quite refreshing. He held the glass up towards the boy and saluted him, indicating the choice was a good one.

"I will think about food and decide in a minute," Tection said.

"I'll be back," the boy replied with a smile, happy to have this stranger as a customer, recognizing it was he who had convinced the traveller to come in, supporting the livelihood of his father's restaurant.

He moved off to take care of a departing local, cleaning off several small plates and collecting payment. Tection saw the amount collected and also saw the stranger give a small amount to the boy. *Good to know the custom*, he thought.

The boy returned and ran through the entire menu list for Tection, illustrating his preferences with a little more zeal than the other dishes. Tection was wary of the pricing for his meal. He did not want this young hustler to take advantage of him, and he did not want a conflict with the restaurant owner. Tection pointed at the table of the man who just departed.

"What did he eat?" Tection asked. "It looked good."

"He had Shakshuka; baked eggs, with tomato and yogurt; an excellent choice."

"Good," Tection replied without hesitation. "Bring me the same."

Tection was confident that he knew the price paid for the meal in question, and could counter any overcharge with such knowledge.

Following his meal, complete with bread and a refill of mint tea, Tection placed some money on the table. It was the same amount the previous patron had paid, plus a small tip for the boy. The boy picked up the money and looked at Tection. *Here comes the overcharge*, Tection thought. *I will have to hassle my way through it.* But the boy actually returned part of the money to Tection, surprising him.

"What's this?" Tection asked, without taking the money back.

"You have paid too much," the boy stated without emotion.

"But I saw the other man," Tection went on, pointing at the table where the other customer had sat. "He paid the same for his meal."

"Aha," the boy said, "but he had Lablabi as well, soup with chick peas."

Tection was embarrassed. He felt his lack of trust in the nature of this young man was further proof of the erosion of his character, a dent in his trust for humanity.

"You keep the change," he said, somehow hoping the offer would ease his guilt.

"I will keep it, if you will have some soup," the boy replied, smiling broadly, innocent to any quick financial gain and oblivious to the struggle Tection was hoping to resolve. Interpreting Tection's hesitation as a delayed decision, he enticed him further. "A small bowl," he added, shaping his thumbs and pointer fingers into the shape of a small bowl opening.

Tection smiled now, how could he resist? "A small bowl," he confirmed.

Tection explored the cityscape and tried to formulate forward plans. He was quite disappointed that he could not read the local language. Reading was a fond pastime for him and he missed it. So, he was most pleased one day when he found a shop near the harbour that had a limited number of books in his language, suitable for indolent tourists, delayed diplomats, or the Tections and Malikas of the world.

Routine became sunny afternoons by the seaside, the occasional coffee, or preferably the mint-tea drink the boy had introduced him to, a good book, and the flow of passing pedestrians. He became familiar with Aziz, the young waiter, and his father Karim. He easily picked up their dialect, as it was not too distant from the language of Selim. Following Tection's seaside afternoons, he usually went to the restaurant for his evening meal and often remained for some time after dinner, when most other diners had departed, chatting with Karim about life and lamentation. Aziz always wanted to remain part of the conversation, but Karim constantly reminded him of his kitchen duties, cleaning and repackaging before they could close down. Aziz was probably twenty, not too much younger than Tection. His mother had passed away a few years earlier, and the sorrow of that event still registered in the eyes of both father and son whenever it entered the discussion.

Tection had found residence in a small house near the square that housed Karim's restaurant, accepting a room from the widow who lived there. It had a separate side-entrance and a toilet and shower area. He agreed to pay her a small amount and assist her with some of the more demanding chores that always accompanied a house. He even managed to complete some repairs, and she was most appreciative. She was the widow of a Foreign Legion officer, one who had received some accommodation for his efforts and his ultimate sacrifice. The Foreign Legion recruiting office was not far from Tection's residence, and he became friendly with the recruiting officers as well. They were openly appreciative of him, once they saw where he lived and the assistance he was providing the wife of their deceased comrade. They thanked him frequently, and he willingly shared with them the pies his landlady always provided after he had done something for her. A very friendly little community.

The recruiting officers often asked Tection if he was interested in joining them and their fight for God and country. He respectfully declined, even though he thought of doing so on occasion, when he was entertaining some of the darkness of his past.

One particular evening, as the sun winked a goodbye, and the occasional wisp of clouds melted into the darkening sky, Tection reclined in his dinner chair and struggled to find reason to get up and depart. He was lost in some esoteric contemplation and did not notice the three scruffy men enter the restaurant. As he focused, he saw Aziz slowly backing away from them, making what appeared to be angry gestures and comments. Tection leaned forward and focused further on the scene. Shortly, Karim came out and engaged the men in a short conversation. The strangers appeared to crowd around Karim and one of them purposely pushed a small plate off the counter, causing it to splinter across the floor. Karim looked worried. He opened the cash drawer and counted out a small amount, which he handed to the apparent leader of the group. The man grabbed the money and then grabbed Karim. He pulled him close and whispered something into his ear before releasing him roughly and turning to exit. His companions followed after.

Tection was unsure of what had happened. He saw Aziz standing by the kitchen doorway and could not help but recognize the look on his face. It was a curious combination of disappointment, anger, and helplessness.

Karim turned back towards the kitchen and Tection saw him and Aziz engaged in an elevated conversation. Soon after, Aziz stormed out of the restaurant, looking teary-eyed. Karim looked over at Tection and shrugged his shoulders. Tection rose. He moved towards Karim and asked what had just happened; who those men were. At first, Karim also shrugged that off, but Tection was persistent.

Finally, Karim relaxed and explained to Tection. "They are local thugs. They demand payment from all the vendors in the square, for protection." Tection looked on with disbelief beginning to mould his features. "Of course, it is actually for protection from them."

Tection was aghast. His sense of fairness and humanity was given a stiff jolt.

"Aren't there local authorities you can count on?" Tection asked, still a little bewildered.

"They do not care about small businesses and stalls in the village square. When we speak to them, they tell us to stop paying and stand up for ourselves. But we cannot match those bastards. We have families, we cannot afford to be off work, even for one day."

Tection felt the anger growing inside. It showed.

Karim looked at him. "Please do not get involved, my friend. They will bring pain into your life and then into ours. They are evil men."

Tection sympathized with Karim and told him so. He gave him a small hug, somehow hoping that would help alleviate the pain and shame of the situation.

"Aziz wants to take some action. He wants to fight them, to attack them, but he would only be badly injured. I have forbidden it. That is why he ran off just now."

"I understand Karim. Young men are full of energy for such situations. He will cool down."

"I hope so. He is all I have in this world." Karim turned away, hiding the sadness that was overwhelming him.

Tection let him retreat to the kitchen and then gathered his coat and headed towards his residence.

As he strolled past the village centre, just beyond the square that housed Karim and his restaurant, he heard a commotion off on a side street. He intended to ignore it, but then he heard a woman's voice calling out. He quickly moved towards the sound and as he turned the corner, he saw the three thugs, obviously a little drunk, and probably empowered by their evening's work of harassing the locals. They were holding a woman and pawing at her.

Tection called out. The men released the woman and she ran past Tection on her way up the street.

"What do you want, kid?" the lead thug barked out. "Get out of here before you get a good whipping."

"I think I saw you gentlemen earlier, over by the square, strong-arming the locals. Was that you?" Tection knew it was.

The three men started moving towards Tection. He measured them easily. Full of bravado. A little drunk. Carelessly confident. Perfect.

"That square belongs to us, kid, and I think it's time for you to learn that for yourself."

The leader slid a small knife from beneath his tunic and moved forward, reaching out for Tection. Tection grabbed his arm and pulled him in close, before smashing his forehead into the man's nose. The thug fell, slightly limp, and Tection twisted his arm, gaining possession of the knife. The other two came at him. He ducked the first blow and drove the knife into the leg of the attacker. He rose and felt a blow hit his shoulder as the third thug swung wildly. Tection steadied himself and sent a straight right hand into the thug's face. The thug crumpled. Tection kicked out at the leader, ensuring his incapacitation, while the thug with the knife in his leg tried to hobble away. Tection quickly caught up to him and easily dragged him back to the others. He removed the knife and used their sashes to tie the three men together, back to back to back, in a sort of three-headed ball. He rifled their pockets, came up with the remaining funds from their night's work, and pocketed a small amount to repay Karim.

"Where's your residence?" he asked the group in general.

"You're dead, kid. We're gonna get you for this!"

"Your residence?" Tection asked again, this time bringing his knee up into the man's stomach.

They showed him where they lived. He went inside and before long he found their stash of money. It wasn't huge, but certainly enough for his purpose. He dressed the wounded leg as well as he could and sat with a glass of mint tea, waiting for the dawn to wander in. The men continued to throw threats, then offers of payment, then renewed threats. Tection made sure they were well bound and drifted off for a short nap.

When he woke, the sun was peeking through the window. He rose with a sarcastic stretch and yawn, and then led the stumbling group down the street. Several locals watched the procession. They knew who the thugs were, and their curiosity about what was happening allowed them to stare openly. The Foreign Legion recruiting office was not yet open, so Tection checked the dressing on the leg wound, made a small adjustment, and sat down on the hard, wooden steps to await the arrival of his friends, and the opportunity to shape the future of the thugs.

His officer friends didn't disappoint. They heard Tection's story and welcomed the very unwilling new recruits. They assured Tection that the new soldiers would be deployed on a distant front, where survival was certainly not guaranteed. Tection handed over the money he had removed from the thug's room.

"I kept a small amount to return to one of the shop owners they robbed last night. The rest in for you to decide upon."

The head recruiter looked at the healthy sum laying on his desk. He raised his eyebrows and looked at Tection. His hand slid across the counter and pulled the purse close. "Thank you Tection, we will make sure it goes to good use." He winked, Tection smiled, and it was done!

That afternoon, Tection lay quietly on his bed, his hands behind his head, and his open eyes seeing nothing but the blurred white of his ceiling.

There is much evil in the world. Everywhere I go I see it. It angers me, but it frightens me. When one evil deed is squashed, it seems two more spring up to replace it. That is a disturbing thought. Yet there is also much good in the world. As a matter of fact, I encounter much more good than evil. Perhaps, each time goodness demonstrates itself, more goodness evolves. Perhaps, eventually, there will be so much good, that evil will no longer have a place to dwell.

Tection drifted off, a small smile on his lips as he reflected on the folly of his considerations.

The long night had left him weary, and when he awoke from his afternoon nap, it was mid-evening and his hunger was evident. He strolled over to the restaurant. It was busy, with Karim and Aziz running around ensuring customers were happy and well served.

As soon as Tection entered, Aziz hustled him over to the back table that was always his. "I almost sat someone here. You are a little late this evening."

"It was a long night last night, and I over-slept my nap this afternoon. Thanks for being patient."

Aziz smiled, went for some mint tea, and then scurried off to fulfil other tasks.

As the evening slowed and the patrons drifted off, a little heavier than on arrival, Tection called Karim over. Karim sat at the table, happy for a moment of respite from the busy evening. Tection removed the small pouch he had placed the recovered money in, and slid it towards Karim.

He looked surprised. "What is this?"

"It is the money from last night. I ran into those thugs on my way home and convinced them to return the funds."

Tection said it matter-of-factly. Karim wasn't sure if he was serious, sarcastic, or whether he had even actually seen the thugs. He knew Tection was a generous man, and feared he might have put his own money in the pouch.

"Those men do not give up their gains; that is a most improbable statement."

"I'll admit that it took a little convincing, but ultimately, they surrendered the money."

"What did you do? They will seek revenge, my friend, if not on you, then on us."

"They will not be back."

"Did you kill them? My God, I hope not."

"Would you not wish that on such despicable men, would you not wish that on those who harm you?"

"I cannot," Karim replied. "It is not for me to decide on who lives or dies. I have suffered death that was too close to me. I cannot bring that to another." He backed away from Tection, his eyes widening in disbelief.

"Well, my friend, relax, sit back down. I can assure you that I did not kill them. They have joined the Foreign Legion, and are to be deployed a significant distance from here. I doubt you will ever hear from them again."

"How did you manage that? Why would anyone join the Legion?"

"It was a perfect match for them. They get to use their anger, and direct it towards a perceived enemy. They get food and lodging and a theatre to act out their aggressive nature. An ideal fit, actually." Tection smiled.

Karim also smiled.

Tection's face took on a more serious, or perhaps melancholy tone. "Karim, I am leaving tomorrow. I have travels yet to make and other places I desire to visit."

"What? You cannot go yet. You love it here. I see that in your eyes."

"I do very much enjoy it here. And you and Aziz are dear friends now, but I am destined to find my own purpose, somewhere farther down the road. One day I will return to my origins as well. I hope one day to find a wife, to have a child. I'm sure you understand that."

Karim nodded. He jerked his head sideways towards the kitchen where Aziz was busy cleaning up. "He will be most disappointed. You have been a great friend and influence on him."

"He is a fantastic son, Karim. You should always be proud. I hope one day my own will be as kind and honest."

Karim teared a bit as the men stood in unison and embraced. It lasted a little longer than expected, and Tection felt a strange sense of loss, even before thy moved apart.

"Please give him my *goodbye*. I will always have a special place for you two in here," he said, putting his hand over his heart.

"Goodbye, my friend."

Thank You, Mr. Mayor

Julian arrived at the restaurant a few minutes early and the maître d' escorted him to the bar for a pre-lunch cocktail. Another couple was sitting there, and Julian thought he recognized them from the night before, but he said nothing. He did smile when the young lady looked at him, with one of those, *yes-I-see you-looking-at-me-and-as-a-human-being-I-am-obliged-to-recognize-you-with-a-smile*, smiles. Nasim had reserved a separate, private room, at the rear of the restaurant, so they could enjoy a secluded meal, free from outside ears. It was not to be opened until he arrived. At twelve sharp he arrived; along with ten or twelve other people, most of whom Julian recognized from the previous evening, but none of whom was named Talia.

Nasim ushered everyone into the room, ensuring they were comfortable and seated where planned. Perhaps a diplomat from one country had requested Nasim to arrange a casual meeting with a counterpart from another country. He could count on Nasim to arrange the seating accordingly, creating an unofficial meeting. This function was basically a collection of favours being answered by

Nasim, setting people in motion with each other, cloaked under the guise of a Sunday lunch. Of course, he would have his own favours to collect back, some on behalf of his own government, and some very much on his own behalf. His bank account was healthy and his purse quite full, no doubt.

Nasim could see the disappointment in Julian's face and took the time to bring him to the side and explain that Talia's father had been called back to his country on some urgent matter, and he was preparing his affairs to leave in the morning. They had arrived by land, on their diplomatic train, and had many days' journey ahead of them. Nasos also had an obligation to stop in a couple of other locations along the way, so time was both limited and of the essence. Julian indicated he understood, but wore his dejection visibly on his face.

Nasim toyed with him a moment longer before delivering some more uplifting news. The young lady in question, Talia, would be shopping that afternoon, and had mentioned that she might stop into a small *maison de thé* along the Front de Mer, called Layali, around three o'clock.

"Do you know it?" Nasim asked.

Julian looked at Nasim, recognizing that he had made this arrangement, just as he had made arrangements for everyone else at the lunch.

"I'll find it," Julian replied as he turned to leave. He stopped and looked back at Nasim. The man had never looked so gentle or harmless, but Julian knew there was a calculating tiger, lying just beneath the layers of laughter and graciousness, stalking those who might purposely, or perhaps even inadvertently, cross him. "Thank you, Nasim."

The older man smiled, leaving a small wink to seal Julian's memory of him.

Julian was nervous as the time ticked by, then pensive, then agitated, then barely holding back a full range of panic, when Talia finally walked in, around four o'clock.

Thank You, Mr. Mayor

She almost ran over to his table, sliding into a seat opposite him, even before he could stand to welcome her. "I'm so sorry to be late like this, I'm actually lucky to get here at all. Thank you for waiting." It all came out so quickly, Julian had no time to respond. "Our train's leaving tomorrow, heading back home. My father had a meeting with the mayor, but it was cancelled for some reason and he has decided to leave early." She finished the statement as thought there was an additional comment imminent, but her stare into Julian's eyes contradicted that.

"I can't believe that," Julian finally mustered. "We've only just met."

"Yet I feel like I've known you forever. You just, I don't know, just seem so easy to talk with, to be with."

Julian felt the same, though he had never articulated it as such. *Just so easy to be with you.* What an enormously accurate explanation of the attraction he felt towards her. The entire internal process that followed took but a few seconds to register in his mind. He was on a life adventure. He could go anywhere his feet, his mind, his spirit, or most importantly right now, his heart, would take him. He had no binds to this town, no obligations, except perhaps a favour returned to Nasim, on which he was sure the elderly gentleman was not counting. There was no reason for him to remain here while Talia sailed off into the sunset.

"If you're on a train, I'm going to travel with you," Julian said, without the slightest pinch of desperation.

Talia looked shocked, then her face melted to small smile, and finally a crooked frown. "You cannot travel with us. It is my father's train and he would never allow that."

Julian reclined into his chair, his mind working at full speed. The mayor had been at the lunch that day, a guest of Nasim, and obviously occupied with another obligation. "What if I get your father an appointment with the mayor for tomorrow?" he finally said.

Talia looked at him with some real surprise. *Who is this man?* she thought. *Can he really arrange that?* "I don't know, I guess he would stay for that, but it still only provides one additional day."

"That may be enough," Julian replied. "Tell your father you met me *by accident*, walking along the *Front de Mer*, and after mentioning the reason for your quickened departure, I told you to have him at the mayor's office tomorrow at eleven-thirty."

Julian had no idea what he was doing, but he figured eleven-thirty was a good time, early enough not to interfere with lunch plans, but late enough to be post morning meetings. He remembered it as a sort of *dead* time at the café he used to own, neither morning nor noon crowds around, staff relaxed, cats asleep, and he himself, wrestling with inventory or accounting matters.

"Are you crazy?" she said.

"I am indeed," Julian replied, standing and reaching out to help her to her feet. He pulled her close, her aroma sparking his senses in a heated message of anticipation. He gave her a gentle kiss on the lips, electric, though barely touching. "Tell him to be there at eleven-thirty."

Then he pushed her away gently. She took a few steps backwards, eyes glued on Julian to understand if this was really happening, or just some unusual day dream. She turned, stepped slowly, then more quickly to the door, running by the time she reached the street.

Julian started his own journey, flush with uncertainty about what he had just promised and apprehensive, no, almost panic stricken, by what he might tell Nasim in order to make his promise a reality. He went to the café. No Nasim, no one had seen him. He ran back to the restaurant; they were long gone. Back to the café, one coffee, two, three, no Nasim. He hung his head low, rubbing his fingers through his hair like rakes, pulling his scalp back tightly, as if trying to yank the unease he was feeling up through his body. He looked up, Nasim!

"Are you OK, young man? How did it go with Talia?"

Thank You, Mr. Mayor

Julian recounted the entire afternoon to him. He told it the way he remembered it, even the soft kiss and the panicked hunt for Nasim.

"It might have been wise to hunt for me, *before* you made the promise," Nasim said, emphasizing the word before. He didn't seem upset, although he admonished Julian for an appropriate time, before finally responding to the issue at hand. "No worries," he said rather nonchalantly, "Mayor Sa'id and I are good friends, I'm sure I can help you out."

Julian fell down in front of him, feeling the emotion of the moment take hold of him, reacting completely out of character. Nasim lifted him back to his chair.

"Thank you, Nasim. I don't know what it is about this girl, but I know I need to find out. It is completely different from Yasmine. I mean, Talia is so beautiful, so righteous, that I can't even think about anything like that right now. I just want to be with her. Nothing more. We don't even have to speak."

Nasim recognized the raw emotion and knew that guilt would follow once Julian regained his faculties and realized the position he had put Nasim in, not to mention Talia, running home to her father with a promised meeting that, at the time, existed only in Julian's mind.

"Be happy now," Nasim said, "but there is a favour that I will ask in return."

"Anything," Julian replied immediately. "What is it?"

"I don't know yet. I will know what it is when I need it."

"Nasim, it is my intention to leave when she does, to find a way to travel with her." He looked at Nasim, anticipating his demand of a favour based on the short time Julian had remaining in the town.

"Life is long," Nasim stated. "I will let you know the favour when I need it, and when *you* can give it."

Julian looked at him, unsure of what he meant, and unable to concentrate on deciphering the riddle. "Of course, Nasim, whenever you need it." He jumped up and hugged the old man again. "Tomorrow, the mayor's office. Eleven-thirty, right?"

"You be there at eleven-fifteen, Julian. Go to his office and thank him for the favour. You will owe him a favour too, that's how it works. That means you will owe two favours, for one delivered, however, Nasos will now owe you a favour." He chuckled a bit as Julian began to understand. "And so, the wheel turns, young man, you get what you give, so always give what you get." The pun spun around a bit, but Julian was a smart fellow and picked up the gist of it. It was a valuable lesson, though not recognized as such at that particular moment.

Julian returned to his room. It was completely destroyed! His clothes were torn, his toiletries smashed, even one of his old shoes forced down into the toilet. He looked on in awe at first, then became quite angry, then almost philosophical as he pictured an angry, half-naked Yasmine, trying to force his shoe into the toilet. Then he laughed, he laughed very loudly. He gathered the mess into a pile and discarded it. He slept with the door tightly bolted and his dreams ripe with anticipation for the morrow. It would be a new beginning, a new adventure, so, why not start with new clothes, new toiletries, and of course, new shoes.

In the morning he returned to Kaporal and another visit with Taysir. He started discussing his various needs but finally just explained the situation, leaving out few details, and leaving it up to Taysir to forge a new wardrobe for him.

"I'm not wealthy, Taysir," Julian reminded him, "the money on Friday was from Nasim, not me."

Taysir laughed out loud. "Crazy kids," he said, "be back here at five. Everything will be ready. I have a special rate for friends of Nasim, we'll discuss money when you come here with some." Julian left to the sounds of Taysir still laughing in the background.

He arrived at the mayor's office at ten-fifty, almost half an hour early. He wore the same suit as the day before, with a shiny new shirt fresh off one of Taysir's racks. He waited on the stairs outside the massive building that was City Hall, three huge archways guarding the entrance. At eleven-fifteen he went in and navigated to where the mayor was. Several people asked him where he was going, but he had a very presentable, custom-made suit on, and a demeanour of slight arrogance, knowing that the mayor was waiting for him, so he passed the unofficial checkpoints with attire as his uniform and his appointment with the mayor as his passport.

The mayor was very official when they met, unsure of who this young man was and how he commanded favours from the powerful Nasim. He asked Julian if he wanted to join the meeting with Nasos and Julian fought back the "Yes," with a "Not necessary." He felt he was already testing the edges of luck and was content with the understanding that he had fostered the meeting. He thanked Mayor Sa'id, but did solicit a promise from him to remind Mr. Nasos that he was meeting with him only at the request of Julian. The mayor agreed, returning Julian's request of him with a reminder that he would make one from Julian in the future.

"Life is long," Julian replied. "Let me know what you need when you need it, and I will deliver it when I'm able." Not exactly what Nasim had said, but close enough to both impress and appease the mayor.

A knock came to the door. Julian, at the mayor's wave, stood and answered it. Nasos stood there, surprised to see the young man, but obviously pleased to be through the mayor's doorway.

"Thanks again, Mayor Sa'id," Julian stated, louder than necessary, walking back and around his desk to shake hands directly in front of him. The mayor was surprised at the lack of protocol, but assumed it to be inexperience, rather that the false bravado it really was.

"No problem, Julian," he added as Julian walked back around the desk, "we'll take good care of Mr. Nasos."

The Journey: Erudite

Perfect comment! Julian thought. He went back towards Nasos. "Your daughter, uhm," Julian hesitated and pointed at Nasos, as if trying to remember her name.

"Talia," Nasos offered.

"Yes, Talia," Julian continued. "She informed me that you would be travelling by train along the coast, heading east I believe."

"That's correct," Nasos answered, a little bewildered as to who this young man was.

"Well, as the mayor knows," now Julian was stretching it, "I will also be travelling that way." He hesitated to see the reaction from either man. The mayor was not really paying attention.

Nasos finally recognized the unspoken request. "Really, well, yes, why don't you accompany us? The train is for my diplomatic mission and there are no other passengers."

Yes! The perfect answer, Julian thought. *The one I dreamed of.* "Oh, I don't think so Mr. Nasos, I mean, I would hate to be a burden on your entourage." *Easy Julian, don't blow it!* he thought.

"Nonsense," Nasos' voice firmed up. "You can ride along with us as far as you need; but the train leaves early tomorrow morning."

"That's so kind of you," Julian responded. "And the timing is perfect; I was very much planning a departure tomorrow as well."

"We're down at the train yard, right by the hotel, say seven o'clock."

"That is indeed most kind, Mr. Nasos. I look forward to seeing you then."

"Now, you're not travelling our way because of my daughter, are you?" Nasos said, only half tongue-in-cheek, but remembering their secluded time together at the party.

"Your daughter is a lovely lady, Mr. Nasos, and her being in your caravan is certainly serendipitous, however, I have an obligation to myself that brings me down the same path as you at this point in time."

Thank You, Mr. Mayor

What a perfect answer, Julian thought. He had not lied, for the obligation unto himself to continue his adventure was indeed a reality, and he had not pretended to be oblivious to Talia.

"I'll see you soon, Mayor Sa'id, and we can take care of that matter we discussed earlier," Julian said, referring to his own obligation towards the mayor. "Good luck, Mr. Nasos, I'm sure the mayor will be most accommodating." Julian left with a little haste, only praying he hadn't pushed matters too far.

"Thanks again, Mr. Julian," Nasos called after him.

Mr. *Julian. Now, that was a first.*

Chasing Illusions

Julian scurried around his flat, jumping randomly from one spot to the other, preparing for his departure, and building his excitement for what he very much perceived as a door opening into a new adventure; the next chapter in his ongoing life. The early morning sun was just cracking the horizon, but his energy level was already in midday form. He had little to account for. The new clothes he had collected from Taysir back at Kaporal were all neatly packed and prepared, even though their acquisition had put a dent in his daily fiscal planning. His journal was also safely stowed, the pages anxious for details of the entire adventure with the mayor.

Birds chirped away at the sunrise. They were often referred to in poetic terms by famous writers from the past, but on this particular morning, they were just a loud nuisance. Their cluttered warbles, ruffling the feathers of an otherwise beautifully dawning day, left Julian's thoughts tangled by their cacophony.

His long goodbye with Nasim, the night before, had easily stretched past the hour of midnight, and he knew he would have a price to pay for that this morning. Silence would've been welcome, but the birds cared not about his hangover. Even though drink clogged his mind, thoughts of Talia swam in his head and provided fuel for the esoteric dreams that swept him from the night that was, to the day that is.

Julian arrived at the rendezvous long before the scheduled time, and went about seeking Nasos for a *good morning* encounter; confirming to Talia's father that Julian had arrived, and confirming to Julian that her father was still extending his invitation to join them on their travels. He found him, busy giving instructions and directing preparations for departure.

When Nasos saw Julian he smiled broadly, and whispered, "Good morning young man. I see you're able to join us."

Julian did not respond with words, but offered a smile of his own in recognition of the greeting, and his confirmation that he had received it. *Nothing in this world could have kept me from joining you, from joining Talia, this morning*, he thought.

He was curious about the meeting with the mayor, and didn't have to wait too long to get a broad confirmation that it had been a great success. Following some additional instructions that moved his entourage to further action, Nasos returned to Julian and rambled on with a short synopsis of the meeting. Julian didn't understand all the content, but it was clear enough that Nasos was pleased with both the opportunity Julian had provided him, and the result that followed it. *I wonder if the value of the opportunity I provided him was in some way measured by the results of the opportunity itself? Of course it was*, Julian reflected. Even though the opportunity to speak with the mayor had been provided with the best intention, though perhaps with an ulterior motive, its value to Nasos was definitely measured by the success it afforded. Consequently, the successful meeting had actually enhanced the value of the favour. The size and scope of the return favour Julian could now request from Nasos was more significant than originally expected. *I like this system, a favour for a favour process; I can see that it is a definite pattern to the flow of* relationships. *He was definitely gaining an understanding of the adage, 'It's not what you know, it's who you know'.*

Nasos directed Julian to his travelling quarters, and explained where he could keep his belongings. Julian thanked him, more profusely than necessary, still holding the advantage of having been the go-between with the mayor, and he stepped up to arrange his baggage.

First, it was a wisp of that auburn-blond hair darting through his peripheral vision, then a quick glimpse of Talia as she disappeared behind his sight line. Julian lunged sideways to change his perspective and caught sight of her. Though her back was turned as she spoke with her father, Julian knew it was she. He had memorized, or more accurately been mesmerized, by the vision of her departing from both the diplomatic affair and the rendezvous café. He would have recognized her from behind at any distance. He stared.

Just as Julian realized he was staring, Nasos looked up and saw him. Julian froze. It was as though Nasos had somehow caught him ogling his daughter, invading her privacy from afar. But Nasos was oblivious to Julian's considerations, and raised his hand to wave him over. Julian raised his hand to his chest as if to say, *me*? Nasos confirmed with another wave of his hand, and Talia turned to see who her father was gesturing to. Julian jumped down and headed towards them, eyes glued to Talia's, and Talia used her most learned diplomatic skills to turn the excitement she felt into a projection of calm aloofness.

"Good morning again," Julian said as he neared the couple. Tipping a casual salute from his forehead towards them, he glanced once at Nasos before returning his gaze to Talia.

"I believe you already know Talia." Nasos stated the obvious.

"Yes, yes," Julian replied as he extended his hand to her. She took it. It was as if he had touched lightning. Their grip sizzled. "Good morning, Talia."

"Good morning, sir, what a pleasant surprise to see you out here so early today."

"Mr. Julian will be travelling with us for a while," her father explained. "I convinced him yesterday that he would be most welcome to do so."

"Well then, we will have to ensure his comforts in every way possible," Talia replied. Perfectly innocent and proper for her father's ears; but the twinkle in her eye and the gentle squeeze of Julian's hand ensured it was both demure and provocative for him.

Julian blushed. "Thank you both for your kind hospitality. I am certain our time together will be most fulfilling." He returned the squeeze.

The preparations for departure were completed and they set off. Julian remained coy in his behaviour, seeking glimpses of Talia at every opportunity, scouting the surrounding travellers to ensure they did not notice his sight line, or suspect his intentions. Her beauty grew rapidly, enjoying leaps in evaluation with every moment of eye contact. Talia was equally drawn to look in Julian's direction, feeling a small twinge in the bottom of her stomach every time she saw him peer her way.

Initial time aboard the train was exhilarating. Julian had never been carried along on steel rails before, and the entire process was fascinating to him. He visited, with previous permission from Nasos, the engine, coal car, dining car, master quarters, staff quarters and caboose. Altogether there were six cars. Julian had a comfortable cot arranged in the caboose, where he slept with the four train crew; the conductor, who was generally in charge of the entire train; the engineer, who was responsible for the motion of the train, whether it was the engine, brakes, or the coupling process; the trainman, who handled the signaling, safety measures, and physical coupling process; and the fireman, who was responsible to ensure the furnace was properly stoked, cleaned, and operating. He was also the replacement for the engineer when he was off duty, or should he fall ill or become otherwise incapacitated.

Besides the train team, Nasos had his own entourage, which included his valet, a male secretary, a diplomatic second, a chef, and a steward. Talia was the only female on board. All the cars were open and accessible via passageway doors, except the master quarters, which had a separate passageway along the starboard side, that allowed the crew to access the coal car and engine without disturbing the occupants. At night that was only Nasos and Talia, but during the day several staff members were busy scurrying about with meals, agendas, and record keeping. Nasos enjoyed dictating long-winded reports, which would be delivered to his superiors once home; effectively a journal of the trip and confirmation that he had indeed fulfilled his diplomatic obligations and, on occasion, expanded his mandate in the development of positive relation with a particular government or individual, like Mayor Sa'id!

Julian continued to record events in his own journal as well, often identifying the important moments with lavish adjectives and personal remarks. Talia received a mounting array of such adjectives.

Although there were facilities on board, which basically consisted of a lid over a hole down to the disappearing tracks, as the train chugged along, they stopped most evenings, slipping onto a side rail near one of the regular stations along the way. There they could shower, enjoy a quiet meal, and gain a decent night's sleep, before continuing the next day, rested and energized. For Julian and Talia, the stops were their best opportunity to continue building their relationship. During the day, despite the many tasks Nasos levied on her, Talia managed to *need a break* and *stretch her legs* frequently, always drifting towards the caboose. With the crew busy and occupied, she and Julian found some time alone. They conversed endlessly, smiled frequently, and managed to touch through casual brushes or warm greetings during arrival and departure. During the stopovers, Nasos invited Julian to join him and his staff for dinner, which was the only time he actually entered the master quarters. There was a dining table with eight places; more than enough. Nasos had Julian at his left, no doubt usurping the diplomatic second's spot. Fortunately, Talia was always on his right, directly across from Julian. While her father regaled everyone with tales from the past and plans for the future, Talia would reach out with her foot, under the table, and caress Julian's lower leg. It was exciting contact. Talia was a little bit shy and slightly immature when it came to matters of male contact. This was obvious to Julian, but at the same time, it was part of what made her attractive. Her striking beauty, demure posture, and childish flirting, were all part of the package that captured him. Her sharp wit and sophisticated lexicon, obviously honed through education and diplomatic sojourns, gave her a distinct appearance of maturity, which was contradicted by her appearance and romantic fumbling. Julian had never asked her age, but the circumstance of her being on the diplomatic mission, and the degree of education she obviously had, hinted at somewhere in her early twenties.

One evening, no different from several others, one for which it was decided not to stop as there was too great a distance to the next station, Julian sat in the dining car. He had eaten there with the crew and some of the staff, as Nasos was slightly ill and wanted to retire early.

"Just a bit of the grippe," Talia had explained.

It was still early, but Julian finally decided to retire, as he would have to walk through the staff sleeping car to get to the caboose, and he didn't want to disturb them once they were in bed. As he rose to go, he heard the door open from the passageway to the master quarters. He stopped and turned. Talia peered in, seeing only Julian there, and stepped into the car, quietly tugging the door closed behind her.

Chasing Illusions

"Hello there," Julian said. "How's your father doing?" He was feeling the adrenalin rush he got every time he saw her, especially alone.

"He's alright. He fell asleep early and is snoring away. I guess he's a little blocked up." She hustled the words out, almost in a nervous tone.

Julian noticed it. "Come, come...sit down," he said, pointing to a chair in front of him.

As she slid into it, he did the same in one beside her, instead of one opposite her. He noticed Talia was wearing an evening wrap and guessed she had her bedclothes on underneath.

"That's a nice wrap for an evening stroll, Talia." He said it with a twinkle in his eye that was not missed by her.

"Have you taken to fashion analysis now?" she replied.

"Only on the most exquisite of models," Julian continued, playing the game with some amusement. "Can you show me the entire ensemble?" he added, raising his eyebrows in a suggestive manner.

Talia looked at him, measuring his seriousness, and probably measuring her own willingness to put herself on display. She smiled, stood up, and slid to the middle of the room, directly opposite Julian.

"A simple throw," she began, mimicking the moderator describing the attire at a fashion show, or défilé de mode as she would call it. She spun once, letting the sleeve fall off her shoulder, and then turned her back to him. "A crested back pull, with fine symmetry and bunching to accent the ...derriere." She giggled at that description, shaking her rear end slightly. Then she turned back and looked at Julian. He was captivated and more than a little interested. She also turned more serious as she moved closer. "With a simple sash, clasped at the side." She undid the sash as she said it, letting the robe hang open in front. "Beneath, a satin tunic, perfect for a comfortable night beneath the covers."

She slid the robe off her shoulders, letting her hands prevent it from falling to the floor. How bold. She looked at Julian. He was looking at her breasts, quite visible through the thin fabric of her nightgown. Her nipples pressing against the soft material, making a statement of their own. Talia threw her head back, perhaps not realizing how reveling the garment actually was, or perhaps realizing exactly how revealing it was. She put her hands behind her head, further accenting her physique, before turning around once again and gently closing the robe, returning the sash to its task of keeping the garment closed.

She turned back to Julian and returned to her chair. "How was that?" she asked.

Julian stood up, his own excitement not easily hidden, and moved in front of her. She glanced down at the front of his pants, and immediately turned an exciting shade of red. He reached down and touched her face, urging her face upwards with a subtle lifting motion. They looked into each other's eyes for a moment. Then Julian leaned in and felt the first thrill of a long, deep, and romantic kiss.

Talia was weakened by her physical response. She had never experienced such a powerful shiver, never felt the surge that was racing through her body. She clung tighter, feeling her breasts push into, and through, Julian's shirt. Then she felt *him* against her stomach; all of him. It was also a first for her.

As the kiss ended, after several lingering pecks and prods, Talia looked up at Julian. She had not expected to be so captivated by a physical moment, so shaken by her own body. Her legs weakened and she leaned backwards. Julian guided her back into her chair.

"That was wonderful," Julian said.

"Very," Talia replied.

He moved his hand over to hers, tangling their fingers, and exchanging momentary squeeze and release grips. They stared at each other, breaking that off only because they heard the door behind them opening. They quickly returned their hands to regular posture and Talia clutched her wrap tightly.

The fireman came into the room on his way to the coal car. He bade them good evening and was gone in a few steps. He had not noticed or considered anything to be out of the normal.

"I guess I should return to my quarters," Talia said, rising up and keeping her head slightly bowed.

Julian stood as well. He cupped her face in both hands and kissed her gently, first once, then a second time, then a third. She smiled, they giggled.

"Good night," she said, as she backed away and then turned to leave the car.

Julian stood there for a moment. It seemed almost surreal. It had happened so quickly. She was so attractive. Her breasts were so perfect. The kiss was so magnetic.

Over the next couple of days, Julian and Talia found many moments together. As a matter of fact, they spent most of their time apart, planning and anticipating their next time together. It was not obvious at first, but gradually everyone knew what was going on. Everyone except Nasos, of course. Whether it was moments caught by a crew member, or a lingering closeness recognized by a staff member, the rumour and innuendo in such a confined condition soon sprouted a life of its own. Throat clearing, occasional winks to Julian, and apologies for interrupting the two of them, became the norm.

It was the diplomatic second, perhaps because of the annoyance at losing his seat next to Nasos, or perhaps because of a sense of loyalty to the diplomat, or perhaps even because of his own attraction to Talia and the jealousy that her budding romance with Julian delivered, who informed Nasos of what was happening. Nasos shrugged it off at first, claiming his second was seeing things, over reacting, creating illusions. Still, his remarks sparked a curiosity in Nasos, and he decided to confront Talia about it. That evening, before he prepared for bed, he decided to get a glass of juice from the dining room. Julian and Talia were in there, enjoying their nightly rendezvous. As Nasos pushed through the door he saw them just breaking off an embrace. They had become more brazen in their embraces, more careless in their secrecy.

Nasos was shocked. "What is going on?" he burst out.

Julian and Talia both separated and wore a look of shame that they did not actually feel.

"Nothing, Nasos," Julian responded. Obviously not telling the truth.

"Mr. Nasos will work, young man. What are you doing with my daughter?"

Julian looked at Talia. "We were just chatting, sir. Just passing some time."

"Don't take me for a fool," Nasos yelled back. He looked at Talia. "To your room, Talia."

"Father, it's alright, we were just talking."

"Perhaps I've been blind, but I'm not stupid. Now, get to your room."

Talia looked at Julian again.

"You better go," he said.

He wasn't sure that was the comment she was hoping for, but Julian did not want to aggravate the situation further by protesting the instructions of her father.

Talia hurried past her father, throwing the heavy door open, and she marched out of sight.

"Have I not been kind to you, Julian? Did I not invite you onto my train and offer a free journey?"

"Indeed, you did, Mr. Nasos, and I'm most appreciative."

"And you repay me by making advances on my child!"

"I can assure you that I have been most respectful. We have only talked and shared some time together. Nothing has happened." Julian tried to keep his voice calm. He wanted to defuse the situation.

"Yet!" Nasos retorted. "Nothing's happened yet. What were you planning? Did you think you could charm her, another conquest for you?"

"No, no, please, it is nothing like that. Talia is a very intelligent young lady, and I have nothing but full respect for her."

"She is not a young lady...she is a child!" Nasos was getting angrier, not calmer.

Julian was annoyed that Nasos referred to her as a child. Perhaps it was a father's right to consider his daughter a child, perhaps forever.

"I don't consider her a child, Mr. Nasos, and I have not done anything inappropriate at all."

"Kissing a seventeen-year-old daughter while her father sits in the next room is most inappropriate, Julian. It is unforgiveable."

"Seventeen?"

"Yes, seventeen, and just turned seventeen. What did you think? Did you bother to find out?"

"Oh my God, I did not know that. I thought she was at least twenty-one. Really...I..." But Julian was lost for words.

"I'll expect you to leave this train at the next stop. In the interim, I request that you stay in the caboose...where you belong!" Nasos turned and marched towards the door. Then he turned again and looked at Julian with a renewed anger. "And you should feel lucky that I don't have you arrested, or better yet, shot by one of my staff!" Then he was gone.

Julian stood still for some time. He could hear the faint rumble of Nasos howling at Talia. He could not make out the words, but he could easily imagine what they were. Seventeen? He kept repeating that in his head. Why hadn't he asked her? She seemed so mature? But of course, that explained why she seemed so...inexperienced in matters of relationships. He had probably been the first man she'd had a discussion with that didn't centre on politics. Certainly, the first man she had kissed. For all of Julian's sense of adventure and hunger for the experiences of life, he had a very strong sense of right and wrong. A distinct set of values; ones he had learned from others, important people in his life, other than his parents; who were both nasty, selfish individuals, full of bitterness, regrets, and usually alcohol.

Julian returned to the caboose. He lay back and tried to sleep, but it was elusive. By now, the whole train knew about the situation. Early in the morning, some time before sun-up, Julian made his decision. He was extremely attracted to Talia, perhaps even in love, although he wasn't sure what that meant, but he felt a consuming guilt about her age. He knew that he would have slept with her in an instant if the opportunity had presented itself, and now that he knew her real age, he wasn't sure that he could suddenly disown those feelings. If he stayed on board, it would be a torment, for him and for her. There was no other choice.

He packed his belongings with as much silence as possible, despite the churning and mumbling of the two crew members sleeping beside him, and drew out a pen and paper. He wrote two notes. One to Nasos, and a second one, longer and more difficult, to Talia. He walked towards the engine, quietly passing through the other cars, including down the passage way outside the now-silent master quarters. When he got to the engine compartment, he met the fireman and trainman, who were on the night shift while the engineer got some sleep.

"You're up a little early this morning, Julian," the trainman said, hardly turning his head away from his chores and responsibilities.

"I need a favour. I need two favours actually."

The trainman and the fireman looked at him.

"What's up?" the trainman said.

"I need to get off the train," Julian said, lifting his packed sack so they could see he meant right away.

"You mean right now?" the fireman said.

"I do, I need you to slow down enough so I can jump."

They saw he was serious.

"We heard about the commotion. Christ, I never thought she was seventeen either. She's pretty grown up for being so young. Hell, why does he even have her out on this trip if she's so young? She should be in school."

There was a period of silence. Julian didn't want to start the whole conversation with them. It was painful enough, and there was really nothing more to say.

The fireman continued. "We're a long way from anywhere, Julian. I think you should reconsider."

"I'll be OK. I've got plenty of water and a great nose for direction. Besides, I have the tracks to follow."

"We're probably sixty or seventy miles from the next station, and it's going to be hot out there. Why don't you hang up here with us, at least for another couple of hours? It'll get you a lot closer."

Julian considered the remark. It made a lot of sense. He could still get off before seeing Nasos or Talia again, and it would make it a lot easier to connect with some alternative transport, even if he didn't know which way he was going to head.

"OK. I appreciate the advice, I'll take it. But when the sun gets up, I'll get off."

"No problem."

Julian explained to the trainman that he had a letter for Nasos, which could be given at the first opportunity, and another for Talia, to be handled more surreptitiously. Something he needed delivered to her without Nasos knowing. It wasn't anything dramatic, but it was personal. The trainman agreed to get it to her, once an opportunity presented itself.

They sat in silence. The fireman peering ahead, ever diligent as the replacement for the engineer, the trainman ensuring the fire was stoked, as replacement for the fireman, and Julian alternatively jotting notes in his journal and then staring down, as the ground

The Journey: Erudite

flew by in a blur of crushed stone and the occasional weed. The day dawned imperceptibly. It was dark, and then it was light.

Julian spun from his trance. "It's time," he said.

The fireman nodded. "Alright, get ready. I see a small curve up ahead; I can slow down a little bit more there. It should be easy enough to get off."

He did, it was. Julian extended his thanks before leaning out the door, tossing out his bag and jumping off, tucking into an easy role as he hit the soft earth. He looked up and saw the trainman wave goodbye, the letter for Talia in his grasp. The train moved by, and as Julian watched the cars, he saw Talia. She was staring out the window at him, tears rolling down her cheeks. He lifted his hand to his lips in a kiss, but he never waved it to her. Then she was gone.

Julian gathered his sack, felt his own tears now flushing his cheeks, and headed in the general direction of the train. He figured he had at least twenty miles to go, perhaps more. In a while, with tears dried and the sun climbing high in the sky, Julian stood at the crest of a small hill. He could see the track extending in a long curve that ultimately changed its direction from east to south. He decided to walk southeast, figuring that he would eventually reconnect with the steel rails.

He didn't know at that point, but it would be a long time before that happened. The lazy, monotonous trek through the barren landscape was about to thrust significant and permanent change onto his adventure, and his life.

Talia Words and Wishes

Nasos was fuming when he returned to the master quarters after his strict treatment of Julian. He admonished Talia for her *shameless* behaviour. Imagine, snuggling with a near stranger, one much older than she, and most importantly, in front of his staff. How embarrassing. How could he trust her? How could she hurt him that way? How could he bring her on future trips? Had they done more than embrace? He went through the whole gambit of issues.

Talia sat quietly, letting the huff and puff bounce off her, while she held court internally with her private god, thinking about Julian, letting most of her father's rhetoric roll off her shoulders.

He is so childish. Such an ordeal. I can mingle with diplomats from around our world, but surely not even hold hands with a gentleman. Julian must be furious, or maybe ashamed. I hope not. I'll see him tomorrow and sort it out. OK, quiet now, Father, I'm tired. I'm going to sleep now.

It annoyed her only that Nasos was more concerned with his own image than with hers, and completely oblivious to her feelings.

The Journey: Erudite

Did he really think she was with Julian under duress? She knew she would not travel with her father any longer. It was time for her to stand alone. So what if she was only seventeen? She had skills beyond her years, and a growing self-confidence. She had always felt as if she and Nasos were spiritually disconnected; neither of them right nor wrong, just very different people. At times it was almost as if he wasn't really her father; they were so different in appearance and demeanour. Tonight, she was proud that she didn't engage her father in an argument about the evening's events. There was no point.

She did not sleep. It was more like a nap to carry off the weariness of emotion. She woke early and stepped out into the passageway, staring randomly out the window, not realizing Julian was only a few steps away, sitting with the trainman and fireman in the engine room. Tears formed on her cheeks, almost as if they were sweat. She could not remember crying them. She mused at the thought that they might be permanent. She weaved scenarios through her mind. Ways she might see Julian without her father's interference. Where would they go from here?

As they slowed noticeably to round a curve, Talia suddenly saw Julian land and tumble onto the terrain beside the train. At first, she thought it must have been an accident. Had he fallen from the train? But as he rose, their eyes met, and his hand raised to his lips confirmed to her that it was no accident. He had jumped off the train. He slowly disappeared into the curve of the train, his fingers still pressing his lips, never tossing the kiss they held, his eyes wide and full of sorrow.

Talia screamed out his name. She didn't even hear it, but her father did. She screamed again. Nasos came stumbling out of the sleeping car, seeking an explanation for the noise.

"He jumped off," she said, quietly, questioning, pointing out the window.

"Who?" her father replied.

"Julian," she barked at him. "Who do you think?"

Nasos was stunned. He had not expected that to happen.

"What did you say to him?" Talia demanded.

"Nothing...I told him you were too young, that he would have to depart at the next station."

"That's nothing?" Talia was angry. She wasn't crying. "Perhaps I should jump off this train as well then."

"Don't be silly. He didn't even know you were so young. He thought you were a woman."

That was a tough remark to swallow. "I *am* a woman," she stated, before punctuating it with, "old man!"

Talia stormed forward towards the engine. She wanted to know what had happened. Nasos began to follow her, mumbling about how it would be OK, about how it was not worth arguing over, about how she should get more sleep, about how she would come to her senses, about how he would tell her mother. It went on.

Finally, Talia turned and looked at him. "Just leave me alone, Nasos." She used his first name, with a not-so-subtle hint of sarcasm. "I'll remain prim and proper for the balance of the journey, but I will never travel with you again." She turned and walked towards the door.

Nasos stood in a stunned silence, but eventually considered the conversation closed. *She'll come to her senses*, he convinced himself. *Women are crazy!*

It was the end of his authority over her. Talia lost any thread of respect she had for her father as her guidance counsellor. It had been brewing for some time. He was so self-centred, so relentlessly pursuing his own agenda, that he had long ago lost her as a valuable part of his life, as an ally. The circus of diplomacy was constantly around, and Nasos could not separate that from his real life, from his family and friends. Because of that, he had no real friends, and he would soon discover, he had no real family either.

The Journey: Erudite

"Why did he jump off?" Talia asked the trainman, almost as a little girl might ask.

"I think he was feeling pretty attached to you, young lady, but you're still young, too young to develop that kind of closeness."

His remarks were right on, but Talia protested just the same, as if it would make any difference. "I'm not too young. Why does everyone keep saying that?"

"It is a difficult time, Talia. You have to let life happen for a while, let yourself make some transitions."

"How do I make transitions when there are so many roadblocks?"

The trainman looked at her. He also had a daughter, though she was now married and about to provide him with a first grandchild. He was careful not to say anything to upset Talia further. He held out his hand, with the letter Julian had left for her.

She looked up with some surprise and hesitated, before snatching it up, like a bird snatching an offered kernel, following some painstaking assessment of potential danger. She turned to go back to her bed; she needed to read it. Before she left, she looked back at the trainman.

He smiled.

"Thank you," she said.

He winked and turned back to his duties. The fireman was always looking ahead, down the never-ending line, with a slight smile on his lips.

Talia, beautiful one,

I must depart. If I stay, I will not be able to control the feelings I have for you. You are a woman. A lovely creature. I am consumed by thoughts of you...but...I was unaware of your age. You look and behave so much older. Do not be upset with your father, he is looking out for you, as he should. Do not be upset with me, for I will punish myself much more that you ever could. I will keep my visions of you close each day and each night, and I will find you. I will find you when you are a little older, when you are free to make your own decisions. I know you feel that you can do that now, but the law says otherwise, and I want us to find a lasting time together. I do not want to run away with you and have the world looking for us. That would be romantic, but not realistic. I will find you. Think of me, and that will lead me to you. I believe I love you...we have just met, but I believe I do love you.

Julian.

The trip home was a long and uncomfortable one for Talia. Her tears dried after several days, and she altered between hopelessness, anger, wistfulness, disbelief, uncertainty...and whatever else could crawl up into her mind. She struggled to smile at the functions they attended along the way. She avoided all conversation with her father, and spent most of her travel days sitting alone at the back of the train. She stared at the disappearing track, wondering of Julian; where he was, what he was doing...and especially, who he was with! It was her first taste of real jealousy, and she didn't like it, but she couldn't escape it.

By the time she arrived home her mood had become one of numbness. She had shut down her emotions in order to live with them for several days. Phoebe was there to meet the train and she was absolutely beaming with the anticipation of seeing Talia. She couldn't even stand still, rushing up as Talia stepped down from the train. But Talia was not as happy to see her. Well, she was, but she wasn't prepared to switch on the emotion of joy. Her mother knew immediately that something was wrong. They embraced, but it was hollow.

"Talia, what is it? Are you alright? Is your father OK? Did something happen?" Phoebe's voice climbed in pitch with each question, almost as though she was elevating the seriousness with each thought.

"No Mother, don't worry. Everyone is fine. Let's just go home, please."

Nasos came down next and he could tell by the look in his wife's eyes that an explanation was in order. He recounted the story briefly, at least from his perspective.

Phoebe just shook her head side to side. "Fool," she said.

He was taken aback by her comment, while she just stared at him. Finally, she dropped her stare and went over to Talia. Talia had her head down, examining the dirt on the ground.

"Tell me about him," Phoebe said.

Talia didn't want to talk about it. She was angry; at her father and at Julian. But Phoebe's question brought a sunshine of memories streaming back into her mind. She looked at her mother, and couldn't resist talking about him. It was as if the memories were her personal property and she wanted to share them with someone else who cared about her. It wasn't exactly introducing Julian to her mother, but it was a sufficient substitute for now.

"Oh, Mother, he was wonderful. He was perfect, beautiful. We had such lovely conversation, and everything we discussed was with the same thought, the same feeling. I can't explain, it was real symmetry."

"You're doing a pretty good job of explaining!"

"And he kissed me." Talia bowed her head as she said it.

"Did it make you tingle?" her mother asked.

Talia was not expecting that. "Yes, it was electric!" Talia shivered at the remembrance.

Her mother reached out and hugged her, holding her close. "That's how it should be," she whispered, remembering her own experiences; wondering where it had all disappeared to.

Talia smiled. She had known her mother would understand.

Talia rambled on about Julian when they got home. Nasos went to the local bar to renew some acquaintances, and no doubt, to avoid the angry stares from the women in his life.

Talia Words and Wishes

As they sat alone in the quiet of their back yard, Talia reached inside her dress and withdrew the letter Julian had left for her. She showed her mother. Phoebe read it with mixed emotions as well.

As she was reading, Talia commented. "He knows where we are from. He knows from Father which place we call home. I'm sure he'll find me; come for me."

Phoebe smiled and cried with Talia, agreeing that it was beautiful and romantic. At the same time, she wanted to caution Talia about the frivolity of false promises, the often casual nature of the term, *I love you*. But now wasn't the time. They could have that conversation further down the road of life. She was fairly certain Talia had seen the last of Julian.

Chasing the Mist Behind

Tection woke to the sound of pounding on his door. It took a moment to focus from his sleep, but it was unmistakable. He rose quickly and went to the door, assuming something, or someone of importance, was in some dire circumstance. He swung it open. Aziz stood in front of him, looking bewildered.

"My father told me you are leaving." He said it almost as if he was seeking either a final confirmation, or a jovial denial and consequential embrace.

Tection smiled. He spread the door open. "Come in, my friend."

Aziz hesitated, but stepped into his room.

"Sit down here, young man," Tection motioned, with a pat on a comfortable bench near the fireplace.

"Is it true?" Aziz demanded.

Tection looked at him through the top of his eyes, with his head slightly bent, as though peering over a pair of glasses he wasn't wearing. He patted the bench again. "Sit."

Aziz moved slowly to the bench. He already knew the answer.

The Journey: Erudite

Tection took the time to provide some explanation to Aziz, with no false promise of return. He could not articulate his entire internal battle with good and evil, but he managed to provide some understanding for the boy. Aziz remained distraught at the idea of losing his friend, but their final embrace was shadowed with understanding as well as sorrow.

Following the heartfelt goodbye, with a lasting stare from Aziz as he walked backwards towards the street, Tection reflected once again, silently and to himself, that the journey he was taking to escape his demons was impossible to complete, while he also carried them with him!

Tection secured transport with a small caravan, in exchange for a minimal sum and a promise of assistance with various labour. The caravan crew was an eclectic mix of herdsmen, traders, scholars, students, and himself, the foreign stranger. They continued to follow the edge of the sea, stopping frequently for trading, travelling east, with the endless desert landscape to their right. In a few weeks, as they rounded the sea and turned north, the desert gave way to a hilly, more fertile terrain. At their next stop, Tection ensured his responsibilities and debts to the caravan owner were covered, and then shared far too much goodbye cheer and drink with his travelling companions. In the morning, he sought transportation east. He knew that the northerly route was the way back to his homeland, around the other side of the sea, but he was not yet halfway through his journey. As long as he travelled away from his home, he was still on the first half of his journey. Once he headed back towards his origins, he was living the second half of it.

Tection did not plan to stay long, but he did want to take a little time to experience the local atmosphere and cuisine. He took a room at a small cottage near the long seaside boardwalk, quite a way south of the first sandy beach that stretched for miles in a northerly direction. He enjoyed the local restaurants in the evening, and his favourite afternoons were by the water, with a comfortable book.

One afternoon, with nothing more than a quiet read in mind, he strolled towards his usual bench. There were seldom any others strolling in this area, as it was away from both the city and the beach. But today there was a young woman sitting on *his* bench. At first it annoyed him. He was not seeking company, especially as the dialect in this area was somewhat foreign to him, and it took an effort to have even a rudimentary conversation. Still, he was not going to let her presence direct his plans. He sat on the bench, politely distant from her, and offered a standard *good day* in the local dialect. She looked over at him.

"I'm sorry," she said, "I am not familiar with your language." Her eyes looked towards the ground in a slightly embarrassed motion.

Tection looked at her again. She was actually speaking his mother language! "You sound like you are very familiar with my language," he said.

She looked up immediately, her hand coming up to cover the smile on her lips. "Oh, I didn't think anyone else here spoke anything besides the local dialect." She was blushing.

Tection couldn't help but stare a bit. She was very attractive. Petite, blonde, and with a young face, yet she was obviously a woman in her late twenties or perhaps even early thirties. Her covered smile, and the shyness it intimated, were equally attractive; seemingly part of her whole demeanour.

"I must admit, I am also a little surprised to find someone here speaking my language; especially someone so attractive." More blushing. Tection let her stew a little in her discomfort before continuing. "You must be a long way from home."

"I am indeed, I'm travelling with a diplomatic mission."

"That sounds very important."

She smiled.

Tection decided to continue with a little sarcasm. "So, this diplomatic mission, it has allowances for lazy afternoons by the seaside… and idle chatter with total strangers?"

She held out her hand. "I'm Phoebe."

"Tection," he replied, taking a comfortable grip of her hand, and holding it slightly longer than necessary. She didn't pull it away, letting it rest in his until he broke the grip. Tection wondered immediately if that was proper diplomatic protocol, as he had expected her to withdraw more quickly.

"Now we're not strangers," she said. It was Tection's turn to smile. "Of course, that doesn't account for the lazy afternoon by the seaside, but that is merely a coincidence of schedule. The mission is in the throes of various meetings, right now, that do not require my presence."

"That would indicate that you are either very important, or not too important at all. Either way, I'm glad that the circumstance, or perhaps fate, has also included my decision to spend a lazy afternoon by the seaside." Tection felt coy and confident.

"Unfortunately, you are just arriving, and I am just about to leave. If fate had truly intervened, you would have been here an hour ago, so we could chat longer, and about more interesting things than cute retorts." They both smiled.

"That is indeed unfortunate. I am just travelling through this town, heading east from here, but I am staying for a couple of days, and do enjoy seaside time most every afternoon." It was an open invitation to Phoebe for a future rendezvous, and she recognized it as such.

"I believe I'll be back here right after lunch tomorrow. It would be lovely if your planned *seaside time* was coincidently around then."

"I believe that is exactly when I was planning to come by."

"Perfect, I'll see you then," she said, rising up and turning away from him to stroll back towards the city street. Tection watched her go, admiring her wit, not to mention the slight exaggeration of her swinging hips.

Their second meeting was much more intimate than the first. They both commented on how they had spent some time through the previous evening thinking of one another. In a very short time, they decided to retire to Tection's room, as her government residence was buzzing with various diplomats, and she was not inclined to have them privy to her affairs, not to mention the husband she had skillfully neglected to reference.

"I am leaving in a couple of days, Phoebe. I want to be honest with you up front."

"As am I. It is precisely why this is so exciting." Her eyes sparkled. They both felt strong stirrings and Tection slid his arm around her waist. She was as light as air and he had no trouble in literally lifting her off her feet, as he drew her close for a long, deep kiss. It had been some time since he enjoyed the comfort of a woman, and his body demonstrated that immediately. Phoebe noticed. She let her legs slide around his hips, her dress crawling up her thighs, as he carried her to his bed.

Phoebe and Tection spend two wonderful afternoons together. Despite his prying, she was evasive about her life, and completely unavailable in the evenings. He realized he had been equally vague about his own past. On the second day, after their very passionate afternoon in bed, she had simply stated that she was leaving in the morning, and reflected on how wonderful their time together had been. Tection thought about protesting, perhaps persuading her to stay longer, perhaps gaining a commitment for a future rendezvous, but in the end, he decided that a simple, but emotional goodbye, was the only appropriate response; along with one last bout of love making, of course.

The Journey: Erudite

Tection's travels towards the east were initially fraught with boredom. He could find no one of interest to chat with, all his books had been read, and the road just continued to jingle and jangle, day after day. He was nearing a point where he might decide to stop in the next town along the way, just to replenish some activity in his life. He was after all, a gregarious individual, with a thirst to meet, engage, and ramble with others. It stemmed from his early upbringing in the orphanage back home. As they arrived at their next stop, Tection's determination to find some excitement was outweighing his commitment to continue travelling east. His mind was all but made up, when a rather boisterous, middle-aged man joined their transport. He appeared to be East Indian, from somewhere on the sub-continent, but he spoke Tection's language perfectly, and was quite different from others Tection had encountered from that area. Mostly, they had been servants, or perhaps labourers, always soft spoken, heads bowed, and forever seeming to be content with navigating through life from start to finish without any conflict. Definitely not the type of person Tection enjoyed. But this man was different. That was evident from the first time Tection heard him speak. He was being assigned a less favourable place, but he spoke up with such volume, enthusiasm, and fluency, that he was quickly relocated; right next to Tection!

His name was Ravi, and he was on his way home, following a lengthy sales trip. The cube Tection had received from Selim managed to peak from beneath his partially unbuttoned shirt, and Ravi noticed it almost instantly. That sparked an initial conversation, one with more thought-provoking commentary than would be expected. The two men hit it off immediately. They were both experienced travellers, both loaded with stories and anecdotes from their pasts, and both more than willing to enjoy a drink or two, or three. They travelled with such harmony, they barely noticed the sun, rising and falling on its endless journey, pushing one day into another. Every once in a while, one of them would reflect on either the time of day, the time of night, or the lovely lady who was walking by. They were not dissimilar to two underage school boys out on the prowl.

There were several stops and transfers, turns and delays, and the people they encountered gradually shifted from Arab, to Persian, to Indian. It became a haze, a throng of travellers, each with a different story, each a different life. Tection loved it. What a cosmopolitan adventure. In his moments of solitude, he examined someone, anyone, with his imagination, exploring their story. It didn't matter if the person was actually a professor of mathematics, if Tection visualized him as a magician, that's where he was slotted. He made a game of it, and many of his subjects afforded multiple reviews, as they were travelling in unison for some time. Occasionally, after several days of detailed analysis, he would shift the individual's story from being, for example, a carpenter, to being a sailor, or some other dynamic shift. Unfortunately, he was occasionally caught gawking at a particular individual, and he soon mastered his *sorry-I-didn't-mean-to-stare* smile. Between his life determinations, the vivid companionship of Ravi, and the appreciation of much sleep, usually fuelled by Arak or more recently, a local drink called Sura, Tection found himself in northern India. The journey had been a blur, with few individual memories to clog up the one large, and most memorable...memory.

Eventually, they neared Ravi's home town, but there was no way they could end their journey.

"Of course you are coming to my home. Not only will my wife and sons be most happy to have you, you are actual proof that I do meet the many crazy characters I always tell them about when I return from my travels."

"Well, with that much importance heaped on me, I have no choice but to accept."

Ravi laughed his large laugh, patted Tection firmly on the back, and then spoke roughly to an attendant at the station, who scurried to load their bags onto a rather cramped rickshaw.

"Welcome to India!"

Ravi's house was large. He had several servants clambering about, all leaving their chores to welcome him home. Tection was immediately introduced to Saachi, Ravi's wife. She was not only a very attractive lady, who must have been stunning in her earlier years, but she was fluent in many languages, including Tection's. He reflected internally, with a little shame, that he had been expecting a bustling little lady, scurrying about her tasks and serving food to her tired husband. Quite the opposite!

"So nice of you to visit, Tection. Please come in and sit down. Ravi, kindly ask

mulazim to bring some chilled refreshments, Tection must be terribly weary."

Tection correctly assumed that *mulazim* was one of the servants about the house. As they moved into a sitting room, Tection caught a movement from the corner of his eye. He sat down on the settee, mindful that someone was peeking at him. As they chatted, the small head peering around the corner shifted higher and lower, then bolder and bolder, until finally, the full head of a beaming young boy became visible.

"Be careful Saachi, I believe we have a spy among us," Tection offered, nodding his head towards the giggling boy.

Saachi looked around, catching a glimpse of her youngest son as he slipped back under cover.

"Sharif, is that you?" No response. "Sharif, we have a visitor, you must come and say hello." No response. Tection was surprised she had used his language, indicating the boy obviously spoke it as well.

Ravi joined them from the other direction and sat down opposite Tection. "Are you comfortable, my friend?"

Tection did not reply. He held his finger to his lips, indicating silence. He then rose and moved over to the edge of the wall that was hiding Ravi's young son. Sure enough, his little head once again peered around the corner. When he realized Tection was no longer in his seat, he leaned in farther, and then it was too late! Tection sprung from the side of the wall and grabbed the startled boy under the arms, easily hoisting him up so he could look at him face to face.

"Are you spying on us," he asked, raising his eyebrows and lightly tickling Sharif's ribs with his baby fingers. He wasn't sure if the boy understood his words, but Ravi and Saachi did.

Once over his initial surprise, the boy began to laugh. He squirmed to escape the tickling grip of this huge stranger, but it was to no avail. Tection carried the writhing little body over to the settee, and sat down, resting him on his knee, but continuing to tickle him. He laughed louder; his head tossed back. His parents laughed. Finally, Sharif managed to slither down Tection's leg and escape to the safety of the carpet. He jumped up and ran back to the corner where he had been captured, taunting Tection to chase him again.

"Not now, Sharif," his mother said. "Come on over here and say hello to your father, he has missed you while he was away."

That was a wake-up call. Sharif suddenly remembered he had indeed not seen his father for several weeks. He dashed out and jumped up onto his waiting lap, throwing his arms around his neck, but with his eyes still glued on Tection. Everyone continued to smile, as Ravi and Sharif exchanged remarks about missing each other, Sharif's amazing growth over the past few weeks, and naturally, a full inquiry into what treasures his father had brought home for him.

"Go find your brother," Ravi said, "and then we can check my bag for possible presents."

"But he's still at school. He finishes later than me," Sharif whined. Then he switched languages and droned on about something else, undoubtably a plea for immediate gift giving.

"Ah yes, well, we will have to wait for him to get home."

Sharif sulked for about twelve seconds, before descending from Ravi's lap and stalking Tection, as if he was the prey for a hungry tiger. Soon enough they were wrestling on the floor. Despite Saachi's admonitions, Tection humoured the lad, playing with him for some time, until Ravi broke up the tussle, and invited Tection into his study for some more serious conversation.

"Run along now, Sharif, we'll see what I have when Ayan gets home."

Tection had travelled much farther east than he expected. He had met someone much more interesting and compatible than he had expected, and his attachment to Ravi's young son, Sharif, was much stronger than expected. He consciously recognized his own internal yearning to be a father; to have a child of his own with a woman he loved, in a place where he was content and happy. It all seemed so distant for him at the moment, and he felt unfulfilled because of it.

In an ironic twist, however, Tection had a first recognition that his searching soul was not only chasing some redemption, or justification, for his action in bringing about the demise of the evil creature he had killed, but was perhaps also seeking a confirmation of purpose and a fulfilment of his powerful urge to have a kind and loving person closely woven into his life. Perhaps that was why he was so receptive to those who seemed vulnerable through their charity of behaviour. His sense of responsibility as a benefactor of sorts for those less able to confront their tormentors, was a common theme in his life. It spoke loudly for the strength of commitment to the battle of good and evil that constantly surrounded him, but also reminded him of the internal battle of the same nature, that endlessly provoked him.

His planned departure took several days to manifest itself. Ravi and Saachi scolded him for even thinking about leaving. Their house was, after all, large enough, with separate guest quarters and ample opportunity for Tection to come and go, live peacefully and explore the city, without disturbing them. Besides, Sharif and Ayan were hopelessly attached to their new found *uncle*, anxiously seeking him out every morning, and every afternoon after school. Tection told them many stories; tales of a distant world, filled with different people and different customs; but he always returned to his main theme, which was the understanding that the more diverse the people he encountered, the more similar he realized they were. All the culture, customs, religion and habits of one particular place, were insignificant when held up against the common values of kindness, hospitality, principles, and most significantly, family; both immediate and extended.

What was it about *family*, that shattered all prejudices and enmity, that breeched the barriers of relationships with ease, and ensured a lasting contact despite distance or distraction? It was easy enough to recognize the powerful bond between parent and child, but this family attachment seemed to be perpetually elastic. During his stay, Tection was fortunate enough to meet several of Ravi and Saachi's relatives; their extended family, as they referred to them. At one gathering there were over one hundred people, all gathered in a town hall of sorts, celebrating the birthday of one of the patriarchs. Tection remembered Ravi's remark.

"It is a lot of people my friend, but only twenty or so are my relations."

"That is still a lot," Tection responded. "Who are the other people?"

"Oh, they're all Saachi's family!"

Tection just smiled and shook his head in wonder.

One take-away for Tection, once again, was a very clear understanding that he definitely wanted a family of his own; there was no doubt. The excitement he felt each morning, anticipating a first encounter with the boys, especially Sharif, was not a new experience for him. He had felt a similar anticipation each day with Selim's daughter Malika, as he taught her a second language, and equally importantly, about life and some expectation she might build. There had been many people in his life that he looked forward to seeing, each and every time they were to meet, but he had not really experienced the kind of attachment he enjoyed with children; first Malika, and now with these boys.

Before departing, Tection found a quiet moment with Sharif. He explained why he had to leave, keeping his comments simple enough for a young boy to understand; perhaps.

"I have a special gift for you, Sharif." The boy's eyes perked up and he smiled in anticipation. Tection removed the small cube that Selim had given him, from around his neck, bringing it forward and placing it in Sharif's hand. "This is a reminder to you. It reminds you to accept all people, to be understanding of all cultures, and most importantly, it is a reminder of Tection, and something to emphasize to you how special you are to me and how much you have helped me on my journey."

Tection was convinced that Selim, when he suggested Tection 'give it to someone you want to share the path with', would have approved of his choice. They were, after all, both admirers of children.

Sharif was a little confused by all the words and not certain he understood what was meant, but he was overjoyed to get something so unique, and most importantly, something so personal, from this huge, travelling man. He put it on and danced around, teasing Tection by holding it out and snatching it back, before scurrying off to show his mother and father. Tection watched him run off, certain that the boy was destined to travel the world. His discernment would eventually be proven to be most accurate, though he could not have imagined the broad spectrum of adventure that awaited the young boy.

A great feast was organized by Saachi to honour Tection, and send him off on his continuing journey. Ravi and Tection found a moment on the morning of his departure, before the family came together in a collective goodbye, with the boys clambering all over him.

"It has been such an honour to have you as our guest, Tection. I have gained some very valuable insights from our conversation, though I must admit, I felt a little jealousy when I saw how attached my sons have become to you, in such a short time."

Tection smiled, almost laughed. "It is easy when I have no responsibility towards them. We only play and have fun. It is you and Saachi who must take all the responsibility to ensure they get their school work done and their chores completed; no wonder they enjoyed me; I was an easy target."

Both men laughed a bit.

"Still, Tection, it has been a wonderful time. They will always remember you, as will we."

"And I will also remember you, Ravi. Kindness, hospitality, wisdom, and generosity! Your family is as fortunate to have you, as you are to have them."

After his departure, as he found himself once again on the road to somewhere, Tection thought about family. He definitely wanted one of his own, picturing himself returning to his homeland, finding a beautiful bride, and bringing forth his own little Malikas and Sharifs. Tection decided at that moment to head back towards his home. The journey was half done. He expected a more expeditious return, but he didn't know then that it would still be years before he finally made his way back.

Safa, Good and Evil

Safa danced a little shuffle as she wound her way down to the river. Her carrying jar was light now, easy to balance on her young head, and comfortable. The sun was high in the sky and relentless in showering the entire landscape with bright, hot radiance. Safa used the jar to shade her head from the downpour of light and paid little attention to her surroundings, content and comfortable in the personal little world of music and mind-play she was enthralled with.

When she reached the water's edge, she lifted her robe, a dress-like wrap, slightly and stepped out into the water, until her calves were almost covered. With one hand she dunked the jar, letting it gurgle full, and then struggled to lift it and carry it along her hip until she stepped back onto dry land, finally dropping her raised hem. She swung the jar up onto her head and began the return march to her father's tent. It was a ritual she performed several times a day, all part of the education she was receiving from her mother, sisters, and cousins, as she grew into womanhood.

She was very happy with her young life, surrounded by loving siblings and relatives, who treated her like a living doll. She was the youngest of six, three sisters who adored her and two brothers she knew much less about. They were older and gone most of the day, charged with their own responsibilities and commitments. Along with her sisters, there were five female cousins, each one anxious to help her grow into her future with progress in both knowledge and happiness. She was the youngest of the bunch by several years and almost like a surrogate child, a proxy for the young ladies who were as yet unmarried. She didn't realize that she was teaching them as much as she was learning, preparing them for motherhood as they prepared her for womanhood. A wonderful time to be alive.

Days and weeks went by, the change in the season as imperceptible as the advancement in knowledge and learning were. Shared meals with laughter and storytelling, hard work with honest rewards, tight family ties, and loving arms at the end of the day, all made the turning of life a joyous experience. Safa ran through the passing of time with the abandon of youth, stumbling occasionally, but ever energized and curious for new experience. The mundane part of daily chores was easily survived through vivid imagination and intimate dreams, while the daily adventure of learning and discovery was inspiration that partnered each morning's rise from slumber. A hard but happy existence.

On this particular morning, on this particular march back to her father's tent, with this particular jar of water, Safa was distracted. A small lamb ran across her path, venturing far from where it should be and obviously agitated by something. Safa lowered her jar down onto the sandy earth and darted after the lamb. It had ascended a small hill, leaving it out of her sight line, and she ran over the crest after it. As she began her descent down the other side, lifting her head to locate the runaway lamb, she bumped directly into an unknown man, a stranger, here in a place where no strangers existed.

The man was large, and he smelled. He grabbed her around the waist and held her tight. She froze at first, unsure of what was happening, and then tilted her head to scream. Too late. His hand was over her mouth and he lifted her off the ground with such ease that she wondered at the strength he must possess. She bent her head to try and see his face but it was covered, his kufiyah draped over his mouth and chin, guarding his identity. He bundled her on his hip and moved quickly across some distance, covering several smaller hills and some turns in direction, finally arriving at a rudimentary camp where another man sat smoking a hookah, or nargileh. This man looked up when they arrived, a little startled and then he stood.

Her captor bent her face forward showing his companion, expounding on her youth and beauty, as the arch between his thumb and finger slid under her chin, lifting her face up. His hand slid up her waist, cupping her adolescent breast through the thick cloth of her robe, while she fought valiantly but fruitlessly against his iron grip. The other man waved his hands and signalled clearly that this was inappropriate and urged his friend to stop. But the beast was already chasing some unseen hysteria, building inside him like a silent volcano. He laughed back, challenging the manhood of the dissenting man while dragging Safa over another small rise, out of sight of the camp.

Her captor brought Safa to the ground and moved on top of her. She was overcome with fear. Her head pounded, bringing on a dizziness that drove reality from her mind. She flailed away, hoping somehow that this was only a lonely nightmare, a cruel bit of humour playing out in her brain. She turned her head. The lost lamb stood a short way off, munching contentedly on the sparse grass stalks that sprouted from the barren soil. He slapped her, blood splattered from the impact, and he brought his mouth down on hers, his tongue licking at her face with a renewed frenzy. Her young mind raced in a frantic gulp of confusion, a complete incomprehension of what was happening. He rose up to look down into the glassy eyes of his victim, surely driven by the helplessness he saw. Then he went limp. His eyes rolled slightly up into his head and he collapsed onto her, dead weight, like a bag of grain, a huge bag of grain.

She closed her eyes. What was happening?

She felt his body lifted off her and pushed to the side, rolling away from her, the fresh air caressing her tears and filling her heaving lungs. She looked up, but the sun was directly in her eyes, and she could make out only the silhouette of her benefactor. Was it her brother, her father? He spoke to her but she didn't understand. The words were not foreign, just different, as if made from the same syllables but arranged in a different manner. He reached out to lift her but she clutched her arms to herself and curled up, closing her eyes in a renewed effort to turn the event into a dream. He retreated and returned with a small canteen, which he brought up to her mouth. She opened her eyes again, sideways now and out of the direct sunlight, peering up into his soft and tender face with his simple but subtle smile asking her to take a drink. She did.

Julian's trek across the dunes, in a direct line to once again meet up with the steel rails, was a fortuitous one. He had been drawn towards the oasis and arrived just in time to foil the despicable attack being perpetrated on this young girl. The man lay unconscious in the sand beside her and Julian removed the assailant's sash and tied his hands behind his back, and then to his bent legs. He felt his pulse to assure his blow hadn't killed him and returned to Safa. She was sitting up, wiping the tears from her face, leaving streaks of dirt in their stead. She stood and moved over to the bound man, lashing out with her feet, kicking him in the side several times. Julian moved slowly to stop her, letting some of her frustration escape and realizing she deserved the opportunity to deliver the blows. As he held her shoulders, calming her actions, they both looked up to see the attacker's companion bolting southward on his horse. They paid him little attention.

Julian could not communicate clearly with Safa through words, but he managed to get her stabilized and she pointed towards her home. She was wary of him just the same, possibly wary of all men for some time to come. They walked together a short distance before Safa stopped and looked back. The lamb was still chasing fresh grass along the hill side and she pointed to it. Julian was uncertain at first, but finally understood that she wanted him to gather it in. He walked over and shooed the beast forward with a wave of his hands along the side of his hips. It headed towards Safa accordingly, not interested in confronting this two-legged creature hustling behind it.

When Safa saw her tent, she bolted for it. Running with screams of something, leaving Julian standing alone, only imagining what the words might be. The surrounding people dropped whatever they were attending to and raced towards her, trying to understand the commotion. They huddled and Safa pointed at Julian. They all looked at him at once and a few young men came running towards him in a very threatening manner. They pulled their knives, their shibriyas, as they charged. Julian froze. He had no chance to run and no weapon to fend them off with. He heard Safa screaming something again, then repeating it as the young men drew near. Suddenly they stopped, looking at Julian with more than a little suspicion. Safa screamed again, pointing back towards the direction they had come from. The men blew past Julian and headed out to find her assailant.

Julian sat cross-legged on the ground inside the large and surprisingly luxurious tent. Five other men sat at the table with him, all of them much older than he, and all of them bearded and very somber looking. They were served meat and peas, with the elder and obvious head of the tribe encouraging Julian to eat. Julian did so, most pleasantly surprised at the very tasty nature of the food. He ate more heartily than expected and the men all followed his action, commenting their approval at his obvious enjoyment, he assumed.

Dinner was consumed without much conversation. The men bantered a little, occasionally pointing at Julian, but always in a respectful and non-threatening way. Julian imagined what they were saying but surmised he could be completely wrong in his interpretations. He understood some of the words but knew enough about the dialect that he spoke, to know inflection was significant in a correct interpretation. The young girl he had saved from assault had not really understood him, although she had looked at him rather curiously, as if part of what he said was intelligible. He wondered if he had that same basic look at the moment.

After the food came some drink, strong drink, and Julian enjoyed that even more. His past life as a café owner had allowed, or more correctly compelled him to drink frequently, and his body had built a strong resistance to the effects of alcohol. He had several drinks and the men seemed surprised at his apparent tolerance to the beverage, some of them becoming slightly askew in their mannerisms long before him. As the evening wore down, slowly descending towards an end, a woman entered the tent. The elder stood and spoke to her, waving his hand at Julian. She hesitated. He spoke louder, almost in a quizzical nature, seeming to admonish her for hesitating. She looked at Julian.

"My father wishes you thank you. Say you brave in action this day; he has honour from you being here, here in his home."

Julian was in shock that she spoke his mother tongue, albeit a little choppy. He hadn't revealed yet that he spoke another language as well, one similar to theirs, except to the young girl. He looked up at the old man who stood with some pride and a look of satisfaction on his face, as though he knew all along that she could speak it. Perhaps he wanted Julian to spend the night in the same ignorant condition with which he had entered their camp. Julian smiled, then he laughed, the alcohol probably providing a little influence. The elder looked at him, confused. Julian had responded to his praise and welcome with laughter. His daughter looked at Julian with worried eyes. The other men looked at their leader, then back at Julian. Julian laughed again, even louder. The elder began to smile, then chuckle, then break into a full laugh of his own. The other men followed suit. The daughter was uncertain what had happened. She was confused. Outside the tent the other members of the tribe were equally startled by the raucous laughter that now engulfed the leader's tent. It was a very rare occurrence for them.

The elder spoke to his daughter again and she translated. Before she spoke, he pointed at her and said, "Malika." Julian gathered that must be her name and nodded his understanding. The elder then pointed at himself, "Selim."

Again, Julian acknowledged the name and, pointing to his own chest, repeated his own, "Julian."

The elder repeated it, mispronouncing it, but it was clearly recognizable.

Malika blushed ever so slightly. "My father is shaykh, leader of all tribe. He says, it is only you, your work, that we, you, are able for laugh now, and for that we are happy, we are...grateful." She struggled with the last word. She waited as Selim spoke further for her additional translation. "We not able for laugh at this trouble, this bad thing, what brings you here, at our table." Again, she waited. "But we are together." She clasped her fingers together, to ensure the correct word had been used. "And join you to celebrate." This time she raised her arms in a flurry. "The joy and result of this day." Her face turned very serious, perhaps even a tear developing in her dark eyes. "Joy grabbed," she said, her hands jerking back at the air, "from teeth of sad, of sorrow." She looked at Julian with the last word, uncertain of her choice, and he nodded that he understood. She smiled and looked at her father. She looked back at him, and even though the end of her words indicated that she had translated what her father said, she added her own addendum; "Thank you."

Julian made an effort to stand up and face the elder but his daughter interrupted. "Please stay in sit. When you stand, we stop, we finish." She was pleased with her recollection of the correct word. "And end of meal."

Julian looked at her and relaxed back down. He spoke slowly, hoping she would understand correctly. "Please tell your father that I have done what any person would do." Julian waved his hand across the room, indicating he meant any of the men present. "I felt fortunate and honoured that I found myself arriving at the right moment, before worse results could be realized." He took a breath to continue but she stopped him, indicating he should wait while she translated his words.

The shaykh, still standing, and the remaining men at the table, lost their smiles, nodding in agreement with his comments. Julian continued, "I hope the young lady will not be badly affected in the future, that this experience will not hurt her soul." He used his fist to gently knock his chest, supporting his use of the word soul with a physical reinforcement. Malika translated, obviously very fluent in her own language.

The elderly man responded, and she translated back, "It is bad, this thing that happened to Safa, to her soul." He returned the chest knocking motion. "But you," he said, pointing at Julian, "you have turned this bad experience, with a strong fight." He slapped his upper arm. "And good soul." Malika translated as his fist once again pounded his chest. Julian began to reply but the old man held his hand up. He spoke further. "She is living and now sleeps." Selim held his left hand out.

Malika translated and Selim waited for her to finish. "On this hand, an evil man, grabbing what is not his, what belongs to Safa. He steals her soul." This time Malika pounded her own chest. "She is not strong enough to fight." Malika looked back at Selim and he let his right arm counter his left, again speaking and waiting for Malika to translate. "You have fought this evil for Safa, you stood to fight the evil and turned it. Not all men can do that, and the evil you fought was a big man, big man full of evil." Malika finished with another pounding of her chest, mirroring Selim.

When she finished her translation, Julian contemplated the words. It was an interesting observation, an intriguing perception. The power of good fighting the power of evil; victorious this time. Julian's mind danced with recollections of his own evil, lurking within, and was puzzled by the realization that he could deliver a perception of powerful good, vanquishing an immense evil, yet could be confused by his own perceived uncertainty about his nature.

Julian looked at Malika and she nodded slightly, indicating it was an appropriate time to respond. "I thank you for your words, Selim, they honour me." He held his open hand over his heart. He waited for Malika to convey what he had said, then continued. "I think most men would find such courage, in the same fight." He waved his hand again, indicating he meant all of them. He wasn't sure if he had somehow insulted the elder by using his first name or by deflecting his praise. But his daughter smiled, indicating he had not. "Let us drink then." Julian raised his glass. "To the courage of men, may they find it when they need it."

Malika translated somehow, possibly not with the exact connotation, but clearly enough. Everyone raised their glasses in unison, various comments coming from them, all of which were not understood by Julian, nor translated by Malika.

Malika left. Julian asked her to stay, to continue providing translation, but Selim waved her off with appreciation, and comments that tomorrow would provide opportunity for more chatter, while tonight required only more drink to translate their words. How could Julian argue with that?

Julian and the Improbable Encounter

Julian was consumed by the revelry that surrounded the events of Safa's fortunate escape from her attacker. He was showered with accolades throughout the night, and, as may have been expected, they grew more boisterous with each glass consumed. The similarities between Selim's language and that previously learned by Julian when he'd first arrived in this new land, were close enough for rudimentary conversation to be possible. Comprehension also magically increased with each new round of beverages.

It was a happy night, filled with the release of tension brought on by the unfortunate episode with Safa, and perhaps an opportunity to bring some diversion into the otherwise mundane existence the tribe endured. *It's funny,* Julian observed, *with little attachment or interaction with the outside world, even the one so close to them, they remain in a generational limbo of sorts, progressing in neither work, nor faith, nor education. Like the closed minds of any culture, the fear of the unknown, the uncertainty of differences, produces ignorance instead of examination, and prejudice instead of tolerance.*

Julian eventually drifted to sleep in the sheltering arms of gratitude, comforted by the not so subtle influence of fermentation. He was relaxed and happy. In the morning, after a pleasant but solitary breakfast of spiced tea, cut vegetables, fresh tahini, hummus and bread, he found time to make some additions to his journal. He had not opened it since detailing the emotional departure from Talia. He mused on the fact that entries with an identical number of words, occupying an identical number of pages, could detail events of such contrary nature, and such diverse importance, like the days of life, each with the same number of hours, but with infinite possibilities of what those hours would deliver.

Around mid-morning, Malika approached him with a request to join Selim in front of the shaykh's tent. As they moved towards it from the rear, Julian could hear a growing commotion of sorts, and when they rounded the corner, Julian saw Safa's assailant, surrounded by a hostile and agitated mass of people, representing a majority of the tribe. The man was on his knees, hands and feet bound, and naked from the waist up. He was mumbling something; a prayer, Julian assumed.

Selim walked forward with a long sword, rather narrow and slightly curved, holding it in two hands, one on the hilt and the other at the point of the blade. He raised it over his head and presented it to the gathered throng as he spoke in a monotone that Julian managed to decipher as a message of offering to God, Allah. They replied with a collective response, punctuated with random call-outs and murmured remarks. Selim turned to Julian and handed him the sword. Julian hesitated. Selim looked at Malika and she moved forward to once again translate his remarks.

"This will bring a final end to the evil against Safa," she translated, as Selim again pushed the handle towards Julian. "Please take it," Malika added in her own words. Julian did.

Julian and the Improbable Encounter

She returned to translating. "The honour to finish his punishment belongs to him that began it."

Selim looked at Julian, bringing his hands forward towards the large man's neck, clearly indicating that Julian should strike a blow to cut off his head!

"Malika." Julian looked at her with shock and terror in his eyes. "I cannot do this; I cannot kill another man."

Selim looked at Malika and she expressed Julian's remarks. Selim looked back at Julian, responding in a calm and measured voice.

Malika followed his tone in her translation. "This man has tried to hurt our daughter, our young daughter. You have saved her. You struck him. You might have killed him with that blow, but he survived. Now you must finish the task, to rid this evil from the world. He cannot hurt another young daughter somewhere."

Julian was torn. He looked at the condemned man, who was teetering back and forth, eyes squeezed shut, chanting, almost singing, a mumbled prayer. Several people in the gathered crowd roared encouragement to Julian with words he did not understand, but action with their arms that mimicked the motion of a beheading. Selim grabbed the man's hair and pulled it slightly, forcing his head forward. He pointed to a spot at the base of his neck. He spoke loudly.

"Now," Malika translated.

Julian looked around at the tribe; all eyes were on him, the pressure of the moment surrounded him. He raised the sword. He looked to his right, Selim with eyes as steady as rocks, to his left, Malika nodding her agreement. At the front of the crowd young Safa stepped forward, her bruised face still swollen, her eyes hungry for revenge. She looked directly into Julian's eyes, her own completely void of any indecision. Julian's body shook as his adrenalin rushed forward, bringing him a slight dizziness and, at the same time, a tremendous building of energy. He brought the sword down with all the force he could muster. The man's head separated from his body under the force of the blow, like a leaf from a dried branch.

Julian dropped the sword. He didn't really hear the cheers that rose from the gathered people, or feel the crush of their embrace. He looked at the head lying on the ground and thought he saw the lips still moving in their mumbled prayer. The small amount of blood was surprising. He stepped backward. Selim said something but Julian didn't acknowledge it, and Malika said something as well, either translating or commenting, but he moved away from their voices. He took a few more steps backwards and then turned and ran to his tent, bursting inside and falling to his knees, shaking uncontrollably and out of breath. Curiously, he shed no tears.

A short while later, Selim and Malika entered the tent. Julian still knelt, with his back towards the door. He wanted to scream out something, but he didn't know what. The man would have raped the young girl if Julian hadn't been there; there was no question of that. Julian also didn't doubt, that if released, the man would again harm a young woman somewhere. He sought justification for the beheading, and he found some. His dilemma was that he could not justify that it was *he* who brandished the sword. He would have approved the task for another, he knew that, but he was shaken by the reality that *he* delivered the blow, or more precisely, by the realization that he was even capable of doing so.

Selim spoke, as always, through Malika's voice. "I can see you have much pain in delivering the justice for Safa. It is once again even more strength that you show. This is not your custom, but you live here right now, and this is our custom. All men wanted to be you today, all except you. You did not want to be you."

Julian took a deep breath. But he did want to be himself. He was in a strange land, a new culture, but he *was* exactly where he wanted to be, and exactly who he wanted to be. *Selim is right* he thought, *I could have easily killed the man with my blow at the sand dune, and I would kill him again to prevent such harm to a young child.*

Julian and the Improbable Encounter

He stood up and turned towards Selim. "It was the right thing," he said, peering directly into Selim's eyes, his own now like rocks in his head, and he touched his open hand to his heart. Selim smiled, but not a smile of joy, or even appreciation. It was a smile of understanding, of knowing that Julian had discovered a great insight into his own character, an appreciation for the power of good over evil, even though Julian may not have realized that himself, just yet.

Julian took advantage of the fresh water and shaded surroundings. He joined the others in shedding his shirt and rinsing the crust of dust from his brow, dipping his head several times into the oasis pool. He splashed water up onto his arms as well, letting the heavy load of weariness wash at least partially away from his upper body. He stood, throwing his head back and pushing his hands through his hair to force out the excess water. *It's amazing how a small rinsing can change the entire posture of the body and mind*, he thought, before looking out to observe the others who were enjoying the same relief. *New friends*, he reflected, *new friends with new ideas, just like this fresh wash of water, pouring small waves of diverse thought and alternative understanding, washing across the soul, delivering new concepts and awareness of the human condition and its convictions.*

Selim strode over to Julian, smiling with the common knowledge of how good the oasis refreshment was, and offered him some dates to help keep his mouth moist and his hunger repressed. Julian accepted them with a nod and returned smile. Suddenly Selim's demeanour changed to something close to astonishment. He stepped forward, carrying some confusion and perhaps even uneasiness to his body language, before reaching out and grasping the medallion around Julian's neck. He raised it and turned it slowly, giving it a full examination before looking back at Julian.

"Tection?" Selim asked, with a curious tilt to his head.

Julian was dumbfounded. How on earth could Selim know that? There was no mistaking that they spoke of the same person; his name was too uncommon.

"Yes," Julian finally uttered, demonstrating his own confusion at how Selim could be in possession of this name. "Yes, Tection." He reached up to remove the medallion from Selim's hand, still holding it out in front of him. A momentary thought crept into Julian's mind. *What if Tection had somehow offended Selim or perhaps even been disliked for some reason*? But that thought was quickly pushed aside. "Do you know Tection?" he asked, pointing at Selim to augment the words, while still holding a look of equal astonishment in his eyes.

Selim crouched down in front of him, slowly letting his body weight compress into a full squat. Julian wasn't sure what to do. He released the medallion and looked down at this man, this shaykh, squatting before him with both hands now on his head, cooing softly in some non-lyrical chant. After a few moments Selim rose up. Others who had witnessed the moment came cautiously closer. Malika stood next to her father. She recognized the medallion as well; it was most precious to her.

Selim looked directly at Julian. "How do you have this medallion?" he asked, his question anxiously translated. He once again reached out to take hold of it, glancing down to reassure himself of its authenticity before he returned his gaze to Julian.

Julian smiled. He had feared that Selim would be angry, perhaps even suspicious of how he had acquired the medallion, but he wasn't. He realized Selim was pleased, even joyous at the discovery of the medallion. "It was a gift from him, a final gift before my departure from where I came, to where I am," he said.

"He is alive?" Selim asked, with as much hope as he could muster.

"Very much so," Julian quickly responded, a little surprised at the question. Tection was not so old, and in good health. There had to be some other reason for Selim's question. "He is not only alive,"

Julian and the Improbable Encounter

Julian added, realizing it would bring much relief and joy to Selim, "but happily reunited with his family, his son."

"You know him?" Selim asked, seemingly oblivious to the obviousness of that very fact.

Julian laughed. "I do," he stated in reassurance. "He is the last person I spoke to before coming to this land."

With Malika ever present to forge a translation, Selim's questions were endless and Julian answered all he could, recounting his meeting with Tection once Tection had returned from his distant voyage, apparently, based on the current situation, one that had included some time with Selim. He spoke of the friendship he and Tection had built. He told Selim of Tection's discovery of his previously unknown son, and the elation and wonder that had ensued when the boy and his mother were reunited in Tection's arms. He explained that it was Tection who had purchased his café, affording him the opportunity to take his own journey, delivering him the medallion as a parting gift in hopes it might provide a connection with some of those Tection had met. Julian never imagined it to be such a fortuitous observation.

Julian learned that Selim's concern for Tection's continued living was nourished by an understanding of the conflict Tection faced in dealing with the killing of a tormentor, a man who had brought much pain to Tection and had been perpetuating that same pain onto others, when Tection took his action. Julian wasn't certain that he knew the story Selim spoke of. He was aware of the immense conflicts Tection carried internally, but he was not aware of the specific events being recounted. He was not aware that Tection had actually killed anybody. It provided much clarity for Julian and his reflections on Tection's demeanour. Julian had wondered what was so traumatic that it had set Tection off on a very lengthy journey of discovery. He had never imagined it was that Tection had killed someone. The thought suddenly struck him; would he also be chased onto a long and winding path by the memories of delivering death with the long, thin sword?

Selim spoke of the recklessness Tection had demonstrated when dealing with those villainous thieves, how he'd held little concern for his own life when confronted with an evil character in another. Tales of the highwaymen who assaulted Selim and his brothers were recounted.

It was this nature of Tection's that brought concern to Selim, for there were endless encounters with evil yet to be had by him, or anyone else for that matter. He was not sure whether, in Tection's case, because he confronted such encounters rather than avoided them, he would one day suffer at their hands.

Then Malika stepped forward and told her own tale. It had been so many years ago. She spoke of Tection with great reverence, recounting the language lessons that now enabled her to translate for Julian, and the sorrow of their parting, with remarks on the hidden demons that Tection seemed to carry.

It did not take long for Selim to build a correlation between Tection and Julian; a common pattern of behaviour, a shared sense of justice, like an inescapable link to each other. Julian did not see the same at first, but soon began to realize that the similarities between them, under the experience and perception of the outside world, might be significant.

Both men had chosen to wander new lands, in search of adventure no doubt, but also for understanding of themselves and humanity in general, perhaps disillusioned by the doctrine and traditions of their immediate society, incomplete within the confines of their culture, uncertain of the offered reward for a devoted life, preferring a road to broader discovery and engagement with the unknown. Running from life while running to it; chasing shadows while simultaneously casting them anew.

Both men had killed. Both had killed for the same reason, although one with reaction and one with reflection. Each had taken

Julian and the Improbable Encounter

a life for the same reason, and would struggle with the conflict of justification and self-forgiveness. Tection's odyssey was much longer and more difficult. He was washing away many of his life's teachings, especially the seminary dogma, battling the conflict that towered inside him.

Julian had no such indoctrination. He constantly strove to remain good and kind; all that which his upbringing had not delivered to him. His killing of the attacker was much more easily digested. While the memory lingered, it faded to near dream-like substance. It occasionally rambled into his consciousness, but dwelled there for only short periods, before slinking quietly back into the depths of his being. He realized that the powerful urge that drove him to despise evil was innate, not learned; the child of cruel parents, yet growing into a champion of understanding and kindness. That was not learned; it was intrinsic to his nature.

Julian enjoyed many more days with Selim, Malika, and the tribe in general. He developed a decent command of their dialect and built some lasting memories of shared life, work, and play. But nomadic tribe life was not his. He was seeking something more, or at least something different. He was seeking many things; much more. His hunger for adventure was still bubbling over. His eventual departure was brief, filled with sorrow, impossible promises, and generous hopes for a bright and joyous future for everyone. Safa was conspicuously absent from his last moments with the tribe. She was nowhere to be seen, but she peered surreptitiously from her lofty viewpoint on a nearby dune.

"And where is young Safa?" Julian asked.

Malika responded, "She reminds me of another young girl." She touched her chest. "One who never came to say goodbye to Tection, when he also made his final departure."

Heading Home

Leaving Ravi and Saachi and the two boys behind was a more difficult task than the mere physical departure. Tection found himself often daydreaming about small discussions or short moments of experience he had shared with the family, especially Sharif, the young rascal who had apparently stolen his heart. His feelings of separation were overpowering at times, even bringing tears to his eyes spontaneously, as if some particular memory was more profound than another. Yet, he recognized that the tears were not drawn by the memories, but rather by the recognition that he longed for such family attachments in his own life.

Tection travelled back towards the west. He was not retracing his steps, but was cognizant of the general direction he was heading. It was one of the few times since the beginning of his journey that he was consciously driving his direction, rather than letting the winds of fate blow him along.

Tection had many adventures over the next few years, always heading towards his home but never feeling pressure to move faster than circumstance warranted. He stopped in many places and met many people. He built new friendships, embraced new lovers, and played with new children. With each encounter, with each person or situation he met, he found himself analyzing the possibility that it might hold a suitable family environment. Was this woman or that a potential mate and mother? Was this town or territory suitable for a child's upbringing? Could he envision living here for the remainder of his life? He never found three positives, as a matter of fact, he never even found two. It was discouraging. Tection's mission seemed to be morphing, from self-imposed exile, to dangerous adventurer, to what now seemed to be a hunt for happiness; always a most elusive target.

Enroute from where he was to where he was going, Tection had to change trains. He found himself sitting quietly in a rather dusty station, his only company an elderly man with a conductor's uniform on, sweeping the dust from the station platform. Tection concluded the man was probably tasked with multiple jobs; sweeper, station master, ticket agent, and repair man. The dust being whisked about filled the air, and Tection was soon thirsty and stepped inside where there was a small refreshment counter. He looked for a sales person but saw none. There was an assortment of drinks available and he contemplated helping himself to one, and leaving some currency in its place. As his decision to do so finally reached affirmative, the elderly man walked into the station. He moved to the counter and lifted the access trestle, stepping behind and speaking to Tection.

"Good day, sir. Can I assist you with something?"

Tection smiled. Of course he was the server as well. "Just a cold beer would be perfect," he said. As the man turned to get the beer, Tection added a comment about the dust. "I must say, all that dust sure does build up a thirst."

"Yup, sure does."

"Seems like an endless job."

"What's that?"

Heading Home

"Sweeping all the dust off the platform." Tection turned towards the door and swung his arm in an arc across the room. "It just seems to return with the breeze. I can imagine it is even more driven by the train traffic."

"It's a funny thing, that dust," the man responded.

"How's that?"

"Well, it is a constant nuisance, but it also provides a good living for me."

"What, sweeping it up every day?"

"It is much more than that. Yes, sweeping it up does take a significant amount of my time. I also handle all the other services around here. But without the dust removal component to my job description, I would probably be only a part-time worker."

"I hadn't thought of that," Tection responded.

"I also have this concession stand," the man said, rapping his knuckles on the counter top in front of Tection, "and you probably would not have had a craving for a beer if there was no dust to influence you. How about another?" he said with a wink.

"Sure, let me have one more. That dust is really making me thirsty."

Both men chuckled. "Besides all that," the man continued, "the passengers, though annoyed by the dusty condition of the station, feel satisfied that there is an effort being made to rectify the problem, even though that will never be the case. It's all about perception."

"I'm glad you have it figured out," Tection said, wondering where all those passengers were. "I had not given it such an in-depth analysis."

"That's not surprising, but one day, you might find it rewarding to analyze something as mundane as dust."

The elderly man began removing drinks from the shelves and opening a few. Tection was curious about that, hoping he wasn't expecting Tection to consume any of them. At that moment, a growing hum could be heard outside. It gradually increased in volume until the distinct sound of human voices became clear, and finally, a wall of young people, all dressed in similar blue and gold school uniforms, crashed through the doorway, surrounding Tection and the service counter. Drink orders were barked, the man was a blur as he accommodated, and in a short flash of time, about fifteen teenagers sat gulping down their favourite sodas. Tection was just watching it play out, concluding that it was as much a ritual, as it was a tradition.

"Yup, tough to imagine this place without the dust," the man concluded.

The train ride forward was pleasant. Tection watched the young folk bantering, teasing, and laughing. He understood from the remarks that they were all heading home for the weekend, obviously from a boarding school somewhere out near the old man's train station. Memories of his own childhood surfaced, clear and concise, but they were not of happy times travelling back and forth from a private school. His were of days of hardship and endurance, under the watchful eye and heavy hand of the orphanage Brothers. Although his thoughts of eventual escape and subsequent blossoming in the real world brought a smile to his face, they inevitably returned to the evil Brother Winter, and the regular physical abuse he suffered at the man's hands. That always sobered Tection's enthusiasm for life.

Upon arrival in the city, Tection scoured the station bulletin boards in hopes of finding suitable lodging. It was his way of finding a decent bed and breakfast, where the costs were reasonable and the accommodations unhurried. He found one small note, written in poor script, but promising a warm bed and full breakfast, near the city centre; perfect.

His knock on the door was met by an elderly lady, at first appearing nervous and timid in her response. Tection assured her he was safe, quiet, and more than a little helpful with household heavy work. The last point caught her attention. She offered a reduction in

Heading Home

the rent if he would commit to some assistance, but Tection refused that, insisting he would pay the asking price for the room, and provide whatever assistance she needed.

"Nonsense, young man. Work accepted without pay creates an obligation, whether spoken or not."

"Fair enough, madame, then let's make a somewhat different deal." She tilted her head slightly, obviously waiting for his pitch. "My rent includes accommodations and breakfast, is that correct?" She nodded, with a little humph to accent it. "OK, then I will assist with heavier work, such as garbage removal, small repairs, yard work and shopping, in exchange for," he hesitated, her eyes widened, waiting for the punch line, hoping it wasn't unreasonable; "supper as well."

She smiled and looked at him. She looked him up and down. "I think you eat a lot."

"Only what is served to me...unless of course, I bring home a large bird or roast that provides for a second helping."

She laughed. She swung the door open and greeted him. "I am Mrs. Kankar, but you can call me Kandy, with a K. Everybody does."

"Perfect, Kandy. I am Tection, and that is what everyone calls me."

"Tection, that is an unusual name. Where are you from, Tection?"

"From a place where our names do not reflect the land we live in." They both laughed.

Life with Kandy was comfortable, very comfortable. She was a fabulous cook, and although many dishes she prepared were new to his pallet, they were very tasty. Shfta, Zatila, anything with warm nan, lamb, always a flavourful meal, always more than enough. Tection, in turn, handled any heavy chore. The yard of her small cottage was now immaculate, even with newly painted edges and trim. Kandy was constantly fawning over Tection, like some long-lost son she never had. It was symbiotic and pleasant.

Tection found an occasional lover among the tourists and travellers, but no one that he formed a close attachment to. Everyone had an agenda, a place to be, something to see. And none of them ever mentioned children. He reflected that he was as much a diversion for them, as they were for him.

Near Kandy's house was a small playground, one of the few inner-city green spaces. Tection discovered it one day while strolling in the afternoon warmth. During mid-afternoon, many youngsters filled the park, playing games, dodging each other, and generally being children. Tection enjoyed watching them, often choosing one particular child and imagining that he or she was his own. It was a silly preoccupation he thought, but a relaxing way to spend a half hour. One day, while he was leaning on one of the trees that surrounded the park, a young lady, a young mother, walked up to him.

"Good day," she said.

"Hello, and good day to you too."

"I notice you are often here looking at the children."

"Yes, I must say, it is most amusing to see them so happy and energetic."

"Are you from around here?"

"Yes, actually, I am rooming with Mrs. Kankar, not far from here."

"Oh yes, the elderly lady with that run-down shack."

Tection was more than a little surprised at the turn in her tone. He stood upright. "Hardly a run-down shack, my dear. I guess you haven't been around there lately."

"I have not, but I do see you here most every day, looking at our children. We wonder why that is."

"I do not have a special reason. I suppose it is merely a remembrance back to youth and its folly." Tection did not like the tone she was carrying.

"Well, we are not comfortable with your presence. We don't feel safe for our children with a strange man staring at them. She

Heading Home

pointed across the park to a small picnic area where several mothers were cloistered, all looking across at them.

Tection was again shocked. He started to respond, but held off. She stood, now with her hands on her hips, displaying some sort of confidence as the bulldog of the group. Tection's shock turned to anger, and then quickly to some kind of inherent understanding. Mothers with their children in the park, playing safely away from the treacherous and deceptive eyes of the world, only to have this unknown man apparently ogling them, as if some greater plan lay afoot.

He lowered himself into a crouch, peering up at the bulldog. "I believe I can understand your concerns. I will avoid being here in the future if it is upsetting to you ladies. Truth be told, I am very much anticipating having my own children, and these few moments watching yours, allows me to reinforced that plan within myself."

She did not soften her stance. Tection figured they must have been discussing him for some time, always with a little concern, before this particular lady gained the courage to confront him. The last thing he wanted to do was bring any apprehension into their happy afternoons. He rose up and smiled, tipped an imaginary hat, and slowly strode away from the park. He felt awkward and out of place. He didn't look back, there was no point.

Soon after the incident in the park, Tection decided it was time to return to his roots, to go to where he was comfortable and hopeful of finding his future bride, who should be, would be, the love of his life. He realized he had stayed too long, much too long. Time to stop scrutinizing things, time to stop trying to fit in somewhere else, and analyzing everyone as to whether they would be a suitable mate. How ridiculous. That was not going to be a successful plan. He was decided; back to his beginnings.

A short time after coming to the recognition that his future lay back in his home area, Tection also realized his internal battle was over. There was no specific moment of clarity, no epiphany, just a recognition that it was gone. It was as if the world was a little lighter, the air he breathed was a little sweeter, food tasted better, laughter came easier and his stride was a little longer.

When he had struck Winter, he'd killed an evil man performing an evil act. Like the mother in the park, who would surely have tried to kill him if he were bringing harm to her child, Tection realized that this was who he was. He did not have to live up to a standard or a definition he had been indoctrinated with. He was more than capable of absorbing that which he had studied and learned, extracting from it whatever he felt an affinity with, but not rendering himself afflicted and obligated by that which did not reflect his own beliefs. His self-castigation was a reflection of a false and projected moral code, one that had been beaten into him at the orphanage and reinforced as he grew to manhood. Reality was, he felt that Winter deserved to die, even though that had not been Tection's intention when he struck him. Recognizing that he had acted in complete accordance and harmony with his own moral compass, freed Tection from the burden of guilt he had been lugging around throughout his journey. Having off-loaded that heavy baggage, he was now fully committed to living in the manner he felt affinity with, and, with that self-actualization recognized was now also able to commit himself to finding a love and a family of his own.

It was a great revelation for him, the only negative aspect being that he admonished himself fervently for not recognizing this fact much earlier. He felt he had wasted significant time in trying to live up to a particular standard, set up by some clerics a thousand years earlier, in the bowels of a world far less understood. He was his own man with his own conscience and morality. Time to see where that would bring him.

Tection finally understood that he belonged back where he came from. He needed to complete his internal battle where it began. His journey, though frequently exciting, intriguing, and certainly valuable, had not delivered resolution. It was, as he had often

Heading Home

postulated, impossible to run from the dilemma while actually carrying it with you!

—

Tection stood in the heat of the desert. Waves of hot air rose from the sand, blurring his sightlines. In the distance he saw what looked like a snake, but it quickly refocused into a caravan of sorts, with riders leading the way, and shepherds driving the flock behind. As they neared, Tection felt a cold chill. It was completely out of character with the desert afternoon, but it was clearly evident. The first rider arrived and said nothing, merely nodding a recognition that Tection even existed. The second rider removed a small canteen and tossed it to Tection. Tection managed a quick attempt to drink, but the canteen was empty. That was unusual, but he tossed it back to the rider, uncertain if he was aware that it was empty. The rider just continued without losing stride. The third rider lifted a spear from his saddle and plunged it into the ground in front of Tection. He also rode on a short way, joining the other two horsemen who were idle, waiting for the caravan to catch up. Tection looked at the spear. It slowly glassed over, turning to a crystal, then a dark metal hue, and finally a bold silver colour. Tection reached out and lifted it. It was light, almost weightless. He held it like a staff, in a non-threatening manner, as the shepherds and animals moved past him, one by one. Some looked at him, some ignored him, and others looked away. The last shepherd looked Tection in the eyes, and then he turned and pointed backwards to the desert from whence they came. Tection followed his finger, but could see nothing but sand. The shepherd then pointed to his ear. Tection listened carefully. The shepherd then pointed to his own heart, and Tection shrugged his shoulders to indicate he was not following the man's meaning. The man just smiled, then laughed, and scurried after a stray lamb, before clustering with the rest of the caravan a short distance away. Tection stood quietly, the silver spear still in his hand. After a few moments he heard a loud noise, almost like a thunder clap, and jerked his head back towards the desert. A single rider was quickly approaching, his horse pounding the desert sand, creating a cloud of dust-mist behind him. As the rider neared, Tection could see the anger in his eyes. His face was hidden by a shemagh, a woven head scarf to protect against the sun and sand, but a madness seemed to consume him. As he neared Tection and the caravan, he produced a bow and arrow, taking careful aim at the last shepherd, and releasing a deadly strike. The shepherd fell to the ground. The rider strung another arrow and took aim at another shepherd. Tection reacted quickly. He raised the spear and hurled it towards the crazed rider. It struck him squarely in the chest, between the breasts. The force of his throw lifted the attacker up and off his horse backwards onto the sand, the spear standing straight up from his torso. Tection looked at the shepherds. They looked as bewildered as him. He walked over to the assailant. Tection reached down to remove his scarf, and see the face of the now deceased attacker. He stumbled backwards at the sight. He fell back onto his behind, stunned. The shepherds all looked at him. They lifted their deceased friend collectively, looked back at their animals, and continued on their way, without a single word or any facial expression. It was as if Tection didn't exist. The rider who had tossed Tection the empty canteen returned on his horse, and stood over Tection for a moment. He smiled and threw the canteen down at him once again. He waited. Tection opened the canteen and raised it to his lips. A cool flow of fresh water danced over his tongue and quenched his dry throat. He returned the cap and motioned to return it to the rider. The man held out his hand to refuse its return and kicked his horse into a gallop, splashing sand as he moved away from Tection and towards his caravan. Tection could hear him laughing loudly as he continued towards the horizon. Tection rose up slowly and returned, with some trepidation, to the dead attacker. He moved over him with his eyes closed, hoping to open them and find a different face below him. He looked at the dead man. The face was Tection's. The attacker was Tection, or at least a complete twin of him. Tection removed the silver spear. He held it up towards the sun, examining the outline and the detail. As he watched, the spear began to *change. It shrank and curved slightly. His hand became attached to the grip of a sword. A long, narrow, slightly curved sword.*

Tection woke up to the smell of fresh bread and coffee. It was so pleasant he didn't want to open his eyes and detract from the aroma with a visual perspective. Finally, he could wait no longer, and he sat up in bed. There was a knock at his door.

"Hello," he said.

The door pushed open and Mrs. Kankar entered with a small tray of the anticipated bread and coffee. It was unusual for her to bring food to his room; he usually had to be downstairs, and be on time, if he wanted breakfast.

"It is very nice of you to bring me such a lovely-smelling breakfast this morning, Kandy."

"I had no choice, Tection, I was so instructed."

"Instructed?"

"Yes, a young lady came by earlier with her young son and delivered these items for you. She asked me to bring them to your room and mention that they were some kind of apology, and that she hopes you have success in finding your own family someday. Whatever that all means."

Tection knew exactly who it was. He smiled. Life was good. People were good. He was good! Time to go home.

The Journey Full Circle

Tection set out in the early morning mist. A cool breeze swept the moisture into his nostrils and the brisk temperature propelled his stride. A train, a boat ride, and a couple of lengthy hikes would bring him back to the place from which his journey had originated. Tection was immensely relieved and relaxed with this fact. Yet, he was full of anticipation, mixed with a little trepidation, at both completing his journey and reconnecting with his past life.

He felt he had come to terms with the events that had initiated his journey; the killing of Winter and the accompanying realization that he was indeed capable of such a violent act. He had resolved that internally. It may have been against the strict principles of the Bible he had studied so diligently, but it was not contrary to the beliefs he had unleashed in his own soul. It was not contrary to the principles he wished to live by, and he knew that another encounter with another man of such evil, would have only the same results; but without the accompanying guilt and self-blame.

It had taken him some time to realize, to recognize, that what he did, felt, perceived, and postulated as an individual, were reflections of who he was. His foundation and core values were built over time. They were not learned through readings, though readings were part of their construction; they were not mirrored from others, though others affected their development; they were not sculpted by circumstance, though circumstance influenced their formation. Tection was, as all people were, a unique agglomeration of reflection and experience that stretched above, below, and within. He finally realized that he was not responsible for the morals and virtues of others, any more than others were for his. Yes, there were certain universal codes of behaviour and attitude that society expected its members to adhere to, though these often fluctuated and oscillated from place to place, from land to land. Tection had established the base of his beliefs. He was comfortable with who he was and could look in the mirror without regret.

It had taken him a long time to reach that point. Much of his hardship had risen from his attachment to the responsibility of emulating his religious learnings. He was glad, now, that they were instrumental in forging his foundation, but he was equally relieved that they were not his master. These teachings were after all, a pasteurized set of expectations, clustered through a long period of time and hardened through many sets of hands and minds. They were a safety net of sorts, able to assist and support when one fell, but they were not a stable ground to stride through life on. The solid foundation Tection now travelled with, was built through his education, experience, expectations, and his internal human paradigm. What a relief it was to be free of self-imposed guilt, self-doubt, and insecurities.

Tection arrived in the small town he had left behind, but it was now much larger and busier than he remembered. Bustling traffic was constant and he was unable to take it all in. His head shifted from side to side, scanning faces for a familiar one, all the while hoping he would not see one. He wasn't sure what reaction others might have, or he himself would have, when coming face to face with someone who knew his past; and his reason for travelling.

As he moved forward, he felt an unusual shiver. It was as if someone of importance were watching him. He turned and spun his head around, only to see a young man staring at him. He thought the man might shift his gaze, but he continued to look straight into Tection's eyes. Tection perceived that as a sign of sincerity, perhaps genuine curiosity, and he decided he would have to meet this young person.

After a few days at the local inn, before he made any contact or research into his past life, Tection decided to wander down the road towards a local café. As he stepped from the inn, he spotted one of the brothers from the seminary he had attended. He was not ready to meet the man, or to have it known that he was back in the area. He ran quickly around the building, hurrying through a long, roundabout route to the café. Some children were lighting a fire on the side of the road, and Tection shooed them off as he stopped to catch his breath. A few moments later, the same young man he had seen a few days earlier suddenly appeared. They nearly collided. Tection slid his hand into his pocket and tried to look nonchalant, not wanting the man to think he was seeking him out.

"Sorry for my haste," the young man said. "I should have been looking a little farther on than I was."

"No need," Tection replied. After a moment of awkward silence, just as the man was about to speak, Tection did so first. "There's a long distance between where I've been and where I'm going." Tection waited, no reply. He continued, "My problem is ensuring that I am not actually returning to where I've already been."

Still no response.

Perhaps the man was deaf, or simple minded, or perhaps he was weary of strangers. In any case, Tection felt certain he wanted to speak with him. The man seemed to be forming a response each time Tection spoke. *Perhaps I should allow him more time to formulate a reply.* Tection thought about it for a moment, then moved past the young man, around the corner, and into the café. He had a feeling the man would follow him, and he sat in the last table with his back to the door. Sure enough, in short order, the young man entered the café. He hesitated and Tection could tell he was giving instructions to the staff. It was clear that this young man was the owner, or at least manager of the establishment. After a few moments, he swung into the seat across from Tection.

"Are you thinking about the last time you took a trip?" Tection asked.

"Not really."

"Are you thinking about what trip I'm taking?"

The man shook his head. "Not necessarily."

"Then what's on your mind?"

"Well, actually, I've been trying to figure out why the dust always settles on my porch in such a great quantity compared to other surfaces along the street?"

It was a completely unexpected remark and Tection took a moment to digest it. His first thought was back to the station master who constantly swept away the dust, but also ran the station and the refreshment counter. 'One day, you might find it rewarding to analyze something as mundane as dust,' he remembered him saying. Tection did not turn around to look at the café. He had recalled every inch of it as he walked in.

"That's almost easy. Your porch attracts a lot of customers, and their movement around the café, walking and sliding in and out of chairs, keeps the chairs dusted, displacing the content and pushing it towards the porch, making the rest of the area look dustier. You also obviously clean quite frequently, which has the same effect as much of the dust is merely displaced by the dry dusters being used. On top of that, the larger traffic itself stirs up more dust, much of

The Journey Full Circle

which comes off the clothing of the weary travelers or carefree frolickers who frequent your establishment, along with their dancing partners, who kick up even more dust. Beyond all that, you are particularly sensitive to the dusty conditions and notice it more when it is attached to your private space; when it appears to tarnish that which you hold dear. And finally, your terrace is located across from the apex of two intersections, so the natural funneling of breezes blows street dust directly towards you."

Tection's companion scanned the room, obviously churning through a visual verification of his comments, though he must have already known Tection's articulation was correct.

"I suppose my style and location will inevitably attract dust then," the man said, with a certain sense of melancholy.

Tection's intention had not been to imply that the dust was a negative component to the café. He held up his hands to prevent the man from continuing in a negative stream.

"Your comment is true, but you have lost the real purpose of the dust. You feel it is there to hinder your life and darken your strength, but the reality is far from that. It is actually a catalyst for your success and enjoyment during the short and confusing time you have on earth."

The man looked at him with more than a little confusion, but did not comment.

"Don't forget that the dust rides in on the breeze. It is this same wind that keeps a nice breeze blowing across your guest's heated brows, and makes your terrace desirable for relaxation and conversation. The dust also keeps them thirsty and prone to greater consumption of your various brews."

The man looked on as if he wanted to say something relevant, but after a moment or two, he simply said, "Can I offer you some lunch?"

Tection relaxed back in his seat. "Sure."

After a short pause to gulp down their nourishment and find a more comfortable spot on the veranda to sip their iced tea, Tection once again spoke. "I answered your question with as much honesty as I could muster. It may not have been what you expected, but it was genuine."

"No doubt," the man replied, "And it was indeed a little bit off the edge."

"Is it reasonable then for me to ask a simple question of you as well?"

The man looked at Tection and spread his hands slightly, while raising his brow and curling his lip, in as certain a sign of *sure* as his body could muster.

Tection wasted no words. "Can you tell me if I'm heading into new territory, or just recycling my previous experiences?"

The man thought for a moment, and before he spoke, he thought again. Finally, he spoke. "Let's order more tea, and then I'll share my thoughts on that question."

They sipped their iced tea and watched the town go by, pedestrians safe and secure in what would happen next and who would wander by, untouched by the insecurity of the moment and impervious to the inner workings of the conversation between the two men in the café. From afar, Tection and the man might have appeared to be discussing the upcoming weekend, or perhaps the weather and its lack of variety, or even the alternate life paths that could have been charted were it not for a little serendipity.

After consuming the iced tea down to the last rattle of ice in the bottom of the glass, the man began his approach to Tection's dilemma. "I would like to respond to your question with vigour and consequence," he began, "but it is not a simple question you have posed, so first I would like to request some elaboration, or rather information, on your irregular past. I have three simple questions that will no doubt help strengthen the sincerity and value of my response."

"All right," Tection replied. "If they will assist you to assist me, I will answer them with candor and limited speculation."

"Firstly, I would like to know from where you came," he said.

The Journey Full Circle

Tection delivered his response quickly as though he fully expected this question, or perhaps he had just answered it several times in the recent past. "I come from somewhere distant and dark. A place where hunger is a weapon and the spirit is captive to the whims of unworthy guardians."

This response was a little more esoteric than the man had expected, but he surmised that Tection was no ordinary stranger, even if he was a veteran stranger, and his few words were not meant for trivial discussion. This would not be a simple, *I come from the east, and I'm heading to the west*, response. Not likely. Still, questioning the response to his question was out of the question. He continued as if Tection's answer was perfectly clear and concise. "Question two concerns your path to this point and what major turns it has taken in the past few years," the man went on.

"That's easy," Tection replied, again without hesitation. "I have travelled from that place of darkness to a new world, one of hope and expression. Once I cancelled the greatest of demons, I climbed from the black hole I was in and turned my heart from anger to calm, and my feelings from spite to pity. I was hoping to afford the guardians forgiveness rather than pity, but I could not find it anywhere within. It is a search I continue to undertake."

"No doubt," the man said. "Forgiveness is a lofty ambition, encumbered by much of our basic instinctual behaviour."

"What is the third question?"

"I would like to know what regrets you have carried and the weight they have built into."

Tection was not quite as prepared for the third question as he was for the first two, especially since it was actually two questions with two very different answers. He began to answer a couple of times, holding back before any actual words came out. Eventually, he took a deep breath and sighed slightly, as he responded in a somewhat apologetic tone. "Not long ago, I had many regrets." He slowed his words slightly with more than a little pensiveness, "But reality is that now I have only one, and it weighs heavily on my life."

The man leaned forward slightly in his seat anticipating Tection's declaration. It did not materialize. He waited a few moments, wondering if Tection was just pausing to collect his thoughts, or if he was expressing his regret. Finally, he lost patience and held his arms out, palms up. "And it is?"

"Oh," said Tection, "I thought that would be obvious. My only real regret is leaving behind those I shared the blackness with and failing to protect my fellow foundlings, who suffered and may still be suffering in that wretched dark hole out of which I was reborn. I should have found the will and the way to free them from the burdens I escaped, but I ran too fast and too far to act upon this regret in time. I pursued a personal reprisal and retribution agenda, at the expense of a more compassionate and collective one."

"Is there no opportunity to return to this *black hole* and remedy that burden?" the man asked.

"Well, that brings me back to my question, doesn't it? Whether I am heading towards new territory or just recycling my past experiences."

The man sighed and Tection realized he was considering the remark.

"I see your point, but I'm not sure I would view it as such. Your answers have provided much food for thought and pondering." After a few more shuffles and more lip pursing, he continued. "I would appreciate the opportunity to respond to your question after having a while to consider what's been revealed. Shall we dine again in the morning? This will give me some time to measure my comments."

"Sure," Tection replied, without surprise.

The man wondered at Tection's easy agreement to a delayed reply. Perhaps Tection was appreciative of the time the man was prepared to give in weighing his situation, or perhaps he wasn't that interested in his response at all.

The Journey Full Circle

The man offered Tection lodging for the night, which Tection accepted readily, freeing him from the clutches of the local inn and the invoice that accompanied the bed. The man could tell Tection was weary, maybe even very weary, but from what was not easily determined. Was it from the travel and tired miles of road, or was it the weight of burdens he was lugging around the countryside?

The spare bedroom was nothing spectacular, but it was certainly comfortable and close to a bathroom and shower. Tection utilized both, washing away the dust of the day, or perhaps even a piece of the decay that comprised his quandary, as he soothed his stress with the hot stream of water.

He woke early and dressed before descending to the café. It was not yet open, but the kitchen was not complicated, and Tection moved over to start a pot of fresh coffee. His experience in large institutional kitchens back in the orphanage was significant, and he had little difficulty in getting things humming.

He glanced around at the surroundings, simple and efficient as they were, and then strolled out into the sitting area to watch the town rolling to life, along with the rising sun. He poured a large cup of the freshly brewed coffee before dropping into a chair next to the window. A few early risers spotted him and wondered what he was doing in the café before opening, but he was relaxed enough to appear as though he belonged there, and they took no action.

Tection barely noticed them, engulfed instead by the underappreciated beauty of a simple dawn and the world of possibilities it was bringing to all as the day grew from it. He was careful not to judge the day or those waking into it. It would be mundane for most, exciting for some, and life-altering for a few. He thought about those still with the guardians and shook his head slightly, knowing that they seldom looked forward to a new day.

Meanwhile, the man woke and realized there should not be an aroma of fresh brewed coffee in the air before he himself made it so. He threw back the covers and hustled downstairs.

The Journey: Erudite

As soon as he spotted Tection over by the window, he felt his body relax, as he realized Tection was probably the one who had ground and brewed the beans. He sauntered over to where Tection was lounging and sat down, while quietly refusing his offer of a cup of coffee. He never let his eyes stray from Tection's brow, hoping for some small revelation into his early morning demeanour before sharing his thoughts on the yet unanswered question.

Tection waited patiently, but when the man suggested breakfast first, he made it clear that the answer was expected before then.

"I will be leaving before breakfast. As a matter of fact, I would have left some while ago were I not waiting for my last piece of luggage."

"What luggage?" the man asked.

"Your answer to my question, of course. I am hoping it will lighten my load."

"Why do you feel I am even capable, never mind worthy, of answering this important question?"

"Because you were concerned about dust, which tells me you pay attention to that which others may take for granted. It tells me you are concerned about the appearance of your café and, therefore, have a fairly high level of self-esteem. Although you have referenced God, indicating a belief in his existence, I note also that you have no overt religious artefacts within your café, telling me you do not conform to either the whims of patrons or threats of clergy. That might indicate I can expect an unbiased response and, at the very least, an honest consideration."

The man appreciated the words of confident evaluation, accurate as they were, and realized the time had come to reply. He had pondered the night before and developed some opinions, though they could not really be considered conclusions.

"Your path is obviously an emerging one and far from a worldly landscape. Therein lies the dilemma. If it were merely a road to be travelled, it would be easy to return to that which weighs on your soul. I surmise then that your route is challenged by both the dangers of wind, storm, and highwaymen, as well as the burdens of soul, faith, and charity. Two distinct yet tangled roads indeed."

Tection nodded slightly, feeling even more certain that this man would be able to provide some beacon in the restless night through which he wandered.

Spurred on by the nod, the man continued. "It is difficult for anyone to depart from what is comfortable, even if that which is comfortable is also brutal. I come from a stinging past, littered with hardship, and what I felt very much was injustice. It was only upon the realization, spurred by the guidance and consultation of close friends, that I recognized I was ultimately responsible for myself, and only valuable as a guide or mentor to others when I was powerful internally, as an individual. I could not walk their miles in my own shoes, so to speak. But there is more than that even, as my good friend the philosopher often details. We must each find an internal resolution, a personal light if you like, which can bring us some sense of purpose and genuine value. We need this internal progress in order to be of value to others, especially those who have not yet pondered such inner assessments."

He paused for a moment, just to be sure Tection was not repelled by his offerings, and to ensure the comments were not being delivered in a monotone-type lecture. Realizing neither was the case, he continued. "That is, once you have come to terms with yourself, your internal nature, and not necessarily with others you hope to provide assistance to, for they would also need to be active participants in any such revelation. The journey to self-realization is empowering and affords the opportunity to bring the most value into the world in general and, more specifically, into the lives of those preferred. Become who you can be and who you want to be first, and then you can help, literally, to save the world. If you try in vain to consume the burdens and hardships of others, like some sort of self-sanctifying atonement, without first building your own character and self-worth, you will be doomed to drown in an inevitable flood of anguish."

The Journey: Erudite

"In direct response to your first query, I suggest it is not what you are doing but rather what you will do. Your confusion about your journey is piled on your doubt about being able to be effective in your self-appointed task of salvation. But the real question is whether you are capable, without first making a strengthening and illuminating journey of self-realization, to find a path towards purifying your past through the liberation and emancipation of those struggling under the same sad destiny that you were once burdened with."

The man had much more to say, both he and Tection knew that, but time was ticking, and the day was fully dawned. The café had to be opened, and the road had to be walked.

Tection smiled in appreciation of the man's offerings. He flipped a small medallion with his thumb, leaving it spinning in the air before landing in his palm.

The man spotted the outline of a crescent moon and five-pointed star. As Tection's hand closed over the medallion, the man reflected that it was unusual.

Tection smiled again and slid it into his vest pocket. He raised his cup for a final swig of cold coffee and then rose up through the strength of his hands pushing against the chair arms. He nodded, and possibly winked, at the man and then strode toward the door.

Before he went out, he turned back and stared directly into the man's eyes. "What is your name, café owner?"

"Julian," the man said.

"Mine is Tection. Hope to see you soon."

Tection wandered out onto the streets of his home town. He turned left, then right, then full circle. It was time. He was full of self-confidence. Not that which he used so deftly to navigate the highways of life, but an internal confidence; one that assured him he was at peace with himself and comfortable with who he was. Demons had been exorcised, the world, at least part of it, had been explored, and he was ready for the next great adventure; love, a mate and a family of his own.

The Human Condition

Sharif remembered the traveller he had met many years before, when he was still a young lad and full of curiosity, easily influenced by tales of a wider world. The traveller he knew as Tection regaled him with dynamic stories of adventure and excitement, all woven in an unusual but captivating way. His father, Ravi, had simply brought the visitor home with him one day. Sharif was not old enough to understand the details of the visit. It was, like most things in his young life, just something his parents presented. This visitor was a large man, taller than anyone Sharif had met. He came somewhere from the distant west and was limited in the local language, but kind and patient with the young excitement of Sharif and his brother, Ayan. Fortunately for Sharif, he had learned a bit of the language of the traveller while he was growing up. His parents had enrolled him in a school specifically intended for language study, without neglect to the standard subjects of literature and mathematics, of course. *Curious*, he reflected when older, *if they didn't want me to travel, why did they ensure I was armed with languages from distant lands?*

The Journey: Erudite

Everything about this traveller was different. His language first of all, but his clothes, his gestures and his name were all unfamiliar to Sharif. Tection; it was a name Sharif had never encountered before, and his repeated queries about its origin invariably induced Tection to offer another rambling narrative from his seemingly limitless repertoire of stories. Whether they were truth or fiction was immaterial, they ignited Sharif's inherent desire to venture out and experience the world.

One evening he heard Tection and his father in a serious discussion. Sharif was young, but wise enough to know when the conversation was not meant for him. He sat on the floor, around the corner from the two men, and listened while Tection talked of death, a man he had actually brought to death, and the circumstances surrounding that. Sharif wasn't sure he understood all of the context, but he knew killing was bad, very bad. Yet his father seemed sympathetic towards Tection, even offering a comment that was curious; *'you did what you had to do.'* Sharif wasn't sure exactly what that meant either, and more than that, he wasn't even sure exactly what the conversation was referring to. His biggest concern was; *when will they stop talking and let me tackle and wrestle with Tection*?

Before departing, in what was an emotional, perhaps even compelling episode for Sharif, Tection gave him a small, six-sided cube. It was almost like the dice he had seen many times when watching others play a board game called gyan chaupar. Instead of numbers on the cube, however, there was a different symbol on each face. One side had a crescent moon with a single star, which Sharif recognized immediately, there was an eight-spoked wheel of Dharma; a cross; an Aum symbol; a taijitu, or ying-yang circle; and a six-pointed star. Sharif didn't recognize the cube as being representative of many world religions; its value to him was all about the fact that it was a gift from this larger-than-life world traveller. There was a tiny ring screwed into a corner point of the cube. Sharif's father eventually restrung it to a smaller size, and Sharif wore it around

The Human Condition

his neck with immense pride and purpose. Sharif's mother, Saachi, was not thrilled that her son now had a piece of jewelry, especially as she had not picked it for him, but she expected he would tire of it eventually. He didn't. It was a fixture around his neck, not even removed for washing.

Sharif would often finger the cube unconsciously, twirling it around as he contemplated things of importance to him. It was a constant reminder that there was a huge world out there. Sharif became more and more infatuated with the lands Tection had spoken of. He read about them, studied them through any literature he could find, and promised himself to see them one day.

During these formative years, Sharif was fortunate to be from a well-to-do family. He lacked for nothing, really, enjoying a full, rich diet, exceptional education, and frequent excursions to the family cottage, or weekend home as they called it. It was not nearly as comfortable as their regular house, but it was full of adventure and imagination. Sharif often played out his travel fantasies by getting *lost* in the forest and meeting imaginary travellers from other lands. As he grew older, his reading skills developed rapidly. His mother tongue was easy enough for him, but he practiced his other languages diligently, often reading in them, especially if it related to information about that particular part of the world.

Sharif's parents were fluent in several languages as well, and decided that he should attend language school to strengthen his understanding of culture and inclusion. They felt too many people were reclusive in their own community, void of opportunities to experience other cultures, and often prejudiced against those who spoke differently. Sharif was a natural. By the time he graduated from secondary school he was fluent in four languages, and somewhat versant in three others. Everyone marvelled at his aptitude for vocabulary and articulation. Armed with language, imagination, and a preoccupation with travel, it was inevitable that he would venture out into the world. His parents knew this, but they were

The Journey: Erudite

not prepared for his decision as it came before finishing his university studies. They imagined him well educated, seeking employment internationally, and starting a young family in the bosom of some distant land, not venturing out like a hobo, dashing through the countryside without purpose or fixed direction.

Sharif reached up and scratched at the bruise on the back of his head. His last recollection of consciousness was when he had leaned over the fountain, hungry for a drink of cool water. A sharp pain had driven his mind to darkness, unexpected and unavoidable. Now, he could feel the partially dried blood and brought his hand into the light in front of him. A red gel covered his fingertips. He tried to stand, but slipped back into a sitting position, moving both his hands up to hold his pulsating head, somehow hoping they would ease the discomfort. They didn't.

The day had begun with a light meal of rice and lentils, all washed down pleasantly with warm mint tea. Sharif had travelled far the day before and his long, luxurious sleep in the hotel was a needed tonic. He gathered his belongings and stuffed everything into his small travel bag. *It's hard to believe everything fits in there*, he thought. He danced around several *'good mornings'* from the hotel staff, and brushed past the doorman, with appreciation for the warm, sunny weather, and the expectation of a long day covering many miles.

The countryside was fairly barren and Sharif found himself lost in thoughts and fantasies unrelated to his physical procession. His feet marched an endless chorus of crunching earth and his arms swung along in harmony, but his mind shuttled between what had been and what might yet be. Leaving his home and the life he was used to was not an easy adventure. Much discussion had been shared with his parents and brother, all of whom tried to dissuade him from departure, at least for a while longer, at least until he completed his studies. *'What is the rush?'* they said. *'Let a few more years ripen your experience before you decide on such a dramatic course.'* But Sharif was already gone. His body had not yet caught up with his plans, but he was definitely engaged with his journey, and little could amend the desire to travel he had built within himself.

He reflected on his mother's repeated warnings of the risks and perils that littered the path to adventure, referencing the nefarious characters and villainous deeds that might cross his path. But he could not be deterred by words. Like a child destined to touch the fire, despite repeated warnings from a parent about the heat and pain that would ensue, Sharif had to experience the adventure of his life beyond those words, written or spoken, describing what was out there in the world. His nature was one of curiosity, and had been from his first cognitive days of life.

Mischievous as a young child, regularly finding that which was forbidden, and playing in places and with things that were off-limits, he always had a smile of accomplishment when discovered. Fortunately for him, his parents were not only loving and understanding of his sense of adventure, but equally unable to quell their amusement at his predicaments, despite their attempts at an angry demeanour. Whether it was using a bag of flour to wash the kitchen floor as a three-year-old, a puddle of mud to clean his clothes as a four-year-old, or even a dangerous mixture of accelerants to fuel an experiment during his teenage years, Sharif was constantly challenging the parameters of restriction placed on him.

His reaction to his mother's warnings of danger and pitfalls out in the real world was considered, but Sharif countered that by imagining that there was surely a greater amount of good. He knew so many people in his life, and all were good. Some were more *good* than others, but none was a scoundrel or miscreant. He had not experienced any real evil in his short stay among the living, so, like the fire beneath his fingers, he was destined to touch that aspect of reality, and no doubt be burned by it.

As his reflections grew with the passing of time, he even had moments of consideration towards the adventure of life without the experience of evil. It didn't seem complete if only the good and comfortable were encountered. The dilemma of opposites reinforcing each other was evident. How much could love be appreciated without an understanding of anger, hate, spite or even indifference? Could joy be fully cherished without an infusion of sorrow to bring it more relevance? The heights of happiness were often built on the rubble of sadness; revenge, regret and perhaps even forgiveness, in a constant circular dance with one another.

He wondered if a particular situation could be lived in different context. Could experiences shift and shape his destiny, or were they merely moments in time, chapters in his book of life, with the final pages already written and unavoidable. He discarded that notion, unable to articulate why, but feeling there must be certain aspects of a life lived that affected the outcome of that life. He took that a step further. Outside influences and encounters would have to be lived through. The question was then, do the outside events in our lives control the development of our individuality, our internal manifestations, or do we become who we are despite, or in spite of, outside experiences? Would an experience lead to the same eventual conclusion if it were kind, indifferent, or cruel?

Sharif wanted to find it all, he wanted to participate completely in life, to know as much of the human condition as he could discover. He wanted to look into the eyes of others, to see their feelings and opinions pour out in tears and laughter. And if his naiveté, his innocence, the reflection of a sheltered and love-filled upbringing, should lead him into the clutches of evil, he was prepared to face that. At least, he thought he was prepared!

Like the day before, and the day before that, Sharif covered many miles during the hours of sunlight. The hotel he had enjoyed the night before was a luxury he afforded himself only occasionally. Usually, he found a comfortable spot somewhere along the roadway, or in the shelter of some building, if a community was nearby. And so it was, lost in thought and inattentive to his surroundings, that Sharif meandered through a small town, closing the gap between himself and his destiny. He was seeking a comfortable doorway, or perhaps a secluded spot in a marketplace area; somewhere to rest for the night. The sun had sunk below the horizon, and darkness was his only companion. The town seemed to be asleep already, even though it was not so late. He was parched after much travel and spotted a fountain with bubbling faucets, proudly guarding the town square, perfect for a refreshing break, and, apparently, for a violent robbery! The blow struck him with intention, but without warning. He lost consciousness.

When Sharif awoke, it took a moment to recall what had happened. It was dark. He looked around, confused and disoriented. It took a moment to remember; for the pain to remind him of what had transpired. So now, his travel bag was gone. His clothing, money, papers, and various personal items all lost to the hands of thieves. The pulsing pain in his head grew stronger with his realization that the impact this situation would have on his forward travels was significant. He would have to work somehow to replenish his purse. That meant he would have to stay stationary for a period, delaying his journey, and crushing some of the excitement and anticipation he had been buoyed by. He would also need a place to sleep, to wash, to live. It was definitely a rather depressing turn of events.

After some time, including a period where Sharif dozed back to darkness involuntarily, he managed to regain his feet. He felt wobbly but used the edge of the fountain to regain his upright posture. There on the ground were his identity papers, scattered around like his brain was. He suddenly felt fortunate. *How ironic,* he thought, *that all my possessions were stolen, and yet, I somehow feel fortunate to have at least my papers.*

The Journey: Erudite

He wasn't sure of the time, but the first crack of morning light was breaking the horizon. He dipped his hands into the fountain to cup some water and splash his face. The water dripped from his face with a red hue, reminding him of the blood he had lost. He looked at his shirt. The shoulder on his left side was also reddened by blood. He reached back behind his head again and felt that it was still moist, looking at his fingers to confirm his suspicions; still bleeding. He needed shelter from the elements and a place to recuperate. He moved towards a building across from the fountain but only made it a few paces before he felt the dizziness return to his head as he fell forward, once again feeling unconsciousness about to consume him.

Inexplicably, his last thoughts were back to the concept of his internal journey, and whether it would be affected diversely by divergent external experiences. How would he survive this current situation? Would he find kindness, would he find indifference, or perhaps even cruelty was holding his destiny? And would any of them, or all of them, change where that destiny lay? Sharif's questions resonated through mystical planes, which bubbled and simmered, rearranging layers of reality to provide him an answer. He was destined to experience all three alternative realities, never sure of which one was real, and which might be a dream.

Sarah

Following his time with the tribe, with Selim, Malika, and young Safa, who seemed to be back to her boisterous bouncy self, Julian travelled from town to town, enjoying some places more than others. He constantly seemed impatient, expecting events of importance, memorable events, to happen on a regular basis. They did not. Much of his travel was boring, often salvaged only by ever-sweetening memories of Talia and fantasies of time they might spend together. One day, in one particular town, near a tavern of no real significance, Julian decided to stop and pursue some daytime libations. He was thirsty, weary, and without fixed direction at the moment. The morning had reminded him of how mundane his recent days had been, and how hungry he was for some excitement, some adventure.

Julian walked slowly into the room. The air was thick with smoke and heat, as the whir of conversation bounced from wall to wall. Concrete walls; impersonal walls, it seemed. The chairs and tables brought some humanity to the room, but it was only the presence of the patrons that gave any personality to the place. *How barren it must be when empty*, he thought. But these could be deceiving walls. Surely, they held secrets from days past, and perhaps a foretelling of stories yet to come, if examined closely enough.

He wandered among the tables, searching for some relief from his boredom, seeking drink, perhaps abuse, staring at the people sitting and chatting, while trying to look like he wasn't doing so. His mind was jammed with regrets and reflection. What had happened? He had cut the head from a man in a single swoosh. He had lost the love of his life, at least for now. And she was still a child. That was so inwardly disappointing. He should have checked. And what of his glorious adventures? Everything had been exciting in the beginning; confrontation, relationships, schemes, and deliverance. How did it spiral into monotony? He cursed, he cried internally, he stumbled, the spin continued. He grabbed the bar for support, as much as to stake a spot for himself.

"Give me a drink," he asked, in a rather distant voice, monotone and non-specific.

The bartender thought he might be drunk. "I think you've had enough, young man," she offered.

Julian looked up and then down at her. She sat behind the bar. He realized his words had been a little muddled, perhaps even incoherent. "Ha," he replied in a clear and distinct voice. "Here I stand, a sober mind and a privileged purse, hoping to reduce both of those facts. My apologies for my disjointed request." He looked directly at her. "Young lady, beautiful young lady, having reached the end of what has been a decidedly unpleasant morning for me, I kindly ask that you serve me a tall glass of ale, with which I can begin the process of drowning my memories of it." He smiled as he delivered the poetic request, the gist of which was: *I had a tough day and need a drink, please accommodate me.*

His words were so clear and concise, his vision pure and unhindered, that the bartender recognized he was not overcome with drink; perhaps with other things, but not drink. She gave him his tall glass of ale, reaching over the bar from her seat, with a verbal caution to relax and appreciate the sanctity of life. He laughed. She smiled.

Julian took a long swallow of the cold beverage, licked his lips, and looked back at her.

"I've only begun." He smiled again and leaned back slightly. Perhaps a little light conversation was just the thing to alleviate some of his angst. "Have you been to places other than here?" he asked, spreading his right arm out in an arc over the room of thirsty citizens. The question was somehow tied indelibly to his past life; that of an innkeeper with a longing to travel and encounter adventure.

She paused momentarily, as if to either consider his question, or more likely, to consider her reply. She was a bartender, familiar with the cackle of banter, proposition, query, and confession, that her patrons made. This was an unusual question to begin a conversation with but not extraordinary. Perhaps this traveller might provide some intelligent dialogue, to sparkle a bit on the mundane and dreary verbal exchanges she usually had.

"This place actually represents only the most recent place I've been," she replied. "I am nomadic, or at least I am not endemic, not to this place or this bar," she concluded, chuckling at the absurdity of her last remark.

Julian scrutinized her again, gaining all he could from a partial view of her. He realized she could also see only half of him; his torso and head that peered at her from above the bar. Small talk seemed unnecessary at this point, it could be filled in later.

"I am lost," Julian paused, that was neither true, nor a projection he wished to make. "No, I'm not lost; I am hiding actually, and afraid to be found," Julian countered.

"That will be difficult, if it is yourself that you are hiding from," she countered immediately, with much more profundity that could have been expected. It was almost as if she had heard the same question so many times, she had developed a pat answer for it.

"Yes, that's an interesting possibility, and not one I have completely discarded, either. Still, when I think about my comment, it might be more accurate to say I am chasing something, not hiding from it. And what I'm chasing is frequently elusive, though not completely unrecognizable."

"OK. Not hiding, and certainly not lost, but chasing." She pressed a hum through her throat, and looked up at Julian, hesitating slightly before she concluded, "Sounds like you're just about normal!"

They both smiled; a smile of consequence, of connectivity. All in all, it was a rapid and highly irregular conversation, not to mention an unusual introduction to a bartender.

"Let me rephrase," Julian offered. "I am Julian, tired traveller, a recipient of harsh news, and a doer of harsh deeds." Talia's age and the sword's victim both sat forefront in his remark. He extended his hand to her, reaching past the far edge of the bar so she could easily accept it.

"That may explain much," the bartender replied, before responding to his outstretched hand. "But, you must realize that I am the least empathetic vessel for bad news, and still, perhaps just such a person as I, is the best possible audience with which to share your distress."

Julian looked at her with quizzical eyes. It was not an expected response. She was a young woman, though certainly not a child in any way. Her dark hair framed her round face, like a shawl drooped over her head, to protect her from an unexpected autumn wind. Her eyes were hazel, and brightened considerably by the darkness of her hair. White teeth glistened with the amber glow of the bar lighting.

"What is your name?" he asked, his demeanour softening and his heart easing from the race it was on, his hand still held out in some uncertain limbo.

Sarah

"I am Sarah," she replied, not moving her eyes from his, but lifting her hand above the bar, and offering it as a connection between them.

Julian gripped it, feeling a strange warmth course up his arm, emanating from her grip. He held her hand for longer than was casual, feeling she was more than a passing moment of conversation. He looked at her eyes. The two spheres were smiling, or perhaps laughing, but not in a mocking tone, simply warm and accepting, pleasant beyond what he had any reason to expect.

"Why are you this perceptive?" he asked, almost without considering what he was saying, before it escaped his restless tongue. Their hands slid apart.

"How so?" she said. "I have only sensed that you are a little restless and ragged, but not inebriated." She let that hang in the air for a minute, then offered a caveat, "Yet!"

Julian chuckled at her caveat, nodding, and recognizing that it was indeed prophetic.

"Has it been such an arduous day for you as well, that you are prevented from standing to greet your restless and ragged guest?" Julian commented, tongue in cheek and a slight, angled smiled reshaping his lips.

"I would greet you with a hug, an embrace, perhaps even a dance, but most unfortunately, I have no legs on which to stand," she countered.

Julian laughed, a little awkwardly. "Have they been worked to the point of fatigue" he asked, "or snatched from you permanently?"

His final comment was complete with a wink and a smile that was intended to ease their chatter, and establish him as a cute and contemporary conversationalist.

"Indeed," she replied without hesitation, or any perception of umbrage, "they were *snatched* from me some time ago." She hesitated for a moment, so Julian could travel through the process of realizing that she was not joking, not carrying the humour of his comment, but rather revealing a distinct truth. "A train now holds them captive, on their way still to somewhere in the distance. As they say; *out of sight*..." she paused with that comment, as Julian absorbed her truth, "...*out of mind*."

Julian froze noticeably, as he realized that she was more than serious. Waves of embarrassment flushed him. How could he be that callous? Of course, she couldn't stand to greet him! But how could he have known?

Sarah watched him ramble through those emotions, questions. She'd seen it play out numerous times before. She let him fumble through it for only a moment, before easing him off the embarrassment his realization was bringing to bear. "Look, Julian, transient to my bar, do not distress yourself with my burdens, and ease your regret, and certainly do not pity me. I am me. I am so wonderfully happy to be me," she stated, obviously recognizing the regret and remorse his comment had delivered him. "Just think," she offered after letting the reality of her situation sink in, "rather than being here, enjoying the company of both saints and sinners, I could be completely unsure about the future, overly concerned about the past, and perhaps even staggered a little by the present." She capped her comment off, watching him as his eyes widened, trying to help his brain absorb her comments, with a slightly cynical note. "Hell, I could even be you!"

Julian looked at her. Her face was not serious, but not comical. It was just the face of someone engaged in a friendly conversation. She was waiting for his response, verbal or physical. She was pensive. He thought, *Whatever I do now will define the future of this conversation, this evening, our relationship, perhaps my life, and maybe even the future of the world.* Of course, that was an absurd thought, but it flowed through him nonetheless. He started to laugh. He laughed loudly at the absurdity of his thought progression.

Sarah looked at him, a light tilt of her head to signify some quizzical nature, before an understanding of the absurdity of the entire

Sarah

situation drove her to a smile, a giggle, and finally a full-throttle laugh, matching Julian's reaction.

The other patrons looked over at them, shaking their heads at the perception of apparent drunken revelry, or alternatively, smiling in unison, without knowledge of the catalyst for this sudden laughter, but happy to be hearing it.

In that two-minute conversation, the day changed for both Julian and Sarah. An instant bond was hatched from some primordial tenet, some common bond of humanity that stated emphatically, that physical circumstance, personal dilemma, and interpersonal confrontation, were all merely snippets in the endless flow of life, objects of imperfection as it were, that derailed the perfect stream of destiny.

Julian had never felt such a distinct and immediate bond with anyone before. Well, perhaps there was one memory that remotely matched this experience. It was the draw of a stranger, an unusual stranger, who had wandered into his café and his life, some years before. He was a strange man, a perfect stranger with a strange past, and a strange name; Tection.

The ale did its job. Julian slid far away from the memories of the execution he had recently performed. He moved outside the sphere of memories of Talia that usually held him captive. Sarah also enjoyed a few drinks, keeping Julian company, and sparring with him, both of them witty and whimsical. In a short while, Julian realized that it was not the ale that drove the shadows from his heart, it only washed away some of the brush and baggage. It was Sarah, her infectious personality, her gallantry, and her humanity that brought him relief.

She neglected her other clients, eliciting the occasional expression of chagrin from them, which she placated with her dancing smile, and an occasional free shot of arak.

Her shift drew to an end, and while she did have to take a few minutes to complete her day's work, she joined Julian at the bar shortly after, this time on the same side as he. They agreed to move over to a table, where they could sit on equal terms, so to speak. She rolled her wheelchair effortlessly across the room, those patrons familiar with her injuries hardly paying attention. Julian tried desperately to avoid looking at her legs, both of which had been amputated just below the knee, but they were like magnets, drawing his line of sight past his internal wishes. As they engaged in their first conversation on the public side of the bar, he glanced down frequently.

Sarah still smiled. She had learned long before that her situation drew continuous glances, frequent stares, and occasional remarks. It was part of her life now.

"I have a great idea, Julian," she said.

He stopped whatever comment he was in the middle of and looked up at her. She rolled herself out from behind the table, moving beside Julian. He was unsure what she was leading to.

"I think you should take a serious look at my legs," she said, lifting them from below the knee, raising them upward and into better view. She wore pants, which were neatly folded over at the bottom and tucked back behind her legs. This action brought both an awkward expression to Julian's face, and silence to his banter. "This is how my legs are, they are part of who I am."

Julian wanted to say something, but did not know what.

Sarah held her finger to his lips, gently, kindly. "Once you have seen them, once you recognize that they are part of me, you will stop glancing at them. You will just see *Sarah*, not Sarah with a wheelchair, or Sarah with no feet, not Sarah, poor Sarah; but just *Sarah*."

Julian started to apologize, trying to somehow indicate that he did not mean to look down; but it was both unnecessary and unsolicited.

"No," Sarah said, "there are no apologies required. I do not apologize for looking into your eyes, or noticing that cute smile you throw around the room like flower petals." She laughed.

Julian could not help but smile. *Who is this lady?*

Sharif in the Clutches of Kindness

Sharif awoke in the soft arms of a foam mattress, bouncing gingerly and playfully beneath his sore limbs and pulsating head. He brought his hands up to hold his head, again expecting some unseen comfort to emanate from them; no help. He turned and raised himself slightly onto his right forearm, ignoring the throbbing sensation and glancing around his room, or more precisely, his closet. It was a very narrow space, covered on the sides by cloth drapery and dangling wares. It took him a moment to realize he was in a wagon, a moving wagon! He tried to push his body further upright but once again felt dizzy. He lay back down, his head sunken into the soft pillow and his body happy for the respite from his futile efforts to raise himself. He passed out.

When Sharif woke next, he was comfortably flat on the same mattress. He had experienced dreams and visions during his unconsciousness and was uncertain of which were reflections of his thoughts, as opposed to snippets of reality. He immediately recalled a beautiful young woman, a soft hand with a damp cloth, and a muddled conversation. If she were a dream, he wished to return to it. If she were real, he prayed for another encounter. Such a wish was soon granted.

When his eyes focused, he saw what first appeared to be a large statue, a dark behemoth of a man clutching a weapon as if attacking, yet solid in stance and stoic in face and form. Suddenly, the statue moved! Sharif was startled and immediately hoped this was not the vision of his bandit attacker. The statue turned towards the room behind Sharif and he heard the words, "He is awake."

Sharif tried to look behind his bed but his head was too sore to swivel. As his eyes rolled upward to bring his vision as close as possible, he saw her float into his line of sight. The young lady of his dreams; clearly not a dream now, or was she? Was he dead, languishing in a soft shelter under heaven's eyes? Many possibilities raced through his now-active brain, dancing between fantasy, confusion, and distraction.

"Can you bring me that water?" she whispered to the statue. She spoke in a language Sharif was fluent in.

The huge man moved off quietly and returned with a basin, gently placing it close to Sharif's head. Sharif could smell something, he wasn't sure what, but it was sticky, almost like rotting wood.

The young lady looked at him as she dipped a cloth into the scented water and wrung the material out with twisting hands. "Turn your head a bit," she asked Sharif, who obeyed her request without the slightest thought of opposing it. She applied the cloth gently to his still throbbing head, smoothing gentle strokes down the back of his skull to his neck. "You have been the victim of a pretty big blow," she offered, not necessarily expecting a response.

Sharif managed only a slight moan. The strokes of her hand were sponges to his pain and the soothing liquid brought him relief.

"It is calendula," she offered, as if reading the thoughts from his mind, "It smells poorly, but it serves to restore and rehabilitate the wound."

Sharif in the Clutches of Kindness

Sharif turned back towards her. She was beautiful, a feature definitely not diminished by the fact that she was nursing his aches. She was also young, perhaps twenty, yet seemingly in control of the situation and in command of the environment. He started to speak, hoping for at least some understanding of where he was and how he had arrived there, but she held her hand over his lips, gently pushing downward to prevent his words.

"Rest first, let the calendula and your will bring some healing. We can speak later." She smiled, radiantly, no, resplendently! Sharif fell back onto his pillows and then down into his dreams.

Amber light filtered through the room and the faint scent of roasting meat caressed Sharif's nostrils. He was immensely hungry. He still didn't know where he lay or who his benefactor was. The statue warrior was gone and a calm silence accompanied the evening light, despite the fact that he could hear voices and activity outside the room he was in. He pushed himself upwards but the thumping in his brain returned. Unfortunately, his need for a bathroom exceeded the dizziness of his head, and he forced himself into a sitting position. His body was not happy with his decision, preferring instead to just relieve itself where it lay. Sharif smiled to himself at the thought. *Wouldn't that be reward for the young lady who has cared for me?* He slid his feet onto the earthen floor and lifted his body. He wobbled and his joints cracked a bit, but he managed to stand upright. He moved towards the flap door and just as he arrived, it was swept open by the large man, or was he a guard, who had previously brought the water basin to his bedside. This time, the man held a plate of food in one hand, no doubt his own dinner, and Sharif's mouth immediately began to water as he smelled the stew.

"You should remain in bed," the man suggested, in a voice much too kind and unassuming for such an extraordinary physical specimen.

Sharif looked up at him. "Bathroom," he said, involuntarily bringing his hand in front of his groin. The man nodded, smiled a bit, and escorted him outside and around the back of the tent. The young lady saw them and started to rise from her table, but quickly realized where they were heading and sat back down, also with the wisp of a smile, Sharif noted.

With that important task accomplished, the man led Sharif over to the table where the young lady and two others, a man and a woman, were enjoying their evening meal.

"Are you hungry?" she asked, with the obvious answer not required.

"Famished," Sharif offered just the same.

She asked the woman across from her to gather a bowl of stew for him, and patted the chair next to hers, indicating he should sit there. "You might as well join us now too, Kadir," she motioned to the large man. She looked at Sharif. "How are you feeling?"

"I am lost at how I will repay your kindness," Sharif answered, looking at her with disbelief and bewilderment.

She laughed. "How about a name before we decide on your repayment terms," she replied sarcastically, holding out her hand. "I am Tanya, this is Kadir." She pointed at the large man again. Sharif shook her hand gently and then followed it as he nodded a hello of sorts. She stretched her hand across the table as the woman arrived with a bowl for Sharif. "And this is Hahn, and Rada, with your supper."

"Thank you, Rada," Sharif smiled as Tanya placed the bowl in front of him. He wanted to devour it immediately but held back. "I am Sharif, a traveller of sorts," he continued, raising his hands and his eyes in a demonstration of his current dilemma. "Surely hungry, and no doubt alive due to your kindness and generosity."

They all smiled, and Tanya gave a slight chuckle. "OK Sharif, eat now and talk later."

Following a very tasty meal, one which Sharif could eat only part of, despite his hunger cravings, he sat with Tanya on a soft, low sofa, hot chai in hand, and heard for the first time the short history

Sharif in the Clutches of Kindness

of their time together. She had plucked him from the city square, still unconscious, though occasional moans and accompanying gibberish were uttered, and tucked him into her travelling wagon. Local hooligans had still been ransacking his garments, seeking anything of value, including his boots, and only the appearance of Kadir had convinced them that Tanya was to be listened to. At first they thought Sharif was drunk, but Tanya had seen the clot of blood on the ground behind his head, and recognized that his life was quite possibly in danger if he was not cared for immediately. Her options were limited, though, as she had to travel with her small entourage to deliver certain goods under a time penalty, and could not delay her trip. That meant either leaving Sharif to the hooligan wolves and barren landscape, or treating his wounds and caring for his condition with any eventual return to the town, or any forward plan, to be discussed once, and if, he survived.

She had no way of knowing if he lived nearby, had family or friends looking for him, or was even heading in an opposite direction. She had queried some local shop keepers and merchants as they began their day, but no one could shed light on who he was. Her decision to include him with her travels was at the risk of interrupting his destination, but she surmised that her choice was his best option at the time. She was, of course, completely correct.

Sharif recounted his recent past to her and Rada, who had now joined them following her post-dinner cleanup. He did not go too far back, did not recount the conflict he faced with his family when he announced his decision to venture out on his own, and he did not express the fears and trepidation he had felt at first. *Curious*, he thought, *this ill fate befell me at precisely the time I began to feel confident that this adventure was the right decision.* He let that thought slip from his mind. He did speak about the short travelling he had done and his ultimate goal of adventure and exploration; a driven desire to see the world up close, experience the life being lived, before it vanished into the arms of commitment, and possibly old age. He had seen the looks of regret on some of the elders in his life, and he knew that destiny could smile or frown upon him at any time. He wanted to grab some experience, build some memories, and perhaps share some entanglement with other dwellers in this world, while his strength of body and mind were agreeable.

"Looks like you have definitely met some other worldly dwellers," Tanya mused sarcastically, "and they are enjoying your beddings and valuables as we speak."

Sharif smiled sheepishly at her remark, feeling a little anger towards his assailants for the first time, and quickly imagining some moment of restitution, a moment that would certainly never come. "It is true that I have met some treacherous individuals, men unworthy of sharing this world with the rest of us, but then, it also afforded me the opportunity to meet you, the beautiful Tanya and your friends. That would seem to be compensation very much in my favour."

Tanya blushed a little, but not too much, as she was not very comfortable with accolades, especially about her appearance, and not entirely sure whether his remarks held a slight tone of romantic interest, rather than just appreciation for her life-saving actions. "Sweet words," she finally replied. "You must be hallucinating slightly; better get off to bed."

Kadir and Hahn were tending to the final process of preparation for the overnight halt to their travels, and Sharif was undeniably feeling suddenly very tired. Tanya had recognized that and shuffled him off to bed with remarks about the lengthy healing process from what was probably a concussion, and continuous responses of reassurance to Sharif's continuous offers of appreciation.

Sharif remained with Tanya and her troop throughout their journey. His head gradually cleared and he was soon participating in their daily activities, at least sharing the workload in appreciation of their support and to ease the guilt he was feeling about receiving their kindness without any available reciprocation. The journey lasted several weeks and Sharif eventually took on the task of repairing tent material and other items that were in some disarray. He was not a tailor by trade, or a handyman by nature, but with a little guidance from Kadir he began to be effective. The tasks he was fulfilling were those that were often left neglected when the group was underway, as everyone had more pressing matters to attend to on a daily basis. In this way, Sharif felt, and Tanya recognized, that he was doing something useful and necessary.

The days melted together and Sharif began to understand the very close-knit nature of this group. He wasn't sure at first if Tanya and Kadir were involved together, but it became obvious that Kadir was more appropriately her big *little* brother, her protector, and an essential component of a caravan that travelled through sometimes risky territory. That suited Sharif, as he was contemplating more than conversation with Tanya when he went to his pillow at night. Her rugged beauty and strength of character were both at work arousing his passions, but he was reticent to initiate anything that could jeopardize her perception of him; that could interrupt the feelings of appreciation he held for her kindness. Hahn and Rada were definitely a couple, and despite their frequent quibbling during the long days, were always in each other's arms when night fell, sharing their tent with only their own murmurs and whispers.

Sharif grew to understand the quiet authority that Tanya possessed, the decisiveness she called upon when required, and the respect she had earned and received. He admired her for such strength and prominence in this often-perilous world of cross-country transport, a world normally carved out by much more vigorous male nomads, complete with their aggressive and pugnacious demeanours. She could, and did, hold her own. Kadir related a few stories about her past, recounting with sadness the story of her father's demise at the hands of bandits and her determination to follow in his footsteps. *To be the 'son' he always wanted, no doubt,* Sharif concluded. *Perhaps I'm a substitute character for the father she couldn't save. Don't be silly, you are about the same age,* he reminded himself. But, her history of conflict with bandits might very well have been the impetus to gather Sharif into the confines of her caravan sanctuary and ensure his recovery and safety.

Eventually they reached the end of their journey. Anxious receivers waited for them, and remarks of Tanya's expedient and reliable service were hurled effortlessly around the room. The goods she carried were quickly inventoried and then dispatched to places unknown. Sharif chuckled to himself as he realized he didn't really know what they had actually been transporting. Payments were made and a return cargo, already secured, was counted and organized accordingly. The shipper confirmed there would be another load the next time Tanya arrived, and so was the continuance of commerce assured.

Sharif was leaving. He was still on his forward journey, but his parting remarks would reflect his feeling that the loss of his funds and possessions, back in the small-town square, was a small price to pay for the great honour and pleasure he had enjoyed in meeting and travelling with the small caravan. He felt fate had been kind to him, exacting a small amount in exchange for the larger benefit of knowing such valuable characters and witnessing such social harmony and gracious kindness.

On his last evening, Tanya came to his room. She presented him with a small travel bag containing various clothing and toiletries. She claimed they were items belonging to her father and had been a burden on her to carry around, intimating that Sharif would be doing her a favour if he took them off her hands. She also handed him a small amount of money, enough to carry him through until he could find some onward work to earn the next leg of his journey. She qualified that by assuring him that the work he had performed was worth much more, and she was actually underpaying him for his services. They both knew that to be untrue, but it did allow Sharif to accept her offering without losing his dignity. He was overwhelmed by her continued benevolence.

He began to find the words to thank her, to gain an understanding of why she had been so kind to him, but she silenced him before he could say too much.

"I have grown in a world full of barbarians and scoundrels," she said, "people living off the misfortune of others. I have also spent much time enjoying the company and camaraderie of kind and generous people; those living for the reward of shared respect and support. There is a huge difference between these people, though I suspect they all began from the same place, from the same point of origin, born with the same internal foundation. It is the world and its unevenness that shapes them, the influence of outside people and forces, parents, friends, and accomplices. You are a kind person Sharif; I knew that when I found you unconscious on the ground. Your face was innocent in the midst of the tragedy that had obviously fallen upon you, and I was right. You have reinforced my faith in the goodness of people, for despite your experience with evil, you have prevailed. I have not heard you lament your situation or hurl words of anger and revenge towards your assailants. I have gained great joy and reassurance from your character, from your time with us, so it is not you who owes me, but I who am ashamed to be paying you such a small amount for the tremendous contribution of inspiration you have afforded me. Now, your responsibility is to find others who are inspirational to you and pass along your generosity to them, so they may do the same for others. It is a wave of forward kindness that might actually catch the wicked by surprise, or better still, convert them back to the kindness that was inherent in them at birth."

Sharif looked at Tanya. Who was this woman? *Who is this woman?* He reached out to hug her, to thank her for everything, but their embrace was slightly awkward, and instead of delivering a warm and comfortable hug, Sharif found his lips drawn to hers, and felt a rise in the stirrings he had kept discreetly tucked away during their travels. Tanya reciprocated his embrace and they found their way to the softness of his bed, entangled in arousal and passion, released for both of them after a significant period of dormancy. Their love making was hard and desperate, something Sharif expected from this fiercely independent woman, and somehow reflective of the finality it represented. Both of them knew they were unlikely to cross paths again, and they attacked each other with the excitement and intensity that such a single encounter, anticipated for such a long time, deserved.

Later, Sharif waved to them until they were out of sight. *How I wish my destiny was to be in a caravan*, he mused. *What a woman.* As good fortune continued to counter-balance the misfortune experienced in the town square, one of the receivers that Tanya dealt with was looking for some help. He had asked Tanya about Sharif and she had given him a glowing recommendation. Sharif was soon employed on a short contract basis, which suited both him and the receiver. He stood on the loading dock, hands on hips, while his mind reflected on the kind journey that had brought him here. *What would my journey have been if I had not landed in the clutches of kindness?*

Sarah, Sarah

Sarah's bar became a regular spot for Julian. He learned her schedule and frequently managed to be there when she finished work.

"I was just passing by; thought I might grab a quick drink."

She loved his rationalizations. Sarah did not have any close friends. Everyone was kind to her, mostly out of some misguided sense of sympathy she guessed, but each relationship was impaired somehow, with the dangling reality of her situation. She could not participate in activities as others did, she did not want to be a burden on them, and, she realized, they did not really want to be responsible for her either. Even when she was pressed to join some outing or excursion, she would inevitably find reason to avoid participation. Special events within the bar or the bar environment were much anticipated, but adventures more distant or remote were seldom embraced.

She had found great comfort in her job, where many patrons were regulars, and she could banter with them; friendly faces who chose to be in the same place she was in. She was with people who were accustomed to her situation, and no longer considered it a separate issue requiring special attention; intended or not. The simple pleasure of interacting with others on equal terms was a luxury for Sarah. One she cherished.

After work usually found her alone at home, reading, painting, and occasionally writing a verse or two. She had never shown anyone her creations. She was fortunate that the bar had some form of celebratory activity on almost every special holiday, so she was not alone at those times. She was entrenched in a life, and lifestyle, that she could navigate and accommodate as much as it accommodated her.

Julian was changing that. They were both a little unsure how that was going to play out. His visits to the bar became more frequent, his attention to her more personal, and his conversations with her more soulful. It was a predictable development, one that was ongoing in every corner of the world between young men and woman who found a certain attraction, respect, and appeal in each other.

He was often there at the end of her shift, ensuring Sarah left safely and covered the few blocks to her small apartment comfortably. She lived close enough to the bar, in a two-room suite that had once been a garage. The kitchen and living area were large enough, but the sleeping room was a little cramped. There was a decent-sized bathroom off to the right as one entered, which had been outfitted to accommodate a wheelchair. One of the bar regulars, Atufa, had remodelled the space to accommodate his ailing mother, who was bound to a wheelchair by several conditions related to her age. The space provided her direct access to the street and a certain sense of independence, despite her deteriorating condition. When she died, he had maintained the space as an empty area, never renting it out to others.

Sarah's arrival in the town had changed that. Her infectious personality had easily won over her fellow patrons at the bar. Her condition made her somehow approachable, somehow engageable, for both young and old, male and female. Women did not see her as a threat to their own attractiveness, for although she was indeed beautiful, she was incomplete physically. Men were not intimidated by her beauty, because she did not have the possibility of romantic engagements, or so they perceived. The older men were not concerned that their attention to her would be considered inappropriate, as much as it would be if she were physically complete.

Atufa warmed to her considerably and saw his vacant, converted garage as a perfect accommodation for her. She had been staying in a single room adjacent to the bar, almost a cubby-hole. When he showed the remodelled garage to her, she cried. He was so overcome with her reaction he wept a little as well, though he tried clumsily to hide the fact. She couldn't believe her good fortune in finding such a perfect spot, and he couldn't have asked for anything better to honour his late mother, than to provide a roof for someone he perceived as unfortunate. Although Sarah had a decent bank account, it would not support her forever. Atufa perceived that. Her rent would be based on her earnings. Fifteen percent of what she made would be given to him. Sarah insisted on twenty percent, but as the owner, he held the trump card. Fifteen it was, and payment would begin as soon as Sarah had some income.

"Perfect, Atufa. Now all I need is a job," she finally stated, smiling broadly and bringing some levity to the situation, hugging him desperately from her seated position, bringing a crimson hue to his cheeks, and a conclusion to the rent discussion.

Her status as a regular was quickly earned, and as much as others enjoyed her company, she also found great warmth, friendship, and acceptance; all things she longed for. When the owner of the bar offered her a job assisting the bartenders, she seized it. Concerns about her mobility and level of support were soon abandoned. She was everywhere at once. When times were quiet, she rolled out from behind the bar and massaged some cleanliness into the tops of the soiled tables. She swung chairs into place and made the setting inviting for the next patron.

It was imperceptible but eventually recognizable that changes had occurred to the bar, along with her entrenchment. As bar items were restocked, they were done so in a way that made them more easily attainable for Sarah, below the bar itself. This in turn made the frontal appearance of the bar cleaner and less cluttered. Patrons also recognized that it was difficult for Sarah to organize the tables and chairs when they departed, and they began taking responsibility for that themselves, to ensure their table was situated correctly and the chairs properly arranged, before they left. Even when their condition was dancing with some unsteadiness due to their alcohol consumption, they made an effort to organize their furniture.

When Angel left her job as bartender to marry and move away, Sarah was encouraged to seek the job as her replacement. The owner said she could fill in during the interim, but he needed to find a professional bartender. Sarah did not sulk about that. She asked the owner to give her a month to prove her worth and capabilities. Several regular customers pushed him on her behalf as well. They liked her, and rode the wave of jubilation that washed through her when he finally agreed.

Sarah studied the *Bartender's Guide*, that had sat below the bar, collecting dust for as long as she had been there. It contained the recipe for every possible cocktail, although the locals drank the same limited assortment of drinks on a regular basis, seldom varying from their norm. Nevertheless, Sarah studied and learned everything. She used part of her wages to purchase the drinks she made, practicing diligently and offering them to patrons, using them as guinea pigs to test her concoctions. Whenever she held bartending class, usually after one of her shifts, several folks gathered around, anticipating free alcohol. Sarah began splitting her self-made cocktails into two or three parts, soliciting multiple opinions on her proficiency, and at the same time, appeasing several regulars. It was a huge success, and the owner could do nothing less than confirm her employment as a full-time bartender. The hangover from that celebration lingered for a couple of days!

Julian had accompanied Sarah home many times, always polite, always the gentleman. Each time he departed, he admonished her never to leave her door unlocked. Sarah often wished that he would stay a while longer with her, help her sort through her evening, bring some relief to the monotony of her schedule, and perhaps even share in some of her creations. Alas, she was always too insecure to ask. Despite her outward personality, one that was safely housed in the bar, she was still quite unsure of herself as an independent person, uncertain of what was real and what was pity or sympathy.

On one particular evening, Julian walked with her, filled with considerable regret that he had not used the facilities before departing the bar. He knew he had a lengthy walk back to his apartment, and his discomfort was noticeable. They laughed as the discussion turned to such issues.

"Come in and use the bathroom," Sarah said as they reached her place. "I don't want to hear that you were arrested somewhere along the way for urinating on some old lady's tree."

Julian laughed, initially feigning his complete control of the situation, but the thought of relief within such a close proximity soon overcame his reluctance. He almost dashed through her living room, barely noticing that everything was at hip level or lower, and found the bathroom door, even before Sarah's explanation of its location had fully reached his ears.

Once done, and returning to the sensibilities of his normal self, Julian noticed more distinctly his surroundings. The bathroom was set up for access by a wheelchair user. Railings and heights appropriate. He looked at the shower-tub, the seat, and low hung controls. For some reason, he imagined Sarah sitting within, naked and lathered. He tried to push that thought out of his mind, but it lingered, as though it resided outside his sphere of influence.

When he returned to the living room, Sarah was trying to lift herself onto her couch. She was struggling a bit, although it was clear that she was more than capable of making the transition from her chair. Julian moved over beside her and offered to assist. She declined, he insisted.

Julian was ever so gentle with her. He lifted her from the chair. She looked at him and giggled.

"What is it?" he said.

"I won't break silly, don't worry about that."

He increased his grip and lifted her straight up. She was much lighter than he imagined. Her left arm slipped around his neck to help secure her in his grip. He moved over the sofa, and leaned forward to put her down, hoping to swing her along beside him at the same time, but that was too awkward. He stood back up again, easily manipulating her, and then went down to his knees, resting his elbows on the sofa, so he could gently lower her, this time into a lying position.

As he turned, he looked at her. Her eyes were fixed on his. They had a very unusual appearance; something sparkling, somehow radiant. He bent forward to lay her down. As he released her, his face drew extremely close to hers. He could smell her, feel her breath, her sweetness; feel the electricity dance between their cheeks.

He wasn't sure why, there was no analysis, but he leaned in to kiss her cheek. At that very moment she turned her head. His kiss landed on her lips. The kiss lingered for just a moment, but in that moment, it turned from a peck of friendly appreciation, to a shared moment of initial passion. They were both startled by their reaction and pulled away.

"I'm sorry," Julian said.

"I'm not," Sarah replied, her eyes saying much more than that. A small tear welled in the corner of one of her eyes. Her faced turned serious, her voice deeper, and her eyes darker. "Don't hurt me," she said.

Julian twisted his head quizzically. "How could I?" he asked almost rhetorically. "I would never do that." He lifted his hand to her face. "I'm not sorry I kissed you either. I was only worried you might think I was out of line."

"I have not been this close to a man in a very long time, Julian. I guess my emotions have transformed with my body." Sarah paused, looking at Julian, seeking some sort of pity in his eyes. There was none. "I have overcome much in these past six years, but my greatest battles have been emotional ones."

She slowly moved her left arm back behind her head, inviting him to remain where he was, expressing her comfort with his closeness.

Julian looked down at her from his kneeling position. He could not remember when she wasn't smiling. This was a new look, a look of passion. He was overwhelmed with a sense of desire and, at the same time, a powerful feeling of empathy. He leaned in again, and brought his lips to hers. She hesitated, before parting her own and dropping her arm once again around his neck, to pull him close and tight. He could feel the energy rumble through her body, it rushed into him from every point of contact, and he was frozen by the strength of the moment. He recalled the first time he'd held her hand, how the feeling of warmth had travelled into him. This was so much stronger.

His hand moved to her breast. She released his neck and slowly slid her hand down his arm, lifting it away from her body. He was unsure where to go next, trapped in the moment. Suddenly he had a rush of realization, an adrenalin-driven fear that he must have offended her. He was immediately concerned that his forward behaviour might have injured her fragile emotional state. How could he be so callous? He felt the guilt build inside him, and began to offer a profuse apology.

Sarah held two fingers to his lips, preventing the words from escaping his mouth. "Do not say anything. I have not kissed a man since my accident," she whispered. She smiled, that beautiful smile, before adding, "And certainly not had anyone put their hand on my breast."

They both giggled. The levity was short lived, but it was perfect inspiration.

"Don't apologize," she said. "It was wonderful. It is a feeling I had long forgotten." Sarah turned very serious, once again a tear resting in the corner of her eye. "It is difficult for me to imagine any man wanting me." Julian tried to look startled by her comment, but it was an obvious revelation. Her eyes moved away from his. "I have buried that side of me, perhaps because I felt far less than beautiful, and perhaps because I am so afraid of truly revealing myself." Sarah's eyes closed. She had no idea what to expect next.

Julian looked down at her. She appeared so vulnerable, so different from the brash, positive, and outgoing woman who safeguarded the bar every day. He could not help himself. He leaned down and returned his lips to hers. She recoiled slightly, before once again moving to meet him, and allowing the kiss to turn passionate. She slid her hand down his arm to find his hand, and then guided it back to her breast.

His breathing accelerated, her breathing accelerated, his mouth moved to her neck, then to her ear. She could hear his breath, more than that, she could feel it, or was it some strange combination of both? His lips and tongue electrified her skin wherever they touched. Soft moans escaped her throat; a foreign sound she had not heard for a long time.

Julian raised his head to look at her. She was flushed. His passion, and his own arousal were only magnified. It was much more powerful than any interference a sensible thought of what was happening could deliver. He reached underneath her and lifted her up, carrying her easily in his arms, his face close to hers, their breath shared.

As he moved towards her bedroom, their eyes were interlocked. She gently whispered again. "Do not hurt me."

Their lovemaking was powerful and passionate. Once the initial awkwardness was dispensed with, their physical contact was relentless. Their bodies crushed one another throughout the evening. Sarah was quite apprehensive. She insisted on both darkness, and the sheet covering them. She was not ready for him to see her completely. She cried gently for some time once they were finished, and assured Julian that they were tears of happiness; *and perhaps gratitude*, she thought.

Sharif in the Clutches of Indifference

Sharif woke on the hard surface of a rough wooden floor, bouncing relentlessly, delivering a cruel battering to his sore limbs and pulsating head. He brought his hands up to hold his head, again expecting some unseen comfort to emanate from them; no help. He turned and raised himself slightly onto his right forearm, ignoring the throbbing sensation and glancing around his room, or more precisely, his cell. It was a very narrow space, opened on the sides to a harsh, dry landscape, that was seemingly being tugged backwards behind it, by their forward movement. It only took him a moment to realized he was in a wagon, a moving wagon! He tried to push his body further upright but once again felt dizzy. He lay back down, his head sinking onto the crux of his right elbow, as his mind tried to focus on some explanation for his predicament, and passed out.

When Sharif woke next, he was confronted with the rather ugly and distorted face of a fellow prisoner, leaning in much more closely than seemed necessary and breathing a foul wind into his face. Sharif had experienced dreams and visions during his unconsciousness, uncertain of which were reflections of his thoughts as opposed to snippets of reality. He immediately recalled the harsh voice of a commander of some type, berating his minions for their lack of effort. He thought he'd heard a whip coursing through the air but was not certain. It was a nightmare he had no wish to return to; a perspective of reality he hoped would be lost in consciousness. He soon discovered it was not.

He pushed out at the ugly man sitting in his face and managed to elicit a suitable distance to allow him remission from the man's breath. He looked around for signs of water but saw nothing. He closed his eyes and faded again.

Sharif finally regained consciousness with the splash of warm water hitting his brow. He jerked his head upwards with the impact but regretted it immediately, as the motion brought renewed agony to his brain. They were no longer moving and he lay on a woven mat on the dirt floor. A dusty behemoth of a man stood over him. He held a vase of sorts and poured another small amount of water onto Sharif's face. Sharif reached up, clawing for the vase, which the man released to him. He brought it to his mouth and drank thirstily, consuming nearly the entire contents of the container. He returned it to the man, who had not budged during Sharif's drink, and he tried to express some appreciation with his eyes. The man took hold of the vase and departed, with no indication as to whether he recognised the "*Thank you.*"

Sharif tried to roll over but he could not. He realized his leg was restrained and he looked down to see a shackle around his left ankle with a short chain that ran to a ring near the centre of the room. He looked around, lifting his head barely above ground level. His view was limited and without perspective. There were several other men, perhaps six of them, similarly shackled and tethered to the ring. He did not see the ugly man at first, but was certain he could smell his odour emanating from the pile of humanity.

Sharif in the Clutches of Indifference

One of his captors entered the room and spoke in a language foreign to Sharif, prompting a reaction from some of the men. He then spoke in Sharif's language as well, instructing those who wished to eat to sit up. Sharif did. His head was pulsating enormously, but his stomach was in command right now. There was the ugly man, just across and slightly down from Sharif. The man looked up as Sharif spotted him and their eyes met momentarily. Sharif looked away immediately, fearful of any perceived interest.

The men were given a plate and a splash of what looked like a creamy stew. Sharif wasn't sure what it was constructed of, but anything right now would be welcome. He was dismayed when the handler and his assistant walked past him without offering a plate, but soon realized why. Once the others were served, he was unshackled and lifted unceremoniously to his feet by the two men, his swirling head making him wobbly and in need of their support.

Sharif was guided, if not practically dragged, outside the shelter, on into another tent across the small enclosure, formed by several other temporary structures. Once inside he was led to a small table and instructed, through physical persuasion, to sit down on the bench. Shortly after, a small, almost statuesque woman entered the room. Her face was covered by her headdress and the men stood up a little straighter as she approached. She dismissed them with a wave of her hand and a few words in a language Sharif did not understand. They stepped back, seemingly hesitant to depart, mumbling back at her in the same language. She barked louder at them and unsheathed a long knife from beneath her robe, stabbing it into the table in front of her, and across from Sharif. The men quickly retired outside the front door, and the lady sat down.

She sat down very gracefully, sliding the covering from her face with a gentle sweeping motion at the same time. She looked directly at Sharif, directly into his eyes. He was certain he should look away, demonstrate some tacit submission, but she held his gaze. She was a beautiful woman; olive skin with dark eyes, almost black, and high, sculpted cheek bones that drew her facial skin taut and youthful. He guessed her to be in her mid-thirties, although her appearance could easily support a younger age than that.

"Are you hungry?" she asked, now speaking his language, without any accent.

"Very."

She called out in her other language and two women entered with trays of food that had Sharif's mouth watering before they were set down.

"Help yourself," she said, waving her arm slowly across the two trays. She voiced another soft command and the women left, returning shortly with water and a fermented liquid Sharif was unfamiliar with.

He ate and drank heartily, trying his best to appear polite and sophisticated as he chomped the food, but painfully aware that his attempts to do so were hindered by his enormous thirst and hunger. She did not speak while he ate, although he looked up at her frequently and her eyes were always on him, her face expressionless. When he slowed his consumption, she called out again and one young lady entered the room with a bowl and towels, moved towards him and began to dress his head wound. He squinted and cringed as she wiped away the dried blood and the throbbing in his head quickly overtook the demands of his now-stuffed stomach. His host continued to watch the process, making the odd comment to the nurse, which always changed her actions slightly. In due time she completed her task, applied a soothing salve of some sort, and wrapped a bandage around Sharif's head. When she was done, his host waved at her and she disappeared.

"Do you need the bathroom?" she asked; her first words to him since the meal was served.

Sharif nodded. She called out again and one of the burly guards came in, lifted him to his feet and brought him outside. The sky was black, night had fallen, and the fires of the evening camp were

Sharif in the Clutches of Indifference

raging as they walked towards the toilets. A bandaged head, a full stomach, and relief were combining to make Sharif's evening more pleasant than he expected. Maybe his host recognized that he had been inappropriately captured, perhaps through mistaken identity, or some misunderstood deed. The guard returned him to the tent. His host was standing as he entered and the guard made it clear to Sharif that he should remain standing as well. He looked at the woman. She reached out and delivered a hard slap to the left side of his face. It was not only painful to his cheek and his pulsating head, but shocking as well, leaving Sharif with his hand covering the area of impact and a look of utter astonishment on his face.

"My name is Nadia. I am the owner and commander of this caravan, this sanctuary in which you now find yourself." Sharif started to form a reply but she held her hand outward, squashing his idea. "I found you near death in the middle of the town square. You had only some papers," she handed his identification to him, "but no currency, and very little blood left." She delivered the last comment with a crooked smile that confirmed he was indeed near death. "My decision to save your life was taken for two reasons. One, because the hooligans who were ransacking you are despicable individuals, unworthy even of the beating one might give a dog, let alone a traveller. Secondly, because I was short one man on my caravan staff; a lazy good for nothing leech, who drank too much and wandered off to jail with his accomplices."

"I'm sorry," Sharif offered, wanting to assure her that he was grateful for her sanctuary, but confused by the shackles and slap. He didn't have the chance to speak further yet.

"I slapped you because I wanted to see your reaction, and I wanted you to know who's running this place."

"I'm sure..."

"Quiet," she barked. "I do not want your story or your thanks or your promises. What I want from you is a hard day's work, obedience to the instructions given you, and no trouble along the way.

Our journey will be over in a few weeks, God willing, and your work will be repayment for the salvation I have provided you."

"Agreed," Sharif nodded in acquiescence, after only a moment's contemplation. He was obviously out of other options and quickly recognized that a one-word answer was appropriate for her.

She looked at him again, moving closer in towards him, her face inches from his. "Do I need to chain you at night?" she asked.

"No, there is no need," Sharif replied.

"What is your name?"

"Sharif."

"Sharif, some of the men are shackled because they are not trustworthy, but they owe me debts for various reasons and are repaying them with labour. I do not trust them to continue their work unless they are controlled. I am going to trust you because your reaction to my slap was surprise, not anger. This tells me that you are not used to aggression, and therefore probably not aggressive yourself. Don't make me regret it."

"I will do my work for you, in return for saving me," Sharif replied, again recognizing that those were the only words she wanted to hear; the only ones he had to offer.

She stayed close to him, her face still inches from his, and barked out in her other language. Two guards came in and she then stepped back, providing them instructions as they came forward. They did not grab Sharif, but directed him with hand motions and words he didn't understand, to follow them.

Sharif looked back at Nadia. "Thank you," he said, plain and simple, unexaggerated, encompassing the fact that she had saved him, dressed his wound and fed him, and the fact that she was expressing some trust by leaving him unshackled.

Sharif was brought to another tent and introduced to four other men. Fortunately for him, one of the men spoke one of Sharif's languages, a fact which made the transition from prisoner to worker much smoother. Sharif's head was still exploding. He found his way

Sharif in the Clutches of Indifference

to his mat as soon as he could, without being anti-social, falling quickly into a tumultuous sleep that danced with dreams of discomfort, misfortune, home, and surprisingly, Nadia.

His work was long and arduous each day. The expectations were high for everybody in the caravan, and Sharif soon understood what a hardship it would be to have even one person less. Somewhere along the way, he reflected that he should be angry with Nadia for effectively making him slave labour; that he should have challenged her or perhaps that he should seek avenues of escape, but each time such thoughts arose, he quelled them with reminders of both his commitment to her and her rescue of him in the city square. *Where would I be if she had left me there? Would I be alive? Do I owe her my life? Perhaps these few weeks of work are little to pay for the generosity she afforded me, whatever her reasons were.* And so, he remained in conformity with the business of the caravan, fulfilling his tasks every day and maintaining harmony with the others in her employ. He seldom saw Nadia; it was usually at night when she crossed the camp or when she walked from her tent to use the toilets. She was a handsome woman, almost noble in her stride, although her physical form was always covered from view by her pirahan, pants, and long robes.

Shortly after his head seemed to be fully recovered, Sharif was confronted during the performance of his work, by the ugly, smelly man who had shared his cell originally. The man spoke to him in Sharif's language, broken and uneducated, but clear in his point. He grabbed Sharif during a moment where their paths intersected during their labour and cupped his hand over Sharif's throat.

"You lady's boy now?" he mocked. Sharif was caught by surprise and unable to respond because of the pressure around his throat. "You break shackle for me, you bring key," he continued, shaking his leg and jiggling the metal sleeve that bound him.

Sharif looked into his eyes. They were dark and cold, almost frenzied. He brought a slight smile to his lips, which confused his assailant. At that moment of relaxation, Sharif brought his knee up into the man's crotch, causing him to release his grip and double over.

"Why would I help you and harm the woman who has been my benefactor?" he whispered in a terse voice.

He turned and moved away from the man, brushing past one of the guards, who looked on, more than a little impressed. Sharif was now forever cognizant of the range the ugly man's shackled leg provided him, remaining diligent not to encroach on its radius in the future.

Sharif was friendly enough with the other workers who were there by choice, but he could only speak to one of them and that left his social interaction limited. With time on his hands in the evenings, he started to do some canvas repair, almost as a hobby, to while away the period between supper and sleep. One of his co-workers showed him a couple of techniques, and Sharif was soon quite proficient in his sewing style. He actually enjoyed the work, appreciating his efforts to turn *damaged* into *useful*, through his own manipulation.

At some point, perhaps three weeks into the journey, Sharif was summoned to Nadia's tent. He was feeling a little nervous about the call, hoping he had not somehow offended the woman.

"Come in, Sharif," she spoke as he entered, her voice gentle and far from the Nadia he had first met.

"Thank you, Nadia," he replied, with uncertainty in his voice.

"We near the end of our journey, Sharif, and I must say you have been a man of your word, having worked hard and given me no reason to regret saving you."

"Thank you, Nadia, I recognize what you have done for me and am pleased with the opportunity to provide some repayment, even if it is minimal."

"Ah, modesty and respect. Traits seldom encountered these days." She smiled at him for the first time. Her face lit like a lantern,

Sharif in the Clutches of Indifference

her teeth in perfect harmony with her bold features. She motioned to him to sit and he did. "I have heard that you have been doing quite a bit of canvas repair during your evening down-time, and that the work is quite good." She looked at him.

Sharif decided to maintain his modesty. "It is only a little effort, something to pass the time."

She smiled. "I also heard about your confrontation with Faolan."

"Who?" Sharif asked.

"The man who asked you, rather physically, to free him from his shackle. The one you dropped with your knee, and told that you would not betray me." She looked at him again and moved closer to him.

"He was ugly and smelly, Nadia," he replied with a smile of his own.

"So, if he was pretty and smelled sweet, you would have considered his request?"

"Certainly not," he replied immediately. "If he smelled sweet, he would not be working in a caravan." He chuckled with his last remark, clearly illuminating the fact that all the men smelled bad.

Nadia laughed as well. "I have arranged a bath for you Sharif, a reward of sorts for your loyalty and extra effort." She looked into his face. Sharif raised his eyebrows with the surprise she had hoped to deliver. "And yes, you do smell rather poorly as well...what with working in a caravan, you know."

With the last remark she raised the back of her hand to her nose, intimating some protection from his odour. Sharif blushed a little. Nadia clapped her hands and two ladies came into the room. They circled Sharif's arms and led him to a small curtained area at the back of the tent, where a large tub of water lay waiting. They began to undress him and he hesitated, reassuring them that he could handle that task himself. Nadia entered.

"You don't want them to bathe you? Most men I know would relish the idea."

"I have to be honest; I mean, I've never been bathed before. I mean, perhaps when I was very young, but not since, well, since then."

Nadia smiled at his predicament and let him suffer with it a little bit longer.

"Very well," she finally remarked, "you can bathe yourself, there is a towel and robe on the chair. There is also a razor on the dressing table. Perhaps it can use some attention." Sharif reached up unconsciously to feel his scraggly beard. "Your clothes will be washed as well." Sharif nodded as she dispatched the servants. "Don't be too long," Nadia commented as she left the area and closed the curtain.

Sharif disrobed. The idea of a warm bath was wonderful. He had been weeks with nothing but a few splash-baths from the occasional wells they passed. He stepped into the water and began to lower himself, when the curtain swished opened. One of the servants entered and snatched his pile of dirty clothing, smiling sheepishly as she hugged them and departed, ostensibly for the laundry. Sharif let himself plop into the water as she entered, reclining backwards to allow his head to submerge momentarily, and relaxed in the luxury of the warm cocoon. *I think this is the most enjoyable thing I could imagine; it has been far too long.*

Mindful of Nadia's request for promptness, he washed and rinsed without much ceremony and stepped out to dry himself. He utilized the razor, feeling the tug and pull as it eliminated his facial hair. After he was done, he rinsed his face once again in the bath. He felt completely invigorated, recognizing what a comfort shaving and bathing were, and once again lamented that it had been too long between opportunities. He dressed in the robe left on the chair and re-entered the main area of the tent. No one was there.

"Come back here," he heard Nadia instruct him, from somewhere behind another curtain on the other side of the bathing area.

He walked forward and parted the curtain to enter. Nadia was there, her back to him, dressed only in her pirahan, a nightshirt of

Sharif in the Clutches of Indifference

semi-transparent fabric that fell just below her buttocks. Her form was clearly visible in the soft candlelight and Sharif was quickly in the awkward position of having to cover the front of his robe in an amateur attempt to hide his excitement.

"Come closer," she said, not asking but instructing, as was her usual tone.

Sharif walked towards her. She turned and sat in the small chair that accompanied her dressing table. Her hair was long and black, her breasts fuller than he would have thought. She looked up at Sharif, raised her hands to his robe, and gently tugged him forward as she separated the cloth.

Their lovemaking was slow and seemingly scripted. Sharif knew his place with her. He reacted to her touch, her whims, without the necessity of words, and ensured her fulfilment long before his own. The evening was magical. *This is much more enjoyable than a warm bath and shave*, he thought, *and it has also been far too long.* When their pleasure had been fulfilled, Nadia rose first, and slipped into an evening robe, her back slowly falling under cover as she raised the cloth over her shoulders.

"They will bring you your clothes in the morning," she said, without looking at him. She left the room.

Sharif was guided to his tent by a servant. He wore a type of loose pajamas he had been given, and slid into his tent under the securitizing eyes of his co-workers. They were anxious for news of his evening but he offered none. They were disappointed, but he paid that no mind, slipping onto his mat and quickly falling into a sound sleep. It was almost surreal. The evening had unfolded without expectation and he even questioned himself whether it was real; it was. When he awoke in the morning his clothes were neatly folded, clean and odour free, sitting at the side of his mat. His co-workers looked at him, wide eyes and more questions, but Sharif offered nothing.

The Journey: Erudite

Several days went by and Sharif did not see or speak to Nadia. One morning, as natural as the sunrise, the journey was over. They pulled into town and receivers hustled after their long-awaited goods. The caravan was emptied and reloaded in a single day. One of Nadia's large guards approached Sharif and told him he was free from his obligation. That was his official and solitary *"good bye."*

As the caravan pulled out of town, Sharif saw the ugly man, Faolan, trudging along beside his wagon, still shackled, and looking back at him with much bitterness in his eyes. One of Sharif's co-workers waved a small salute, as a new replacement worker shuffled along beside him.

Sharif still needed to find funds, to continue his forward travels. He approached one of the receivers that Nadia had dealt with to see if he was looking for some help. Nadia had not mentioned Sharif, but the receiver was overwhelmed with the newly arrived merchandise, and Sharif was soon employed on a short contract basis, which suited both him and the receiver. More hard work, but this time for pay. He stood on the loading dock, hands on hips, while his mind reflected on the journey of indifference that had brought him here. *What would my journey have been if I had not landed in the clutches of such indifference?*

Sarah, Sarah, Sarah

The development of a physical relationship between Sarah and Julian changed their entire interaction. All banter now had varying connotations. Their eye contact had morphed from sparkling attachments into quizzical reflections. The transition from friends to lovers was anything but subtle, and raised the eyebrows of many who populated their lives. They made no public declarations, and did not engage in any intimacy at the bar, but those who knew them became aware of the situation just the same.

For Julian, it meant little in the way he was perceived and encountered, but for Sarah it was another story. Suddenly, she was a viable and vibrant woman again. The cloud of pity that hovered so tightly above her head, was shredded. The feelings of insecurity her condition strangled her with, were blown up. She exploded from a world of self-pity and hibernation; a world she had not realized she had built for herself. It was exhilarating, like a rebirth, like that final pull, lifting her from the bog that had been consuming her, slowly suffocating her soul.

She changed noticeably. To the world around her, she was full of spirit, snappy in her conversation, and even flirtatious from time to time. It was not a negative change, not something that left patrons wishing for the *old* Sarah, but it was also not necessarily a totally endearing change. It was a new Sarah, one with both good and bad qualities, but one with much more personality and much more confidence.

Julian could see the changes. Sarah grew emboldened, almost aggressive in her desires, both physical and communal. As the Olive Oil Harvest Festival approached, she took the lead in organizing the events the bar would host. She arranged external outings and celebrations, in which she intended full participation. Many were happy to see her out and active, others were confused by her shift in personality.

As their relationship developed, Julian realized that his attraction to Sarah was driven by several things. Her physical beauty was obvious, although there were many beautiful women within hailing distance in the city. Her vulnerability, her self-empowerment, and her strength of character were key ingredients for him. Her outward lack of self-pity had always been an expression of her true character, though he was well aware that her internal world held significant turmoil. Sometimes that reminded him of himself, though certainly on a less dramatic scale.

The hindrances of her condition and the occasional public scrutiny of their shared emotion was not of concern to him. He was certain that Sarah's accident had released a part of her character that might otherwise have remained dormant throughout her life. He speculated often on that fact and wondered if such was true for most people, people who had not faced such trauma in their lives. *Do such extraordinary events unleash internal strengths that would otherwise remain dormant? How can one call upon these strengths without enduring such trauma? Can we learn to actually harness our significant internal powers?* These thoughts often wandered into his mind.

One thing Julian did realize; he did not love Sarah, not in the way he should if he intended to remain with her. He enjoyed her company, anticipated seeing her, he was constantly aroused by even a glimpse of her curves, but he was not in love with her. He did not dream of a lifetime with her. He did not fantasize of children and a happy backyard. Sarah was his lover. Her physical limitations were a blur to him, almost an afterthought. She was a woman, erotic in her way, and stimulating to his mind and body; but he was not *in* love. He knew that. His heart still belonged to Talia.

Sarah was not *in* love with Julian. He was her saviour of sorts. A man, a beautiful man, who had yanked her from the dark depths her soul had slowly been sinking into. Before they met, as her outward vibrancy grew, to shield her from the cruelty of the surrounding world, her inward depression had mounted accordingly. She wasn't sure which one fed the other. Julian had broken that vicious spiral. He had brought her to laughter, real laughter. He had spilled happiness into her life with an abundance, which she could not measure. And he had rekindled her passions, renewed her self-worth as a woman, and shattered her doubt about her attractiveness. She knew his passion for her was not driven by pity. She could tell by the voracity of his love making, and the frequency of his arousal. But she was not *in* love with him. She did not long for him when he left her in the early morning hours. She didn't feel the need to share every part of her world with him. He was her lover, her redeemer, and her appreciation of him was immense. She wondered, sometimes, if that was what held them together; her own sense of obligation to him for all that he had returned to her, all he had given her.

Julian was overcome with guilt and trepidation about how to express his true feelings to Sarah. He was so afraid of hurting her, crushing her, sending her back into the world of insecurity she had so recently left behind. But he had much to fulfil in his own life. He still longed to travel, to see other lands and peoples, to find something he was searching for, and to eventually return to find Talia. He didn't know what it was that he searched for between then, but he knew he had not found it.

Sarah was often consumed by her feelings towards Julian. She wanted to tell him that she was free from so many burdens now, that she would always be grateful for his strength and courage, that she would forever consider him her gallant champion, but she could not commit to a long-term relationship with him. Her confidence and self-worth regained, she was anxious to return to the world, away from the bar, from the same old faces, and from Julian himself. *How can I express that to him? Surely, he will be heartbroken, angry, perhaps even devastated,* she anguished.

One particular afternoon, on a day off for Sarah, the sun near its meridian and the breeze barely tickling the hedges along the street, Atufa sauntered down the road. Sarah was surprised to see him. It was normal working hours and Atufa was a diligent worker. He was a manager in a factory, with many workers under his jurisdiction. Weekdays away from his job were a rarity.

"Is everything OK?" she asked as he neared.

"Good afternoon, young lady," he replied, avoiding her question completely. He smiled his usual smile, and strode towards his own separate entrance to the house.

"Atufa," she called again. "No work today? I'm not used to seeing you strolling the streets in the mid-afternoon."

Atufa started opening the door and then stopped. He turned and walked across the yard towards Sarah, avoiding the stone walk, and using the shorter route across the grass. This was also most unusual for him. He worked hard to maintain the lawn, and respected it more than most would.

Sarah looked at him, sensing something was amiss. "Is everything OK?" she asked again, keeping her voice level and light.

"Yes, yes," he replied. "I'm just facing a bit of a dilemma."

"What has you concerned, Atty?" she asked, using a shortened version of his name, one that was usual for him at the bar.

"Well, there's this lady I've been seeing." Sarah perked up. She wasn't aware of anyone in his life. "Ha," he laughed a bit at her reaction, "yes, I have a few little secrets my dear."

"I'm happy for you, Atty, I always felt some lady would be lucky to catch on to a gentleman like you."

Atufa looked at her with his most sarcastic glance. She smiled.

"Well, this particular *lucky lady* is not turning out to be who I thought she was," he continued.

"Oh?" said Sarah, her voice framing a question, inviting additional information.

"Yes, we've been seeing each other for a while, and she is not really the person I thought when we first met." Atufa paused, waiting perhaps for Sarah to ask a specific question.

She just tilted her head a bit, waiting for him to continue as he wished.

"She seemed like such a fun person when we first met. We could go places, dinner, you know, do things together, and there was never too much ceremony about it. I mean, she never asked me for anything, or pried into my life."

"Has that changed now?" Sarah asked, recognizing his point was made, and anxious to find out what the issue was.

"Today she asked me to visit her, to take a day off work and be with her." Sarah waved her arm in a circular motion, asking him to move forward with the story. "She told me I should be spending less time at the bar." Atufa raised his arms in a sort of surrender. "I mean, how does she even say that to me? And why a day off work? I thought there was some quandary or difficulty she needed assistance with, but it was just an opportunity for her to demonstrate some kind of control over our situation."

Sarah waited to be sure he was finished with that particular thought. "And, what did you reply?'" she asked.

"I told her she was out of line, and that I did not require her permission to do anything."

Sarah looked at him. He was proud to recount the conversation, proud that he had stood his ground.

Sarah was proud of him for telling her so. "Good for you," she said.

"Not really," Atufa declared. "Now I'm back to the bachelor life; just me, work and the bar. I wonder if I should have adjusted a little bit to appease her?"

"Nonsense, Atty, you did the right thing. There'll be another lady along soon enough. One who will be happy with you just the way you are. It's important that you be honest and up front with someone you're seeing, someone you care about." As Sarah said the words, she thought about Julian, and the fact that she was being a little deceitful with him about her true feelings.

Atufa mumbled something about agreeing with her, although he didn't seem too happy about the situation. "I'm getting changed and heading to the bar early," he said, but Sarah's mind was elsewhere.

She decided at that moment that she had to be honest with Julian and tell him how she felt. They had plans to meet for dinner; a perfect opportunity, out in public, no drama, no opportunity for excessive guilt.

As usual, Sarah was fiercely independent and insisted on meeting Julian at the restaurant. She would invariably go early so that she could demonstrate her self-sufficiency in maneuvering the pathways of the city. Julian recognized that and didn't try to dissuade her.

After a light meal of hummus and fattoush, they relaxed with some sahlab, sipping slowly, as their conversation settled into a casual stream. Sarah looked over at Julian. He was half in the conversation, and half in thought.

"I love you," she said, matter-of-factly, and without much emotional connotation.

Julian's eyes perked up. He adjusted his seat and looked back at her. "I love you too, Sarah."

"But..." Sarah stumbled. She wasn't sure what to say next, but with the *word* already dropped onto the table, there was no turning back.

Julian leaned forward, his body towards the table, his head turned up towards her. He raised his eyebrows and repeated the word. "But..."

Sarah had to say it, she had to be true to herself, to Julian, and to their future. "I'm not *in* love with you." Her eyes strayed from his. She bowed her head, almost praying that he was not going to be overly emotional about her statement. He said nothing. Sarah raised her head and looked at him.

He was smiling. A genuine smile. "I do love you, Sarah," he finally said. "I love you more now, just because you have just said those words." He laughed.

She didn't get it. Sarah looked at him. She was surprised. It was a turning-point moment. *What should I do? Is he saying that because of what I said? Did I misread his emotions towards me? Was he just pitying me all this time?* These thoughts raced through her mind in a flash. She reached a conclusion. She smiled, then started to laugh. Julian returned to his own laughter.

"It's funny?" she asked, stifling her own outburst, feigning seriousness.

"It is not," he replied. "But..." he waited for a half moment, "I have been searching for a way to tell you the same thing." His face became serious. "I love you in so many ways. Your strength, your courage, not to mention your..." he trailed off, letting his eyes descend to look at her breasts. She smiled, unconsciously moving her arm across her chest. "I do love you so much. You have been everything to me, during a time when I *needed* everything. You saved me from some deep darkness that was capturing me."

"I saved *you*," Sarah said, elevating her voice in some slight sarcasm. "You have been *my* saviour. It is you who have brought me back from a living death." Julian looked at her, raising his eyebrows once again. "Well," she corrected herself, "perhaps not death, but certainly some borrowed existence, void of happiness and joy. I mean, you have brought back into my life; the joy and happiness. I will always love you for that!"

"It would seem that we have done each other much good, Sarah."

"We have," she agreed. "But I know that I need to take this *new* me, and revisit the world. I have to escape from this dungeon I locked myself into. You have opened the door, but I have to step through...you cannot carry me." She rambled on, working her analogy to its full potential.

Eventually Julian hushed her. He slid his chair around the table to be next to her. "And I still have that which I'm chasing, that *something* I seek, still unsure of what it is."

They embraced, both slightly tearful, completely oblivious to any unwelcome stares from other diners.

"Let's go back to your place," Julian whispered, his eyes clearly revealing his welling passion.

"Yes," she agreed loudly. "We can celebrate the fact that we love each other, but we're not *in* love!"

The other patrons were confused no doubt, and possibly amused as well.

A few weeks later, as life for the two lovers who weren't *in* love continued, Julian wondered over to Sarah's place, fresh-picked poppies gathered in his hand, and *good morning* wishes on his mind. He knocked and waited. After a short while he knocked again.

Atufa appeared at the door. "Good morning, young man," he said, glancing at the flowers Julian held. "Are those for me?" he said, giggling a bit at his own comment.

"Absolutely," Julian replied, playing along with the charade. Atufa reached for them. Julian released the bouquet and glanced around the man, peering into the room. "Is there a young lady hiding in there somewhere?" he asked.

"She's gone," Atufa said.

Julian smiled, not recognizing the sincerity of Atufa's comment. Not grasping that he was serious. "What do you mean?" Julian asked. "She's off today."

"No Julian, I mean gone." Atufa raised his hand and waved it towards the horizon.

Julian was shocked, speechless as the comment finally reached him.

"Wait here for a moment, I have something for you." Atufa walked back into the room over by the counter and gathered an envelope. "She asked me to give this to you."

Julian took the envelope, realizing immediately that it was a good-bye note. He looked at Atufa, whose face was serious.

Julian smiled, nodding his head in some understanding of the situation. "Good for her," he finally said.

Atufa looked at him, a little surprised at his comment. "Well, I guess you knew this was coming, then."

"I knew, at least I hoped. I just didn't know it was today."

"She also asked me to give you a little kiss, but I think I'll let that parting gift remain undelivered."

They both laughed. Julian turned to walk back to his place. "Those flowers need water," he said over his shoulder, "if you want them to flourish."

The Journey: Erudite

—

Julian, my lover…

We have said our goodbyes several times during the last few days, under the warmth and comfort of my sheets. It is the way I would like to remember you. There were no other words necessary.

I am afraid. Perhaps terrified. I do not know what the future holds for me. But I am confident at the same time. I feel so completely free. First of all, I am travelling to find new feet. How crazy is that remark? My mobility is paramount. I have sat sulking in this chair long enough. I love you.

You have allowed me to be reborn. It is not too dramatic; it is absolutely the way I feel. I don't know what I would have done without our time together. When I reflect now on how I felt a few months ago, tethered to a rickety bar and a carved-out apartment, I cringe. But the physical liberation is only a small part of my transition. You have helped me understand that I am valuable, I am loveable, and I am attractive. You cannot imagine what a gift that is. I love you.

I have prayed for several things this day, my last day here. First and foremost, I prayed for you. For you to find what you seek; to find some contentment in your restless spirit. I prayed for you to live long, longer than most. I believe you will bring much joy into this world, wherever you touch it. I love you.

I also prayed for me. That my renewed dreams are not folly. That my reborn self will not cower when I eventually face those hardships that are part of my destiny. I prayed that I can be strong enough eventually, to provide the kind of joy and happiness for another, the way you have for me. If I can, it will confirm my complete transition. After all, it is transition we both seek.

Think of me from time to time, even as the memory slowly fades. I fear I will think of you much too often.

I love you.

Sarah

Sharif in the Clutches of Cruelty

Bouncing relentlessly, Sharif awoke on the lumpy surface of a rough woolen mat, delivering a cruel battering to his sore limbs and pulsating head. He brought his hands up to hold his head, again expecting some unseen comfort to emanate from them; no help. He turned and raised himself slightly onto his right forearm, ignoring the throbbing sensation and glancing around his cell, or more precisely, his cage. It was a very narrow space, covered on all sides with sturdy metal bars. Beyond the bars was a harsh, dry landscape, which was seemingly being tugged backwards behind him by their forward movement. It only took him a moment to realized he was in a wagon, a prison wagon! He tried to push his body further upright but once again felt dizzy and lay back down, his head sinking onto the crux of his right elbow, as his mind tried to focus on some explanation for his predicament. Someone spoke to him. He passed out.

When Sharif woke next, he felt the grip of a strong hand shaking his shoulder. He opened one eye and tried to focus on who was shaking him, but the outline remained blurry. He sensed the arrival of water before the full impact hit his face. Dirty water. It smelled, forcing him to jerk upwards in a reflex motion, spitting out any residue clinging to his lips, but quickly regretting the motion enormously. His head burst with pain. Sharif grimaced and tried to lie back down, but the man who was shaking him now grabbed him firmly and swung him off the pile he lay on, lifting him to his feet. His head hit the low roof of the prison wagon, delivering even more pain, causing him to grab the sore area as he crouched slightly in order to fit under its limited height.

The man who had dragged him to his feet now lay down on the pile. It consisted of a folded, quite tattered tent, apparently woven with wool and possibly goat hair, covering a small mound of wooden ground stakes. Sharif looked at him, a little confused.

"Find another spot, kid. This belongs to me." With that, he closed his eyes and nestled backwards into a more comfortable position.

Sharif leaned back against the bars and slowly slid down into a sitting position. He was in no condition to battle for the make-shift bed. Besides, the man was rather large and menacing. Sharif glanced around the cell. There were three other men besides himself and the bed thief. They all had sad, almost distant expressions on their face. They didn't look at Sharif. It was as though he didn't exist. Sharif drifted back to unconsciousness in his awkward sitting position, his mind spinning with dizzy uncertainty, and his thoughts spouting questions without answers.

Sharif woke once again with warm water splashing on him. He turned his head to avoid the stream and looked back. It wasn't water. The man who had taken his bed was now standing in a crouch beside him, his head bowed to avoid the low ceiling, urinating directly on him. Sharif lashed out, missing the man, and tried to rise up. The other men in the cell laughed. Sharif swung out again,

Sharif in the Clutches of Cruelty

catching the man's shoulder. He finished his stream and reached in for Sharif. He was indeed a big man and Sharif was still wobbly; no match for such a confrontation.

"Careful kid, or I'll crack open the other side of your head and take a crap in it." He pushed Sharif back onto the bars.

The others laughed again.

Sharif did his best to clean his face and hair with the sleeve of his shirt, but it was not a very effective wipe. As the afternoon moved ahead, the cell fell into a silent rocking motion, dancing to the turning of wheels and choppy terrain. Sharif slowly became accustomed to the odour, both of the cell passengers, and his own urine-soaked clothes. He longed for some answers, some explanation for his current dilemma, but was reticent to say anything to anyone.

Soon enough, Sharif had to relieve himself as well. His former assailant lay sleeping. The other men were drowsing off as well. He raised himself to his knees, lowered the front of his pants, and let his stream dart out into the afternoon dust; directly onto the face of his previous attacker. Like Sharif, the man took a short moment to realize what was happening. Once he did, he waved at the incoming urine, and burst off his bed, hitting his head hard against the ceiling. For a brief moment, he looked at Sharif with an incredulous stare. Then other men suddenly came to full consciousness and looked on in complete disbelief. Sharif had not finished, but he tucked himself back into his pants and returned the stare. His mind was rapidly weighing the potential repercussions of his actions, with all scenarios ending badly for Sharif. The man lunged forward. Instinctively, Sharif grabbed one of wooden stakes peeking out from below the tent and held it against the floor by his waist as he recoiled from the oncoming attack. The man plunged forward, pure evil in his eyes, and landed on Sharif. Unfortunately for him, he also landed on the sharp end of the wooden stake. He pinned Sharif to the floor, and himself to the stake, now deeply embedded in his stomach. A look of bewilderment crossed his face as he realized his life was about to end. It turned to one of sadness, helplessness, before his eyes glassed over into a cold, unattached stare.

Sharif was shaking. He had not intended to kill the man, only to protect himself. He immediately questioned his decision to urinate on him. He couldn't clearly recall making the decision. After a few moments he slid from beneath the man, letting him fall face first onto the floor. Sharif swung around and sat on the makeshift bed, blood now mixed with the urine soaking his clothes. He glanced at the other three men, who sat huddled at the front of the cell. They glanced away. Sharif's head was pounding like never before. He was trying to clarify whether this was reality, or just a dream induced by his apparent concussion. He wasn't sure. He lay back, closed his eyes, and fell immediately into unconsciousness.

Sharif felt the gentle tug at his leg. He began to regain consciousness, peering out into the growing darkness of late evening. The earlier events rushed back into his brain and he sat up, wide awake. The man who had been tugging his leg jumped back.

"I'm sorry, sorry...but you must wake. We are at the auction."

"Auction?"

The man did not reply. He slid out of the now-open cell door. The other two were already gone. Sharif glanced at the dead body, if for no other reason than to remind himself of what had happened.

A large man, brandishing a serious-looking Lebel bolt action rifle, came up to the wagon. "Get moving," he said, waving the gun to reinforce his command. "Over there by the fire, c'mon. And wake up your friend," he added, nodding his head towards the dead man.

"I've never met him," Sharif replied.

"I don't care, get him up and moving."

Sharif shook the dead man, somehow incapable of stating that he was no longer able to move. He shook again. "Let's go," he said to the dead man, trying to inject some urgency in his tone. He looked back at the guard and shrugged.

"Get out here," the guard said.

Sharif in the Clutches of Cruelty

Sharif climbed down from the cell. The guard hit the man through the bars with the butt of his rifle. No reaction. He moved in closer to examine him, offering his own version of *get up*, as he peered into the cage. Glassy, staring eyes looking back at him, told him the man was dead.

He turned to Sharif. "What happened?"

"He fell. I think he must have landed on one of those spikes. I don't know. Is he OK?"

"Get over there," the guard said, pushing Sharif with his rifle towards the large fire.

Sharif scrambled off. A commotion ensued. Several other soldiers came over to the wagon. One rather distinguished-looking lady also strode forward, calmly looking at the dead body and giving some instructions that were too far off for Sharif to hear clearly. Soon the body was removed and things seemed to return to normal. It was as though this was a regular occurrence. Sharif looked around and spotted the other three men who had shared his cell. They were looking at him as well, but quickly averted their gaze once eye contact was made. Sharif was obviously concerned that there might be repercussions, but there was little he could do about it now. He took a deep breath, reminded himself that his head was a throbbing point of discomfort, and stared vacantly into the fire.

In short order, a heavily tattooed monster of a man, came from behind a large, elaborately decorated wagon. He spoke loudly in a language Sharif did not know. Several men started moving forward. Sharif began to do the same.

"Line up beside the rocks," the tattooed man said, now in a familiar dialect.

Sharif looked over to where he was pointing and saw a small cluster of boulders with one larger stone standing conspicuously in the centre. The other prisoners were scurrying over to line up where told and Sharif followed, ever aware of both the pain in his head and the size of the man giving the instructions. The prisoners huddled together in a semi-cohesive group.

After a short period, distant traffic could be heard. Sharif looked towards the growing rumble and eventually saw several wagons arrive, with some very distinguished travellers emerging from them. They chatted amongst themselves. It was clear to Sharif that some old acquaintances were being renewed and some new ones being forged.

Suddenly, the hiss of a whip sailed through the night, and the scream of a prisoner pierced the air. Sharif spun and saw the man trying desperately, and fruitlessly, to reach for his back, no doubt to sooth the sting. Others began to shift away from the man wielding the whip, but several guards with rifles ordered everyone to remain as they were.

"Everyone must taste my whip when they start working for our clients, just so you will know what awaits you if you misbehave, or try to escape. One lash now as an appetizer, ten for disobedience, one hundred for any attempt at escape."

The men were lined up and administered a single lash each. Some handled it more defiantly that others, some screamed, some sat stone-faced.

As Sharif's turn approached, he felt an eerie anticipation mounting in his chest. His eyes darted about, seeking some potential relief, some respite from the inevitable. There was none. When his turn came, he turned and stared blankly out towards the onlooking crowd. He thought of his mother. He reminded himself it would be over soon, and he reached up to turn his six-sided cube in his hand. The blow struck. It stung immensely, but Sharif maintained his stoic look. Inside, his entire being screamed with pain and confusion, but the only outward evidence of this was the sharp refocusing of his eyes and their unusual shift to anger! It was not the only lash he would endure on this journey.

Sharif in the Clutches of Cruelty

The event of the evening was indeed an auction. The visiting audience first inspected the twenty or so men who were to be sold. They were made to strip, as both men and women walked among them, verifying their potential as labourers, or perhaps not. Once the inspection period was over and the men re-clothed, they were asked if they possessed any special skills. Anything that would make them more valuable, and perhaps save them from a dusty and dangerous life in someone's fields.

One man claimed he was a chef. He was warned of the consequences if he was stretching the truth, but he assured his captors that he was an experienced cook of some renown in his homeland. He was quizzed extensively on various cooking and baking methods, fluently answering all questions, and even enhancing some of the suggestions with elaborate gestures and recipe recitations. He was obviously quite knowledgeable in matters of the kitchen. His value certainly rose sharply, and the overseer was very happy with the price he received.

Another claimed to know horses; how to train them, care for them and race them. That was most interesting to one particular customer, and following much discussion and inquisition, he too drew a handsome sum for the seller. Another was a carpenter, which was not as valuable as a chef, but did, nonetheless, elevate him beyond the hardship and torment of routine slave labour. Sharif had no particular skills. He tried to explain that he was an excellent reader and spoke four languages, but that only drew laughs and chuckles from the audience. Still, he was young and strong, so he was sold for a fair price.

Eventually everyone was sold. Sharif was not sure what had actually happened and still convinced himself that he would explain carefully to his new *owner*, who would then release him with apologies for the misunderstanding. That dream was short-lived. The man who bought him and two other slaves, both previously unknown to Sharif, marched them back to the rear of his wagon…actually, the wagon of his madame. She had not been present at the auction, preferring not to soil her hands with such distasteful activity. Sharif recognized that she was a woman of education and clearly in charge. She was quite beautiful. Mid-thirties perhaps, a slim figure with an apparently ample bosom. Her exact outline was difficult to determine with the clothes she wore. He saw this as an opportunity to explain the unfortunate series of errors that had placed him in this predicament.

"Good evening, Madame," he began.

A short crop that she held in her hand came up immediately and swung with a back-hand stroke across Sharif's face. It happened quickly, before he realized what she was doing. It took a moment for the pain to register in his brain, but he grabbed for the point of the blow. Blood oozed from his cheek.

The lady did not stop, she continued walking along in front of her new slaves, before pivoting and returning to her quarters, which was a large tent, erected in front of the elaborate wagon she had arrived in. The new overseer who had purchased him came up to Sharif. He was a very large man, nasty and unkempt in appearance. He had gold teeth, rough skin, and numerous piercings in his ears and nose. He moved close. His odour was evident, though probably not as bad as Sharif's.

"If you speak to her again, unless spoken to first, your punishment will be more severe than you can dream of, including removal of your manhood." His hand moved forward and cupped Sharif's groin in a grip more than sufficient to convey the sincerity of his threat.

Sharif cringed. He bowed his head and moved backwards, gently escaping the grip while quickly making an internal decision to reconsider his plan to explain the misunderstanding that had landed him in his current circumstances.

The three slaves were led to a small creek, not far from the clearing. They were ordered to strip and wash themselves. A young woman came out of the tent, delivered some soap and collected their soiled clothing, leaving in their place a fresh set of attire.

Sharif in the Clutches of Cruelty

As they washed, Sharif glanced up and saw the madame watching from the inside of her tent. Their eyes met momentarily, but Sharif quickly averted his, returning vigorously to his task at hand. Once relatively clean, and following a close inspection by the overseer, the men dressed in their new clothes and returned to the rear of the wagon. A shackle was attached to each of their left legs, then to a master chain, and eventually to the back of the wagon. Their overseer handed out some food and water, instructing them to rest.

"Tomorrow will be a long day of travel. You will need much energy."

Sharif was exhausted, he was confused. A short time earlier he had been completing a comfortable day, sipping from a cool fountain in a town square. Now, he was sitting with a woozy head, a whipped back, and a slashed cheek, shackled to a chain, with nothing but foreboding as company. The night was restless. Some wagons departed, some buyers drank and laughed into the late evening. Some slaves could be heard in the distance, receiving punishment for undetermined infractions.

The morning brought little respite from the headache, but the three slaves were more than surprised when they were instructed to sit on the back edge of the wagon. They had been anticipating a long day of walking.

Their overseer explained. "My name is Iken. You will receive your instructions from me, and answer to me for all shortcomings. You now belong to Madame Lunja, she is a descendant of Queen Kahina, a great Amazigh priestess and warrior. She is demanding, but fair, as long as you obey without question. You will not be whipped without cause, nor starved without consideration. In return, you will reward Madame Lunja with your loyalty, hard work, and acquiescence to any demand made. Remember, she owns you and can do with you as she wishes. It is your honour to serve her. Any questions?"

His final comment was spoken with a snarl, leaving the three men with nothing to say but, "No, sir."

The Language of Opportunity

Following a lengthy time of travel, Sharif and the other slaves arrived at a mountainous plateau, with expansive agriculture for as far as the eye could see. At the entrance to the plateau stood several rectangular buildings, constructed of brick and clay.

"This is your new home, be grateful it is not a bagnio," Iken stated, waving his hand in a full circle towards all the land visible.

He then pointed specifically at one of the rectangular buildings. Sharif did not know what a 'bagnio' was, but assumed it was something unpleasant.

"Find a bed that does not have a bag on it. You will find your own bag underneath the bed you choose. It will contain two more sets of clothing and some utensils. Clothes you will work in. The clothes you currently have on will be worn only when you are not working, and are in the presence of Madame Lunja or her entourage. Is that clear?"

The men nodded in a quiet understanding.

Iken unfurled his whip. "Is that clear?" he asked again, with a more exaggerated tone.

"Yes, yes, sir," Sharif responded immediately. The other two slaves also reacted immediately.

Iken pointed with his whip, indicating they should find their beds.

Sharif entered the building. It was a long, barracks-type interior, with more than thirty beds lining the back and side walls. There were five or six empty ones scattered amongst those that already had bags on them. He chose one which was not too close to the door, reached under the bed, and found a bag. The other two found their own spots as well.

"It is too late to work today. No need to change. Put your bag on your bed to identify it, and follow me."

Iken led them down the edge of the building. Between each building was a latrine. It smelled most foul. "For your daily needs. Your barracks is responsible for your latrine."

He then marched them across the road to a larger square building. It was a large dining room, or more precisely, a large room full of eating mats. There were several people scurrying about in the back, which Sharif assumed was the kitchen. They stopped and bowed to Iken when they saw him, before returning to their tasks.

"Meals are here. You will sit where you find a place. There is a plate and cup in your bag. Meals are served in the morning before labour, and in the evening after labour. If you are late, you don't eat. Understood?"

The now standard, "Yes sir," followed.

"Your fellow slaves will soon return from their day of toil. You will then meet your driver. He will organize you, direct you, and ensure you provide a full day of work. Understood?"

"Yes sir," was the response, although none of them actually knew what he was referring to.

Eventually they settled into a difficult and arduous routine. The driver of their barracks was one of the few decent people Sharif encountered, and although he was obviously ferocious when

The Language of Opportunity

necessary and delivered harsh lashes when he felt warranted, he was fair and protective of his *flock*. Sharif felt his whip a few times, whenever he found himself slipping towards a day-dream. He was amazed that the driver would somehow be cognizant of his mental drift.

The normal day began before sunrise, the driver always calling out a wake-up message. Sharif wondered how he knew to be up at the same time every day, until he himself was awake one morning and saw the night guard enter and wake the driver. Almost like a shift change taking place. A lineup at the door, based on your bed location, preceded a trip to the latrine. The horrible smell soon became unnoticeable. A breakfast of bread, garbanzo beans, and occasionally amlou, washed down with some weak mint tea, followed. Then they marched to the fields. Tasks were assigned on a rotating basis. The day was long and difficult. Mid-morning and mid-afternoon tea breaks split the day into three parts. Following the march back to the barracks, an evening meal of flat bread with tajine or couscous was served, again washed down with mint tea. Occasionally, a small piece of meat accompanied the evening meal.

Although evenings were short and basically transitional from work-to-meal-to-sleep, some camaraderie did develop. Not all barracks were as cohesive as Sharif's, and that was usually a reflection of the driver. Occasionally, a scream could be heard from someone receiving lashes, but it was not common. In the time Sharif was there, Iken only once used his whip. One particular slave, known as a trouble maker, tried to escape. He was caught and lashed one hundred times. His cries of anguish soon became shallow, as he lost consciousness. By the last blow, he was dead.

One nondescript evening, as the slaves settled into their beds, with a light buzz of chatter permeating the room, the door swung open. Iken stepped in. He held a paper up high, letting the light from his candle illuminate the writing.

"Can anyone read this?"

He slowly walked around the room, allowing each slave to see the writing clearly. No one responded with more than a shaking of their head. When the text came into focus for Sharif, he couldn't believe it. The writing was his native language, one he had learned originally as a child, even though he seldom used it.

Sharif raised his hand.

Iken almost missed it, but turned back to him and held the paper closer. "Can you read this?"

"I can."

"You had better be sure."

"It is my native language. I learned it when I was a boy," Sharif confirmed.

Iken smiled, the first time Sharif had ever seen that, then returned to his usual sober demeanour. "Put on your visit clothes and come with me."

Sharif took a moment to register what was happening. Was this a trap? Was he going to be punished, perhaps killed, for knowing this language?

His hesitation brought on a loud command from Iken. "Now, slave!"

Sharif was led in a trot across several small fields. Iken led the way. They eventually arrived at the main building; one Sharif had only seen from afar. Once inside, Iken spoke quietly with a demure and effeminate young man. The man looked at Sharif, then returned to his conversation.

Sharif was ushered away by the man, after receiving a strong recommendation from Iken to follow all instructions he received immediately, without hesitation. He was reminded that any hesitation would be rewarded with a most severe punishment. Sharif had no intentions of risking that.

Their first stop was a small bath chamber. Two women waited there, both raising their hands to their noses when Sharif walked in. They quickly disrobed him and led him to a warm bath of scented water. As they washed and shaved him, he became aroused. It had been a long time since a woman had washed him there. Actually, no woman had ever washed him there. They giggled as they stood him up to exit the bath and dry off. His state of arousal was clear.

The man who had guided him to the bath was looking directly at his member, a large smile covering his face. "You do clean up quite well," he said, before moving closer and brandishing a small, spoon-shaped instrument, with which he proceeded to slap the end of Sharif's erection. Sharif jumped back; his arousal quickly diminished. The ladies still giggled.

He was dressed in a long robe, tied at the waist, and then sprinkled with a soft perfume. His guide led him through two more chambers, pushed aside a series of curtains and then moved aside. Sharif stood directly in front of Madame Lunja. The guide pushed down on his shoulder and Sharif fell to his knees.

Madam Lunja reached for her tea and spoke, as if addressing the teacup. "You speak the language of the page?"

Sharif nodded, then realized she would not have seen that, and replied. "Yes, Madame."

"What did it state?"

"I did not really read it, I just saw briefly that it was my mother language, one I learned when I was young."

Madame Lunja looked down at Sharif, then up at his guide. "Bring the pages here."

The guide scurried off, leaving them alone for the moment.

"Stand up and remove your robes."

Sharif hesitated. Madame Lunja scowled at him but said nothing. He rose and undid the cord, letting the robe fall, leaving him fully naked. Madame Lunja didn't look at him. She returned her attention to her tea, taking several sips, before returning the cup to its saucer. Sharif tried desperately to remain calm. He tried not to look at her, but he was unable to avert his eyes. Standing in front of her naked was stirring his arousal again. He moved his hands in front to cover his growing excitement.

"Hands at your sides," she said, without striking eye contact.

Sharif slid his hands back to his sides, completely embarrassed by his now fully extended presence. He was certain he would be punished for his insolence, perhaps killed. Still, he could not do anything but stand there, frozen in the moment.

His guide returned, saw the situation, huffed in mock dismay, and once again flicked a slap to the tip of his organ. Sharif wilted, the smile on Lady Lunja's face not unnoticed. The guide handed Sharif the page and Lady Lunja waved him away.

"Sit here," Madame Lunja said, waving her arm again to indicate the area at her feet, "and read me the page."

Sharif did. It was an introductory message from someone named Nasar, referring to the British Raj and various trading opportunities. It was very flattering towards Madame Lunja, detailing the importance of her land and inviting her for a meeting with representatives from India, later in the spring.

Lady Lunja was most pleased with the contents of the letter and had Sharif read it several times, stopping him on occasion to ask a question, glean a clarification, or query if there was another possible interpretation for a particular comment. Once she was satisfied with the full translation, she leaned back in her chair, gazing upward as if she was alone in her thoughts. Sharif sat quietly, once again painfully aware of his nakedness, and feeling quite foolish, if not helpless.

Momentarily, Lady Lunja held out one of her legs. "Massage my foot," she said, as if it was a simple request to hand her a piece of paper.

Sharif took her foot in his hands and began to knead the ball through her very ornate leather shoes.

She looked at him curiously. "Remove the shoe," she said, softly, without irritation.

The Language of Opportunity

Sharif slowly, carefully, slid the shoe off her foot. He provided a lengthy massage to her delicate foot, enjoying the process despite its appearance as a degrading act. He did her other foot as well. All the while, she barely glanced his way, preferring to recline and expend her attention elsewhere. At one point, she moved her foot alongside Sharif's face, and used her large toe to trace the line of the scar that still lingered from the crop she had used on him when he first spoke to her. He noticed a slight smile cross her lips, before her eyes returned to some point of interest on the ceiling of the tent.

After she felt sufficiently massaged, she clapped her hands. Sharif stopped massaging, wondering what he should do next. His uncertainty was answered shortly when the two women who bathed him entered the room. In a language Sharif could not understand, Lady Lunja instructed them in a soft, whimsical voice. They raised him up, gathered his robe, and hurried him to another room. There he was laid down backwards on a long bench, still naked, his legs astride it. One of the women began massaging him, once again bringing him to a state of intense arousal. His hands were lowered down on either side of the bench and tied underneath it. The bindings were not tight or uncomfortable, but they definitely immobilized his arms. His legs were left untied. His robe was used to cover his face, blocking all possibility to see what was happening. Short intervals only aroused him more, occasional touches, an odd brush of flesh, and an ever-increasing need. In due course, he felt two hands grip his hips, as someone slowly lowered herself on to him. The fit was sublime. Soft, yet fiercely hungry. He thrust, she moved in harmony. He finished first, but she continued grinding until several low moans escaped her, and she tensed several times. Then it was over.

His hands were loosened and the robe was removed from Sharif's face. As he rose from the bench, he was certain he saw Lady Lunja swishing out of sight behind one of the many curtains surrounding the room. He wondered.

Several days went by. Sharif returned to his labours, never mentioning the experience, other than to confirm he had translated the page for her. He did not reveal the contents of the message, a point not missed by Iken. After a week or so, he was once again summoned to Lady Lunja. Again, he was bathed, ogled by his guide, and carefully slapped to ensure his excitement was only momentary. He anticipated another evening of pleasure, but was soon disappointed. He was handed a response to the letter. It was written in the language he now spoke, or more accurately had learned. His rudimentary understanding of it had been greatly enhanced through the process of living and working with it. His task was to write a translation of it as a reply to the original message.

"You can write, can't you?"

"Yes, I can."

"Do you understand the message I want to send?"

"Yes, I do."

"Very well, sit here and compose a direct version in your mother language."

Sharif did so. It didn't take long. Lady Lunja was pleased with his penmanship, mentioning so to his guide, but not directly to him. He was escorted back to his barracks without further ceremony.

Another week passed. The memory of his interaction with Lady Lunja all but forgotten.

One particular morning, he was confronted by Iken. "No work for you today. Dress in your visit clothes and remain here until I come for you."

Sharif waited. The other slaves went about their morning ritual of latrine and breakfast. He had to relieve himself quite badly. Still no Iken. Finally, he slipped out of the barracks and quickly strode to the latrine. As he left the toilet, the great relief he felt was quickly dismantled by the scowl from Iken. Sharif dropped his gaze to the ground and hurried back to the barracks. He waited nervously for Iken to enter.

The Language of Opportunity

"Most fortunate for you that Lady Lunja requests your presence this morning. Disobedience usually requires ten lashes."

Sharif said nothing. He followed Iken to the main dwelling, followed his guide to the bath, received a cleansing from the two women, without extending an arousal, much to the chagrin of his guide, and was dressed in rather fancy leggings, shirt, shoes, and robes. He asked no questions, and was given no explanation.

After some time waiting in a side room, Sharif was joined by a man he had not previously seen. "You are the translator," the man stated, carrying a distinct air of authority.

"I guess so," Sharif replied.

"You do, or you do not speak the language of the letter?"

"I do."

And that was the end of Sharif's life as a common slave. He joined Lady Lunja's entourage as they set out for the meeting with the mysterious Nasar. They travelled for several days. Sharif rode comfortably in the back of a support wagon, occasionally enjoying the fresh air from the passenger seat, gulping down three good meals a day, and sleeping comfortably among the chit chat of Lady Lunja's various servants, who were definitely not to be confused with slaves. At night, his leg was unceremoniously shackled to the foot of his bed.

The meeting with Nasar was full of ceremony, opulent in surroundings, and very formal initially. Sharif was constantly at Lady Lunja's side, translating everything that was said. It often seemed as though he was the one actually having a conversation with Nasar, Lady Lunja present only as a bystander. One time he responded to a simple question without first waiting for a comment from Lady Lunja This had him chastised and threatened, with a nice superficial smile crossing her lips. He only required one such warning.

The entire summit lasted three days. Much was discussed, some was agreed upon, and a few actual transactions were completed. After the final goodbyes were given, after the final meal was eaten,

The Journey: Erudite

after the last words were translated, Sharif found himself once again in his quarters. He was alone. Several other servants were attending to Lady Lunja and her aides, gentlemen cooking and serving, ladies preparing baths and refreshments, music being played, and a canopy of relaxation permeating the small caravan.

Suddenly, Sharif had a revelation. It was an open invitation to freedom! He used a small knife to slit a hole in the rear of the tent. He peered out. No one. He slipped through the opening and dashed aimlessly towards the hustle and bustle of the town. He wove through several streets, drawing curious looks from pedestrians, amused by his wardrobe and his confusion. He turned down a seemingly deserted alley, bumping into a portly gentleman, knocking him sideways. Sharif stopped. He reached out for the man, apologizing profusely for being so reckless.

The man grinned and chuckled through a quiet moan. "Why such a hurry, young man?"

Sharif wasn't sure what to explain. He was confused and pumping adrenalin. He was thinking about Iken's whip. "I am running for my life," he finally stuttered, realizing how silly that must have sounded, but how true it actually was.

"That's rather dramatic."

"You don't understand. I was kidnapped some time ago. Made a slave. I just escaped because we came to town and I was valued as a translator. I did everything I was asked. The chance to run was unexpected. I took it. They will kill me if they catch me." It all came out in a blur.

The man looked on, losing his own breath under the influence of Sharif's verbal barrage. "Calm, calm. Come into my place, no one will find you here."

Sharif quickly evaluated it as his best option. Inside, the small apartment was dim, but Sharif could make out a small cooking area, a table and chairs, and a doorway to a rear room, probably for sleeping, perhaps a toilet.

The Language of Opportunity

"Here," the man said, pulling out one of the chairs. "Sit down and regain your breath. You are safe here. My name is Aderfi."

"I am Sharif. Thank you, Mr. Aderfi."

"Just Aderfi will suffice." He moved over to the stove and poured some water into a kettle.

Sharif relaxed noticeably. They shared tea and Sharif recounted more of his tale; his descent into slavery and servitude. Aderfi listened attentively, with brief nods and the occasional *uh-huh*.

Sharif stayed in the small room for three days, fearful of revealing himself to anyone on the street. He had no choice but to put his full faith in Aderfi. He slept on a straw mattress quickly put together, and changed into some of Aderfi's clothes, even though they were a few sizes too large. Aderfi reported that there was indeed a buzz through the town. A healthy reward had been posted for Sharif's return. The reward included a statement inferring he had stolen from Lady Lunja. Sharif denied that vociferously. Aderfi did not question his sincerity.

Eventually, the fervour died down. Lady Lunja departed with her entourage in tow. Aderfi acquired some suitable clothing for Sharif and helped him dress in a concealed manner. It was time for Sharif to move on, to travel to some distant place, where he would not be recognized or hunted down. He found no way to repay Aderfi for his kindness, but soon realized nothing was expected. Aderfi even gave him a small sum to restart his life, which Sharif only accepted after much protest. He made a vow to repay the gentleman at some point.

"Just be kind to others," was the only response he received.

Sharif secured travel with a small group of men who were heading to a larger town, quite a way off, searching for employment. They had heard that jobs were available, as the various trading caravans would soon be arriving with their seasonal harvest and livestock. Sharif felt lucky to be concealed by the band of travellers, and he was careful to always be nondescript, his head bowed, his eyes always darting around, looking for Iken or his men. The travellers thought he was a rather unusual individual, but he had paid for passage, so they left him to his own world.

When they arrived at their destination, Sharif followed the crowd to the hiring office and was fortunate enough to land a job right away. He was no stranger to hard physical labour and impressed his foreman from the first day. He stood on the loading dock, hands on hips, while his mind reflected on the cruel journey that had brought him here. *What would my journey have been if I had not landed in the clutches of cruelty?*

The caravan experience was complete. First in the clutches of kindness, then of indifference, and finally of cruelty, with all three resulting in the same conclusion. Here he stood on the loading dock of the receiver, regardless of which pathway had brought him here.

Sharif laboured with a small team of workers who were tasked with moving merchandise from the main yard onto the individual transport equipment that the receiver's customers used, to depart with their particular portion of the bounty. One of the young men working with him noticed the cube around Sharif's neck.

"That is a very interesting piece," he said. "Do you mind if I look at it?"

Sharif didn't mind. He was actually quite proud of it, as it was both universal in symbolism and unique in construction. "You'll have to look at it here," he said, holding the cube forward, but still on the cord around his neck. "I never remove it."

His co-worker stepped forward and examined the cube, turning it over and around several times. "That's an amazing array of religious symbols, my friend. Where did you get it?"

"From a world traveller, some time ago. He gave it to me as a parting gift and I have worn it since."

"That is a good thing. It definitely gives you an appearance of tolerance and understanding."

Sharif reflected on that comment. For him it was still a gift, a unique remembrance of Tection. "I had not thought of it that way, but I suppose you're right."

"And, is that an accurate description of you?" the co-worker asked.

Sharif contemplated for a moment. Was he tolerant and understanding? Of course he was. "It is almost precisely who I am," he responded. "Plus, a little curious and adventuresome," he added with a broad smile.

"Well, I am of a similar frame of mind, my friend." His co-worker offered his hand. "What's your name?"

"Sharif. And you are?"

"I'm Julian. Nice to make your acquaintance."

Sharif soon replenished his travelling purse, at least enough to continue his journey onward. Onward with Julian.

Sharif and the Improbable Encounter

Julian was a little distraught over Sarah's departure. He cried frequently, often shook his head in some amazement, and even laughed occasionally at the thought of her barging down the road, commanding the unfortunate souls who had two feet but no heart, to *move aside*. There were so many things he wished to tell her, to discuss with her. Her departure left him empty. He languished without purpose for a while, not feeling the excitement of a new day, nor the whispers of the dancing streets outside. Yet, her letter was also most fulfilling. It made him feel good and useful and perhaps even special. Quite a paradox! She filled a whole section of his ever-growing journal.

Eventually, he realized that she was absolutely right. Their passion was fleeting, their connection was not permanent. Maybe it ended too soon or maybe it ended just in time, before either of them was hurt or even damaged. He tucked the many fond memories of her deep into his pockets; the future was waiting. Destiny was calling. Julian had a way of stepping back and recognizing that experiences in his life were part of the great conclusion, part of the sum of all he would become. He reflected on his beginnings, his childhood, his café, his journey, Yasmine, and Talia. He knew at that moment, as he thought about Talia and Sarah, that the attraction was different.

Sarah was infectious. She had forced him to her with her vulnerability, despite her outward façade. She was emotionally unavoidable. She was erotic, once she broke through her own barriers. She was independent and realistic; all things needed in order to survive.

Talia, on the other hand, was intriguing, beautiful like a flower, soft, and graceful. She was innocent, despite the outpouring of diplomatic verbiage. A branch, waiting for a tree to claim her. Julian immediately felt some guilt about her age. He should have checked. But it could not dampen the fire he felt for her.

Once Julian satisfied his uncertainty about Sarah, he realized it was time to move on. He knew there were various travelling caravans heading east, and he decided to seek one out. At the main bazaar, there were numerous receiving points for incoming caravans. He approached several to find out when an opportunity might present itself. One caravan had just left, but another was expected in a couple of weeks. Julian accepted an offer of employment with the receiver, at least until the next caravan was unloaded. He immediately went to work on transferring the various goods that had arrived onto the transports of smaller, local merchants.

One of his co-workers was a young man of East Indian descent. Julian could not help but notice a small cube pendant that hung loosely about his neck.

"That is a very interesting piece," Julian said. "Do you mind if I look at it?"

His co-worker lifted the cube in his hand, holding it out towards Julian. "You'll have to look at it here," he said. "I never remove it."

Sharif and the Improbable Encounter

Julian turned the cube over several times. "That's an amazing array of religious symbols, my friend. Where did you get it?"

"From a world traveller, some time ago. He gave it to me as a parting gift and I have worn it ever since."

"That is a good thing. It definitely gives you an appearance of tolerance and understanding."

His co-worker cocked his head slightly, obviously reflecting on his comment. "I had not thought of it that way, but I suppose you're right."

"And, is that an accurate description of you?" Julian asked.

More contemplation followed. "It is almost precisely who I am," he finally said, a mischievous smile creeping onto his lips. "Plus, a little curious and adventuresome."

"Well, I am of a similar frame of mind, my friend," Julian replied, holding out his hand. "What's your name?"

"Sharif. And you are?"

"I'm Julian. Nice to make your acquaintance."

After some time together, which included much narration and reflection, laughter and curiosity, the two young men realized that they were heading in the same direction. Not specifically directed by a compass or map, but more broadly interpreted as a similar interest in joining the turning world, and letting it ebb and flow into their lives. There was no specific destination, no city or settlement targeted, although they were heading generally east, which Sharif consciously recognised as the way back to where he came from.

He did not want to go home with his tail between his legs, listening to his parents deliver their soothing *I-told-you-so*, in that nurturing, yet condescending tone they always seemed to deploy. His excursion out into the world had only begun. His adventures on the roads of kindness, indifference and cruelty were only just beginning. So why was it that he so easily agreed on an easterly direction, when Julian indicated it was the way he was heading? Perhaps it was an unconscious ambition to return to the safety of home. Maybe it was simply a desire to share some time with Julian or just a coincidence of circumstance. Most likely, it was some sort of mélange of all of that, and more.

Julian was definitely heading east. He was not sure if he was running away from the memories of Sarah, or running towards an undetermined destiny. He knew much of what lay behind him and his quest was far from over. The sea lay to the north, the desert to the south, and memories to the west. East was the only option for him. He was glad to hear that Sharif was also planning to travel east; it made their decision to travel together, at least for a time, a simple one. Still, Julian wondered about his own direction. He thought of Talia often, musing that he dreamed of her often as well. Was he unconsciously hoping to come across her again? Was she somehow, deep in his vast internal landscape, beckoning him to come find her? He hoped so, unable not to smile at the thought of reunion. But then again, she was far to the northwest from where he was, and his next itinerary was heading farther away from her.

One evening, not too far into their travels, as they sat quietly beside a comfortable fire, tasked with lighting their faces and warming their coffee, Julian once again noticed the cube that hung around Sharif's neck.

"A world traveller you said?"

Sharif looked up from the hypnotic flames. "Sorry?"

"A world traveller; you said the cube was a gift from a world traveller."

Sharif's hand automatically went to the cube. He twirled it. "Yes, exactly. A traveller who visited my home some time ago."

"Tell me about him," Julian asked. "I am fascinated by the thought of travelling and encountering new worlds, new people. Where did he come from?"

"I was small, just a child. One day, my father walked in with him. He seemed like a giant to me." Sharif laughed a bit, running through the memory of meeting Tection for the first time.

Sharif and the Improbable Encounter

"Did he scare you?"

"You know...he should have; but he didn't. He had, I don't know, he had a face, a demeanour that was...it was just friendly. He made you feel like he was an old friend, even though you'd just met."

Julian nodded, not so much in agreement, but rather in understanding. Such people were not frequently encountered.

"He had me rolling around in a wrestling match within minutes of his arrival. And soon after, my brother Ayan as well. I remember my mother laughing so hard she had to sit down. We were squealing and racing around, I don't think he moved more than three or four steps during the whole exercise, he let us provide all the energy." Sharif was looking into the fire, but he was seeing Tection, smiling back at him.

"Where did he come from?" Julian asked, wanting to keep the story flowing.

"I'm not sure. Like I said, I was young. He taught me many things, though. He would tell us stories with such a vivid vocabulary. We would sit and listen as he transported us to some distant place."

"That sounds fascinating."

"Tection had a certain way of explaining the..."

"Tection!" Julian jumped to his feet.

Sharif fell backwards, putting his hands out to prevent him from falling off his rocky chair.

"Tection?" Julian repeated loudly. Could it be? It *had* to be. How many Tections were there in the world?

"Do you know him?" Sharif asked, skeptical about Julian's dramatic reaction.

Julian looked at him. "Sorry, Sharif. Forgive me. I know a Tection, yes. It has to be the same man. The name is so uncommon, I have never heard of another." He sat back down, relaxing Sharif as well.

Julian began to describe Tection and Sharif nodded in agreement with each new feature mentioned, enhancing the description with his own memories. There was absolutely no doubt that they were talking about the same man. They were consumed by the impossible coincidence. How could they both know this man, nearly fifteen years apart, from cultures in opposite corners of the globe? The serendipity of it was unfathomable.

After they regained some sense of normalcy, with their heads still shaking in wonderment, Julian looked over at Sharif. "I'm sorry I interrupted your story; it was just impossible not to react when I heard his name. He was such an important part of my life."

Sharif tilted his head further. "I keep thinking something will come up that tells us we are talking about two different people, but I'm sure that will not happen."

"Please, finish the story of your meeting with him, and the cube."

"No, no, I have to hear how you know him. Is he still alive? Where does he live? I would love to see him again. Is he close to here?" A lot of questions were flying out of Sharif's mouth, completely unable to keep up with the ones dancing in his head.

"He's far from here, Sharif. When I began my journey, he was the last one I saw. Actually, he is the reason I am able to take this journey."

"How is that?" Sharif leaned forward, anxious for any information on Tection.

"It's a long story, but I guess I can provide a short version."

"Why?" Sharif asked. "The fire is burning, dawn is far away, tell me everything."

Julian laughed at his enthusiasm. It was obvious that he had a shared history with Tection. "I met him one day in the small town I lived in."

"Was it near here? How far away?"

Julian smiled again at his eagerness. "Hold on, my friend, I will tell you everything."

Sharif leaned forward, holding his legs with his arms, his eyes peering up at Julian.

Sharif and the Improbable Encounter

"I lived in a town on the other side of the sea. It was not far from the shore, but it was not really a port. It was a town of farmers mostly. My good friend John P and I travelled there when we were quite young, though that is another story altogether."

Julian paused noticeably at the mention of John P. He wondered if he was doing alright. They had parted under such sad circumstances. John P had only discovered who his father was at the very moment of the old man's death.

"And he lived there too?" Sharif asked, jerking Julian back to the present.

"Well, he did eventually. I actually met Tection one day when he first arrived in town. I had a small café, and he just appeared near it one day."

"You had a café; one of your own?"

"I did, but that is also a different story. Let's stick to Tection for now."

Sharif nodded.

"The first time I met him, he was aloof and mysterious, yet somehow magnetic as well. We talked a bit, we drank a bit, and eventually he stayed in the room above my café. We quickly became friends. Like you said, he had a demeanour that was friendly, if not infectious. I knew he had travelled for some time, and was just returning to his homeland. I guess that would explain your time with him."

Sharif nodded and smiled.

"But I never knew where he had been specifically, or at least not the specific names of people he met along his travels. He just told stories that were exciting and believable, even when they were *unbelievable*, if you know what I mean."

"I know exactly what you mean," Sharif nodded, his smile almost permanently carved onto his face.

"Anyway, after we built a friendship, Tection often managed the café, allowing me to share some time with other matters in

The Journey: Erudite

my life. And, he was very friendly to my cat." Julian laughed at his last remark.

"So, how is it you are out here," Sharif waved his arms out like wings, indicating everything around them, "in this forsaken landscape?"

"I'm getting to that. I always wanted to travel. I was fascinated by Tection's stories and they only enhanced my desire to venture out. He knew how I felt and often advised me to follow my dreams, so to speak, as opposed to settling for a life that was comfortable, but ultimately unrewarding; warning me not to become something or someone I was never meant to be."

"Exactly, well put," Sharif chimed in, recognizing the feeling.

"It was an amazing day when Tection discovered he had a son. He was…"

"He had a son!" Sharif sat upright, even more intensely engaged.

"He did."

"He told me he wished to have a son, and that he would be exactly like me," Sharif recounted, proudly touching his hand to his chest.

"Well, he had one, although he only discovered that when the boy was grown up. It seems he had him before he travelled, which would mean he had him when he met you, but he didn't know it."

"Or maybe he knew it deep down, maybe he felt it, but didn't know it for a fact."

"That could well be true, Sharif. Anyway, he was reunited with his son and the young man's mother. It was perfect timing for all of us. He needed a home base in our town, so he could complete the reunion with his family and live a life more suited to a weary traveller, and I was just so anxious to begin my own adventure."

"So, what happened?"

"So, I sold him my café, which was where he was living anyway, and used the funds to sail off across the sea. I have been travelling in this land ever since; several years now."

"I am so happy to hear that he is well and, hopefully happy."

Sharif and the Improbable Encounter

"He was very happy when I last saw him," Julian confirmed.

"I was young," Sharif said, "but I heard him tell my father one time that he had killed a man. Not killed him during a battle or something, but killed him under some other circumstances. I think that fact was the first impetus for him to travel."

Through Selim, Julian knew Tection had such a history, that he had killed someone evil, but he did not know specific details. He was hungry for them. From their relationship, he would not have thought Tection capable of such action, but he realized it had indeed happened. After all, Julian had also killed someone. That thought sobered him for a moment. "I am aware that he endured such an act. Are you aware of the specific circumstances?"

Sharif was surprised with the term *endured*. It seemed unusual, but he couldn't know that Julian had also *endured* such a life-altering event. "Well, I don't really know much about it. He never spoke to me about it. I mean, I was still a young child. I do remember hearing my father tell him that he was absolutely right in what he did, so I guess there were justifiable circumstances that they agreed on. I don't know what they were. I was more interested in them getting through the serious conversation so I could wrestle with him again."

They both laughed at Sharif's last, hopelessly honest remark.

Their shared experience and recollections of Tection bound them closer together than hours of idle chat could have. They both realized how important Tection had been to them, albeit in different ways and at different points in their lives.

As they moved farther east, they came to a decision to travel to Sharif's homeland. It was not a conscious decision, hacked out during some organized meeting of their minds, but rather a slowly steeped one, filtered through days of shared time, and recognized as a destiny already in play, before it was articulated.

A few small side trips, some discovery and diversion, some clumsy romances with local girls, and the occasional odd job, left them remarkably close to Sharif's home.

The reunion with his parents and brother was over the top! Their hugs and kisses never ceased, questions rolled out like hornets from a hive, and the introduction of Julian took much longer than anticipated. Julian just stood back and watched the process, realizing how much Sharif was loved, and how much he loved back. Coming from his own hostile and cold upbringing, Julian wondered if he would have ever travelled if his home had been so warm and loving. Eventually he would come to the determination that he would still have travelled; it was his destiny.

His introduction to Sharif's father, Ravi, was complete with a lengthy monologue related to their mutual acquaintance with Tection. Ravi was no less amazed at the coincidence than Sharif had been originally. Ayan wanted to hear the whole story as well. So it was, after their first meal together, Julian recounted his history with Tection, in much more detail than before. As he reached the part where he was departing for his journey, he mentioned that Tection had given him a medallion. Before he could pull it out, Ravi spoke.

"A round coin with a crescent moon and pointed star?"

"Exactly," Julian replied, pulling the medallion out from his shirt for all to see.

"I saw that same medallion around the neck of Tection. He valued it greatly, so he must have also valued you greatly, in giving it to you," Ravi said.

Julian could only smile. He had always felt that the medallion was a very personal gift, but Ravi's description seemed to highlight it as even more valuable than that. It was a statement of trust and respect, something Julian would also have to be careful to respect as he continued to be the caretaker of it.

The stories and excitement surrounding the discussions inspired Ravi to share his own experiences with the tall traveller, also in more detail than he had offered his boys previously. At some point, Julian brought up the question of Tection having killed someone.

Ravi fell silent. He looked at Sharif, who was completely useless at hiding anything from his father.

"I heard you talking with Tection one time. You were discussing just such matters. I was young, but I remember well."

"Well Sharif, Julian, as Tection has not shared any such info with you, I would not be willing to do so either."

"Please, Father…" Sharif continued.

Ravi just looked at him with that stern, commanding glare he mustered on occasion. Nothing more than that was necessary.

"I was already aware that Tection had endured such a dilemma in his life. I'm sure whatever happened was more than justified," Julian said, breaking the uncomfortable silence. "After all, Tection is one of the kindest people I've ever known. Let's just remember that."

Sharif once again pondered the choice of words. Endured?

Ravi smiled at Julian. "You are absolutely right, young man, now, let's see what's happening down in the town tonight!"

Talia and the Traumatic Truth

Talia woke slowly from her sleep, eyes shut, morning breeze rustling leaves outside, and the bang of a loose shutter somewhere, bouncing off the frame of its anchored sister. She lay there for a while, eyes still shut, letting her mind create a picture of the room, the yard, the horizon; a picture of how it should be, not necessarily how it was. She knew, once she opened her eyes, everything would be defined and unalterable. The furniture would be where it was the night before, her clothes in the same pile, and her reflection in the mirror would hold the same face; no variation. With her eyes closed, however, she could change the room, the brightness, the horizon, and even her own reflection.

There was a soft knock at her door. Talia opened her eyes. The knock was repeated, and she mumbled a familiar, incoherent noise, which confirmed to whoever was on the other side of the door that she was indeed awake. Her mother came in, always in a sort of shuffle, soft and quiet, *just like a mouse*, Talia thought, smiling to herself, *a really nice mouse that I love dearly, but a mouse nonetheless.*

"I need to speak with you about something," her mother said, sitting gently on the chair beside her bed table, which was still draped with clothes from the night before. She picked up a sweater and began folding it, completely unconscious of the fact, as her mind worked on putting together her words in the best possible manner.

Talia noticed the seriousness of her mood and propped up on one elbow. Usually their morning chatter centred on some rumour in the town, or a circumstance of some relative. Not today.

"What is it?" she asked her mother, taking on a similarly serious demeanour, in an expression of understanding that something of significance was to be said.

"School will be done in another two weeks, Talia!"

"Yes, I can't wait!" she confirmed.

"After that I will be taking a trip, and I want you to travel with me."

"A trip. What do you mean, where are we going?"

Talia's mother looked up at her. A tear rolled down her cheek.

Talia sat up on the edge of her bed, tossing the cover off her legs and leaning in towards her mother. "What's wrong? Did something happen?"

Her mother looked at her. She was trying to speak but her voice was not available. She took a deep breath and she closed her eyes tightly, pushing additional tears down the sides of her face.

Talia leaned forward and took her mother's hands in her own. "What is it, Mother?" she asked, with mounting concern flooding her voice.

Her mother took another very deep breath, her chest heaving slightly, and then spoke rapidly, her words combined into one long word. "I'm leaving your father."

Talia looked at her, nodding slowly, half confirming her mother's statement and half grasping the finality of it. Talia didn't really catch it at first. What did she mean *leaving*? Going on a trip? It took a moment, but the implication of her remark soon had its impact.

"What?" was all that Talia could muster. It was one word but it carried all the questions and curiosity that were expected.

"I cannot continue," Phoebe whispered, bowing her head and her eyes. Her hands were shaking, and Talia gripped them tighter.

Phoebe looked up at her daughter. "He is not faithful to me. He has not been for a long time." She bowed her head again and Talia got down on her knees in front of her, sliding her arms around her mother's waist. Her mother's face fell into the nape of Talia's neck. "I am sorry, Talia, I am sorry."

Talia rubbed her hand slowly across her mother's back. "It is not you who should be sorry," she said, almost in a whisper, conveying sympathy and understanding to her mother, with the simple sentence and gentle massage.

"I'm sorry for you," her mother said, fresh tears renewing the flow.

Talia moved in even closer and wrapped both her arms firmly around her mother. Their embrace tightened as they rocked gently, a low hum escaping her mother's throat. They were definitely living in the *eyes-open* world.

They stayed that way for some time, each of them absorbing the revelation in a different way; Talia's mother relieved to have the burden of her decision unloaded, and Talia bringing reality into focus. She knew her father saw other women during his trips. She didn't know he was intimate with them. Still, after her mother's comments, she realized it was naive to believe otherwise.

Eventually they broke the embrace, and went on with the business of the morning without setting any firm time frame or details. Talia's father had already left for work, and Talia sat patiently at the kitchen table as her mother kept busy with cooking, nibbling, and then cleaning.

When Phoebe finally sat down with a rather exaggerated sigh, she looked up at Talia. "I have known about your father's infidelity for some time, Talia. It is not something new."

"Then why have you not done something about it before?" Talia was confused about her uncertainty.

"I was afraid."

"Afraid of what?"

"Afraid of life. Afraid of his reaction. Afraid of the future. Afraid of losing you." She looked at Talia and new tears welled up in her eyes. "I didn't know what to do. I fought the urge to stand up to him; kept telling myself it was the last time he would be with another woman, but I knew it wasn't."

"Why did you wait so long, Mother? Why wait if you knew?"

Phoebe looked over at her. Tears rolled down her cheeks. She bowed her head and said nothing for a few moments. Talia waited for some response.

Finally, Phoebe almost whispered, "I felt guilty."

Talia was confused by that comment. "Guilty about what? You did nothing wrong. He was the one who cheated on you!" Talia was feeling an anger build inside her. She clenched her teeth.

"I also cheated," her mother whispered.

Talia wasn't sure she heard correctly. "What?"

"When I was very young, when we were first married, before you were born, Talia. Your father was always away, I was always alone. One day, after a walk through some distant town, as I relaxed on a lovely bench near the seaside, I met a very charming and handsome young traveller." Phoebe hesitated. She looked up at Talia. Tears formed again in her eyes and she blurted it out. "The next day we met again. We went to his room." Her head bowed again, her hands covering it. "Talia, I'm so sorry." Then she burst into yet another set of tears.

Talia rose and went to her, cradling her head on her stomach as she stood over her mother. "Have you felt that guilt all these years?"

"How could I blame him, when I had also been unfaithful?"

"Yours was a moment, Mother, just a weak moment. He has probably been carrying on with other women for years. It is not the same." Talia waited, but her mother said nothing. "Forgive yourself, Mother. It is the very least you can do."

That last comment struck a note in Phoebe. She realized her guilt actually had nothing to do with Nasos or her perceived act of betrayal to their marriage. It wasn't about herself. It was about another secret she still harboured. Talia couldn't know the guilt was not driven by the actual indiscretion. She didn't know her mother had gotten over that. What Talia did not know, what she would find out only later, was that Phoebe's guilt centred on the fact that Talia was the child of that encounter. She was not the blood daughter of Nasos. Her mother knew because of the timing. When Talia was born, everyone just assumed she was a few weeks premature. Nasos never suspected anyone else had been involved. But Talia's mother knew, she always had. Folks reflected that Talia's blond hair and lighter skin was surely just a genetic factor from a distant, fair-skinned uncle.

Even so, with Talia's last comment, *"Forgive yourself Mother. It's the least you can do,"* Phoebe realized that because her own guilt was a self-condemnation, she could conversely provide her own forgiveness. The power to cast both guilt and absolution was internal. What a revelation!

Talia's words were both correct and relevant. Phoebe looked up at Talia; this woman-child, the fruit of her womb. How amazing she had become, how wise she seemed. Maybe all the travel with her father had been good for her, provided her with a maturity beyond her years.

"You're right. Talia. You're absolutely right. I have paid enough for that lapse in judgement." She released herself from Talia and stood up. She walked towards the front door, renewed with this sudden absolution of guilt, and turned to Talia before exiting the house. "Be ready, two days after school ends."

She waited for Talia to nod her agreement, and then strode out into the village.

Footsteps and Shadows

A feeling grew in Julian that he was walking in Tection's footsteps. Tection was an unavoidable part of Julian's life. Every turn seemed to lead in a mutual direction, no matter how spontaneously selected. In moments of deeper reflection, Julian even contemplated whether he was under Tection's wing, somehow moving in his shadow, somehow under his protection. *Protection.* It seemed like a comfortable way to harbour Tection's ever-present aura.

Julian was vaguely aware that Tection had actually had his name coined by a young orphan who could not properly pronounce the very word, *pro-tection*. It seemed one of the brothers at the orphanage had mentioned in jest that Tection was under the protection of God himself. The young boy heard this from his hiding spot and brought the conversation back to the older boys, under the impression that it was a serious and truthful comment. They did not understand him at first, as his vocabulary was quite limited. Finally, they recognized that he was saying 'tection, but actually meaning *protection*, and thus, the name Tection stuck. It was unique, larger than life, and carried a full religious weight in the minds of the orphaned boys, who believed Tection actually was protected by God.

Julian had spent some time at Sharif's place. As with Tection, he was most welcome and provided fairly separated living quarters, with free access and mobility at his whim. The young men often spoke of their next adventure, where, when, and how. But in the end, Julian was miles and miles from his home, while Sharif was safe in the loving bosom of his own; very different motivations. Sharif continued to manifest his building desire to travel, but he decided, with much suggestion from his parents and vivid memories of his fate at the hands of highwaymen, to wait for a few years. After school was complete and life was a little more lived, he would reconnect with his ambition to travel. Julian understood that and verbally reflected that he too would have been more reticent to venture out if he had had such a wise and loving family, but he had to move on, to head back towards his homeland, back towards Tection. He didn't mention his greatest desire, which was to pass through the town where Talia lived and reconnect with her; with the adult her. Sharif promised that his first journey, once he was back in travel mode, would be to join Julian and Tection for a reunion. Julian carefully explained where they lived, including points of reference on a map and written information of routes and resting places.

Their last goodbye was, naturally, filled with sorrow, but also with anticipation of the future.

"I have something for you, Julian."

"No need, Sharif. We will not be apart for too long. I am sure of that."

"I agree, so this is especially important then. It is not really a gift; it is a loan."

Julian looked at Sharif with a quizzical smile.

"Close your eyes."

Julian did. Sharif reached out and slipped the necklace containing his six-sided cube over Julian's head.

Footsteps and Shadows

Julian opened his eyes immediately. "No. You can't part with this. You never take it off."

"I am not parting with it. You are only keeping it safe for me. It will be a magnet for me. I will track you down to reclaim it soon enough. Besides, Tection will have no possibility of doubting your story when he sees it. He will be completely amazed."

Julian smiled at the thought. Tection would be shocked indeed. Not only with the cube, and the stories surrounding it, but also with the encounter with Selim and Malika. So much had passed, so much interweaving of their travels. He didn't know that these coincidences were only the beginning.

"I will guard it, Sharif, and if you don't come to get it soon enough, I will be forced to return it to you!"

As Julian looked at the cube, sitting comfortably just below the medallion he had received from Tection, the next action seemed obvious. He removed the medallion and handed it to Sharif. Sharif was stunned. He knew the importance of the medallion and remembered his father's words to Julian. *Tection valued it greatly, so he must have also valued you greatly in giving it to you.*

"This is such a personal item, Julian. It should not be shared."

"It is no more personal than your cube, Sharif. This will give us both a reason and some incentive to reconnect soon. Besides, I am sure Tection would be happy with my decision. Your cube will confirm our friendship and mutual comradeship. And, I will assure him that it is only a loan, soon to be returned to Sharif himself, and exchanged once again for the medallion."

They laughed and agreed that it was a great idea. Tection would surely approve, and Sharif and Julian would both have a constant reminder that they shared an obligation to reconnect. Julian's journal entry cemented the commitment.

The Journey: Erudite

The road towards home, towards Talia, seemed longer than anticipated. It was one of the few times Julian actually had a planned destination, rather than merely flowing with the twists and turns of the day. Having a specific objective multiplied his distaste for every small diversion. Late schedules were annoying, wrong turns irritating, and all tardiness aggravating. He realized the journey was much less enjoyable when it was enclosed with specific deadlines and destinations. So, he decided to remain aware of his direction towards Talia, but the pace of his travel was not going to be pushed so hard. He would get there when he did, and if she felt the same about him as he did about her, they would both be overjoyed at the reunion.

With a newfound nonchalance, Julian decided to visit the next tavern he came to. Who knew what adventure might lie within? That thought, as he reached for the door, delivered a hard reminder of Sarah, and the flurry of experience that she had opened him up to. He hesitated, but ultimately decided that whatever lay inside was just part of his destiny. He mused that Tection had perhaps stopped in this very establishment. After all, their paths seemed to constantly meet at crossroads.

The interior of the tavern was dimly lit, and Julian had to wait a few moments for his eyes to adjust from the bright afternoon sunlight. There were only a couple of patrons lounging casually around a long bar, with nobody at all sitting at the various tables. Julian decided to follow the others and took a seat two stools away from anyone else. He had learned the proper protocol of visiting an establishment for the first time. Sitting directly beside someone else was way too familiar; one seat away was an invitation or intention to chat, without knowing the other patron's wishes, and two seats away was perfect. Still close enough to chat if the feeling was mutual, but far enough away to not be considered nosey. Julian selected a chair close to the corner of the bar, two seats down from an elderly gentleman who seemed to be massaging his glass of whisky. The man said nothing and showed no change in demeanour, not even a glance in Julian's direction. *Guess he's not a chatterbox.*

The bartender was a very young woman. Julian wondered if she were old enough to even be in such a place. He decided not to chat with her, preferring to order his drink and get a better understanding of the place. She wandered back to her task, drying and re-drying the glasses, with some faraway look in her eyes, apparently wishing to be anywhere, doing anything, except what she was currently doing.

Somewhere between drinks two and three, the door opened and a rather attractive, middle-aged woman entered the room. She seemed apprehensive and certainly not like a veteran of afternoon excursions to the tavern. She walked up to the bar and sat around the corner, one seat away from Julian. Her seat selection indicated she wanted to chat, or perhaps confirmed that she was not an experienced bar-sitter.

Sure enough, her proximity invited conversation, and soon the two of them were exchanging comments and anecdotes. The woman was pleasant enough, but harbouring some sort of melancholy, some kind of weariness with life. They exchanged names and enjoyed the anonymity of a bar conversation. You could be anybody you wanted to be at the bar. You could tell the truth, exaggerate the truth, or tell a lie, or exaggerate a lie. You could give your real name, a false name, or even the name you wished your parents had given you. There were no rules.

After a fair amount of innocuous chatter, the woman finally managed to let slip a bit of what was bringing her negativity. Julian cautiously, yet skillfully, pried into her affairs, and eventually learned her story. She was getting divorced. Effectively, she had run away with her daughter and was in transit as well as transition. Julian provided a soft shoulder for her, and before long, after a bathroom break, she sat next to him and shed some tears onto his sleeve. He comforted her. Even though she was many years older than he, the warmth of her skin and sensitivity of her character began to arouse him. He did not want to take advantage of her during a vulnerable time and decided to just go slowly and see where things went.

Julian, in turn, opened up a little. He spoke of a young woman he loved dearly, one who actually had been too young for him at the time of their first encounters. But she was old enough now, and he was on a pilgrimage of sorts to find her again. The woman commented on how romantic his story was. Julian was in full bar mode, easily revealing some of his deepest thoughts to this person he would probably never see again.

It was clear, after a while, that they might be destined to spend some more personal time together in private, and were it not for a vicious fight that broke out between two men at the bar, they probably would have. *He must have sat too close to the other guy*, Julian mused.

The commotion completely broke the mood, and the lady left the bar quite rapidly, as Julian stepped in to break up the fight. With the two men safely apart, Julian ran outside to try and find his barmate, but she was nowhere to be seen. When he returned to the bar, the two combatants were now shaking hands and buying each other a drink. It would seem the only big loser in the fight was Julian.

Julian grabbed his travel bag and stumbled out of the tavern early in the evening, after an excessive amount of drink. He was enjoying his decision to relax the effort to scurry to Talia's hometown. He much preferred a casual travel schedule, without deadlines and commitments. What he needed at the moment, though, was a place to stay. As he walked towards the water, closer to the town centre, he spied an elderly lady carrying a few bags of groceries. He immediately moved to her side and offered to assist her. She was reticent at first, but the weight of the bags finally convinced her. Once up to her small house, she thanked Julian and turned to go inside.

Before entering she turned back to him. "Where are you staying, young man, or are you just carrying that travel bag around for fun?"

Footsteps and Shadows

Julian truly didn't know. He had no plan. The fact that he was carrying his travel bag had made his situation rather obvious. "No plans as of yet, ma'am."

"Do you have any money?"

"That I have. No place to spend it yet, but I have it ready just the same."

She smiled. "I have a room for rent downstairs if you are interested."

It was a perfect offer. "I am very interested."

She put down her groceries, waved Julian into her yard, and walked around the side of the house. There was a small stairway down to a door that opened into a semi-basement room. Inside there was a small kitchen area, a bed and a separate bathroom.

"This used to be where my son stayed, before he moved asway. It's been empty for a while, but I'm sure it is more than comfortable."

"It looks perfect. I'll take it, at least for a while. I will be moving on soon."

"Yes, that seems to be what all young men are doing these days," she said, seemingly referring to her own son. "Breakfast is included, but you have to be upstairs between seven and eight. Nothing after that."

Julian settled in and developed quite a friendly rapport with Mrs. Vankov, or as he called her, Miss V. Eventually they agreed on other tasks for Julian to perform, in exchange for dinner as well. Always between six and seven she said again, otherwise nothing. The house was in the city, but there was a nice park down by the water and Julian spent several sunny afternoons there. Evenings occasionally found him back at his now favourite tavern, though his *older woman* encounter was never to be repeated.

One morning Julian woke with an understanding that he had already stayed longer than planned, and his intention was to move on in the next few days was established. He was sure he was not

The Journey: Erudite

more than a few days travel from Talia's home town, and that tug at his plans was becoming a more powerful lure every day.

Talia Full Circle

"**But she will** miss her graduation."

"What do you care? You will be off in some foreign country anyway."

"Yes, but she should be there; all her friends, her classmates."

"Name me one of her classmates, Nasos," Phoebe said with such heavy sarcasm that Nasos had to look away.

"Whatever," he finally muttered, and returned to his morning paper.

Phoebe moved about her morning tasks, as though everything was exactly as it was supposed to be. Neither of them was aware that Talia was just around the corner listening. Phoebe had only told Nasos that she was taking a long vacation with Talia. She did not mention that she was actually leaving their marriage. That bit of news could be transmitted at a later date, while he was off somewhere chasing a negotiated settlement, on some foreign trade issue. But Talia knew exactly what her mother was intending.

After Nasos left for work, Talia sat down in the kitchen and chatted with her mother. They did not speak specifically about the dissolving marriage, but it was tangled in the innuendo of every comment they made. This would not be a vacation; it was an exodus.

Talia bid goodbye to her father as he left for the train station on his next diplomatic mission. It was still a week away from graduation, but he would be gone for a month, and she would be away with her mother by the time he returned. She gave a little extra squeeze with her goodbye hug; a fact that he noticed.

"Don't worry, my little angel, I'll be back before you know it."

Talia didn't respond, just one last squeeze.

Phoebe had stuffed as much as possible into the four trunks that would accompany them on their trip. Talia took very few items, with her mother promising to buy her lovely new clothing once they settled somewhere. Moments of sadness littered the generally joyous momentum of departure day, as small treasures of a long life lived in one spot, were left behind. Talia had an emotional goodbye with her bedroom furniture, her bed, and all her small stuffed toys. Despite Phoebe's request that she take only the necessities, she secretly slid one special stuffed rabbit into her portion of the trunk. The neighbours were properly informed of the extended vacation, and well wishes were spoken over the surprise at the departure just before Talia's graduation ceremony, and so close to her nineteenth birthday.

Their first destination was a seaside city that Nasos often travelled to, and where he had a very close relationship with the regional governor. They had been offered the use of a diplomatic guest apartment for as long as they wished. It was, actually, the very apartment that Phoebe and Nasos had been staying in when Phoebe had her one indiscretion, some twenty years earlier. Her one short fling with a handsome traveller; and one long life with a beautiful daughter! She was going back to the beginning, consciously or not. She told herself the destination was only because of the availability of the accommodations, but her heart was unravelling an entirely different narrative. She was not yet ready to tell Talia that Nasos was not her blood father. She was more afraid of Talia's reaction to that news than anything else she had ever encountered. The possibility of Talia reacting badly, retreating from her mother, and all the accompanying dilemmas, was such a huge risk.

Their first few days were bittersweet. The impact of their permanent departure had not yet hit all the way home. It still felt like a vacation. They were in guest quarters with meal sittings, if they wished to partake, and daily maid service. Breakfast was on their terrace, with waiters to refill their coffee cups, and messengers to deliver their daily paper. Not really the life of a mother secretly escaping with her daughter from a mundane life with an unfaithful husband.

Talia's graduation day was celebrated with wine and fruit. Just the two of them on the terrace, with Phoebe making a simplified commencement speech, littered with claps and giggles, and Talia responding with the valedictorian's remarks.

"It is with great honour that I respond on behalf of my graduating class. Unfortunately, they were unable to be with us today."

Phoebe laughed heartily.

"The years of hard work and dedication have finally paid off. For today we stand before you, before our families and our gods, before our teachers and our peers, to promise the world that we will use the tools we have mastered in this hallowed institution to finally leave behind our childhood lives and stretch forward into the vast unknown, towards the destiny that lies beyond these walls."

Phoebe's mood became noticeably somber.

Talia looked at her and smiled. She spoke again with renewed vigour. "Today we begin a most anticipated journey. An adventure to create a new beginning. To throw off the shackles of an uncertain past, and devour the fruits of a new land. It is ..."

"Enough," Phoebe interrupted. "Come here, my crazy daughter."

They embraced together. They laughed, then they both cried, before finally laughing again.

"Just wait for my birthday speech next week," Talia said.

Her nineteenth birthday was a significant one for Talia. Everyone had always said that eighteen was the big one, but that just never rang true for her. At eighteen she was still at home, still in school, and still very much under the dominion of her father; and still without Julian! She remembered thinking that she was now old enough to legally make her own decisions, but she knew she was both emotionally and mentally unprepared to form her own individual life.

Nineteen was so different. What a transition those twelve months had made. She realized the last trip with her father had matured her beyond her age. Her comfort with social settings, confidence in the value of her opinions, and her general intellect, were evident. Her passion for Julian had awoken feelings she was not fully prepared for. The idle flirtations of a teenage mind had graduated as well, into recognition of a more powerful stimulation. The first revelations of love she suspected; such an aching, such a desire. And now, probably most importantly, was her newly perceived role of protector and confidant to her mother. It was as if they were both finally leaving home at the same time. At eighteen she had wanted a huge party, friends and family, food and drink, music and merriment. At nineteen, she was immensely happier, with just the realization that she was beginning her adult life's journey; a journey with empty drawers and cupboards just waiting to be filled with whatever she wished to place in them. The fact that others might also place things in her cupboards that were not as favourable to her, was something she had not yet considered.

Phoebe and Talia drank a little bit too much champagne on her birthday. They paid a heavy price the following morning, soothed only by much water and many hours under the covers. It was dusk, the sun beginning her tumble from the sky, and the room washed in a darkening hue, but not yet ready for artificial light. Phoebe decided she would have to tell Talia the truth. They sat quietly in the living room, Talia softly humming something and Phoebe forming her thoughts.

"This is where we stayed when I had my little episode with another man." She immediately regretted using the word episode. It was cold and unattached, nothing like the memory felt for her.

Talia looked up at her. She wasn't prepared for such an ominous remark, and was lost for a sensible reply.

"Perhaps not an episode, Talia, perhaps an adventure is more appropriate."

"Did you love him?"

Phoebe laughed, although Talia didn't appreciate it. Her remark had been genuine and serious. Phoebe saw that she wasn't pleased with her reaction.

"Love? No, I wasn't in love with him, at least not for more than a couple of days."

Talia sat upright and leaned forward. She sensed that her mother was ready, perhaps even anxious, to share more of her story. "Tell me about it, and I mean details."

"No, I'm not giving you details," Phoebe said with a little smile. "What do you know of such things?" There was a pause. Phoebe suddenly got serious. "You don't know of such things, do you?" Her last remark was definitely a question.

Talia waited for a moment, letting her mother begin to wonder about it. "Of course not, Mother. I'm just teasing. But you mentioned it, and you've already told me it happened. You might as well get it all out, I'm pretty sure you want to."

Talia sat back, pleased with herself for recognizing her mother's desire to reveal some details.

"I was walking by the sea. Your father was in another of his endless, long meetings. I had just realized that he probably did more than just chat with some of the secretaries and dilettantes who roamed in his circle. I had no proof, but I definitely suspected."

"Were you trying to get back at him?" Talia asked, a little disappointed in that possibility.

"Oh, no, not at all. That was far from my mind. I kept telling myself that it was just my imagination. I hadn't allowed myself to be convinced that anything was really going on with him."

Talia smiled at her. She was happy her mother's tryst was not a revenge affair.

"No, my little affair was pure magic. I mean, your father was always away. Even when I travelled with him, he was away, if you know what I mean."

Talia pursed her lips into a slight sarcastic smile, fully understanding her mother. "So, what happened, and give me some details."

Phoebe looked at her, feigning some shock. "As I said, I was walking by the sea. I had a couple of hours before dinner, so I just sat on a bench. Come here," she said, taking Talia by the hand. She led her out onto the terrace and pointed down to the sea. "There," she said, pointing to a distant bench, barely visible in the distance. Talia bent down to look along her outstretched hand, spotting the bench in question.

"I see it."

"Anyway, I was sitting there, almost asleep actually, and at some point, this man came and sat down on the same bench."

"Did he sit right beside you? Were you worried?"

"No, no, he sat on the opposite end of the bench, very proper. There was nowhere else to sit, really, unless he walked much farther up the boardwalk. Anyway, he sat down and after a while he said hello, or something like that, in the local language. I answered in our language, not expecting him to answer, really, but it turned out that our language was his mother tongue as well."

"Where was he from?"

Phoebe thought for a moment. "I don't know exactly. Isn't that funny? I just don't know."

"Never mind, go on."

Talia Full Circle

"Well stop interrupting then." They both giggled. It was as if they were young girlfriends talking about their first kiss, not a mother telling her daughter about her first affair. "I was heading back to the conference, but we agreed to meet the next day. And that was it. We had a wonderful time for two days."

"Whoa, you're not getting away with that. I'll need a lot more info, please."

"I'm not giving you details," Phoebe replied, once again feigning shock at the request.

"I don't mean details of your time together, but at least what you did, where you went, how you felt after, all that? You didn't even tell me his name!"

Phoebe hesitated, but she knew she wanted to share the story, reliving it herself at the same time.

"Tection," she said, almost as if she was talking to no one in particular. She looked at Talia, refocussing, absorbing in a mere moment, the rush of memories that flowed over her. "His name was Tection. We met after lunch the next day. I mean, we could do nothing, really, except maybe chat or go for coffee, and that was not what we were thinking of. We just ended up kissing. He was tall and very strong, very handsome. I was surprised he was even talking to me."

Talia looked at her. "Hey, you are a gorgeous lady. Any man would be lucky beyond reason to be spending time with you."

"Tell your father that."

Talia looked back, nodding her head slightly in disapproval at her remark. "Go on, without the negative comments."

"We went to his room, but I had to be back for dinner at the consulate, so it was only for a couple of hours."

"A couple of hours, what did you do?"

"No, I'm not getting into *those* details." They both laughed. "We met again the next afternoon. We planned on having lunch,

299

but once we were together, we went straight to his room again." Phoebe smiled.

"Mother, you didn't," Talia said, a little screech of sarcasm dressing her words. "Weren't you afraid of getting pregnant?"

Phoebe suddenly lost her smile. She stood up and turned towards the terrace. Talia watched her, wondering at first why her remark was having such an effect. Then it hit her. Her mother *did* get pregnant. There was such a rush of adrenalin that Talia had to sit. She froze in place for several moments. She looked out at the terrace. Phoebe was there, looking out towards the sea, perhaps towards the bench.

Talia slowly moved over behind her and slid her arms around her mother's waist, leaning her head close to her ear. "Is he my father?" she whispered, barely audible.

Phoebe nodded once, almost imperceptibly. She started to cry, gently heaving, without any sound escaping her lips, except for the occasional rush of air into her lungs. Talia held her. She had absolutely no idea what to say. Everything was flashing through her like lightning. Every moment of her upbringing. Every conversation with her father. She was in shock. She grew angry, letting go of her mother.

Phoebe turned, the tears washing her cheeks. "I'm sorry," was all she could muster.

Talia stepped back farther. So much to process. But she loved her mother. She loved her father too, or at least the man she thought was her father. Did he know?

"Does Father know?"

Phoebe looked at her, her face blank. "He has no idea," she said, before bursting out in a new set of tears. "Please don't hate me."

Talia wasn't sure she had heard the words correctly. Suddenly, she realized how difficult it had been for her mother to reveal such stunning news. What a burden it must have been to carry around

Talia Full Circle

all these years. She moved forward, enveloping Phoebe in her arms. They stayed that way for several moments, swaying gently together.

"I could never hate you, Mother. You're everything to me."

Phoebe was overcome with relief. She squeezed Talia with all her might. "You are everything to me, Talia, everything."

Several days went by. Talia came to terms with reality. The two ladies discussed the situation in great detail, riding the emotional bumps in unison, supporting one another through the revelation. One particular day, as they strolled along the boardwalk, arm in arm, with Phoebe recovering from yet another set of tears, Talia's grip suddenly tightened, and then she released her mother's arm. Phoebe looked up. A smile was creeping across Talia's face. Phoebe looked forward. A young man stood some distance from them, his face also forming a new smile.

"Talia, is everything OK?"

Julian and the Rays of Fate

Julian slouched on the bench, his head resting on the back support, and let the glowing sun bathe his face in a pleasant warmth. The air was hot, sometimes sticky, and he was very much aware of the odours on the breeze, and the waves splashing in a repeating pattern. But the sun's rays seemed to have a different quality, almost unearthly, and disassociated from the whirl of the everyday. It was as though they were falling onto his face directly from the heavens, somewhere above and beyond where he was.

He tried to lift his body, it felt heavy, tried to open his eyes, they felt glued together by the warmth, but there was no anxiety. Actually, he was relieved, pleased that he did not have to open his lids or lift his torso. He thought he might be in a dream-like state, but his total awareness of his surroundings contradicted that. Was it a trance? No, it was more like a journey, a voyage from the heat and dust of the day to a warmer glow of something else. The future? He wasn't sure. It was a very profound, yet confusing state. He languished in it, without fear or flight. After some time, he felt the warm rays cooling, their forces receding.

Finally, he looked up. A thin band of clouds slid across the sky, blocking the direct rays of the sun. It wasn't a large enough formation to darken the skies, but just to temper the warmth flowing down, and it was an extremely unusual pattern. He watched carefully as the band of clouds followed its destiny, squinting carefully as the light filled his eyes. As the tail of the cloud stream passed, the sun's rays returned to full light and Julian was forced to look away. He could have just closed his eyes, but he knew the near-magical moment had been lost. It intrigued him, though it was not something he had previously encountered. He lifted his head, and his body followed into a sitting position.

The bench on which he had been reclining sat on a long boardwalk that snaked away along the sea, in both directions. He looked right, but saw no one, except for some distant movement, perhaps others strolling along the seaside, oblivious to him and his experience with the sun. He turned left. Walking the other way was a young lady, carefully holding the arm of the more mature lady with her, who seemed distressed. As they neared, the young lady looked up and over at Julian. She froze, he froze. Their eyes widened. Talia? Talia!

She let the older woman's arm drop, causing her to look up as well. Both Julian and Talia were frozen, smiles slowly creeping onto their lips.

The older woman spoke first. "Talia, is everything OK?"

That comment confirmed to Julian that it was indeed Talia, not just some twin or apparition. Talia didn't answer immediately. The lady looked at Julian, and he returned her gaze with another smile, breaking eye contact with Talia, and noting that Phoebe had indeed been crying.

"Julian, is it you? Are you here? What are you doing here?" All the questions came out at once. Talia turned to her mother. "It's him. It's the boy I told you about!"

Her mother looked at her, then back at Julian. He moved forward towards them, inwardly smiling at the term *boy* she had used.

"Phoebe?"

"Julian!"

"What?" Talia interjected, stepping back a little and looking on with amazement. "You two know each other?"

Phoebe had a look of fear in her eyes. Julian looked directly at her, smiling warmly and reassuring her with his eyes that all was OK.

"We actually met purely by coincidence," Julian finally said.

"What? Where?" Talia asked.

"In a restaurant, not far from here." Julian cautiously substituted restaurant for bar. Phoebe pursed her lips in appreciation. "I told her of this beautiful young lady I was travelling to find!" Talia smiled broadly. "Anyway, later, we can discuss that later, but Talia, I can't believe it's you. What are *you* doing here?"

She shrugged, uncertain of what to answer. They moved closer, then she ran the last few steps to him. Julian hugged her with some force, perhaps too much. He didn't realize just how much he missed her, until that moment. He spun her around in several circles, until nearly falling down. He opened his eyes. Phoebe was staring at him with bewilderment on her face, but she smiled when Julian did.

Julian pulled back. "Oh my, you look so wonderful, Talia. You are like..."

"I'm like, nineteen now," she blurted out!

Julian laughed, as did she. She lifted up and kissed him on the lips, much to her mother's surprise. Julian accepted the kiss but did not return it. She looked at him. He nodded his head towards her mother.

"Yes, of course. Mother," she said, pulling Julian by the arm, towards her. "It seems you already know Julian." She presented him like a prized possession. "Julian," she said sarcastically, "you already know my mother, Phoebe."

"Very pleased to meet you, Miss Phoebe." Julian held out his hand.

She took it gently. "And I, you," she replied warmly.

They all laughed and moved together towards the bench. Sitting down was a little awkward, first with the mother in between, then Julian in between, and finally with Talia in the middle. They laughed again at the reorganization process, realizing they were all a little flustered.

Talia turned to Julian. "I can't believe it's you...but how do you know my mother?"

Julian recounted their encounter in the tavern, again referring to it as a restaurant, leaving out some key parts that were unimportant.

"We happened to be sitting at the same counter in a restaurant, a few towns over. Must have been a week or so ago, before I came to this place. We chatted about this and that; about you!"

Talia looked at Phoebe with a mischievous smile. "I didn't know you were off in other towns, chatting with young men."

Phoebe blushed a little. She also did not want to reveal everything about that day. "It was just a warm day that deserved a light meal, and I'm not a complete prude, you know."

Talia turned to Julian. She hugged his arm closely. "I can't believe it's you!"

After the wonderment and happenstance of their meeting, after more hugs and a tear or two, Talia explained that she and her mother were on vacation. She was not yet ready to divulge the true circumstances of their travel, although Julian already had a good idea of what was going on. As a matter of fact, from his bar chat with Phoebe, he knew exactly what was going on.

Julian explained that he was travelling back west, towards his homeland, with every hope and intention of stopping in her town on the way, to seek her out.

He was initially uncomfortable discussing their strong emotions for each other in front of Phoebe, but her relaxed response and open acceptance soon had him talking freely. After all, he had told Phoebe much during their restaurant encounter. He had thought of Talia often, always fearing she had blossomed to full age and found some dashing young man from her area. Never! She had thought of Julian often, always fearing he had found some more mature and exciting young lady to share his adventures. Never!

"Where are you staying, young man?"

Julian appreciated that he had apparently been elevated from *boy* to *young man*.

"I have a small room nearby. I am renting it from an elderly widow. A little money for the room and a lot of yard work for my supper." They laughed at that. "As a matter of fact, I have promised to collect some groceries for her today, and I have to get that done before supper time." Talia looked at him with disappointment in her eyes. "If I get that done now, I can finish in time to take you ladies to dinner. How does that sound?"

"That sounds excellent," Talia quickly replied.

Her mother smiled at her rapid reply, then feigned weariness and begged off the invitation.

"It has been a long day for me, and somehow, I think you two would prefer a quiet dinner together, without an old lady chaperoning."

"Not at all," Julian replied, "I'm so happy to meet you again, it would be great to spend a little time with the woman who was able to give this beautiful young lady to the world!"

Talia tilted her head in a sarcastic nod toward Julian, and her mother smiled even wider.

"That may be a little bit dramatic, Mr. Julian, but appreciated just the same. I think I will rest tonight, and hopefully we can renew our acquaintance tomorrow."

He smiled and nodded, before turning to Talia. "Where are you staying?"

"We are at the diplomatic residence. There," she said, pointing to a three-storey building that peeked over the bushes at the end of the park.

"Excellent. I will be outside the door at six, if that's not too early."

"Six is a little early Julian, it's almost five now. How about six-thirty?"

They parted. A gentle kiss to Phoebe's cheeks, and a significantly firmer one to Talia's lips.

Groceries delivered, shower and shave accomplished, finest clothes, which were still a little scruffy, and a brisk walk, left Julian in front of the diplomatic residence at six-twenty. He waited until six-forty. It was worth it. Talia burst through the front door, appropriately held by a properly uniformed doorman, and glided down the few stairs, until she was close, very close to Julian. He took her arms and held her back slightly, gazing up and down her body in a slow scan, and a smile that increased as he moved upwards. "You look amazing," he said; "absolutely amazing."

Talia blushed coyly. "Why, thank you, young man." She spun around in a circle once, before melting back into his arms. They kissed. Passionately this time, oblivious to the on-looking doorman and to the smiling mother staring down from her second-floor apartment.

"Do you have a favourite dinner spot?" Julian asked.

Talia looked up into his eyes. "Actually," she said, "I was hoping to get a look at your residence before dinner." Her smile turned serious. Her eyes turned dark.

"That sounds like an excellent idea."

Their *dinner* was a delicious three-course meal, full of fruits and passion, tastes and textures, slipping and sliding, rising and falling.

Talia lay on top of Julian, her head safely planted against her arm on his chest, her outstretched hand idly combing his hair behind his ear, her other hand toying with his breast. He rested his hand on her cheek, his other tucked behind his head.

"I have waited two years for a night such as this, Talia. I have thought about it so often."

"I have waited my whole life," she replied softly, almost in a whisper, tears slowly splashing from her eyes onto his chest.

Julian shifted to look at her. "You're crying."

"I'm happy."

"But you're crying."

"Because I'm happy."

Dessert was similarly outstanding, though a slightly smaller course.

Later that night, with Talia safely home from their lovely meal, and armed with a rendezvous schedule for the morning, Julian lay back on his bed, feeling great joy and release from the reunion. As he drifted towards sleep, he recalled the afternoon's events, just before Talia had arrived, clutching onto her distressed mother. He recalled the warm embrace from the sun, how it had delayed his departure and kept him glued to the very spot he was in; glued with his eyes shut until Talia was about to pass by. The band of clouds holding him until the very moment they would meet. He remembered the feeling that he was on a journey towards the future. *A future with Talia*? He wondered. He laughed to himself. How could the sun possibly know what was going to happen? Then again, how unbelievable was it that they met at that moment, in that place, after a specific delay? It was not inconceivable that some other force was in play. Destiny, perhaps. Serendipity, certainly. Inevitability, hopefully! *What an amazing adventure life is!*

Jubilation, Revelation, Destination

The days with Talia were full of excitement and joy. Phoebe was happy to see her daughter blossom with the relationship. She knew Talia and Julian were sleeping together, but she was not overly concerned about that other than the odd reminder about using proper precaution and hygiene. She remembered her own first forays into the world of passion and reminisced silently at the butterflies of first touch and the heavy heart of each departure.

The decision to leave her husband had weighed heavily on her. The fact that Nasos was not Talia's father had also been suffocating. But now, both of these perceived traumas were being rapidly diluted. She felt a great freedom, something that had eluded her for longer than she cared to remember. She had not officially told Nasos that she was leaving him for good, but she knew in her heart that it was so. She wasn't anxious to find another lover, as she wasn't really confident in her ability to find and sustain a relationship, but she was enthralled with the relationship evolving for her daughter.

Phoebe realized the fact that Nasos was not Talia's father had dramatically clutched at her, even though it was a pull that resided somewhere below the surface. Revealing the truth to Talia had worried her, but that too had proven to be an overdramatized burden. Things were indeed flowing smoothly.

Talia was gone much of the day, spending time with Julian, as they explored the beach, the city, and each other. Each evening she recounted her day to Phoebe, leaving out some of the particular details, but also adding some personal observations to frame her comments.

One evening, several weeks into their time together, Julian invited Talia and Phoebe to a small dinner club, where he had heard music and laughter frequently tumbling out of the doorway, along with the occasional over-indulger. He passed the club regularly on his way home at the end of another day but had never ventured inside. The ladies were thrilled with the idea and they all went early to ensure decent seating. They enjoyed a delightful meal, full of chatter and laughter, finishing well before the actual show began. They filled the interval with drink and discussion. Several people came only for the performances, and the small club filled to overflowing in no time at all. The atmosphere was buzzing with tidbits of conversation, observations, and preparations.

The performance was excellent, though not to be confused with a truly professional theatre production. A skit about infidelity invoked much applause, while Talia and Phoebe exchanged the occasional knowing glance. There were also a couple of singers and a storyteller to keep things flowing and maintain the festive mood.

Once the performance was over, the audience thinned noticeably, as bedtimes had been exceeded for some, and further merriment elsewhere remained for others. Julian, Talia, and Phoebe decided to partake in at least one more drink. They were savouring the jovial atmosphere and really enjoying each other's company. As the drink loosened the vocal cords, and the discussion circled

Jubilation, Revelation, Destination

around the infidelity skit, Phoebe, full of confidence with her new *single* life and bolstered by the uplifting changes in her daughter's demeanour, blurted out that she had been unfaithful once as well, when she was much younger.

"Mother," Talia said, expressing shock at the revelation.

"What?" she replied. "You are well aware of the situation, and Julian surely won't be shocked."

"You have been drinking, Mother. We've all been drinking. I certainly hope you are not going to reveal anything you'll regret in the morning."

"Nonsense, I think we have shared enough time and experience to share this fact as well."

Talia just raised her eyebrows and shrugged her shoulders.

"It all sounds fascinating Phoebe, but I don't want you to share anything that is too personal," Julian added.

"More nonsense. Shall I tell the story or not?"

Julian looked at Talia. She couldn't help but smile. Julian looked back at Phoebe, who had her own mischievous grin creeping onto her lips.

"Let's hear it," Julian said.

Phoebe suddenly changed her demeanour. The smile shifted from mischievous to one of distant reminiscence. She looked around the room. "It was in this very town. Nearly twenty years ago. Just a short adventure. A couple of days."

Her sentences were short and choppy. She seemed to be remembering it in great detail, but only verbalizing the memory in short, point-form remarks. She gathered herself, the alcohol surely affecting her emotions, and allowed small, lingering tears to trickle down her cheek. She smiled and brushed them back with a murmured apology.

"Perhaps it's not the best time to be sharing such matters, Mother."

"No, no...it is exactly the right time to share it." She looked up at Talia. "We have taken the leap, my daughter, now we have to swim in the water."

Julian wasn't certain what these remarks meant, but was wise enough to know it was something between them and something he realized he should stay out of.

"Well," Talia looked at Julian, "I do believe I love this man...and I guess we might as well be straight up from the beginning." Talia returned her eyes towards her mother.

Now Julian was completely confused. He wanted to return the statement of love to Talia, but she did not seem to be expecting it. He figured he would save it for a more appropriate point in the conversation.

"OK then," Phoebe continued. "Let's get the story finished. As I said, it was only a short, two-day fling, or actually one and a half days. I was down by the water, sitting on the bench, and a very tall, good-looking man sat down on the other end of the same bench. I was already married to Nasos, and we were here for a diplomatic function, but Nasos was always busy or always tired. It seemed that was the situation from the day we married; work and sleep, not much else. I don't know why, at that moment with that man, but it just felt right. Tection was very kind and gentle, full of life and..."

"Who?" Julian blurted out, lifting himself slightly upward.

Phoebe and Talia were both surprised by his outburst. Nearby tables glanced over as well, before returning to their own chatter.

"Who what?" Talia asked, gently touching his arm and easing him back into his seat.

"Who did you say? Did you say Tection? Was that the man's name?"

Phoebe looked at Talia, then back at Julian. "Yes...ya, Tection, a very unusual name."

Julian began to laugh, he muttered something, shook his head and laughed in more amazement.

Jubilation, Revelation, Destination

"What?" Talia said. She looked at her mother. Phoebe shrugged. Julian slapped his hand on the table. Others looked over again. *How can this possibly be?* The women just watched in stunned silence. Julian stood up, took a few steps, turned around twice, then sat back down. The remaining patrons stared at him, whispering and wondering. He sat back down. Everything settled. Phoebe and Talia were speechless. Momentarily, Julian composed himself, stood again, slowly, and stepped over to Phoebe. He reached out and held her face in his hands before leaning forward and placing an exaggerated kiss, firmly on her forehead.

"What?" Talia said again, both women smiling now at his antics.

"Tection, your Tection, no doubt, is a great friend of mine, a mentor of sorts and the very reason I have been able to make this journey."

"How do you know it is him?" Talia asked.

"There is only one Tection," Julian stated rather matter-of-factly.

"There *is* only one Tection," said Phoebe in full agreement.

They all laughed at the absolute serendipity of the situation, shaking their heads in wonderment and disbelief. Julian recounted a few details of his relationship with Tection, but soon realized he had interrupted Phoebe's great revelation.

"I'm sorry, Phoebe, I didn't mean to leap into your story like that. I was just absolutely shocked when you said his name."

"That's OK, young man, I can imagine your surprise."

"So," Julian said, hoping to bring the discussion back to her affair with Tection, "what happened?"

Phoebe sat back in her chair. She looked directly across at Talia, a look filled with as much love and admiration as Talia had ever seen in her eyes before. She didn't look back at Julian. She just opened her arms in a gesture towards Talia, as though asking her to come to her embrace.

Julian didn't understand at first. He thought she was perhaps asking Talia to continue the story. Then Talia looked at him and it became clear. *Talia* **was** *what happened.* She herself, was the result of the affair.

"No. Impossible...," was all he could say at first. He looked back and forth between the two women before finally reaching out to take Talia's hand. "I believe I love you too."

Over the next few days, Phoebe was incessant with her questions about Tection. She was disappointed, though not surprised, that he was now married. When Julian recounted the story of Tection returning from his travels, only to find he had a child named Nicholas from a previous affair, she couldn't help but remark that he seemed to have fathered children in several places.

"I wonder how many others there are?" she asked, to no one in particular.

Julian sidestepped her remarks. They were very true, but immaterial at this point. The next shock-wave came when Julian revealed that Tection had been an ordained priest and had walked away from his calling. He did not mention the fact that Tection had taken another's life. It too seemed immaterial. Perhaps Phoebe had actually been his first lover in a very long time. Based on Talia's age, and Julian's time knowing Tection, their affair must have been some twenty years earlier, relatively soon after Tection first went on his journey.

Julian recounted the bond that had developed between him and Tection, after the elder man had returned to his home. As he shared some of the stories with Phoebe and Talia, he recognized how inexorably his and Tection's lives were intertwined. Not just from their early days back in Julian's café, but continuously, throughout his travels. The impossible serendipity of his encounter with Safa, Malika, and Selim, the inexplicable mutual connection in India with Sharif and Ravi, and now, the most amazing coincidence of all; Talia!

Julian spent much time reflecting on the parallel experiences he was sharing with Tection. It was as if Tection's journey through life was providing a pathway for Julian to follow, even thought there

Jubilation, Revelation, Destination

was no visible, or even suggested indication of where that path was. This realization opened a whole new perspective for Julian; was this all God's plan, or was there some mystical, magical, collective experience that was recognized and manipulated on some level below or beyond the conscious thought process? What else could explain the continual bumping into Tection's past, all leading forward to this seemingly destined encounter with Tection's unknown child, his second unknown child. Julian had to smile at the inconceivable strength of reality, at its unimaginable deliverances and its astonishing conclusions. At the end of each day, Julian found himself anxious for the next encounter, anticipating another great revelation in the life-living process.

To the contrary, Talia was noticeably quiet during the ensuing days. She was still lovely and in full *butterfly* mode, but there was a certain melancholy in her stride. The stories surrounding Tection and anyone, or everyone, he knew, or even everyone he was, permeated all conversation. So many questions, so much speculation. 'What if', 'who knows', 'might have been', 'other circumstances', 'twist of fate', 'ironic nature'...but one thing was for sure; Talia was most anxious to actually meet her blood father. That possibility had not been anticipated, and the crazy reality of Tection and Phoebe's short liaison was, some twenty years later, about to reset the life course of at least three people, perhaps more.

The Journey Parallel

"I can't wait to see Tection's face when he meets his daughter. It will be an outstanding moment. And all the other stories I have; the gifts I bring him." His hand went to the cube around his neck. "The impossible cross adventures...." Julian looked up. Talia was not nearly as excited. "What is it Talia? Are you not anxious to meet Tection?"

"I am Julian, I am. But it is not as simple as you make it sound."

"What am I missing? Are you worried about travelling with me?"

"It's not about you, Julian. I guess that's the biggest problem. It's just not about you. We are not married, and I'm not saying we have to be, but travelling to distant lands with you is not something I feel comfortable with on such a whim."

"Yes, yes, you're right, Talia. It is a little thoughtless of me. I'm sorry."

"No apology required. I know you are so excited about seeing your friend and mentor again, with lots of stories and things to share. But I'm *not* a thing. I've had a father growing up all my life. He is not my blood, perhaps, but he is my father. Tection is only my biological father, not the one who tucked me in every night, championed my efforts, and scolded my folly. Nasos did that for me. Right or wrong sometimes, he was still there for me all my life."

Julian truly felt ashamed. *How stupid I am!*

"You are absolutely tight Talia. I have been thinking of me and anticipating the reunion. It is not like me to be this selfish, so please forgive me. We have much to discuss."

Talia looked up at him, a tear forming in her eye, one reflecting the uncertainty and confusion the situation was delivering.

"All I know for sure," Julian continued, "is that I want to be with you. If my reunion with Tection happens soon, later, or not at all, it will never be as important to me as you are."

Talia smiled. It was, after all, exactly what she wanted to hear. She just hadn't realized that fact until she actually heard it.

Julian moved closer and they wrapped each other up in their arms. They swayed for a while, each with their own thoughts. After a while, Talia broke the embrace and leaned back.

"And what about Mother? She has just stepped out into the world again. She cannot traipse all over, following us on some adventure...specially to meet a man who was her casual lover and is now married and with family. It doesn't make any sense. I can't put her through that. I can't ask her."

Julian was silent. Her comments were without fault.

"And I can't leave her here alone. She needs me right now. She is trying to figure out where she fits in this world, or more importantly, where she will fit in the future. She needs my support."

Again, Talia's words were sobering, but completely true. Julian knew that. He thought for a moment before responding, but realizing there was no contradiction to make, that this was an emotional moment, and the Tection discussion could resurface at a more appropriate time, he simply said, "Talia, I am here with you. I do not need to be anywhere else. And we will never abandon Phoebe, never."

The Journey Parallel

Talia liked that he said *we* will never abandon Phoebe. Later that night Julian wrote in his journal. *I will have to marry this woman. My love for her aches.*

———

The next few months were glorious. Phoebe rented a small cottage on a month-by-month basis. It had a basement apartment, ostensibly for Julian, but actually for Julian and Talia. They basically lived as husband and wife, although the separate quarters lent an appearance of respectability to the scenario. Days easily rolled into weeks and then into months.

Phoebe had sent Nasos several long letters with various explanations about her plans and intentions. She wanted a divorce, although there was no rush. She had no male friends of interest, but she was pleasantly surprised at the number of suitors who approached her, seeking dinners, drinks, or walks along the water. She accepted some and refused others, but did not find anyone who really captivated her. She wondered, aloud sometimes, if there was ever going to be a special person in her life again. Talia constantly reinforced her as a woman, and Julian always found a way to charm a smile out of her with his own remarks about her feminine attributes.

Nasos did not reply for some time. He did not rush to their town and promise to change, begging her to return to him, ensuring her he would be attentive and loving. Phoebe dreamed of that response, but it did not materialize. She knew in her heart that Nasos was more than pleased with her decision; leaving him free to pursue his next generation of lovers.

One day a messenger arrived. His package contained various documents describing their divorce and her entitlements. All she had to do was sign. Nasos had provided a decent amount of funds for her, more than she had expected actually, but it was Julian who insisted that she should demand the house for herself. After all, she was caring for their daughter, and it had been her parents' house when they'd married, and her main residence before the separation, not to mention that it was the most valuable asset they held. With Julian's encouragement, Phoebe drafted a supporting document, making an addendum to the divorce papers, claiming the house as her sole property. She signed and returned the package to Nasos, uncertain of his reaction. Another couple of weeks went by. One bright morning, the cloudless blue sky still protecting the world, and Phoebe happily transplanting her plant cuttings, the messenger returned. Phoebe accepted the package and brought it into the kitchen. It sat on the table. It would not be opened until everyone was home.

Phoebe could not look. She slid the envelope across to Julian. He undid it slowly, enjoying the drama of the situation.

Talia reached for it. "Give it to me, you're too slow!"

Julian yanked it back before she could grab it. "Patience please, it will be open and reviewed in just a moment." A smug smile crossed his lips, Talia looked at him sarcastically, and Phoebe just continued to pump her right leg up and down in a blur.

Julian slid the papers out and perused them silently. He knew the women were watching his face carefully, searching for some hint of the results. Julian maintained a stoic look, and after completing his review, slid the documents to the middle of the table.

Talia was worried. She picked them up. After her own short review, she put them down and looked at Julian. "He's giving her the house."

She looked at Phoebe. "He's giving you the house!"

Julian whooped, Talia jumped up and reached for Phoebe, and Phoebe just stared at the papers, slowly letting a smile cross her lips. Julian joined them, and they were soon laughing, cheering, giggling, and dancing.

Then Phoebe started crying. Talia and Julian slowed down.

Phoebe sat down. "He would never give up that house unless he had an awful lot of money stored away somewhere."

Talia looked at Julian. "Who cares, Mother?"

"I just wonder how long he's been hiding his money from me, from us. His riches tucked away, his girlfriends no doubt hungry for it; he and his friends laughing about me."

"Whoa," Talia interjected. "That's crazy. We don't know any of that." She was not enjoying the disparaging remarks about her father.

Phoebe recognized that.

So did Julian. "Look," he stepped in, "you have what you need to make your new life happen, Phoebe. Let's celebrate that and let the past melt away."

"Please, mother."

Phoebe looked at them both. She sniffled once, took a deep breath, and stood up. "Let's party," she screamed, throwing the divorce papers up in the air.

The value of the house, once sold, was enough to support Phoebe for the rest of her life. The lifting of that great weight was just being realized and she was emotionally spent by it. The divorce was done, the house was hers, and Nasos had indirectly confirmed to Phoebe that her decision to leave him was the right one. The initial celebrations waned, but they ignited a long period of relaxed joy and quiet comfort.

One otherwise eventless evening, after a hearty dinner, Phoebe and Talia were relaxing on the front veranda in rocking chairs. Julian excused himself and went downstairs before returning shortly after. He stood in front of Talia for a moment. She looked up at him. His eyes were magnetic. She noticed right away that they were more clear than usual.

She stopped rocking. "What is it?"

Julian slowly sank onto his right knee, simultaneously bringing a small box out in front of him. Talia brought her hands to her face. She knew what was coming, but she could not really articulate it internally.

Julian's other hand moved to the box and lifted the lid. A beautiful ring sat royally on a throne of felt. "Marry me, Talia. I love you so much, I cannot ever see my life without you."

Talia looked at Julian. She wanted to shout *Yes*, but her mouth would not make the word. She opened and closed her mouth, still no sound. Finally, she just nodded her head several times and dove into Julian's arms, knocking him and the ring back onto the veranda. He laughed. Phoebe laughed. Talia cried. After some composure was regained, Julian slid the ring onto Talia's finger. She admired it for some time, then covered it with her other hand and brought it close, over her heart.

"Thank you! I am so happy. I have been waiting to hear those words for a long time…probably since I was ten years old"

They enjoyed the now-official family unit. The wedding was small and fairly inconspicuous, except for the official notice in the local paper, which was a requirement of the local authorities. For some time afterwards, even strangers passing them on the street would nod a congratulatory word. Their landlord had borne witness to the marriage, along with Phoebe, and his habit of gossiping was no doubt a driving force in igniting the slight notoriety they received. Phoebe assumed the downstairs accommodation, and the newlyweds the main house. Harmony was easy.

As time evolved, discussion of the future began to take shape. Location, employment, and even children, all topics of increasing attention. The six-month honeymoon was definitely heading to a conclusion. Julian was still most anxious to reconnect with Tection. Talia was concerned about Phoebe, but her mother was not stressed by the possibility of seeing Tection. Phoebe had originally maintained that the young couple should begin to navigate the world on their own, insisting she would be fine by herself. Both of them quickly discarded that notion, reiterating that she was a key part of their lives, and absolutely no discussion of separation would be entertained.

Their first step was a return to Talia's home. She wanted to see her father again. She missed him, even though they had been at odds in recent times. Unfortunately, Nasos was not in town. He was on an extended mission somewhere back in North Africa. Then there was the matter of selling the house and land, though Phoebe was not concerned about it. Their neighbour, Georgios, had been trying to buy them out for twenty years. No doubt he would be exhilarated to finally get the opportunity. He was! It all happened quickly, more quickly than they were prepared for. Georgios was thrilled with the agreement to buy the land, although he tried to beg off buying the house. Phoebe insisted. She drove a fairly hard bargain actually, and Julian was impressed with her negotiating skills. Georgios finally agreed with her after she surmised that it would be a great residence for his son, once he married and delivered hungry grandchildren.

Theo, Georgios's brother, was a local publisher of some renown. He had a large publishing house in the city and was constantly looking for new material. When the discussion of the many travels and adventures Julian had experienced came up, he was most curious. Regionally, there was a newly developing hunger for information from outside the local world. People had begun to seek a wider understanding of distant places. Travel, not the local kind to visit relatives, but in a broader sense, to more distant lands, was becoming more prevalent. In context of the discussion, Julian mentioned his journal. Theo was fascinated by it. He absolutely had to read it. Julian promised him he could, but only after some editing and finalization. Of course, Julian wanted to change some names, dates, and locations, to protect Talia and her family from some of the stories, not the least of which were his adventures with Sarah and some other ladies.

When he was finally done, spurred on by Theo's constant reminders, he handed it over. Theo couldn't put it down. Over the next several days he constantly visited with Julian to get updates, clarifications, and confirmations that all which he had written was real and true, not at all fabricated. Julian assured him it was real, though certain names, scenarios and locations had been altered to protect the characters involved. Especially me, Julian mused. When Theo was finished, he had a proposition for Julian. Allow Theo to have professional writers draft a new version of the journal, perhaps with some poetic license and vivid imagination ameliorating the tales, and he would publish it under Julian's name.

Julian was flabbergasted. He hesitated at first, until Theo mentioned the financial rewards he would receive, not to mention royalties and certain notoriety. Julian finally agreed, provided the new version was published as fiction, not an autobiography. Theo agreed. It would still be written in an autobiographical stream, but names would be changed and it would clearly be labeled a work of fiction. Done.

The process of cleaning up all their affairs, transferring the property to Georgios, and getting Julian's book published took a few months. During that time Nasos returned to town, but only for a few days. Another mission called him away again.

His first encounters with Phoebe were undramatic. It seemed as though they were both completely indifferent to each other. Julian reflected again on the determinations he had made earlier in his journey, that indifference was the opposite of both love and hate. Nothing he saw here changed that. They were courteous, succinct, and generally evasive of each other.

For Talia it was different. She had no intention of telling Nasos that he was not her real father, because he was. She did not know Tection, though she was anxious, yet feeling some trepidation about their first encounter. But Nasos was still her father. They had some time together, a couple of lunches, and some soft tears. Julian joined them on occasion as well. Nasos was extremely gracious toward Julian, full of heartfelt congratulation on their marriage, and admitting that he never expected to see the young man again. In turn, Julian praised Nasos for his protective posture when it came to Talia, and apologized numerous times for approaching her when she was so young. Nasos recognized that she appeared much older, and all was considered water under a long-forgotten bridge. The three of them said their last goodbyes together, as Nasos departed back to his world of being a diplomatic nomad, and the married couple turned towards their own destiny.

And so it was. They departed towards Julian's home, and a rendezvous with Tection. Phoebe was now a fairly wealthy woman, full of confidence and receptive to a new beginning.

Julian was in love, freshly married, and in possession of more funds than he had ever dreamed of. His *book* was a huge success. Sales were beyond expectations, and a second novel was already in demand. He promised it for Theo within the year, and accepted a hefty advance to secure his commitment.

Talia was uncertain of what had happened to her. She had returned from her last diplomatic mission with Nasos as an angry teenager, full of resentment and hostility towards him. She was heartbroken about, and perhaps even in love with, a man she never expected to see again. Since then, she had learned her blood father was another man, a passing stranger; she had helped her mother separate and eventually divorce her real father; she had reconnected with her lost love and become engaged; and was now married and contemplating children. What a whirlwind.

The Journey: Erudite

As they waited for the boat that would carry them over the last leg of their voyage to Julian's home town, Talia sat patiently and remarked to no one in particular. "You know, we should get something nice for Tection. A gift, to get our introductions off to a friendly start. I wonder what he likes?"

Julian looked at her. He smiled. "We have a gift for him." She tilted her head in a quizzical manner. "You Talia. You are the greatest gift he could ever dream of."

-END-

About the Author

David Cocklin is a consultant and occasional lecturer, who is now retired from mainstream corporate life. His passion for writing continues to build a growing legacy for his children and for future generations. Apart from writing, David remains dedicated to the pursuit of happiness; he seeks experiences that promote growth and sharing gained wisdom, supports charitable endeavours, and retreats from circumstances that convolute life. *The Journey: Erudite* is his third book. *The Cottage: Recondite* and *Vargas Hamilton: Life Is a Gas* were also published by FriesenPress. He shares his time between Montreal and Fort Lauderdale.